Rachel Abbott is the bestselling author of both the Tom Douglas and the Stephanie King series. Together, her books have sold over 5 million copies.

Born and raised in Manchester, Abbott founded her own interactive media company in the 1980s before retiring in 2005. She then moved to Italy where she wrote her first novel, *Only the Innocent*, which became an international bestseller, reaching number one in the Amazon charts both in the UK and US. She has now published sixteen psychological thrillers, plus a novella.

She is one of the top-selling digital authors of all time in the UK (published and self-published), and her novels have been translated into 21 languages.

Abbott now lives in Alderney in the Channel Islands.

Praise for Rachel Abbott

'It's obvious why Abbott has attracted her huge audience.' *The Times*

'Abbott applies elegant control to her storytelling. Even her walk-on characters are vivid creations' *Daily Mail*

'a powerhouse combination of psychological thriller and intense drama. The twists don't stop coming' *Heat Magazine*

'Abbott leaves you guessing until the final few pages' *The Glasgow Herald*

'It's easy to see from this gripping story's frequent twists and bluffs, in a narrative that's rooted in psychology ... why Abbott stands out in a crowded market'
Morning Star

'Cleverly plotted and intriguing, all the characters are well-fleshed! Utterly compelling and truly unputdownable!' *Mystery People*

'It's easy to see why readers keep coming back for this author's thrills' *Observer*

'A dark, extremely readable, well-plotted psychological thriller' *The Times*

'The queen of psychological thrillers' *Fabulous Magazine*

'Abbott is a gifted storyteller and this book is a total delight!' *Daily Mail*

'Absorbing, complex and brilliantly planned' *Novelicious*

'A Must Read' *Sunday Express*

'A brilliant read, full of suspense' *Closer*

ALSO BY RACHEL ABBOTT

DCI Tom Douglas Series

Only the Innocent

The Back Road

Sleep Tight

Stranger Child

Nowhere Child

Kill Me Again

The Sixth Window

Come a Little Closer

The Shape of Lies

Right Behind You

Close Your Eyes

No More Lies

Stephanie King Series

And So It Begins

The Murder Game

Don't Look Away

The Last Time I Saw Him

WHATEVER IT TAKES

Rachel Abbott

black dot
publishing

Whatever It Takes
Published in 2025 by Black Dot Publishing Ltd.
Copyright © Rachel Abbott 202t.

Rachel Abbott has asserted her right to be identified as the author of this work in
accordance with the Copyright, Designs and Patents Act 1988.

This is a work of fiction. Names, characters, places and incidents are a product of the
author's imagination. Locales and public names are sometimes used for atmospheric
purposes. Any resemblance to actual people, living or dead, or to businesses,
companies, events, institutions or locales is completely coincidental.

ISBN 978-1-9999437-6-9

Find out more about the author and her other books at
http://www.rachel-abbott.com/

1

You're dead, aren't you?

You must be. It's the only thing that makes sense. If you were still alive, you would have found your way back to me. You wouldn't have left me out of choice, knowing it would destroy me, that I would be waiting, day after day, night after night, for some word. But there was just one text – eight words I didn't understand – and then silence. I never thought it meant goodbye.

That first night, when you didn't come home, I persuaded myself you'd gone to dinner with a client, one of the rich guys who relied on your skills to increase their wealth but made you jump through hoops to prove yourself worthy of their business. Or maybe you'd left your phone in the office, or the battery was flat. I made excuses, even though I had never known you to be home late without calling. I sat, staring at the wall, a swarm of restless butterflies fluttering in my chest, waiting for the flicker of joy I always felt when you walked, smiling, through the door. But you never came.

And no one knew where you'd gone.

Every night for weeks my heart raced at the slightest sound outside, praying I was about to hear your key in the lock. By day I tore the flat apart, wondering if there was something you were hiding from me: a reason, an excuse, for why you would disappear.

All I had was that one message before your phone was permanently disconnected:

I thought I could escape.
I was wrong.

What does that mean? Who were you running from? What have they done to you?

I ask you these questions repeatedly in my head. Never out loud, because that would feel like madness. And I may be many things, but I'm not mad.

Talking to you like this, it's as if you're listening to me, and I'd love to know what you think, because if I'm going to find you – or at least discover what happened to you – there are things I must do. Things you might find hard to understand.

Right now I'm poised on the edge, staring at the void below, my toes curling over the brink, clinging on. There's still time to back out, to walk away. But if I take the final step, risk everything – it will be the biggest gamble of my life.

What's the saying? 'Take the leap and build your wings on the way down.'

Let's hope I can fly, because my plan is complex and as dangerous as an actual cliff edge, but I can't hesitate. Every move is plotted, every contingency considered. It can't go wrong. I can't afford for it to go wrong. But if I pull this off, it could give me answers to the questions that have tormented me for years. Did they kill you? And if so, why? Maybe you knew too much. Or maybe you had to disappear, to go somewhere they can't find you. Is that it? Did you run to save me?

There are questions I have asked of myself, too.

Do I believe in what I'm doing? Absolutely.

Do I like what I've had to do to reach this point? No.

Am I breaking every rule of decency drilled into me – rules that I once thought mattered? Yes, but sometimes the stakes are so high, the consequences of failure so great, that conscience has to be abandoned.

All I know is that I have to find you, Alessandro. Alive or dead, I need to know what happened, and someone has to answer for it.

2

The crack of a gunshot ripped through the wood, scattering the birds from the trees, and Tom Douglas began to run. Not away from the sound, but towards it, lifting both hands to either side of his head, palms out, as if in surrender.

'I'm unarmed,' he called. 'I'm a police officer. Let's try to calm things down, shall we?'

From that moment, everything seemed to happen in slow motion – the girl pointing the gun, the man lunging to knock it out of her hand, the explosion of sound as the gun fired, the searing pain in his chest, the silence as the world turned black.

A muffled sound slowly penetrated Tom's ears as a gentle hand rested on his stomach.

'Tom, wake up, darling. You're dreaming.'

Louisa.

The tension drained from his body as he realised he wasn't in the woodlands at Rivington. No one was pointing a gun at him. He was at home, in his comfortable bed, Louisa's warm body next to his.

He groaned. 'Sorry I woke you.'

'Don't be silly.' She snuggled up closer, draping her arm across him, avoiding the wound in his still-painful chest. 'I'm not surprised you have the odd nightmare, given what happened. And it doesn't help that you're stressed about Jack too.'

'I'm probably being ridiculous. I spend far too many hours worrying about my bloody brother as it is, but this silence is not like him. Not now. Not when I've been splashed all over the papers.'

News that Detective Chief Inspector Tom Douglas of the Greater Manchester Police had been shot had dominated the headlines and been on every news channel. That was more than two weeks ago, and there had been no word from Jack. Not a peep.

Louisa frowned. 'I understand why you're disappointed he's not been in contact, but you never seem to know where he is or what he's doing. You always have to wait for him to get in touch with you, and we both know he's unpredictable.'

'True, and I understand why he has to live in the shadows. But you know how much he cares about family – you saw it yourself on holiday. So why the silence?'

'I can't answer that, but if anyone can work it out, you can.'

Tom scoffed. 'I'm getting nowhere. Call myself a detective? That feels a bit of a joke at the moment.'

Louisa tightened her grip. 'Give yourself a break, Tom. It's only been a few days since you got out of hospital, and Jack isn't making it easy with his fixation on secrecy. Get some sleep, darling,' she murmured. 'You can't do anything until morning.'

She was right, but sleep evaded him. He lay quietly, racking his brain for ideas on how to find his brother, cursing him for his obsession with security. Tom had no way to contact Jack, and he was certain something must have happened for him to disappear so completely. So certain, in fact, that he'd taken time off work to find him, extending his sick leave after the shooting.

His brother's past was complex, dangerous, and as the man who had brought down one of the most powerful organised crime groups in Manchester, he was constantly under threat of exposure, certain there was a price on his head.

Jack had never intended to become part of the criminal under-world but – a gifted black-hat hacker – he was adept at gaining unauthorised access to computer systems. As a teenager it had been his hobby – illegal, but he swore he'd never intended to cause harm. The more complex the security, the bigger the challenge and the greater the sense of achievement.

When his talents had attracted the attention of organised crime, he'd found himself faced with an ultimatum: do as they demanded, or his family would pay the price. Forced into a far darker world, he had seen only one way out. To free himself from their clutches and save the people he loved, Jack had faked his own death in a speed-boat accident.

Years passed before the devastated Tom had discovered his brother was alive, and it was a source of regret that they still couldn't spend time together as a normal family. Jack had a new identity, but if the brothers were seen together the truth of his survival would soon emerge, and although the senior figures in the gang who had controlled him were now dead, there were still some who blamed Jack for putting an end to their lucrative exploits. So he kept his distance. It was better if Tom didn't know where he lived – safer that way – but that was now proving a problem. Nothing about Jack's silence felt right to Tom, because despite not being able to see each other often, they still managed to communicate through Tom's laptop. Jack had hacked into it years ago, moving files around and leaving cryptic messages to let Tom know he was alive.

For the last two weeks, there had been nothing.

Tom's last contact with his brother had come from an unrecognised number. Typical Jack. The news, however, hadn't been good. As was his habit, Jack had been scanning the dark web for any chatter about himself and he'd found something that disturbed him. He didn't share the details with Tom. He just said he and his family were going off-grid for a while – but he promised to be in touch.

That promise had been broken, and Tom had to find a way to break through the wall of silence.

He lay still, turning over every possible next step, until Louisa stirred.

'You didn't go back to sleep, did you?' she said, rolling towards him and resting a hand on his hip.

Tom smiled. 'No, and I have a favour to ask. Do you think you could speak to Kate about her part in all this? I know it's a big ask, but if I talk to her I'll lose my temper, and you seem to cope much better with her.'

He heard a soft chuckle. 'She's your ex-wife, Tom. You're unlikely to be neutral.'

'I know, but I do wish she wouldn't wind me up so much.'

'You know why she does it. She's never forgiven you for not leaping at the chance to take her back when that guy she left you for turned out to be less of a catch than she thought. She likes to punish you, and much as I struggle with her antics, she's Lucy's mother so I try to keep things civilised. What do you need me to say?'

'Apart from telling her she's an evil witch with a wicked tongue...' At the look on Louisa's face, Tom held a hand up. 'Sorry, I know that's over the top, but she pushes the retribution angle too often, given our divorce was her choice. Telling the whole bloody world and his wife that my brother – the criminal, as she called him – isn't dead, and is actually hiding from an organised crime group, is unforgivable. Not to mention that I – a detective – am apparently complicit. Knowing her friends, that's gossip they'd love to share.'

If Tom hadn't been shot shortly after he'd discovered that his ex-wife had revealed Jack's death to be an elaborate lie, he'd have done more to check out the people she'd told. None of them appeared to have any affiliations to organised crime, but they might know someone with an unhealthy interest in Jack Douglas. When he'd pushed the point, Kate had clammed up, refusing to give him anything more than the names of those she had spoken to.

Louisa raised her eyebrows. 'And you want me to ask Kate who are the biggest gossips? Or which of them might be involved in the criminal underworld?'

'Okay – I get it. That's not going to work. Any ideas?'

'I could suggest we meet for coffee. I know things have been difficult between her and Lucy since she told those people that you're guilty of sheltering your criminal brother! I could say that maybe she and I can come up with a plan to put things right.'

Tom wasn't convinced this would work, although he appreciated the offer. 'Kate doesn't think she did anything wrong, so she won't apologise. Lucy thinks her mum was being malicious and won't back down. We need to end the stand-off for Lucy's sake. But maybe when you have this chat, you could see whether she'll tell you anything more about who she gabbed to.'

Louisa frowned. 'Okay, but are you sure your brother's actually disappeared? He told you he was going to make himself scarce, so perhaps that's all he's doing. Maybe the more you ask about him, the more exposed he could be.'

She had a point. 'I get that, but I find it hard to believe he didn't try to contact me when I was shot – even if he'd asked Clare to phone you.'

'It didn't occur to me at the time, but once I stopped panicking that you were going to die, I did wonder why she hadn't been in touch. You said he was moving them all, though – Clare and the kids. Maybe they've gone completely off-grid and never knew about the shooting.'

Tom shook his head. 'He might take the whole family's mobile phones offline – I can see him doing that – but he wouldn't go anywhere without Internet access. He's constantly checking stuff online. Something's not right. This is more than just one of his disappearing acts.'

'I have to admit that I've tried to call Clare without success, but when we were planning the holiday she warned me that their numbers are constantly changing. Maybe that's why I've not been able to get through.'

For just a moment Tom was back on the holiday Louisa and Clare had secretly organised on a remote island in the Adriatic, giving the brothers and their families a chance to spend time together. Was that really only a few weeks ago?

Louisa rolled away from him to pick up her mobile from the bedside table. 'When I call, it just rings out. I texted her too, but she hasn't responded. Look, I know it's early, but Clare told me that since the fire she's usually up by five. Do you want me to try again now?'

Tom nodded, praying that Clare would answer this time.

'Oh!' Louisa turned to him, frowning. 'That's changed. It was ringing out before, but now I'm getting a message saying the number's not in service.'

Tom felt a knot tighten in his chest. Where the hell was Jack?

3

Lucy had been staying with her dad and Louisa more often since the argument with her mum, and the slam of the front door announced she was home from a morning's shopping with her friend Akira.

'Hi, Dad. Louisa and Harry not here?' Throwing her backpack onto a kitchen chair, she headed for the fridge.

'They've gone to the park. Did you buy anything?'

'No. Akira's got a sudden urge to be a jewellery designer, so we mooched around the Craft and Design Centre for a bit, then went to a café for a weird-coloured smoothie. Not sure what was in it. What are you up to? Did you manage to get hold of Pete?'

Tom shook his head. Lucy always referred to her uncle as Pete – the name he had adopted when the world believed Jack Douglas was dead – and since Lucy hadn't seen him since she was a small child, she'd found it easy to accept the new identity, although in Tom's mind his brother would always be Jack.

He'd adjusted more easily to the new identities for the rest of the family. Emma was now Clare, Ollie was Billy, and Sophia had been born after the family's escape, so her name had never needed to change. But Ava was different. Tom had first known her as Natasha Joseph – Tasha – a deeply troubled young girl, and her name had been inseparable from the case that still haunted him. But since she and Lucy had become friendly during the recent holiday, he was finding it more natural to think of her as Ava.

He hadn't wanted to burden Lucy with his concerns about her uncle until now – she knew only that her dad was getting frustrated at the lack of contact – but it was time to see if she could help.

'Can I ask you something, Lucy? When I came out of hospital I asked if you'd heard from Ava. You said you hadn't, but you'd sent her a couple of messages. Anything since?'

Lucy leaned back against the fridge door, a chunk of cheese in her hand. 'Nope. Funny, though – she's usually really quick to reply. I didn't notice that she'd gone quiet while you were in hospital – there was enough going on, to be honest – but it hit me today that she's still not responded. We spoke quite a bit after the holiday, then you got shot. I messaged her to say you were home, and again yesterday when I knew you were trying to get hold of Pete. She didn't reply. Are you worried about him, Dad? I thought you said he often goes quiet.'

Tom looked at his daughter nibbling the cheese, usually so relaxed, so comfortable with herself, but two worry lines had appeared between her brows – the last thing he wanted. She wasn't a child, though. She'd be sixteen in a few weeks, and she'd know if he was lying.

'Come on, Dad. What's going on?'

'Sit down a minute, love. I need to give you the whole picture.'

Lucy dragged out a chair. 'I knew you were more stressed than you were letting on. Is this because of Mum yapping to her friends? You shouldn't worry about them, to be honest. They're so dull – all they ever talk about is who has the most expensive clothes.'

Tom tried not to smile. 'Lucy, don't be rude about your mum's friends. I'm sure they're nice people.'

'Huh! Nice enough, I guess. Nothing offensive. A bit shallow. Mum made me join them one evening because I'm "growing up".' She rolled her eyes. 'I tried to talk about some interesting stuff. We'd been doing a project on climate change at school, so I asked what they did with their clothes when they got bored with them. Like, do they even *know* how much waste they create and how that impacts the environment?'

Tom could imagine the moment. 'And what did they say?'

'They looked at me as if I was mad, and Mum sent me to the kitchen for more wine. I made homework excuses and disappeared. Honestly, Dad, they might gossip about Pete for five minutes, but they'll forget all about him as soon as someone mentions a new place to shop.'

'Maybe. And I don't want you fretting about what your mum said. You need to make things right with her, Luce.' He took a deep breath. 'I didn't want to bother you with how worried I am about Pete – the whole family, in fact. He said they were going to keep their heads down for a bit, but he's not given me any indication that they're okay, and that's out of character – especially since I got shot. Louisa can't get any answer from Clare either. Something's off.'

Tom saw a flicker of unease in Lucy's eyes.

'I can keep trying Ava, if you like?' she suggested. 'Even if they're staying under the radar, that can't mean no mobiles.'

'Perish the thought! No social media!' Tom said, attempting to lighten the atmosphere.

'She's not allowed to use social media. At least, in theory.'

'What do you mean?'

'Her dad – she means Pete, although I know he's not her dad,' Lucy chuckled, 'and for that matter not called Pete either! Anyway, he says she shouldn't put her face all over the Internet. Or his. Or Clare's.'

Tom couldn't help thinking how difficult that must be for a teenager. How had she managed to square it with her friends? Jack was right, though. Ava didn't look much different from the child she used to be, a child who was thought to be dead – killed in a house fire, along with Clare and Billy. Sometimes Tom wished life around his brother could be a whole lot simpler.

'You do understand why he's asking her to do this?'

'Of course. She told me about her upbringing – once she'd cleared it with Clare. I know she was kidnapped when she was six and brought up in a criminal family, asked to do all kinds of things that would scare the hell out of me.'

Tom closed his eyes for a second at the thought of Lucy going through even ten per cent of what Ava had experienced. 'It must have been horrific for her, but if it's any consolation, I don't think it was all bad. There were a lot of kids in that house, and I think they genuinely supported each other, even though most of them weren't actually related.'

'Wow, Dad, that's putting a bit of a positive spin on what must have been a crappy childhood. You should have been a politician.'

Tom had to concede that she was right. 'I know. I guess I'm trying to protect you from imagining what she went through. God only knows how confused she must have been – she was so young when they took her. But she's part of a happy family now, even though they do have to keep secrets.'

'What, like the secret that she's alive? She told me about that too, about how Pete – with help from you – rescued all of them from the fire that was supposed to kill them.'

'It was a long time ago, Lucy. The important thing is that we work out where they are now.'

'What can I do?'

Tom leaned back in his chair. 'How would you feel about sharing stuff that Ava's sent you? Photos, texts – anything that might give me a clue about where they could be. Even if they're not there now, it might give me somewhere to start.'

Lucy stared at him for a moment, clearly thinking about the content of the messages. He had no idea what secrets girls that age might share, and he didn't want to pry.

'Can you tell me what you're looking for? If I knew that, I could maybe find all the relevant stuff?'

'That seems fair. Any photos – no matter how innocuous they might seem – would be really useful. Comments about school or friends' names. Also her mobile number – the one she used to contact you last. I've no doubt it's changed now, but I might be able to trace where it was last used.'

Tom wasn't sure he could pull that off, as he was on leave and couldn't use police resources. But if he could prove that Jack and his family were officially missing, it would be a different story.

Lucy pulled her phone out of her pocket. 'We mainly used WhatsApp. How about if I export the chat, edit out stuff you don't need to see, and then send it to you?'

'Sounds fair enough, and I'm sorry to ask. I'm not being nosey, Luce, I promise. Just get me any photos, anything that might suggest where they are – even if it's the name of some boy she fancies at school. I don't need the specifics – just his name.'

Lucy's eyes widened. Tom really didn't want to read that conversation.

'I'll go and check. I'll let you know if there's anything.'

With that, Lucy pushed the rest of the cheese into her mouth and headed for the stairs, eyes glued to her phone.

4

Harry had dropped off to sleep by the time Louisa arrived at the café by the park where she had agreed to meet Kate. Tom thought she handled his ex-wife well, but Louisa wasn't so sure. She was determined not to create battle lines, but Kate sometimes made life difficult. It was clear she harboured deep resentment against Tom, even though *she* had left *him*, not the other way round. What really seemed to gall her, though, was that he was happy, and Louisa always felt she had to tiptoe around the pair of them in an endless effort to keep the peace.

There was no sign of Kate, and Louisa wasn't sure whether to go inside or stay outside in the sunshine. She preferred outside, but knowing how contrary Kate could be, Louisa was almost certain she would suggest they move.

'Louisa, there you are!' The voice came from behind her. 'I should have guessed you'd be outside. Is the sun not a little too strong?'

Louisa almost laughed but decided to stick to her guns. 'It's better if we sit here – for Harry, at least. He's sheltered from the sun and wind in his pushchair, and fresh air is better, isn't it?'

Kate frowned but pulled out a chair. 'What's this about, Louisa?

You don't usually suggest that we meet, so I suspect there's some ulterior motive. Tom's, no doubt.'

'If your daughter's an ulterior motive, then yes. We love having her with us and she can stay any time she wants. Harry adores her and misses her when she's not there, but we'd never try to persuade her to stay. Tom knows it's important that you and Lucy maintain the strong bond you've always had, and he's concerned that the business with Jack has come between you. I want to know if I can help.'

'You mean Tom does. How very magnanimous of him, considering he's the one that's caused all this trouble – making mountains out of molehills, allowing my daughter to think her mother's at fault. I didn't make anything up – I only spoke the truth – but somehow I'm the guilty party, even though *I'm* not the one covering the tracks of a known criminal.'

Louisa cast an anxious look around to check if anyone was listening. Fortunately, everyone nearby seemed to be chatting happily.

'You know Tom's not been able to make contact with Jack, don't you? Lucy said she told you.'

'*Blamed* me, more like. And what a lot of fuss about nothing. Maybe he's going to pretend he's dead again – a repeat performance – breaking everyone's heart. I was there when Tom learned Jack had been "killed" in that freak accident.' Kate emphasised 'killed' with finger quotes – a gesture that irritated Louisa. 'Tom was devastated, and I've no idea how he can forgive Jack, brother or no brother.'

Before Louisa could answer, a waiter approached the table, giving her a moment to let her anger settle. She was tempted to order a gin and tonic but settled for a cup of coffee instead.

'Okay – coming up – one cappuccino and one matcha latte,' the waiter said before turning away. Louisa took a steadying breath, resisting the urge to ask what the hell a matcha latte tasted like. Wasn't it made from ground-up green tea? She pulled her thoughts back to the problem at hand.

'Kate, it's been explained to you many times that Jack faked his death to protect the people he loved – including your daughter. It was either that or continue to be under the control of the gang. He knows he made mistakes, but he put his life on the line to bring down those criminals, and ever since, he's done whatever it takes to protect his family. Which, in his eyes, includes Lucy.'

Louisa could hear her voice rising, so she paused, took a few breaths and counted to ten.

'What do you expect me to do?' Kate asked. 'Beg for forgiveness?'

'Your relationship with your daughter is your business – I wouldn't dream of suggesting how you approach it. But the present situation is a problem, and the best solution for all concerned would be for Tom to find Jack, establish that he's not in any danger, and then it will be over. Do you agree?'

'It's a solution, I suppose. But God knows how you think I can help with that.'

The drinks arrived, giving Louisa a few seconds to rethink her strategy. She had come prepared with a speech, but now that Kate had opened the door a crack, she realised a different approach might work: making her feel valued.

'There's one thing you can do. We have no way of knowing whether Jack's disappearance had anything to do with the people you mentioned him to, but Tom's trying to rule out all the options. I think he'd appreciate your help. He wonders if you believe any of your friends could have criminal connections – at any level.'

Kate laughed. 'Only Tom would think that. Of course they're not criminals!'

'No, I didn't mean that. Maybe one of them has connections to the prison service or other police officers. People talk, and word can spread so easily. Or someone in their families might have links to crime. I read somewhere – this didn't come from Tom – that one in a thousand people in the UK are involved in some way with organised crime. Not just petty crime. The big stuff.'

'And how in God's name am I supposed to know that? They don't exactly wear a badge, do they?'

'Maybe you have a friend who seems to have more money than you'd expect, given their job – or their partner's job. Flashy car, exclusive clubs, lots of jewellery?'

Kate tutted. 'I feel like a spy. I won't interrogate them. And now I'll be questioning how my friends can afford their clothes, wondering if their husbands are part of the underworld. No! I won't do it, Louisa.' She took a sip of her drink, and Louisa could have sworn she winced. If Kate had to choose something she didn't like just to stand out, Louisa couldn't help feeling a bit sorry for her.

'I understand why you're not keen, Kate. I wouldn't want to second-guess people either. If they're genuine friends then I'm sure you'd know if they were likely to be the source of the leak. Don't worry. I'll tell Tom you can't think who it might be.'

Kate couldn't quite meet Louisa's eyes as she stirred her latte. 'They're not good friends, really. I've only met most of them since I came back from Australia.' She looked up. 'But I gave Tom all their names. He can check for himself, can't he?'

'He's on leave and without access to the police system, so it would help if there was a hint of something worth investigating.'

'Well, we both know Tom thinks he's above the law, so why can't he ask one of his juniors to do a search?'

Louisa flinched at the word 'juniors'. This wasn't going the way she had intended, and it wouldn't help to get into a discussion about Tom's unwillingness to break the rules.

'What about the guy you were on the date with? How much do you know about him?'

Kate leaned across the table, her gaze steady. Her lips pressed into a thin line. 'Next to nothing, thanks to Tom. He wasn't impressed that my ex-husband interrupted dinner to ask about me supposedly spreading rumours, and suggested it wasn't a good time to get to know each other. So do thank him for me, Louisa.'

Louisa felt a stab of sympathy. 'He wouldn't have wanted that to happen. You know that.'

Kate gave a dismissive huff and bent to pick up her bag. Leaving her drink unfinished, she stood up.

'I can't help. Tell Tom I accept that it may have been inadvisable to mention his brother to strangers, but also point out that I'm not the criminal here. If there was nothing to hide, there wouldn't be a problem.'

With that, Kate gave a tight-lipped smile and left Louisa to settle the bill.

5

Lucy looked sheepish when she came to find Tom, who was still poring over his computer at the kitchen table. One glance at her expression and he guessed she'd had to edit quite a bit of teenage banter out of the chat.

'I've found some stuff, Dad; I don't know if it's useful or not.' She put a couple of sheets of paper on the table in front of him. 'There's a bit about school. She didn't want to learn Welsh and was relieved it wasn't necessary. It was bad enough that she'd had to learn Spanish, but that was in another life, she said. Not sure if that helps.'

Tom knew all about the other life, and he would never forget the night he whisked Ava – or Tasha, as she was then – to the airport with the rest of the family. They had been booked on a flight, but he didn't even bother to check the destination because he was certain that as soon as it landed they would transfer to another plane, with passports in new names. He'd always assumed they'd ended up in South America, based on the few bits of information Jack had shared since, and it explained why Ava spoke Spanish.

'She panicked when she told me that – swore me to secrecy because she wasn't supposed to let even that much slip. I can't imagine what her life's like. She says her friends give her hell for not sharing stuff on social. She's told them it's lame and she's over it, but it must be tricky. She's been tagged in a few photos, but if she tells her dad, he does something to limit who can see the picture without her friends knowing it's kind of hidden. No idea what that's about.'

'It makes sense. The people who took Ava when she was six believe she's dead, and while it might seem a long time ago to you, it's only a few years since she escaped. She was thirteen when she got away from them. Your uncle's trying to keep her safe – and he can make technology sing if you ask him to. Always could. I've never understood how he does it. We don't share the same type of brain, I'm sorry to say.'

Lucy huffed. 'I don't think that's true. You solve crimes. That takes loads of logic – just a different sort.'

Tom gave her a fleeting smile. 'You're very kind, but there are so many processes now, so many ways of tracking criminals, that my input isn't as critical as it used to be. Anyway, forget that. Maybe I can use my detective skills now. Let's have a look at the messages you've printed.'

'They're not going to cause you any problems, I promise.' Lucy grinned, and Tom couldn't decide if he loved or hated the fact that she was growing up. 'There are some photos that might help – ones she sent me but obviously couldn't share anywhere else. I can't see anything useful, but you might.'

Tom looked at the printout. 'You'd be surprised. Sometimes there's a clue in something that seems absolutely innocuous.' He picked up a page. 'Take this photo, for example. In the background there's a bridge, and I can just make out the sign of a pub or hotel. Can you send me the original? I can blow it up and see if we can read the name, or I can put it into a reverse image search. If we can find the village where this was taken, it's a start. Ava says in the attached message that the river she's standing by is half an hour's walk from home. That gives us a radius to work with, based on walking at about three miles per hour. It could be hilly, or a winding road – but it's still helpful.'

'Wow! Told you you're a good detective.'

Tom smiled as he scanned the printed pages. In another message Ava had mentioned they lived 'miles from anywhere', which, given the thirty-minute walk to the village in the picture, Tom assumed meant anywhere of interest to a teenage girl.

His mobile pinged as the picture arrived from Lucy's phone. He pulled it into a photo app and expanded it.

'I can read the name of the pub. That's helpful. I'm just going to run this through the image search.'

Lucy came to stand behind him, resting her chin on his shoulder.

'That's it!' she squealed as the screen showed some very close matches.

'Yep, it seems to be Beddgelert, a village in Snowdonia. I'll check the pub name to be sure.' There was a pause as Tom typed it into the search engine. 'That's the one. Brilliant, Lucy! We know she lived within a thirty-minute walk of here. We also know she goes to a school where she doesn't have to speak Welsh, and it has to be a school with a sixth form, given her age. While I do some digging, do you want to do a bit of detective work yourself? See if she ever talks about her journey to school or mentions any friends by name. Anything that might help.'

Lucy pulled out the chair next to Tom, phone in hand, her eyes glued to her screen as he began a search of schools in North Wales. Maybe, just maybe, they were going to find a clue to where Jack had been living – and from there, perhaps discover what the hell had happened to him.

'I might have found something,' Lucy said, half an hour later. 'You said anything might be important, though I'm not sure what you'll make of this.'

Tom felt a tingle of optimism. 'Try me.'

'She moans about her dad in one of the messages – I didn't show you that one,' she admitted with an apologetic grimace.

'Don't worry, just tell me what she says. You can paraphrase, as long as you don't miss out anything important.'

Lucy nodded. 'Basically, she says her dad's a...pain. He insists on either picking her up from school every day – always from a different spot – or she can catch the bus, but she has to get off at a different stop each time, and he's always there waiting. Doesn't he trust her, Dad?'

'I don't think it's that, Luce. I suspect he's worried that someone will follow her.'

'Gosh, that must be awful. Poor Ava.'

Tom agreed, but it was still better than the life she'd had before. Just about anything would be.

'I think I may have found the school too,' Tom said. 'The fact that Ava doesn't need to speak Welsh was the biggest clue. There's an independent school in Bangor where Welsh is a second language. Now, I need to figure out how to get them to give up her address.'

'You're a detective; they're bound to tell you.'

Tom pulled a face. 'Well, I'm on leave, so that complicates things. They'll want to verify who I am before they give out any details – and quite rightly so.'

Lucy frowned. 'Are you sure all this is necessary, Dad? Aren't you worrying more than you need to?'

Tom shook his head as he picked up his mobile. 'I don't know, love, but I don't want you to get stressed by it. Leave that to me. I think I know someone who might help.'

Selecting a number from his contacts, he hit the Call button and waited.

'Well, good afternoon, DCI Robinson,' he said.

'Tom! What a nice surprise,' Becky answered. 'Don't tell me you're coming back already. I've only had my temporary promotion for a few days.'

'Don't worry. Your job's safe, and anyway, you deserve a permanent promotion. How's everyone doing?' Tom asked, missing his team more than he cared to admit.

'Well, Rob is still bouncing around like an overgrown puppy, and Keith still has the tidiest desk I've ever seen. He's straightening papers as we speak. In other words, nothing much has changed. What are you up to? Any news about…?'

Becky wouldn't mention Jack's name in the office. She was one of only two people who knew why Tom had taken leave, the other being Detective Superintendent Philippa Stanley.

'Nothing, but that's why I'm calling. I need to ask a favour. I think I've tracked down which school Ava – the stepdaughter – goes to.'

There was silence at the other end as Becky tried to piece it together. He wasn't sure if he'd ever mentioned the name Ava before. Becky knew her as Tasha, but she'd work it out.

'That will be…the stepdaughter who's now, by my reckoning, about seventeen?' she asked.

'That's her, though technically Ava is *Clare's* stepdaughter. His stepson is *Billy* – now around five.' He could almost hear Becky's mind spinning as she matched new names to each member of the family.

'Ri…ight,' Becky said. 'So Clare's the wife? Then there's Ava, and Billy. And their dad's name is…'

'Pete. I'll send the surname in a message. Is this making sense?'

'Just about. Any other children I need to know about?'

'A baby sister, Sophia. Not quite two, so not at school yet.'

'And you think you know which school Ava goes to?'

'I do. By a process of elimination. I'll message you the details.'

Jack had always warned him to be cautious on the phone. Tom's house and car had been bugged at least once, so he didn't share anything that could be useful to a third party.

'And you want me to…'

'Could you call the school and check if she's been attending for the past week or so? Maybe see if they'll provide her home address? I'd do it myself, but if they call the office to check me out, they might refuse.'

'And I want to know because…'

'You could say a family member is of interest to the major incident team, but you're having difficulty tracking them down. Their home address would be helpful.'

'I'm guessing you've done all the obvious things to locate his address?'

'Yep. No driving licence in his or Clare's name, nothing in the Land Registry or electoral roll.'

Becky tutted. 'Course not. And do you know how Pete earns a living these days?'

'Not a clue, Becky. But he must be making money because – well, you know his past.'

Tom was suddenly hit by the memory of the day he was told his brother had died and that he had inherited all his money – millions he didn't want and had barely touched. It had been years before he learned Jack was alive.

'I guess there was never any way of getting his money back to him,' Becky said.

'Not easily. Not without questions that might lead to his door. And that's one door that needs to remain locked.'

'Leave it with me then.' There was a pause. 'Look, Tom, I know you're worried. *More* than worried. You wouldn't have taken extra time off if you weren't. But Pete's been in plenty of scrapes before and managed to survive.'

'This is different, Becky. For years, people – particularly Philippa – have laughed at me when I've said what my gut's telling me. Rightly or wrongly, it's telling me now that something bad has happened. He's in trouble. Worse than the usual trouble. I can *feel* it.'

6

I stare into the mirror, not liking what I see. Dark circles smudge my eyes, evidence of sleepless nights and relentless days. The woman staring back is a ghost of who I used to be, a testament to who I've become. Five years of hiding in the shadows have stripped away the person I once was, but I've had to accept that only the ruthless survive in the world I've chosen to inhabit.

I glance over my shoulder at the apartment I've called home for the last few weeks. The high ceilings make the room feel spacious. Soft evening light filters through large windows, casting shadows on the tiled floor. It should feel comfortable, but I can't wait to be out of here.

I cross the room and throw the windows wide, listening to the voices from the path below – tourists, enjoying the city. With each peal of laughter, I feel more alone. My eyes stray towards your photo, the one I take with me everywhere. Your brown eyes are laughing at me, crinkling at the corners, your thick black hair mussed where you lie against the pillow, the stubble on your jaw catching the light. I remember taking it, wanting to freeze the way you looked at me. I press my fingers against my chest, feeling the bite of the cold diamond of my engagement ring against my skin, a constant reminder of why I'm doing this.

I'll never forget the night you proposed, Alessandro. You understood *how I shy away from having my life on public display, a lingering echo from my childhood. You made the occasion perfect by whisking me away to a secluded hillside under the stars – the two of us alone, under the night sky. You took my hand and asked me to be your wife. No embarrassing scene in a crowded restaurant, no grand gesture, just a moment that belonged only to us.*

Now it feels as if the answers to my relentless questions are almost within reach, as if I might finally learn why you were taken from me.

I walk over to the table and pull out a chair. In front of me sits my master plan – everything I've done, everything I still need to do. It's all coming together and everyone is exactly where I want them to be. No one is in any doubt about what they need to do. But it doesn't mean they like it.

It doesn't mean I like it either.

I trace the steps of my plan with my finger. So much achieved, so much still to do. I've crossed many lines, but my purpose is clear: to discover the truth.

I knew something was bothering you. I thought it was your work – something to do with the people you dealt with daily, not all of whom you trusted. But why didn't you talk to me?

'It's nothing, darling,' you said, reaching out an arm to pull me towards you. 'Just a tricky client who's never satisfied with the investments I recommend.' It was more than that, though. When I looked into your eyes, you seemed lost.

Sometimes I worry that I'll find you alive, but that you'll turn away – appalled at the changes in the woman whose morality you admired so much, the woman who battled against some of the most dangerous people in the world in search of justice. Would I now even recognise the person I was back then?

I wonder what you'll see when you look at me: a woman who rarely smiles, whose edges are so sharp you could cut yourself, who has built fences to repel anyone who tries to get close. And not many risk it.

All I hope is that when I find you, you will understand why I've made the choices I have, and you will forgive me.

Maybe you will. At least for most of it.

I rest my finger on a step on my plan written in red.

The girl.

Can I forgive myself for the girl? That's another question I can't answer – one I hope I'll never have to.

7

Tom bounced along the narrow track, relieved he'd chosen to drive to Wales in his old Jeep. It might be fourteen years old, but it felt much safer on this terrain than his brand-new BMW.

He'd been tempted to head for Wales as soon as he'd heard from Becky the previous afternoon, but it was late in the day so he'd delayed his departure until the morning. In the end, he hadn't been able to sleep and had left at 5.30 a.m.

His hands tightened on the wheel as he thought about what he might find when he reached the farmhouse where Jack and his family had apparently been living. He could only hope that they had simply disappeared somewhere to stay safe. If that was true, maybe he'd find a clue to where they had gone, but his mind couldn't help turning over and over his belief that something bad had happened, and that he was about to discover what. Nothing else explained the silence.

Glancing at the satnav, he wished he could ask it if it was sure this was the right way. The track appeared barely used, and yet Ava had said her dad took her to school. Given the location of their home, those journeys had to have been by car, so maybe there was another way to reach the house, known only to locals.

Although it was half-term, it had taken Becky less than an hour to get an answer from Ava's school. The information provided was alarming. Not only had Ava failed to attend for a couple of weeks prior to the break, but the head teacher confirmed that a local primary school had been in touch with her. It seemed Billy had been absent too, and they'd been unable to contact his parents.

'The children weren't considered at risk,' Becky told Tom. 'But when neither school could contact the parents, they decided their absence should be followed up. They arranged for a welfare officer to visit the house, but they couldn't get an answer or see any signs of life. Both schools are waiting until the end of half-term to see if the kids return to class, thinking maybe it's an unauthorised holiday. If not, and the family still can't be located, the police will be asked to look into it.'

Tom had groaned. 'We need to prevent that if we can. I'll go to Wales myself.'

'The head gave me the address, once she'd checked I was who I said I was, and I suggested that, as the family are of interest to Greater Manchester Police, we should pursue their absence in the first instance. No need to involve anyone else yet.'

Becky had overstepped the mark by checking this out for Tom. Clearly there was no current Greater Manchester Police investigation, and should the North Wales force become involved in the search for the family, they would query her actions. For her sake, he had to sort this out before it became a problem.

Now he was here, and he was struggling to understand why Jack had chosen this location. He had expected somewhere remote, which this certainly was, but he'd assumed it would have a wide view of the surrounding countryside so Jack could spot anyone approaching, and yet the only access seemed to be via a twisting overgrown track through dense woodland.

Just as he was wondering when the house would come into view, he rounded a bend and stamped on the brakes.

'Bollocks,' he muttered, slamming his hands on the steering wheel with frustration.

Dense foliage had been encroaching further and further onto the track with each hundred metres, and he was now faced with a full-sized fallen tree trunk blocking the way forward.

He jumped out of the Jeep. The trunk was too big to move, its bark peeling and covered in moss. The ground around it was littered with decomposing leaves. It had lain here for weeks – months, probably – and he couldn't see any way of getting round it. The Jeep could handle most types of terrain, but it couldn't get between the tightly packed conifers on either side of the track.

Resisting the temptation to give the tree a hard kick, he realised that, short of retracing his journey and trying to find another route in, he was going to have to travel the rest of the way on foot. According to the pin on his phone, it was less than half a mile to the farmhouse, so he took a long drink of water and picked up the bag he'd packed the previous night. Aware that he might have to break into the property, Tom had brought everything from a lock pick to a mini crowbar. Wincing at a sharp stab of pain in his chest as he shouldered the bag, he climbed over the trunk and continued along what was left of the track.

With each step the forest seemed to close in around him, the undergrowth thickening. Twisted roots snaked across the path, ready to trip him up, and the air grew cooler and damper, the scent of earth and decaying leaves hanging heavily. Birds sang from the treetops far above, their cheerful calls a stark contrast to the sombre silence at ground level. Somewhere nearby, a woodpecker drummed persistently on a tree, the rapid taps echoing through the forest.

Pushing aside a low-hanging branch, Tom glanced up at the thick canopy, the interlocking branches creating a web of shadows, and he quickened his pace, driven by a gnawing unease urging him to reach the farmhouse as quickly as possible. None of this made sense. No one had been on this path for a long time. Had Jack provided a false address to the school? Was this a wild goose chase?

He couldn't decide whether or not he hoped it was. He wanted to find Jack and his family, but he wanted them fit and healthy and a long way from this forest.

. . .

Tom sensed that he was getting close. There was a subtle change in the light up ahead as sunlight filtered through the leaves. The birdsong grew louder, and as he rounded another bend the forest abruptly opened up.

Sitting in the middle of a large clearing was a double-fronted traditional stone farmhouse, its slate roof reflecting the sunlight. Tom stopped to rest his aching body and stared at the window boxes filled with spring pansies. A rose growing around the bright blue front door was coming into bud. He waited, hoping the door was about to be flung open, his brother stepping out to greet him.

Was this Jack's house?

The thought that Jack and his family had been living just over two hours from Tom's own home sent tingles up his spine. He could imagine them here – Billy on the swing in the garden, Clare watering the window boxes, Ava playing with her baby sister. And Jack? What would he have been doing?

Tom found it hard to think of his brother taking care of the jobs needed to maintain such a property. He was a computer nerd, a man who had always been happier with technology than tackling practical jobs. It felt weird, disturbing. But the possibility that Jack's seemingly idyllic life here may have unravelled was even more unsettling.

There were many things puzzling Tom, but top of the list was how Jack could have protected the house against unwelcome visitors. Given his obsession with privacy and secrecy, he must have had security in place, otherwise anyone could have sneaked up to the house unseen, unheard, and that didn't sound like Jack. Tom couldn't see any cameras, but there could be infrared sensors hidden in hollows in trees or bushes, or motion detectors underfoot. If there were, and Jack was in the house now, he would know someone was coming.

And Tom still didn't understand how the property was accessed by car. There had to be another track, so he scanned the grounds. To the right of the house he noticed a gravelled area leading into the forest. It wasn't on the map he had brought, or on Google Maps, but

Tom could just make out an arched wooden structure with trees trained to grow over it. It would be invisible from above, and it might explain how the family and those familiar with the area got in and out.

His eyes travelled back to the farmhouse. He was standing in full view of the windows, and had Jack been there, he would by now have come out to greet him. But there was no sign of life. Apart from the birds and the occasional rustling of small creatures in the undergrowth, there was silence – the type that shrieked abandonment.

Tom swallowed. He was going to have to get inside the house and face whatever he found. He wished he hadn't come alone. Throughout his time at GMP, he had almost always had one of his team by his side. He remembered racing through woods with Keith Sims, sneaking up a dark stairway with Becky Robinson. A hundred other similar occasions leaped into his mind, when he had always been confident that someone had his back.

But now, there was no one.

8

Becky Robinson arrived at her desk at eight o'clock to find a Post-it stuck to her monitor.

> Det Supt Stanley called – wants to see
> you ASAP

That was all she needed first thing, but she decided she might as well get it over with.

'Come,' was the response to Becky's knock. She remembered how Tom had hated that, and it made her smile for a moment as she pushed the door open.

'I'm not sure what you're grinning about, DCI Robinson, but you and I need to talk. I've had North Wales Police on the telephone, asking about our interest in a family called Johnson. I had to lie – something I'm not fond of doing – and tell them it was an under-cover operation. Basically, I didn't have a clue what they were talking about, and that doesn't please me. Would you care to explain?'

Becky groaned inwardly. It had been a risk, but she had thought it might be sorted by the end of the day and no one would be any the wiser.

'Did they say what *their* interest in the family is, ma'am?' she asked.

'I'm asking the questions, not you.'

'I'm sorry. It was something Tom had been working on before he left. I was trying to tie up a few loose ends.'

Philippa glared at her. 'DCI Robinson, if you wish to retain that title, you are going to have to do better than that. I understand loyalty, but at this moment your loyalty should be to me and to this force. Not to Tom Douglas. Do you understand me?'

'Yes, ma'am,' Becky said, looking straight ahead, not wanting to meet Philippa's eyes.

'I'll spare you the trouble, as you've already managed to disappoint me. Two schools have expressed concern about the absence of pupils from the same family. Yes, it's possible the parents have taken them on holiday without prior authorisation, but apparently this is distinctly out of character. The schools have failed to make contact with either parent, and North Wales Police have been notified. However, this morning one of the head teachers concerned asked them to stand down because the disappearance of these children – and potentially their parents – is being investigated by Greater Manchester Police. And in particular by a certain Detective Chief Inspector Robinson. Is this ringing any bells with you?'

Becky continued to stare straight ahead, aware of the rising tone of irritation in Philippa's voice. 'I'm sorry, ma'am. The school said they hadn't reported this to the local force yet, so I didn't think I was treading on any toes.'

'It seems one of the children's teachers is married to an officer, so although it wasn't official, she asked him to bring it to the attention of his boss. You may not have thought you were treading on any toes, but where exactly *were* you treading? Because it doesn't relate to any case that I know of.' Before Becky could answer, Philippa leaned back, arms folded. 'This isn't a case Tom was working on, is it? It's his personal investigation. I *knew* it! So who is this family?'

Becky was never sure how much Philippa knew. All she was aware of was that Philippa had supported Tom when Jack first left the country with his family four years ago. She didn't know how up to date she was with the situation. Did she even know Jack was back in the country?

'I'm sorry, ma'am, but this isn't entirely my tale to tell.'

'Oh, stop avoiding the question, Becky. I know why Tom has taken leave. He was honest with me about that. Who are these people in Wales?'

Becky finally met her boss's eyes. 'They're a family who left the UK four years ago, but returned two years later for the birth of their daughter, Sophia. They have two other children – the ones the schools are concerned about. Ava is now seventeen. Billy is five. They have been living in Wales for the last two years, apparently.'

Philippa's eyes narrowed and she gave a slight nod. 'Understood. And am I also to understand that prior to your call to the head teacher yesterday, Tom had no idea of the address for this family?'

Becky nodded.

'Well, he should *not* have asked you to get involved. I'll speak to him. Do we know his plan?'

'He was aiming to go to the house in Wales today. He doesn't want the police involved – there's so little he's able to tell them, and the last thing he wants is family photos in the media. For obvious reasons.'

Philippa's lips had settled into a thin line. 'This was supposed to be a time for Tom to sort out his *own* problems. Not to drag us and other forces into this mess. Probably the only solution is for me to speak to my opposite number in North Wales and explain that a member of the family in question – without being precise – is a covert human intelligence source.'

Only Philippa would use the full title, rather than saying 'CHIS' like everyone else on the force, but she was probably right. They couldn't say the family were under police protection, because the local force's witness protection team would have been informed if that were the case.

'Can I suggest we play it down, ma'am? Maybe something local to us that doesn't affect them in Wales. That way, they can call off the hunt but tell the head teachers at each school that it's in hand.'

Philippa put her head on one side and glared at Becky. 'I think I know what to do, thank you.' With that, she leaned forward and bent over the papers on her desk.

Realising she had been dismissed, Becky headed towards the door. She hadn't even been offered a seat, so the boss was obviously less than pleased.

As she was about to leave the room, Philippa spoke again, her voice a fraction softer.

'Becky, don't let Tom use you. I know you want to help him, as do I, but you need to protect your own job too. This wasn't a major misdemeanour, but don't let it escalate. I'll speak to Tom and tell him any further requests for help have to come through me. There's no reason for you to speak to him any further about this. Do we understand each other?'

'Yes, ma'am,' Becky said, knowing full well that the first moment she got, she was going to call Tom.

9

In the ten minutes since the farmhouse had revealed itself, Tom had been rooted to the spot, hoping – with dwindling confidence – that the door would open and Jack would rush out to greet him. But there was no sign of life within the house; the windows were dark, blank, staring back at him like empty eyes.

His heart jumped when he glimpsed movement to the left of the building. But it was nothing more than a squirrel darting up the trunk of a tree.

Tom thought he had imagined every possible scenario: from the horrific thought that the family were lying dead in the house, murdered – the fate that had been planned for them four years ago – to finding them recovering from a virus that had left them bedridden. One thing he hadn't considered until this moment was that someone could be holding them captive and would be watching, monitoring his every move. Whatever the situation, he couldn't just stand there; he was going to have to try to get inside. He had no idea if Jack's alarm system was linked to the local police, but he doubted it. He would have his own security system in place, and how Tom would get past that, he had no idea.

He pulled the bag off his shoulder, grabbed his water bottle and took a large gulp, aware he was putting off the moment, knowing he should alert someone to his whereabouts in case he was about to be ambushed. With a guilty conscience, he marked his location on Google Maps and opened a message to Becky.

> Becky – one more favour. Please don't reply
> or call. But if you don't hear from me in one
> hour, this is where I am. Sorry!

He pressed Send, uncomfortable with involving her again, but feeling it was his only option.

He started to move, slowly at first, then picking up his pace, suddenly needing to run, to find his brother, his family – to make sure they were safe. Jogging towards the door, his eyes scanned the house to see if he had triggered an alarm that had brought someone to a window. But there wasn't so much as the twitch of a curtain.

As he approached the blue front door, Tom stopped and turned in a slow circle. Was someone watching him from the trees? He saw nothing but the beauty of the surroundings, the mountains of Snowdonia rising majestically above the forest. The silence was almost unnerving, so with a slight shiver he turned back to face the door.

He scoured its surface. Not only was there no lock that he might stand a chance of picking, there was no lock *at all*. Nor was there a handle. The door was a solid-looking structure of closely fitted painted wooden boards, which Tom suspected hid a central core of steel. He looked around, expecting to see a keypad or scanner – some means of entering the house. Nothing. He reached into his bag for the mini crowbar, not certain it would be strong enough for the job, but it was the best he had.

Just as he was about to attempt to insert it between door and frame, he heard a soft but distinct *clunk* of locks disengaging. Tom took a quick step back, holding fast to the crowbar. The door inched open, but no one appeared. He spun round again, certain he was being watched, but the trees were as still as ever. There was no sign of life.

Who had let him into the house? Where were they?

He reached out a hand and pushed the door with his fingertips, listening for the screech of an alarm. It swung inwards without a sound. Beyond it, the hall stood empty, silent. Taking a hesitant step over the threshold, Tom stood, listening. The air smelled stale but there were no putrid odours, and he exhaled slowly with a flicker of relief. There was a dead feeling to the house, but there were no bodies here.

A vase of drying daffodils and wilted tulips, their withered petals scattered over the top of a side table, told him what he needed to know: Jack and his family weren't here. They had gone.

So who had opened the door? Was someone waiting, lurking around a corner, ready to pounce?

He advanced slowly, a step at a time, wishing he had more than the small crowbar to protect himself. There was no point calling out. Had anyone wanted to greet him, they would have made themselves known by now. Tom made his way through the downstairs rooms one by one, pushing back each door in turn, glancing inside quickly, letting out his breath as each room proved empty, barely taking in the details of the comfortable home Jack and Clare had created.

A few toys were scattered around as if they had been abandoned mid-game. In the kitchen, washed dishes had been left to dry and there were crumbs on the table, a pepper mill lying on its side, a half-drunk cup of coffee. He opened the fridge. No perishables, and the waste bin was empty but the bin liner hadn't been replaced.

It looked to Tom as if they had done the minimum to clear up before leaving, which suggested they left out of choice, but in a hurry. Or they could have been taken, their abductors staging the scene to make it *look* as if they'd left abruptly. There was no way of knowing.

At the far end of the kitchen was a door. Assuming it led to a cellar, Tom pushed it open – but there were no steps down, just a small windowless room crammed into the centre of the house. The complex locking system on the inside of the door told Tom this was Jack's panic room. Two bunk beds and a sofa were made up with duvets and pillows. A desk was pushed against one wall, strewn with disconnected wires suggesting a computer had been there – maybe a laptop. But it wasn't there now. Bottled water was stacked in the corner, while packets of crackers, tins of tuna, protein bars and similar ready-to-eat foods lay on a shelf. There was no evidence that this or any other part of the downstairs of the house had been ransacked by an intruder – no mess, no open drawers, and the bedding on the bunks was tidy. Only the technology was missing.

Leaving the room as he found it, Tom made his way back through the kitchen to the stairs, increasingly certain that the house was empty. There was an uncanny stillness to the space, no background hum of life. No rustles of movement or creaks of floorboards. Tom had always felt that an empty house had a distinctive texture – a sense of solitude. That was what he felt now.

Despite his certainty, his heart was thudding as he climbed slowly, quietly, up the stairs, clutching his makeshift weapon. He moved along the corridor, pushing open each door in turn. Stuffed animals lined the window ledge in what was surely Sophia's room, Lego littered the floor of Billy's, and the dressing table of Ava's was cluttered with make-up and a few colourful bracelets. The final room – which seemed to be Jack and Clare's – looked as if it would normally have been a haven of peace. But not now.

One wardrobe door was wide open, hangers scattered as if clothes had been dragged off them. Drawers gaped, underwear spilling out. Tom walked over to open the other door of the wardrobe. To his surprise, there were a couple of men's suits with some formal shirts, and he struggled to imagine Jack wearing anything like this. There were T-shirts and jeans – far more in character – but what was obvious was that Jack's side of the wardrobe was largely undisturbed. It was Clare's clothes that had been pulled from hangers; her underwear drawer that had been raided. Not Jack's.

Did this mean that Clare and the children were the ones who had left in a hurry? Where was Jack in this picture? Did he leave with them? Maybe he didn't have time to pack. Or maybe when they left, he had already gone.

Tom lowered himself onto the edge of the bed, his eyes never leaving the bedroom door. Despite his certainty that he was alone, he couldn't understand how the front door had opened without him so much as touching it. It couldn't be triggered automatically each time someone approached the house, otherwise any random caller could gain access.

Leaning back on his hands, Tom wondered if he had achieved anything by coming here. The only thing he now knew for sure was that the family had gone; they weren't lying injured or dead – or at least, not here. Was this hurried departure down to Kate spreading gossip about Tom's criminal brother? Had word got back to the underworld of Manchester that Jack Douglas was alive and well?

If so, Jack's death warrant had been signed. And possibly not only his.

10

Tom had almost forgotten to contact Becky. He'd been so intent on trying to make sense of what little evidence there was in the house that it had been almost an hour since he'd told her to call in the cavalry if she didn't hear from him. Wary of speaking in a house that could be bugged, for all he knew, he propped the front door open and escaped to the garden.

'Becky,' he said, relieved to hear her voice. 'Sorry if I put you in a difficult position, but I was about to enter the house in Wales, and I didn't know if there might be someone waiting inside. Someone I didn't want to meet.'

'You sound out of breath. Is everything okay?' Becky asked.

'Yes and no. I don't want to say too much over the phone, but at some stage I'd really value your take – face to face – on what I've discovered. Or not discovered, in fact.'

'The house is empty?'

'It is. I can't say more right now, but it would be great to see you and just chew over what I've found – which isn't much. I'm going back in to look round a bit more. Are you around tonight? Just an hour would really help me sort this out in my head.'

'Give me a minute. I need to head away from the office. I'll call you back.'

Tom made his way across to a garden bench and sat down. He didn't know what to make of everything he'd found. He couldn't see any obvious signs of a struggle, so was he worrying unnecessarily? Maybe there was a good reason why Jack hadn't been in touch. Perhaps Louisa was right – if Tom kept digging, he might expose Jack to more danger.

He lifted his face to the sun, hoping for inspiration. It didn't come, but fortunately he didn't have long to wait for Becky to call him back.

'Tom, you need to know that Philippa's on the warpath. Someone at the school had already notified the police of their concerns, so Philippa's oppo in North Wales contacted her to ask about the investigation we're running. I think she bluffed her way through, but she's not impressed.'

'Bollocks. Sorry, I shouldn't have roped you in. I won't ask you to do anything else, except perhaps listen to me and help me work out what the hell is going on.'

'She says any further requests should go through her, and I shouldn't discuss this with you again. I'll ignore that last bit.'

Tom groaned. 'You mustn't. Don't jeopardise your new job, Becky. If I need anything else, I'll contact Philippa.'

'Oh shut up, Tom. There's absolutely no reason why you shouldn't call round and see Buster, is there? And Mark's cooking curry tonight, so bring Louisa if you can get a babysitter.'

'That's good of you, but Louisa's working tonight and she's already organised a babysitter – she didn't know if I'd be back. So it will just be me. To be honest, I'd rather she didn't hear some of the possibilities we'll have to consider. I'm going to go back into the farmhouse and check the study more thoroughly, although I guess the computer system will be impenetrable. Can I let you know later if I'm going to be back in time to come round?'

'Course. Just…maybe while you're there, send me a text every so often so I know you haven't had any unwelcome visitors. Okay?'

Tom smiled. 'Okay. See you later, and thanks, Becky.'

With that, Tom ended the call. It was almost certainly unnecessary to speak in code, but it had become second nature not to mention Jack's name. He wished he'd been able to talk to Becky about the door, though. He could only think of three possible explanations: that the door always opened automatically when someone drew close, which he discounted immediately; that somehow his face had been programmed into the security system and had recognised him – anything was possible when it came to Jack; or that someone was watching the house through Jack's security system and had remotely activated the door lock. That seemed the most likely – but was that Jack, or had someone else gained control of his system?

Going back into the house for the second time was only marginally less daunting. Despite his certainty that there was no one else there, Tom nevertheless felt as if he was being watched. He scoured the walls, the ceilings, looking for evidence to support his prickling sense of unease, then scoffed at himself. Any surveillance equipment would be hidden in everyday items, maybe disguised as a power socket, a light switch, or in a smoke detector. Developments in nanotechnology meant cameras could be as small as a pinhead, so there was no point trying to find them. He just had to assume they were there, and that someone was following his every move.

He made his way towards the back of the house, to a room he had merely glanced into to check it was clear. It had to be Jack's study, although his brother would probably have called it his command centre – the place where he could concentrate, focus his incisive brain, analyse problems, think several steps ahead.

On the desk were two monitors and a hi-spec computer, plus a weird keyboard, split down the middle with wooden wrist rests on each side. This didn't feel like enough technology for Jack, and Tom glanced around. Behind the desk, double doors were embedded into a shelving unit. There was no handle, so he pressed on the join. The doors slid sideways, revealing a bank of blank monitors with pull-out shelves holding further keyboards.

Tom smiled. This was so much more like Jack, who always had at least three screens going at a time when he was a teenager. He ran his fingers over the trackpad to the side of one of the keyboards and two of the screens sprang to life. But all that appeared was an endless array of numbers and letters scrolling quickly up the screen.

Turning back to the desk, Tom wiggled the computer mouse and a desk monitor lit up, asking for a password.

'Come on, Jack. Be consistent,' Tom mumbled, sitting down and reaching for the strange keyboard.

It had been some years since he'd used Jack's complex password code structure to gain access to a file, but he remembered it well and started to type.

S!L<E?S£H€}€

Jack's hacker alias had always been Silver Sphere, and he replaced certain letters with symbols. But if Tom got it wrong, there was a chance that the computer would self-destruct. He hesitated when he typed in the final symbol and then, with a deep breath, he pressed Enter.

The password box cleared, but nothing happened. Then the cursor started to flash again in the box. It hadn't worked.

'Bugger,' he muttered. He had no idea what he was expecting to find on the computer, but he'd hoped there'd be *something*.

Leaning back in the chair, he examined the desk. Without hope or expectation, he pulled on the handle of the single drawer. It opened to reveal a mess of papers, bills and handwritten notes. It was unlikely there was anything important in an unlocked drawer, but nevertheless he lifted everything out and laid it on the desk, separating it into piles. The bills were all in the name of P. Johnson, as he would have expected. The notes were covered in complex figures and symbols, some with flowchart structures and mathematical equations.

Among the random items were a few business cards, and he looked at each one in turn, wondering if they would provide any clues, but most were for companies offering services for the home – window cleaning, gardening and the like. A dark blue card stood out from the rest, and Tom held it between finger and thumb: *Blake Securities*.

Blake wasn't an unusual name, but it was the one Jack had used when he was working undercover to bring down the organised crime group. Coupled with 'Securities', surely it had something to do with him?

Tapping the company's address into Google Maps, Tom discovered its office was situated just outside Chester close to the A55, less than a couple of hours' drive away. This had to be *something*.

Telling himself not to pin all his hopes on a random business card, he typed the web address into his phone.

Blake Securities specialises in bespoke security solutions for high-value assets.

With our extensive experience in cutting-edge technology, we offer impenetrable systems for luxury estates, private art collections, high-end retail and corporate assets.

Our services include advanced surveillance, AI-driven predictive behaviour analysis, facial recognition, access control and 24/7 monitoring, all tailored to meet the unique needs of each client.

Tom slumped back in the chair. This had to be Jack. If anyone could create a system to predict behaviour, it was him. The AI reported in the media might seem to be advancing in leaps and bounds, but Jack would be several steps ahead in a field Tom found hard to grasp. If this was his brother's company, maybe it held the key to what had happened to him.

Where are you, Jack?

The certainty that his brother was in danger wouldn't leave him. The house told its own story: the sense of a hurried departure, scattered clothes, dying flowers, half-empty coffee cup.

Keying the phone number of Blake Securities into his mobile, Tom held his breath. After a few seconds, the ringtone cut out to be replaced by an automated message from a man with a clear, authoritative voice and a slightly condescending tone. Definitely not Jack.

'We are currently unable to take your call. Leave a short message, and we will respond accordingly.'

The voice seemed familiar, and Tom gave a shaky laugh, the sound incongruous in the silent house. It was the voice of Orac from *Blake's 7*. He and Jack had watched every episode together when they were kids, and he could still remember when Orac was described as a supercomputer capable of accessing every other computer in the universe, knowing everything there was to know.

Jack had said, 'It will happen someday.' Tom had laughed at him. But that was forty years ago, and his brother hadn't been wrong.

'You clever bastard,' Tom muttered. Jack must have sampled Orac's voice and reused it with his own words. 'If you're listening, what am I supposed to do now?'

He wasn't expecting an answer, yet *someone* was watching. They had to be. Otherwise how had he got through the front door?

11

I've taken to walking the streets at night, dodging down dark alleys where every footstep echoes off the surrounding buildings. It's foolish, but it's the danger that excites me, makes me feel alive. Tonight there's a thin drizzle falling, but it doesn't deter me. I love the feel of the water on my skin, and I turn my face up to the sky.

The solitude of these narrow traffic-free streets clears my mind, allowing me to reflect on what truly matters. There is little for me to do now, except wait. That's the hardest part.

I pause on a narrow footbridge, leaning against the cold stone parapet. Below, dark water ripples faintly, the drizzle peppering its surface. There's no one around. The weather has driven everyone indoors and the only movement comes from the shimmering reflections of street-lights dancing on the rain-soaked cobbles.

I tell myself I'll be relieved when this is all over. But sometimes I'm not so sure. Maybe I've become addicted to this life, the way it sharpens every-thing and gives me a purpose beyond anything I've ever known. Each time I take a step closer to finding the truth I get a hit of pure, blinding focus. It's like a drug.

You always told me that one of the things you loved about me was my tenacity – like a dog with a bone, you said. But persistent as I might be in my working life, I never wanted to be that person with you. I believed you'd tell me what was worrying you when you were ready, and much as I itched to interrogate you, I tried to respect your boundaries. That was a mistake.

Do you remember when we first met, how prickly you thought I was? But when you understood my childhood, how traumatic it had been to be brought up in a war zone, you tried to protect me from worry. I think of the nights I lay in bed, scared to close my eyes, expecting at any moment to hear the sharp crack of gunfire or the distant thud of shellfire. You lay beside me, whispering that the past was far away, that I was safe, and you'd talk about the future we would build together.

You were the only person I could relax with, the only one I believed didn't have another agenda – but in those last weeks you were pulling away, your laughter no longer ringing true but sounding like a hollow bell.

I think you'd like it here, in these deserted streets. The bars and restaurants are closed, the lights out, the silence broken only by the soft sound of music filtering through a window, ajar to let in a breath of cool night air. I wonder if you've ever been here.

My eyes fill with tears that I rarely allow myself. They run unheeded down my cheeks, mingling with the thin rain. I sometimes ask myself what I'll do when all this is over, when I have answers. Who will I become then?

I don't know if I can walk away from this life, or if it's already seeped too deep into my bones. Just like walking deserted streets at night, maybe it's the risk that drives me, the knowledge that at any moment the truth about me might surface. Or maybe it's the belief that I'm cleverer than my victims. Even the smartest behave predictably, fall into the traps I've skilfully laid, and they don't see what's coming until it's too late.

My target this time was no exception. Executing my plan was easier than expected, because ultimately his emotional response sealed his fate.

He took the bait, as I knew he would.

12

'Where are you?' Philippa jumped right in, typically skipping the niceties at the start of a phone conversation.

Tom turned to watch the front door of the farmhouse close behind him before he responded. It seemed to swing to of its own accord. Not knowing what to make of that, he answered, 'I'm in North Wales, Philippa, as you are no doubt aware.'

'I am indeed. I realise that right now it's not my business to know precisely where you are, but it *becomes* my business if you create chaos and mayhem.'

'And how, exactly, have I done that?'

'By forcing me to lie, Tom. And that's not something I do as a rule. For some reason it only seems to happen when your brother enters the fray.'

'Sorry about that, but you know I don't like discussing him over an open line.'

'And equally, you know that I think you're being paranoid. But I'll avoid the use of names, if that makes you less twitchy. Unfortunately, North Wales Police *will* be mentioning his name – at least, his current name – if I can't get back to them with a reasonable explanation as to why one of my team, and let's face it, you're not even that at the moment, is poking around in their business.'

Tom felt a jolt of concern. 'Christ, Philippa, we can't let that happen. They can't get involved. Not yet, anyway. If they release photos, both you and I know that at least two faces could instantly be recognised by the wrong people.'

Tom thought about Ava, who was even more recognisable than Jack. She didn't look so different now from the thirteen-year-old Tasha who was supposed to have died in a fire.

'Can't we say the stress of being a CHIS was getting to the man we're looking for, so he's taken himself and his family out of the country for a few days?' he suggested.

There was a short huff of irritation down the phone. 'Are you asking a superior officer to lie for you?'

'You know what's at stake, and I'd rather you weren't involved. I don't work for you right now, so you're just a friend doing me a favour.'

There was a moment's silence, as if Philippa was trying to decide if 'friend' was an acceptable assumption on Tom's part. *'I'll* decide if I'm involved or not. Tell me what you've discovered,' she finally said, totally ignoring his comment.

'Weird stuff.'

'Well, that's not surprising, given who we're dealing with.'

Tom didn't rise to the bait. 'I get the impression that some of the family left in a hurry.'

'Explain.'

'One room showed signs of hurried packing. Although not the children's rooms, surprisingly.'

'Not surprising at all. You're a parent. Would you want to panic your children by tearing around like a mad thing, or would you project an air of calm while you selected what to put in a bag?'

Unusually perceptive, but Philippa was right. Clare would have tried to hide her anxiety, selecting a few items from each child's bedroom with a smile on her face as if they were going on an adventure, then dashing into her own room, not caring about the mess as she rushed to get them out of the house.

But what about Jack's clothes? Why were there no signs that he too had fled? Ava would probably have chosen her own clothes, but her room was suspiciously tidy for a teenager, and Clare would have found it almost impossible to fool the girl, who had witnessed more horrors than anyone should be subjected to in a lifetime.

The more Tom thought about everything he'd seen, the more worried he became.

'Next steps, Tom? Or is it better if I don't know?'

He debated how much to say, but Philippa might be able to help. 'I found a business card that could offer a possible lead. I'm going to follow that up.'

'Follow it where, precisely?'

'It's a bit of a long shot, but there are some clues in the name. And it's not in North Wales, so I'm not going to piss off the locals any more than I've done already.'

'Fine. It pains me, but I'll back you up this time, and hopefully I can convince North Wales that they don't have to take any further steps. But you're aware that if we need them in the future in this investigation of yours, it might be rather more difficult to get them to cooperate?'

'I'll take that risk.'

'So what's special about this supposed lead?'

'Nothing that I can say right now, but I'm going to find out what I can about the company and head there next.'

Philippa sighed. 'I know you're not going to tell me over the phone, but send me an encrypted message with the details. I'll look up the company for you.'

'That's very kind, thank you.'

'I'm not being kind. I want this escapade of yours over so I can get you back to work.'

Tom didn't believe her for a moment. Philippa hated anyone to believe she was human, even though he had seen plenty of evidence of her thoughtfulness over the years.

Agreeing to forward her the information, he ended the call and quickly typed a message, outlining the significance of the name, the specialisms of the company and the voice on the phone.

Within seconds, he had a response.

> Good God. Why does everything with your
> brother have to be a game?

Tom pushed his phone into his pocket and hurried back through the forest to the Jeep, turning once to check that the front door had remained closed behind him.

It had.

He shook his head. Philippa might think this was some game of Jack's, but it wasn't.

13

It had taken Tom a little over an hour and a half to get from the farmhouse to the business centre where Blake Securities was based, and the unease he had felt since he had started this hunt for Jack wasn't abating. If anything, it was building. He was glad Philippa knew where he was going. If she didn't hear from him again, she'd know where to start looking.

He pulled into a car park in front of a large red-brick building with dark blue window frames that proclaimed itself to be the offices of Dee River Holdings, but Tom was searching for a single unit. He got out of the car and looked around. The area was divided by beds of shrubs and relatively mature trees, and the buildings appeared well maintained, although to Tom it looked a soulless place to work. Pretty much like GMP headquarters, he realised on reflection.

To his right, a building bore a sign saying 'Units to Let', so he assumed it consisted of individual offices and was perhaps where Blake Securities would be found. With no idea how he was going to get in if the office was empty, he set off in the direction of the building. As he arrived at the main door, his phone rang.

'Philippa,' he said. 'Not calling to tell me off again, are you?'

Philippa gave an audible tut. 'Actually, I'm ringing with information. I wasn't able to find out much about the company or its clients, and because it's a small business it doesn't have to file full accounts. I did discover, though, that there's one director. Ethan Blake, if that means anything to you.'

Tom stifled a burst of laughter. Jack really was something else.

'That's very helpful, Philippa and you've saved me some time. I appreciate it.'

He was about to end the call when Philippa spoke, her voice a little less abrasive.

'Tom, I don't want you dragging my officers into this mess, as I've already said, but I do recognise your concerns. If you need me to help find the family, let me know. I understand why you don't want photographs to be part of the hunt, but there's a lot that the North Wales force could do – not least accessing ANPR or CCTV in the area. Don't rule it out, and if necessary I'll perpetuate the myth that the man concerned is an important intelligence source who has to remain incognito. I know you don't trust anyone, but it's always an option.'

Tom was surprised, although he wasn't sure why he should be. Philippa had bailed out both him and Jack in the past. Thanking her again, he ended the call.

'Bloody hell, Jack,' Tom muttered. '*Ethan Blake!*'

Any doubts Tom had about this company belonging to his brother had evaporated. The man who had forced Jack to work for his organised crime group was called Guy Bentley. But Guy was a nickname Jack had given him at school. His real name was Ethan, and Jack's undercover alias – Blake – was known to only two or three people on the planet.

Tom couldn't help feeling there was something orchestrated in all of this. Jack could have used any name under the sun, but he'd chosen one that Tom would instantly recognise. Blake Securities wasn't a new business, so this identity hadn't been created in the last few weeks. Had Jack always thought that Tom might have to track him down at some point? Did the danger he lived with haunt him every day?

Tom looked again at the business card. Unit 2A, Abbeygate House. The name on the door he was standing in front of matched, so he pushed it open and made his way up to the second floor.

The office facing him at the top of the stairs was 2A, but there was an air of desertion about the whole building and Tom found himself peering warily down the dark corridors to either side. There were no lights, no sounds. Were all the units empty? The door to Blake Securities had a frosted glass window, and although there were no signs of life behind it, as Tom drew close he could hear music coming from inside.

He approached the door, knocked a few times and tried the handle. It didn't give. If there was no one there, why was music playing? It was a track Tom recognised but couldn't immediately place. To the left of the door was a keypad, but how on earth was he supposed to know what keys to press? Jack wouldn't have used a family birthday. Too obvious. But if the name Ethan Blake had been chosen to bring Tom here, that suggested he should be able to figure out the code. Alternatively, he could smash the glass in the door, which might yet prove to be the only option.

He scoured his mind for anything Jack had said to him during recent conversations – something that seemed out of the ordinary. Perhaps he had never expected Tom to have to do this, but everything pointed to him guiding Tom to some truth, whatever that might be.

Peering closely at the pad to see if any of the keys showed more use than others, Tom couldn't detect any discernible difference. None of them was shinier or more scuffed. He turned to lean his back against the wall and closed his eyes.

'He's not in.'

Tom jumped as he heard a voice, and his eyes snapped open.

'He's not been here for at least a couple of weeks, maybe more.' The voice belonged to a young Asian woman in a wheelchair, heading for the lift. 'I've missed him. It's been too quiet up here, and he knows it's hard for me to carry coffee from the machine in the lobby so he always gets it for me on the days he's here. No idea where he's gone, before you ask.'

Tom looked down at her smiling face. 'Disappointing. I was really hoping to see him. Can I get your coffee for you?'

'S'okay. I'm leaving for the day. I'm only part-time.'

Tom thought for a moment. 'When you say it's been too quiet, what do you mean? I can't imagine he made much noise.'

'Hah! He was glued to his computers every day but he likes loud music, and as most of these offices are empty, there's no one to complain. Except me, and I like it too. Well, to be fair, I liked the beat and the guitar bits but I wasn't too keen on the singer – the one he played most, anyway. Sounded like he needed a Strepsil to me. The same track's been playing on a loop since I last saw him, but quietly. It would have driven me bonkers otherwise. When he's here, it's usually blasting out. It's better than silence, though. It's a bit spooky being the only person on the floor.'

The lift pinged, and she wheeled herself in. 'If you see him, tell him I miss him!'

Tom nodded to the woman, then leaned back and closed his eyes again. He had to think, to concentrate. Tom remembered as if it were yesterday the nights in his early teens, when he was allowed into Jack's room as he tinkered with one of the computers he'd built from scratch, components lying everywhere. The music blasting out *was* Jack – wild and unpredictable – and it made those evenings exciting. Led Zeppelin, ZZ Top and AC/DC were among his favourites, and Tom still listened to them occasionally to take himself back to that time in his life.

Could the clue be in the music? Why else would he repeat the same track?

He listened through the door, pressing his ear to the glass. What was it?

The track came to an end and started again, this time the opening guitar riff jolting Tom's memory. Jack's old favourite, 'Back in Black'.

Why did that feel significant?

Tom had a sudden flash of memory. One evening during their recent holiday, sitting up late and talking long into the night, Jack had admitted that he never felt entirely safe, but he'd put measures in place to protect Clare and the children, should anything happen to him.

'Do you think they'd try and force you back into that world?'

'Back in black? No chance. My days as a black-hat hacker are done, Tom. But remember what I told you when you were a kid? Rule 1921 of the hacker's code – wherever you break in, always plan your exit route.'

Tom had laughed, thinking Jack was being cryptic. 'What *is* rule 1921?'

Jack grinned. 'I made it up. There's no real rule 1921, but I *always* make sure I have a way out. And if ever you need to find me, you'll work out what it is. You're a detective, aren't you?'

The memory fell into place. The music wasn't a coincidence. Jack must have known that if Tom came here looking for him, he would eventually recognise the song – especially when he realised it was playing on a loop – and remember their conversation.

With a growing sense of apprehension, Tom spun round and pressed 1921 on the keypad. The door clicked, and he pushed it open.

'What are you up to, Jack?' he whispered.

If his brother had *wanted* him to find all this, why hadn't he just sent an email or left a note on Tom's laptop?

'Why do I have to play bloody Sherlock?' he muttered.

He knew the answer. Every clue had to be specific to Tom, something that no one else could work out. If Jack had thought it safe to tell Tom where he was, he would have done so. That could only mean one thing: this was Jack's fallback plan, the trail he'd laid for a time when either himself or his family would need saving.

14

Tom's mobile buzzed in his pocket. *Louisa.*

'Hi, darling. I thought I'd give you a call to see how it's going, if you've discovered anything.' Since he'd been shot, Louisa had been twitchy, worrying about him more.

'Well, I was able to get into the house – which is lovely, by the way. The location and the views are spectacular. No one was there, which is a good thing.' He hoped Louisa would read between the lines, knowing he had been afraid he might find them dead. 'I'm halfway home now, so I should be back tonight. I thought I'd go to Becky's to chat a few things through, if that's okay with you.'

Tom had decided not to mention any of the weird stuff, such as doors that automatically opened on his arrival or Clare's clothes all over the place. It would worry Louisa even more.

'Good idea. Two heads are always better than one.' There was a brief pause. 'I know how much this matters to you, but please don't put yourself in danger.'

'I'm in an office on a huge business park, so I doubt anyone's running round with a gun.'

'Don't laugh at me, Tom. That was a very scary time.'

Tom bit his bottom lip. 'Sorry, you're right. I'm being flippant because I'm worried, but that's not fair on you. I'll see you later, love.'

Despite his words of reassurance, as Tom looked out through the frosted glass window of the office door he had to wonder. *Was* he in danger? There were no shadows approaching the door. It seemed he was alone on this floor – at least, for now.

He thought back to how Jack's front door had opened. Perhaps the people he'd believed were looking for him had found the farmhouse, cracked his security systems and let Tom in. If Jack was in hiding, maybe they didn't know where to look next. They wouldn't have understood Jack's secret codes. Had Tom led them straight here?

He had been so absorbed in thoughts of his brother that he'd never thought to check his rear-view mirror for anyone following him. Pretty smart for a detective.

Tom sat down behind Jack's desk, empty apart from a computer, two monitors and a keyboard. Floor-to-ceiling doors covered one wall of the office, and they were locked. Tom guessed that behind them were other computers, or perhaps files. There was no sign of paperwork anywhere.

The desk drawers held nothing more interesting than a tangle of cables and adaptors, so Tom wiggled the mouse and wasn't surprised when one of the screens sprang to life. An icon in the top left of the screen showed the track currently playing, and he clicked to turn it off. The music had been distracting but the silence was even more disturbing, so he switched it back on.

Using the mouse, he moved the cursor around but nothing happened. Apart from the controls for the music, nothing on the screen appeared to be live, apart from a flashing cursor asking for a password.

What now, Jack?

His brother had led Tom here, but he could find no keys to the cupboards, and the drawers were empty of papers. The computer might offer some clues, but having tried the only password he knew on the workstation in Wales, he didn't hold out much hope. If it was wrong again, he was out of ideas.

Slowly, methodically, he typed each letter and symbol, certain he had remembered it correctly.

'Here goes nothing,' he said, pressing Enter gently, as if that would make a difference.

There was a brief pause, then the screen lit up with menus, folders on the desktop, applications auto-loading.

Tom sat back and stared. *What was he supposed to do with all of this?*

He clicked on one of three available browsers and accessed the Internet history. According to the girl in the corridor, Jack hadn't been here for a while and yet the browser showed activity within the past few hours.

'Yes!' he whispered to himself. It could only mean one thing: Jack had another device linked to this one, sharing its Internet history. Did that mean he was alive?

Tom's excitement faded as he noticed the recently visited sites were oddly out of character. The Premier League on the BBC Sports site? Jack had never shown any interest in sport, let alone football. The *Sun* newspaper? Definitely not his preferred way of staying informed. Along with a weather forecast site and a link to British Gas, the list seemed completely incongruous and Tom's optimism plummeted. Whoever was accessing this browser, it wasn't Jack.

Pushing aside thoughts of the peculiar browser history, he focused on the fact that *someone* had to be using a device – a laptop or mobile – synched to this computer. If he could find that device, he would have a starting point for his search, so with a sudden surge of hope, Tom opened the Find My app. Only one device showed – 'Laptop' - maybe the one Tom suspected was missing from the panic room. A map loaded, showing streets – Calle Avogaria, Calle Balastro – that were definitely not in the UK. He zoomed out, his pulse quickening as the map revealed a location far from both Jack's home and office.

Venice!

What the hell was Jack's laptop doing in Venice?

There was only one way to find out. Tom grabbed his phone. There was a flight from Manchester to Venice the following morning.

Clinging to the hope – however tenuous – that *maybe* Jack was alive, and that his Internet searches – however bizarre – were evidence of the fact, Tom confirmed his reservation and headed for the door, ignoring the voice in his head telling him that this was far from the only conclusion he could draw.

All he knew was that someone in Venice had access to Jack's laptop, and he had to find them.

15

A sense of calm settles on me, but it's deceptive – the calm before the storm. I know better than anyone that however perfect my preparations, plans can spiral out of control, and I can't allow that to happen.

So far, every small detail has slotted into place. I insisted we move slowly, that nothing should be rushed. I had to study all the players, as I always do, to understand who I am working with. I have to know their limits, and I am well aware that one of those involved apparently has none. That makes him dangerous.

I've witnessed how he handles betrayal – or what he judges to be failure. A simple remark can spark his rage and his brutality makes me shudder. I can't afford to antagonise him. He's the key to the success of this plan, and I have to handle him with infinite care. He will not hesitate to punish me if I fail.

But I won't.

I wish you were with me, Alessandro, whispering words of reassurance, because although I've wormed my way into organisations that operate in the shadows and have worked for some of the worst people on this earth to get here, no one scares me more than this man. His unpredictable, volatile nature presents a constant threat, because I never know what he'll do next.

And the other player, the one I need to bend to my will? He has one weakness. His family. He will rush to their side without a second thought, regardless of his own safety. He walked straight into the trap I laid, just as I knew he would.

I can't help him now. He's sealed his own fate.

I sigh as I push the plan across the table, telling myself that sacrifices are necessary. It's the only way I'll win this game.

16

As Tom fastened his seat belt for take-off, he mulled over the conversation he'd had with Louisa the night before, after he returned from Becky's. It hadn't gone as well as he'd hoped.

'If you know where his laptop is, why can't you let the police in Venice check it out?' Louisa had asked, her eyes round with concern.

'Because I don't know what's going on. If it's not Jack who has it, I need to tread carefully. And if it *is* him and he's in trouble, a police raid could make it worse.'

Louisa tutted, folding her arms. 'I didn't mean a *raid*, Tom. I meant a general enquiry to his well-being.'

He understood why she didn't want him to go. She had struggled at the outset to accept the baggage that came with Jack, and Tom's dishonesty about his brother at the start of their relationship had nearly finished them. She knew, as Tom did, that the current situation was unlikely to turn out to be a case of Jack taking his family on a cultural trip to Italy.

It was clear that the breadcrumbs left by his brother weren't a trail he'd put in place recently. The clues seemed well planned, a failsafe, puzzles Jack could rely on Tom solving if anything happened to him. And now it seemed something *had* happened to him – to all of them. The question was, what?

'I'll be careful, I promise. I've diced with death enough for one year, and I didn't enjoy it much. I'm not about to do anything stupid.'

'Are you going to just rock up at this location and ask if he's there, then?' she asked, an unusual edge in her voice. It wasn't an entirely daft question.

'I don't know. I need to work it out. I can watch, see who comes and goes, make a judgement call. But I won't go charging in on a rescue mission, alone and unarmed. If I find evidence that he's there and is being held against his will, I'll talk to the local police or the *carabinieri.*'

Louisa had given a shaky sigh. 'I'm sorry, Tom. I'm sure you think I'm being a nag, but I thought I'd lost you when you were shot, and I couldn't bear to feel like that again. Where your brother's concerned, things are never simple. I like him – a lot – and Clare's become a friend, so obviously I don't want anything to have happened to any of them. But neither do I want you to risk your life.'

'I get all that. But if I don't do anything and subsequently discover I could have somehow averted a disaster, you wouldn't want to live with me anyway. I couldn't forgive myself if something happened and I'd done nothing.'

'Can't you wait and see what comes from the conversation I had with Kate? I know she wasn't very helpful, but she might come round.'

Tom had lifted his eyebrows and given her an 'as if' look.

Realising she was fighting a losing battle, Louisa had stomped around the kitchen for a while, pouring herself an unusually large whisky. Tom knew he was being unfair on her, Lucy and Harry. If anything happened to him, they'd be the ones who would have to live with the consequences.

When Louisa reluctantly agreed they should go to bed, he'd held her tightly, unable to sleep as he worried he was being selfish, choosing his own peace of mind over hers. When morning came, she had tried to smile as she kissed him goodbye, holding on to their hug a little longer than normal.

And now he was on a plane heading to Venice, a city he hadn't visited for many years. Had there been any other reason for him to be making this journey, he would have been thrilled.

As soon as his travel arrangements had been confirmed, Tom had put the details of his flight, the water taxi company he'd booked and the hotel where he was staying into a folder on his desktop, which he'd labelled 'Venice trip'. With no idea whether Jack was still able to access his laptop remotely, he'd thought it worth a punt. But if he was hoping for some form of acknowledgement, which usually entailed Jack moving the folder to another part of the desktop, he was out of luck.

Apart from Louisa, right now the only other person who knew about his journey was Becky. He'd asked her to tell Philippa later and to stress that he wasn't looking for any help, but it would be useful for someone to know his whereabouts. He hadn't voiced concern that he could be walking into danger, but he didn't need to. When he'd told Becky what he'd discovered at Jack's farmhouse, she'd instantly been alert to the potential threat.

'You don't know who opened that door, Tom. You don't know if anyone was, or still is, watching the house, or who may have taken control of Jack's systems. I know you think the clues Jack left were things only the two of you could have known about, but signs of the whole family leaving worry me. Do you think they're *all* in Venice?'

'No idea. I was debating whether I could come up with some sort of justification to check flight manifests, but if I know my brother, he'll have another alias for travel purposes – one I don't know – and he's too smart to travel with his wife and three children. They'll have gone in separate groups – perhaps him with Billy, and Clare with Sophia and Ava. There's no way we could check every flight to Venice over a time period we can only guess at. And I doubt he'd have flown direct. He'll have gone to Turin or somewhere, and travelled on from there.'

'God, he makes things difficult.'

'That's the idea. He's not hiding his whereabouts from me specifically; he doesn't want *anyone* to know where he is. The fallout from Guy Bentley's OCG may have been a few years ago now, but the people whose livelihoods he destroyed, evil and corrupt as they were, won't have forgotten him or what he did. Anonymity is his only weapon. That and his planet-sized brain.'

Now, as the plane soared into the sky, Tom sat back and closed his eyes, trying to get comfortable in the hard seat of the budget airline. His legs were too long for the space, but at least he would have two and a half hours of uninterrupted thinking time to plan what he was going to do next. The truth was, he didn't have a clue.

17

Venice Airport was heaving, and Tom was glad he'd booked a water taxi in advance. He'd only brought hand luggage, but hadn't allowed for the queues at passport control. As he waited, his phone pinged. Three messages, the first from Louisa.

> Sorry to be such a worry-guts. Please stay
> safe, and I hope you find what you're looking
> for. Love you xx

Louisa was very good at not mentioning names in texts, and Tom felt a twinge of guilt that she had to be dragged into his family drama.

The next was from Becky.

> Always here if you need me. And bugger
> Philippa. I'll do what I think is right.
> Take care. B

The final message was from the water taxi company.

> Please proceed to Bay 5 where your water
> taxi is waiting.

He quickly responded to Louisa and Becky, then he was through and into the bustle of the main terminal. Manoeuvring his way around rolling suitcases and somehow managing to avoid being battered by heavy backpacks swinging from the shoulders of travellers, he spotted the sign for the water taxis and made his way towards an escalator.

The sun was beating down, and Tom felt ridiculous in his leather jacket. He had based his packing on the weather in Manchester in May without giving it enough thought, and he paused to strip off his jacket and roll up the sleeves of his shirt before following the signs to Bay 5.

'Signor Douglas?' a smiling taxi driver said, reaching up to help Tom into his boat. 'I have something for you.' He handed Tom a package. 'Please take a seat and enjoy the ride!'

Tom was bewildered. 'I'm sorry, where did this come from?'

'A man – un pilota – asked me to give it to you.'

'What man? What pilot?'

The driver gave a typical Italian shrug, his shoulders rising dramatically, his hands spread wide. 'Non lo so.'

Tom remembered that this meant 'I don't know,' and it wasn't helpful.

'How long ago?'

Another shrug. 'Cinque minuti?' He had obviously given up trying to charm his English passenger.

Five minutes. Was this Jack? Or was someone else expecting him?

Tom's eyes scanned the crowd. The place was swarming with air crew. If it *was* Jack, why would he just leave a parcel rather than wait to talk to Tom himself? But if it wasn't Jack, who else could know he was here?

Reluctantly, sensing impatience from the driver, Tom followed his outstretched arm and went into the cabin to take a seat as the engine roared to life.

The package was wrapped in brown paper secured with far too much Sellotape, and Tom tore at the tape, cursing that he had nothing to cut it with. Resorting to his teeth, he finally managed to get the package undone. Inside was a small black mobile phone.

Pointlessly checking that the driver wasn't watching, he switched the phone on. Nothing. It was charged and there was a signal, but the contacts folder was empty and there were no apps loaded.

Who had left the phone? Why?

He continued to stare at the phone, hoping it would spring to life, and was about to give up and go outside to watch their arrival in the city when it pinged with a message.

Do not respond. Go to hotel and wait.

Tom's mind raced. It felt like a warning. For all he knew, someone had been following him from the moment he left Jack's home in Wales. Should he do as the message instructed, or should he try to track down the laptop? Someone knew he was here, and the only option seemed to be to do as he was being told and hope-fully find out who was behind the message. It might be dangerous, but he didn't feel there was any other choice.

Leaving the cabin, he took a seat at the back of the water taxi, forcing himself to put his fears behind him until he reached the hotel. The sun beat down from a cloudless blue sky as the boat zipped across the shimmering water. Ahead, he could see the skyline transform as they drew closer to Venice, the city's silhouette rising from the water. Despite all his worries, he felt a thrill as the magnificent buildings drew nearer, and the breathtaking sight of St Mark's Square came into view: the basilica, the doge's palace, the campanile. It was so long since he had last visited, but it was all coming back to him.

The driver veered off the Grand Canal to enter the network of smaller canals. A gondola glided past, the occupants staring around them in wonder as they passed under a stone bridge. The centuries-old buildings with their weathered bricks loomed above the taxi, and Tom got the occasional whiff of food – something deliciously rich with herbs – coming from a restaurant kitchen.

The air was cooler here, the sunlight struggling to penetrate as the canals became ever narrower. The driver had cut his engine to little more than a whisper, slowing to the speed limit of around three miles per hour, and a shout of laughter drifted from an open window above, the sound spilling out into the quiet waterway.

'Signore, we are here,' the driver said as they drew to a halt by a flight of stone steps leading up to a modest but delightful-looking hotel, its walls covered with climbing ivy, window boxes bursting with colour.

Thanking the driver and giving him what he hoped was an appropriate tip, Tom made his way up the steps onto the cobbled path above and stepped into the small foyer of the hotel, where a smiling receptionist was waiting to greet him.

'Buon giorno, Signor Douglas.' Her smile widened at his look of surprise. 'We only have two arrivals today, the other being a couple from Taiwan, so I assumed it would be – what do you call it in English? A safe bet?'

Tom returned her smile and completed the registration process, handing over his passport.

'Do you, by any chance, have any messages for me?' he asked as she handed him a key – a real key, he was pleased to see, not a piece of plastic.

She looked at her computer screen. 'Nothing showing here, sir, but I will check with my colleague. Please excuse me for a moment.'

As she disappeared through a door behind the reception desk, Tom looked around the small foyer: the dark wood of the walls, the floors tiled in old terracotta, an arrangement of multicoloured roses on an antique round table. Their fragrance filled the air, and the sense of peace and calm settled his nerves a little. But with no idea what the next few hours and days would bring, he couldn't quite overcome a jittery sense of anticipation.

'Nothing, I'm afraid. Were you expecting something?' the receptionist said on her return.

'No, not really.' Tom was about to say that he might have a visitor later, but realised she might ask for a name, so assuring her that he needed no help with his one small piece of luggage, he picked up his key and made his way to the lift. Pleased to find it was absolutely in keeping with the hotel, he pulled back the wrought-iron gate and pressed a large brass button for floor three.

The room was everything he could have expected: the opposite of the clinical anonymity of a modern chain hotel with not a single item in a shade of beige. He dropped his suitcase by the wardrobe and sank into a comfortable armchair, reaching for an apple from the fruit bowl and pouring himself a glass of water. If it hadn't been for everything else going on at that moment, he would have thought he had found perfection.

As it was, though, he was going to have to sit there for as long as it took, never taking his eyes off the door, waiting for someone to knock.

It was ten thirty that night before Tom heard a scratching sound outside his room. Nerves frayed from the long wait, he jumped to his feet. He heard a key turn, and the door was thrust open.

A figure moved into the room, quickly turning to close and lock the door behind himself before Tom had the chance to make out the face shaded by the hood of a jacket. But he had no doubt who this was.

'Jack,' he whispered, his breath almost deserting him. 'Thank God.'

The brothers walked towards each other, and Tom felt himself being pulled into a fierce hug.

'What the hell, Jack?'

Jack put his hands on Tom's shoulders and gently pushed him away. His face was pale, his eyes bloodshot.

'They've got Ava,' he said softly.

18

Tom was so overwhelmed by his relief at seeing Jack alive that it took him a few seconds to register the significance of his words.

'What do you mean, they've got Ava? *Who's* got her? Did someone find out who she is? Is this Kate's fault for telling the world that you're alive?'

Tom had a million questions, but Jack held up a hand to silence him. 'This has nothing to do with Kate. I'm almost certain it's nothing to do with the fact that I'm Jack Douglas, or that Ava is Natasha Joseph, either. The online chatter that I told you about a couple of weeks ago was a lie.'

'What?'

'I made it up. When I phoned to tell you I was going to disappear, I didn't know Kate had been gossiping. I said we were going dark because I knew Ava had been taken.'

Tom glared at his brother. 'Why the fuck didn't you tell me?'

'Because you'd have had the whole of the Greater Manchester Police force leaping into action, and I didn't know who I was dealing with. You might think there are no leaks, but I wasn't prepared to take that risk until I knew who had taken her and what they wanted. If I'd made the wrong decision, who knows *what* that could have meant for Ava, so it was easier to just tell you I was going dark – at least until I knew more.'

Tom was mystified. 'Why did they take her? Why are you here? Where are Clare and the kids?'

'Too many questions, little brother,' Jack said, using the affectionate nickname he'd used when he was a teenager and Tom was in awe of his older brother. 'Give me a chance to explain.' He nodded towards a low table by the window. 'Is there any wine left in that bottle?'

'Help yourself. But why all the cloak and dagger, Jack? I didn't even know if it was you who left the mobile with the water taxi driver. I've been half-expecting the door to be kicked in and to have a gun pointed at me again.'

'I thought you'd know it was me, but I couldn't be sure if the driver would pass you the package or keep it for himself. So no names. And I didn't want to be seen with you because I don't know if I'm being followed.'

Overwhelmed by a flood of disturbing questions, Tom didn't know where to start. 'Why don't you tell me everything that's happened, starting with how the hell you just got into my room?'

Jack waved his hand dismissively. 'I hacked the hotel's reservation system to find your room and came in through the staff entrance, flashing a badge to say I was from the Azienda Sanitaria Locale, here to check hygiene. Then I picked up the key from the housekeeping board on the way through.'

Tom found it slightly terrifying to think his brother was capable of this level of subterfuge. But now wasn't the time to comment.

'I know my behaviour offends you, Tom, but needs must and all that. Ava's in danger, so gaining illegal entry to a hotel room is hardly significant. Anyway, I don't give a stuff what I have to do to save that kid. She's been through more than enough in her life.'

'But if it's not because of who she was, or who you were, why would they take her?'

'It's because of who I am *now* – Ethan Blake. They want me for my expertise with security systems, and to make me obey their wishes, they've taken Ava.'

Tom groaned. Jack had been threatened for years that his family would be harmed if he didn't obey a man called Finn McGuinness – the enforcer of the OCG he was involved with – and even though McGuinness was now dead, it felt as if they were right back where they started.

'I can't just disappear this time to escape the clutches of the evil bastards, because they have Ava. So you'll be pleased to hear I won't be faking my own death again. If I did, they'd kill her, so I've got no choice. I have to go along with what they want.'

'But who are *they*?' Tom's mind was spinning through all the possible options.

'Just sit down and I'll explain,' Jack said, filling his glass and topping up Tom's. 'I started a company specialising in high-end security systems when we moved to Wales. We couldn't live off fresh air, and it's what I do best.'

Tom leaned forward. 'You didn't need to do that! I would have given you money. It's your money, anyway. Can we use it now? Can the people who've taken Ava be bought off?'

'Don't think I haven't thought about that, but I'm not sure money alone would achieve what they want.'

'Before you tell me what that is, do you know if Ava's safe?'

Jack gave a despondent shrug. 'A photo. There's no evidence it was taken in the last few hours, so before I do what they're asking I'll want proof she's alive – something they're unable to manipulate.'

'And Clare and the kids?'

'They're fine, although Clare will be struggling to hold it together. If anything happens to Ava, neither of us will ever forgive ourselves.' Jack gave a bitter chuckle. 'Too late, was the cry!'

'It's not too late. She's bound to be going through a shit time, though, so we need to focus on how to get her back safely. Perhaps Louisa could get in touch with Clare and offer some support?'

Jack's eyes opened wide. 'No! Nobody must try to communicate with her. I don't know how good these guys are, or what they're capable of. She's with the kids in a house just outside Heywood. We've had it a while, just in case we ever had to move quickly.'

'Why Heywood?' Tom asked, thinking there must be other places that would make more sense.

'Because it's covered by Greater Manchester Police. I wanted our escape – our safe house – to be in a place where I could call on you for help, if needed. Can you imagine if I had to explain myself to any other police force?'

Tom couldn't, and under different circumstances he would have found the idea amusing.

'Why didn't you tell me all this was happening, Jack? Why let me work it out for myself?'

Jack released a long slow breath. 'Initially, I had no idea what they knew about me. I didn't know if there was any connection to you that I'd missed, careful as we've been.'

'Who, though? Only three of my colleagues know: Phillipa, Becky and Paul Green from the Organised Crime Unit, and they're all rock solid.'

'Well, to be fair, you know them and I don't. Any one of them might have broadcast the scandal that one of GMP's stars is linked to a member of the criminal underworld. It was juicy enough for Kate, after all.'

Tom decided to ignore that. 'I couldn't understand why you hadn't made some attempt to contact me after I was shot. You do *know* I was shot, don't you?'

'Of course, and I knew you were okay. I'm sorry if my silence hurt you, Tom, but don't think for a moment I didn't know how you were doing. Lucy was posting updates on you all the time – with photos and videos.'

Tom said nothing, knowing there was more to come, and Jack looked uncomfortable.

'I felt bad about it, but I needed to find out what was happening and what they wanted before I involved you. And then you were shot, and you're only just recovering from what I gather was a fairly sizeable hole in your chest. There's also the fact that if I do what they're demanding – and that's looking highly likely – I'll be breaking the law. Where's that going to leave your conscience, little brother?'

Tom cringed. 'I get all that, but it would have been good to know you were alive.'

'Look, it was selfish of me, I know that. I should have let you believe everything was fine, but it isn't, and I couldn't get past the thought that if something happened to me, there would be no one to help Ava. So I left the door open a crack, thinking that when you were well enough you might come looking for me, even if only to confirm that I was dead. But it had to be your choice.'

Tom shuddered at the thought. 'Well, you didn't make it easy! I'm assuming you opened the door at the farm using some remote-access camera system, but what if something had already happened to you and you weren't able to let me into the house?'

Jack gave a ghost of a smile. 'The sensor would have scoured the images I've uploaded – faces of people known to me. The door would have opened, but I got there quicker.'

Tom leaned forward to pour more wine into his brother's glass. 'I don't get this, Jack. Did you set all this up – the door, the hints and clues you left – in *case* I tried to find you?'

Jack gave a dry laugh. 'Ever since we've been back in the UK, I've been creating and modifying trails that only you could follow. I've always known something might happen to me or my family, and I had to be sure that if I was silent for too long, you'd investigate.'

'Why such obscure clues, though? Why not give me a guidebook in advance?'

'Come on, Tom, you know the answer to that. Any information you have makes you vulnerable. It's the same reason you've never had my address – the less you know, the better. I didn't know if there'd ever be a time when I needed to be found, even if it was just my body, so I had to think like you.'

'Jesus.'

'It's always been a possibility, so don't look so shocked. As for the office, if you hadn't remembered the 1921 rule – which there was every chance you wouldn't – I assumed you'd just break the door down.'

Tom raised his eyebrows and was rewarded with a soft chuckle. They sat in silence for a moment while Tom tried to absorb everything Jack had said.

'Your Internet history nearly had me fooled. I thought someone had stolen your computer.'

'I kept a current history so you'd realise my laptop was still active. It was boring stuff because I didn't know who might have a back door into my browser.' Jack leaned towards Tom and grasped his wrist. 'You did everything I knew you would and more, little brother. I admit I didn't expect you to come so quickly, although I half-hoped you might. And I'm bloody glad you're here now.'

19

Seeing Jack looking so tired and drawn was unnerving. He had always seemed weirdly together, considering the life he led. Calm, eccentric and cavalier were the words Tom would have chosen to describe him. But now, with one of his adopted children under threat, he was just a worried dad.

'When was Ava taken?'

'The day before you were shot.'

'Christ, Jack! That was more than two *weeks* ago. And you think she's here, in Venice?'

Jack gave a hopeless shrug. 'I don't know. I'm here because this is where I was told to come, but whether she's here too, I can't be sure. I've run every piece of analysis I can on the photo they sent. The walls in the picture are brick, which isn't particularly helpful, but they're obviously old, and longer and thinner than most British bricks, with lots of dry powdery residue as if the walls have been damp and dried out. Might suggest Venice, but that's nothing more than a guess. Being locked up in what looks like a cellar must be bringing back some dreadful memories. When she was a kid, that bastard Rory Slater used to throw her into a dark hole – she called it The Pit – every time she wouldn't do some dreadful thing he demanded. When we get her back, it's going to take some time for her to recover.'

Tom knew Jack was really thinking *if*, not *when*, but he would never say that out loud.

'What do they want you to do? And why is it taking so long?'

Jack pulled a folded sheet of paper from his back pocket and handed it over. Flattening it out, Tom could see a painting which, although abstract, leaped from the page and shouted 'Venice'.

> *Serenata Selvaggi (Wild Serenade)*
> *Orlando Ricci*
> *Orlando Ricci is an influential Italian abstract painter from the early 20th century. Known for his bold use of colour and texture, Ricci's works are celebrated for their emotional intensity and unique interpretation of landscapes. Serenata Selvaggi is a striking example of his style, with thick, vibrant layers of oil paint creating an almost dreamlike representation of Venice. The painting hints at the city's iconic canals and architecture, but its abstract nature leaves much to the viewer's imagination. This masterpiece, held in a private collection in Venice, is valued at around 3 million dollars due to Ricci's esteemed reputation and the painting's evocative beauty.*

Tom looked at Jack. 'This is about a painting?'

'Kind of. It's about stealing one, anyway.'

'They want you to *steal* it?'

Jack's mouth pressed into a thin line. 'Not me personally, but I have to facilitate the theft. The private collection in question is protected by one of my security systems, and they can't get past it without my help.'

'If that's the case and someone *does* get past it, won't you be implicated?'

Jack slowly nodded. 'Undoubtedly. I did tell you I'd be breaking the law.'

Tom ignored this. 'What's so special about your system? People have circumvented unbelievable levels of security in the past.

Remember the Antwerp diamond heist a few years ago? There were infrared heat detectors, Doppler radar, magnetic fields, all sorts of security. What's so wonderful about yours that it can't be beaten?'

'I'll explain it at some point, but all that matters now is figuring out how to get Ava back unharmed. If I subsequently end up under investigation for my part in the heist, we'll disappear back to South America.'

That was the last thing Tom wanted, but now wasn't the time for that conversation.

'Who's doing this, Jack? And why this particular painting? It can't be easy to sell it on, can it? I know there's money to be made from illegal art, but surely there are better targets?'

'Art theft is a multi-billion-dollar industry, but I'm guessing this painting's not being stolen for resale. I'm now as certain as I can be that the theft is gang-related, and this time we're playing with the heavyweights. The 'Ndrangheta.'

Tom felt as if someone had tipped the contents of an ice bucket down the back of his shirt. The 'Ndrangheta made Guy Bentley's organised crime group, which had controlled drugs and prostitution rings in parts of Greater Manchester, look like a high school pranksters' club. This wasn't just another level – it was a whole different ball game.

'Do you want to explain?' He resisted the compulsion to yell at his brother for getting himself – and now, by default, Tom – into something as terrifying as this.

'I'm sure you're up to speed on organised crime in Europe, but despite everybody believing the Cosa Nostra is confined to Sicily and that the Camorra restricts itself to operations in Naples, the truth is that they've all spread their wings far and wide – none more than the 'Ndrangheta. They've been getting a lot of press attention recently because of some high-profile arrests, but their tentacles stretch way beyond their roots in Calabria. They're all over the world. They've spread throughout Europe like a cancer and infiltrated North America – particularly Canada. They've even reached Australia now.'

'I know all this, Jack. INTERPOL briefed my team some time ago. They have an international unit working to combat what they call a "growing Mafia phenomenon". I understand it's the structure of the 'Ndrangheta that makes it so difficult to tackle. They have small family-based groups – *'ndrine* – scattered bloody well everywhere. Even in Manchester, I'm horrified to say. What's their hold in Venice?'

'As far as I can make out, the 'Ndrangheta has taken control of the top end of the drugs market here, shipping in from the usual sources – South America, probably – with a local *'ndrina* managing trafficking in the area. The other Venetian Mafia groups rely on extortion, prostitution and lower-level drugs for their income. There's probably a complex web of alliances, rivalries and collaborations, but as far as I know, no one else touches high-end drugs. They daren't.'

'Why steal art, though? I didn't think it was a core activity of theirs.'

Jack breathed out a heavy sigh. 'I'm still trying to figure it out. I've got feelers out to try to get a sense of who's who, but I think the gang that has Ava is lower down the food chain and trying to align themselves with the big boys. If they want an alliance with the 'Ndrangheta, they might need to prove themselves. And perhaps this painting has some significance. That's why I don't think paying them off will get Ava back, and I'm doing everything I can to discover their motives while simultaneously working out how I'm going to corrupt my own security system to give them access.'

Tom still didn't get it. 'But Ava was taken two weeks ago! Why is it taking so long?'

'That's one thing I *can* answer. There's to be a private showing of my client's art and he's invited other collectors to show their pieces. Much of his stuff is currently stored in a vault that I'd defy anyone to break into, but it's going to be brought out for an exhibition protected by the best security – as provided by yours truly.' Jack's lips twisted into a wry smile. 'It's being displayed in his palazzo for one night only with a grand Venetian reception for the rich and famous, all invited to admire the wonderful paintings and the magnificent wealth of their host. Oh, and it's a masked event too. Venetians love their theatrics. It should have happened last week and it would have been over by now, with Ava safely home, but one of the paintings hasn't arrived and my client believes it's crucial to the success of his event, so the whole plan's been delayed. I have to be ready as and when the date is confirmed, but it will happen sometime soon.'

Tom looked straight into Jack's eyes. 'And now I'm going to ask the most obvious question. Why the hell haven't you reported all of this to the local police or the *carabinieri*? They have specialist teams to deal with organised crime.'

Jack broke eye contact, standing up and prowling the room. 'And that, little brother, is precisely why I wasn't sure if I wanted your help. You may remember I said I "half-hoped" you'd come and find me? The other half of that hope was me saying to myself, "No, no, no – he'll want to call the cops." And I can't do that. Not only can't, I *won't*. This is the Mafia, Tom. If I call the police, they'll know, and they'll kill Ava without a moment's hesitation. I know you deal with the chaos caused by criminal gangs, but I've been right in the thick of it, and I know how they think. Life is cheap. What does one teenage girl matter? I'll tell you the answer, shall I? She doesn't.'

20

Ava's legs give way as the door slams shut. The men are gone, but she still holds her breath. The bolt slides into place with a clang, and she slithers down the wall to the cold, hard floor. She'd thought – hoped – they were coming to free her, but she was wrong. Each time they come, her heart leaps, filled with the same optimism. But all they offer her is food. The greasy paper bag they left is out of reach, and she doesn't have the strength to crawl across the floor to get the dry, saltless bread and lump of cheese.

A sudden metallic crash echoes through the space, and she sits up, startled. It's coming from outside the building, and she hasn't heard it before. For a moment her heart leaps.

Is someone coming to rescue me? Is it Dad?

She holds her breath, straining to hear more. But hope fades as quickly as it grows, and she collapses back against the wall. No one is coming. It's been too long. If her dad was going to rescue her, he'd have been here by now. Ava swallows a sob. If she allows herself to cry, she'll never stop.

She focuses on the other noises to distract herself: a gentle, rhythmic sound that repeats day and night; footsteps on a hard surface; a vibrating noise that fades in and out – an engine, maybe?

As it passes slowly, the constant *swish* grows louder, as if it has caused a disturbance, then fades.

The air smells musty, earthy, and sometimes she thinks there's a whiff of salt water. Is she by the sea? Perhaps. She has no memory of her arrival and can't tell how long she's been here. *Too* long. She has tried to work it out based on the number of times she is fed, but are they feeding her once a day or twice? She sleeps in between, so she has no sense of time. They must be putting something in her food, but she doesn't care. At least when she's asleep, she doesn't have to think about why she's here and what they're going to do with her. There are no windows, just a couple of bricks with holes high up on the wall that let in sounds and smells, but no light. She doesn't know if it's night or day.

She remembers the first few days – the terror, confusion, shock that this was happening to her *again*. But now she feels numb. Does fear have a time limit? Is there only so much of it that a body can take? She feels empty, as if her brain can only handle so much distress before replacing it with the hollow ache of despair.

She's given up all hope of escape. She can't fight the men who come. She's too weak, too scared. There are two of them. One leans against the door, watching, while the other tosses the bag of food onto the floor at the far end of the room. They don't speak. Both have dark hair and unshaven faces. One is skinny, with a long body and short legs. The other is stocky, with muscular arms. He's the one who blocks the doorway. She couldn't get past him.

The single light bulb dangling overhead is too high to reach and is always on, probably so she can find her way to the bucket in the corner. She's thought about jumping up to pull the bulb out, plunging the room into darkness. But then the men would come, and she wouldn't be able to see them. That idea scares her even more.

This is her fault, she knows that. She broke one of the rules she'd promised to follow, after grumbling for months that her dad's precautions were overkill. Who would remember her anyway, after all this time? And yet here she is.

What did I do wrong?

She knows the answer. The day they plucked her off the street she was being stubborn, obstinate, defiant. She thought her dad was being overprotective when all he was doing was trying to keep her safe.

She should have listened. Maybe that's why he hasn't come for her.

Fifteen days ago

'See you tomorrow,' Ava called to Jade and Sita as they walked out through the school gates.

'Sure you don't want to come?' Jade asked, already knowing the answer.

Ava shrugged, and they pulled sad faces as she turned left and they turned right. They were going into town to browse the shops and maybe grab a slice of pizza before heading home, and it was a pain to have to explain again why she couldn't join them.

She always made the same excuse: 'My dad has to pick me up because we live in the middle of nowhere.' She didn't add that her dad worried about her being out in town, where she could easily be watched or followed.

'We're going to have to find a way to get round this,' he'd said. 'I know you can't live your life this way, and we want you to be happy. For now, maybe your friends could come here. I'd be happy to pick them up.'

Was it fair to ask them to stay for a sleepover? What would happen if there was a middle-of-the-night scare and they all had to rush into the panic room? How was she going to explain that?

As she trudged, head down, along the main road towards today's pick-up point – the station car park – she remembered overhearing Dad and Mum talking.

'We can't wrap her in cotton wool,' he'd said. 'She deserves a life as close to normal as we can make it, but how do we keep her safe and at the same time let her be a teenager?'

'The trouble is, she hasn't changed enough to be unrecognisable,' Mum had answered. 'It's not just Rory Slater we need to worry about. All the other kids she lived with would know her in an instant, as would Finn McGuinness's guys – the ones who didn't get locked up.'

Dad had sighed. 'Their lucrative lifestyles must have taken quite a hit, but they think she's dead, so hopefully they won't be looking.'

'So how do we make things easier for her?'

The question was met with silence.

She knew they'd tried their best, encouraging her to join school clubs – but only those that kept her inside the building or within the school grounds with lots of people around her. That had helped, and she'd made friends. She'd been invited to sleepovers, but she didn't bother to ask if that might be allowed. What if someone followed her to a friend's house?

Her dad had put systems in place – secure communications with encrypted phones, regular check-ins – but she'd been feeling the urge to escape the constraints for so long and had begun to break the rules. Sixth-formers were allowed out at lunchtime, but she was supposed to stay in school. She was sick of saying no, so that term she'd sneaked out with Jade and Sita to a café for an hour. It was fantastic. She'd felt normal. However guilty she felt, she didn't want to be that sad girl who had no friends and was no fun.

For a moment she wished she'd ignored her dad's message giving her today's pick-up point and gone into town with the others. It would have been worth it. The funny thing about her dad was he never got cross with her. He seemed to understand every-thing she did, and why she did it. She had to wonder if he'd been a bit wild when he was a kid.

It would have been better if he got angry. It felt much worse to think that each time she broke the rules, she was disappointing him.

Ava stomped along, feeling cross with the world. She could see the station in the distance. She was supposed to walk all the way along the main road and turn where the cars drove in, but there was a shortcut. She could nip through the pedestrian entrance and cut across the car park. Her dad would be parked around the other side, so he wouldn't see. It was a small act of defiance, but it felt like a minor victory in her fight for freedom.

As she turned through the gap in the fence, she heard a vehicle on the road behind her, revving its engine as if someone had their foot hard on the accelerator. She glanced over her shoulder as a dark blue van sped past and swerved into the car park. Suddenly afraid, she broke into a run. The van was now heading straight for her. She spun round, wondering if she could get back through the fence and onto the road. It was too far, and this part of the car park was quiet, with no one to witness what was happening.

She scrabbled in her bag for her mobile so she could send an alert to her dad but fumbled, and the phone dropped to the ground. The van screeched to a halt before she could pick it up. She turned to run again. The side doors slid open. Two men jumped out, grabbed her around the waist and dragged her in. A hand was clamped over her mouth, cutting off her scream. The doors to the van slammed shut and she was thrown to the floor, where she lay bruised, shocked and terrified.

Her stomach lurched. The walls of the van seemed to close in around her.

What are they going to do to me?

Its engine roaring as it sped out of the car park, the van tore her away from the safety of her family.

21

The hotel room felt empty after Jack had gone. 'No point trying to go through all the details tonight,' he'd said. But he'd been clear about one thing: Tom's involvement could only be on Jack's terms.

'You've seen what men like this can do, Tom, and witnessed the destruction they leave behind. But you haven't been inside their world. I have, and this lot don't follow the rules. Your average criminal might have a code, but the 'Ndrangheta? They've thrown out the rule book. Trust me. Whatever you think you know, it won't be dark enough.'

Tom hadn't wanted Jack to leave. Not knowing where his brother was staying, he couldn't shake the concern that he might not hear from him again, and Jack had been reluctant to reveal too much in case Tom decided to take matters into his own hands and involve the police. Fear was etched into his face, and Tom worried that if he pushed him too far, he might disappear again – this time for good. For now, he would watch, listen and learn.

The last detail he'd been able to glean from Jack was the story of how these bastards had found him and abducted Ava.

'My fault entirely. I was so busy trying to disguise my identity as Jack Douglas that I never considered *Ethan Blake* might be of interest to a criminal gang. They must have followed me when I left the office in Chester. I guess they saw me pick up Ava, grabbed a photo – and just like that, they had a target.'

'They knew where you picked her up every day?' Tom asked.

'No! That's the thing. Each day she'd walk to a different spot. Never the same place two days running; never the same on a specific day of the week. Supermarket, train station, bus stop.'

'How did they track her, then?'

'I'm not sure I'll ever tell her how I think it happened, but we had a ban on using social media – for obvious reasons. She understood, although it must have been hard for her with other kids. How could she explain that she didn't want her photo in any of their posts? She told them that social media was, and I quote, "so last decade", but she'd been caught in pictures on friends' streams once or twice. The gang probably ran the photo they took through a facial rec program, discovered who her friends were and used their social profiles to find out where they went to school. There's no uniform in the sixth form, so it's the only way they could have worked it out. Then I'm guessing they watched her walk out through the school gates, followed her, and waited for an opportunity.'

'Poor kid,' Tom said, a hollow ache in his chest at the thought of Ava, terrified and alone. 'How did they let you know they had her?'

'I knew something was up. She was late sometimes, but only ten minutes. I wondered if she'd decided to break the rules and go into town with her friends – and who could blame her? So I tracked her phone, and found it lying on the tarmac in the car park.' Jack paused as if reliving the moment. He swallowed, then continued: 'I got a call. The Blake Securities number wasn't private – wouldn't be a very viable company if it was. A man's voice told me they'd taken Ava and they'd be in touch. They called again early the next morning and told me to come to Venice. I've only got one client here, so it seemed obvious it was something to do with the system I'd put in the palazzo.'

'And you came, not knowing what to expect?'

'I tried every trick in the book to find out who'd called me, but I didn't have much joy. They've got bloody good security. I hacked the train station CCTV and discovered Ava had been abducted in a van, but it was undoubtedly stolen so there was no point trying to trace it. They'd have swapped vehicles or changed the plates as soon as they could.'

'What happened then?'

'They said I'd be told what they wanted when I arrived in Venice, so I grabbed my laptop and not much else, and took a roundabout route here. I rented a room where I didn't need to provide my passport – one of the many "no questions asked" accommodation sites – then I was contacted and told what they wanted me to do. They said Ava would be released when they have the painting. Simple, really.'

It was difficult for Tom to know what to say; he had never seen Jack look so nervy. His eyes usually danced with laughter, finding amusement in the most unlikely situations. But now they were shimmering with tension.

Jack had then thumped his glass down on the table and left as abruptly as he'd arrived, telling Tom to keep the mobile he'd given him by his side at all times. He'd be in touch.

It was with mixed feelings that Tom called Louisa. He dreaded the inevitable questions he wouldn't be able to answer, and knew exactly how she would respond if he tried to dodge the truth.

Her phone rang just once. Clearly, she'd been waiting to hear from him.

'Hi, darling. How was the trip?' The forced joviality didn't fool Tom, but he played along.

'Small seats for tall men – the usual. How are you?'

'Okay. Worried, but I won't waste time talking about my day. Harry and Lucy are both fine, so let's get straight to the important stuff. Have you found him?'

This was the question he had been dreading. Not long ago, Louisa had left him because he'd lied about Jack being dead, and it had taken a promise of total honesty to persuade her to come back.

Now he faced a dilemma. If he told her about Ava, she would be frantic with worry and would want to contact Clare. Lucy would sense something was up and would start asking questions. But if he lied to Louisa to save her the stress, he had a fairly good idea how she would react when she eventually found out the truth.

He took a deep breath. 'You know I promised always to be honest with you?'

'Don't like the sound of this, Tom. Don't lie to me, whatever you do.'

'I'm not going to lie to you. For now, though, that means I can't tell you what's going on. I won't confirm or deny anything, and there's a very good reason for this. I promise you, the minute it's safe I'll tell you everything, but in the meantime I won't tell you any lies.'

'Christ, Tom, do you really think this is fair?'

'Probably not, but I'm asking you to trust me. I only know some of what's going on. I've had a conversation.' Tom was certain she would understand that he meant with Jack, so at least she would know he was alive. 'But it's a complex situation, and one I'm not sure how to handle. I'm hoping tomorrow might bring some clarity.'

There was silence from the other end of the phone. 'You've said you won't lie, so tell me – are you in any danger?'

'Not right now, and I intend to stay that way.'

'Are others in danger?'

It was Tom's turn to be silent.

'You're not going to answer that, are you?'

'No. Sorry, love, and if you prefer, I won't call you until this is over.'

'Don't be so bloody ridiculous, Tom!' she said with a sharp sigh.

He was handling this badly, probably because of his worries for his brother and Ava. His mind kept imagining where she was being kept, wondering if she was even alive. The thought of a teenage girl being held in captivity made him shiver. *This could be Lucy.* The thought plagued him and he couldn't pass this level of stress on to Louisa.

'I'll call you every day, I promise. The hotel is lovely, by the way.'

'For God's sake, don't start making polite conversation! I am not remotely interested in the hotel. Just keep yourself, and those you love, as safe as you can.' Her voice softened. 'I'll be thinking of you.'

With that, she hung up, and despite her final words, he was in no doubt that she was pissed with him. But he also knew that, given time, she would understand his decision. At least, he hoped so.

22

It had been a long night and, comfortable as the hotel bed was, the tangled bedclothes were testament to Tom's restless tossing and turning. At one point, feeling hot and sticky, he'd got out of bed and had a cool shower, barely drying himself before stretching out naked on the bed, hoping it would help.

It didn't.

As sunlight filtered through a gap in the curtains, Tom rolled over, reached into the bedside table drawer, and retrieved the phone Jack had left at the water taxi. There was a message and a dropped pin.

10 a.m. Usual precautions.

This, he assumed, meant he had to check he wasn't being followed, although why that might happen was a mystery to him. There was no obvious connection between Ethan Blake, security expert, and Tom Douglas, British detective, but he would do as his brother asked, doubling back, stopping to look in shop windows, checking reflections for signs that someone else had paused their journey.

The problem was, any organised crime group – Mafia or not –

would use tag teams to follow him, so when he stopped, the first person would continue past while another seamlessly took over the tail.

A quick glance at the dropped pin on his phone showed that the building he was being directed to was tucked away at the end of an alley, flanked by several other properties, making it difficult for anyone following him to know exactly which building he entered unless they were close behind. The back of the building faced on to a small canal and he could see a modest jetty, but he dismissed the idea of approaching by water. He wouldn't know whether people in passing boats were simply cruising by or watching him.

According to Google Maps, it was less than a twenty-minute walk to the address Jack had provided, so Tom had plenty of time. He quickly got dressed and headed downstairs to the hotel exit. He needed to get his bearings, to know where the path along the canal outside his hotel led and how, if necessary, he would be able to make his way from this quiet area of the city to a bustling square where he could lose himself among the crowds. He was leaving nothing to chance.

There was already warmth in the air as he stepped out of the hotel, and Tom breathed in the distinctive smell of Venice. It was the scent of old stone, slightly brackish water, and this morning the aroma of freshly baked bread. The cobbled pathway was quiet, and a church bell tolled the quarter-hour as Tom arrived in a tiny square. His gaze drifted to every shadowed corner and dark passageway, mapping out potential paths, marking subtle landmarks to guide him should the need arise.

Following his planned route, he entered a narrow alley where the buildings stood close together, swallowing the light and muffling the sound of his footsteps. Then, turning a corner, he suddenly emerged into the dazzling expanse of St Mark's Square. Tables spilled out onto the piazza in the bright morning sunshine, and the air was filled with the lively hum of conversation. Pausing for a moment to take it in, he made his way to a spot where he could sit and watch the world go by, scouring the crowds to check if anyone was paying him undue attention.

Barely able to absorb the buzzing morning scene, his mind was spinning with questions. He was desperate to get to Jack, to discover everything his brother hadn't yet shared, but Jack had said ten o'clock. With time to kill, Tom ordered a cappuccino and a brioche and waited as the minutes dragged by.

He'd accomplished his first mission of the day and would remember the route between here and his hotel without the need to consult a map. Later, he'd walk the same route at night, and tomorrow – if he was still in Venice – he would find a different route, turning out of the hotel in the opposite direction.

The last thing he wanted was to feel trapped in a city he didn't know.

Tom managed one bite of the brioche before pushing it away. He couldn't stomach the thought of eating at a time like this, so he just sipped his coffee until it was time to set off on a convoluted route towards the address Jack had provided.

Even though he didn't believe anyone had reason to follow him, he nevertheless made his way down alleys, made random turns, stopped, gazed around, and turned back, phone in hand as if he were just another tourist. Much as he hated selfies, he snapped a few to see if any faces showed up more than once in the background.

As he had suspected, there was no evidence that anyone was taking the slightest interest in him, so as the time grew close to ten, he rewound his steps and headed towards his brother.

The lane leading to the building Jack had marked on the map was neither narrower nor darker than any of the others Tom had walked along that day, but he shivered, knowing that each step was drawing him deeper into a situation he couldn't control. A window above him was thrust open, startling him. Looking up he saw an elderly woman reeling in a washing line stretched across the width of the alley. She gave him a toothless smile and a small wave, as if she was pleased to see a tourist venturing into her lane.

'Hai perso la strada?' she shouted.

Tom wished he understood. He thought *strada* meant road or street, but the rest was a mystery. It was clearly a question, so he just nodded vaguely and gave her a thumbs up to show he was okay.

She cackled and disappeared from the window, probably muttering about daft tourists as she went.

A narrow, weathered building stood at the end of the lane, its single door covered in flaking light grey paint. Worn shutters hung loosely over blank dark windows on each of the three floors, and there was no sign of life. Tom pushed against the door. It was locked. For a moment he expected it to open, like the door at the farmhouse. No such luck.

He pulled out the phone Jack had given him and sent a text.

Outside

He waited, and after a minute or two he heard the slap of bare feet on a stone floor, and the door flew open.

Without pausing for the niceties of a greeting, Jack stood back and ushered Tom in.

'I wasn't followed,' Tom said.

'I know. I was watching.' He pointed upwards, and for a moment Tom wanted to ask what Jack would have done if he'd seen someone pursuing him down a dead-end alley, but decided not to push it. 'Come up.'

Jack turned and ran back up the stairs, taking them two at a time. Tom glanced at the door behind him to make sure it was locked. He was relieved to see a steel shaft running top to bottom. No one was getting past that easily.

Reaching the top floor, Jack threw back a door to reveal a room with peeling off-white paint, bare floorboards and a few mismatched bits of scruffy furniture. An old sofa along one wall looked as if it doubled as Jack's bed, given the throw and a couple of pillows. In one corner stood a decrepit fridge. A single electric hob ring and kettle sat on a worktop. The door to a small bathroom stood open.

One part of the room had been cleared of clutter and was dedicated to two tables pushed together, bearing three monitors and two computers, all apparently box-new. A comfortable-looking high-backed office chair sat facing the monitors, two of which were filled with images that appeared to be from CCTV, while the third displayed an endless stream of scrolling letters and numbers.

'HQ,' Jack said, pointing vaguely at the technology. 'I brought my laptop and a few small devices with me, but I had to buy all these computers and install them when I got here. Do you want coffee? Has to be black, I'm afraid. Never thought to buy milk. And it's instant, which seems sacrilege in Italy.'

'Black's fine. Do you want me to make it? Looks like you're busy.'

'No, the system's doing its own stuff right now, so I've got about half an hour to fill you in properly.'

It was the first time Tom had seen Jack in daylight, and he was dismayed to see how pale he was. The tan he'd acquired during their holiday in the Adriatic hadn't faded completely, but the pallor beneath shone through, giving him a jaundiced look. His hair had grown a little, back to its natural curls rather than the wild mane he'd had in his teens or the shaved head of a few years ago, and he had a feverish look about him that Tom hadn't seen for years – not since he was a teenager obsessed with technology.

Back then, Jack had built his own computer from scratch and spent every waking moment pushing it to its limits, driven by a relentless curiosity to see what he could make it do. His eyes had burned with a passionate desire to learn and understand – a commitment unfortunately evident in neither his schoolwork nor his classroom attendance.

In the rare moments that Jack took a break he would sit on the floor, relaxing with a beer, rock music blasting out. He had an air of almost cynical amusement about him, as if he was laughing at himself. Now, though, this nonchalance had evaporated.

'I've got news. We have a date. They plan to take the painting on Monday night.' Jack pointed to a number flashing at the top of one of his monitors. 'Just over sixty-five hours, Tom. Then I can get Ava back. And I need to be ready.'

23

65:01:34. Tom stared at the flashing digits on Jack's monitor, watching as the numbers fell, each second drawing them closer to the critical moment. When they'd talked the previous night about the theft of the painting taking place 'sometime soon' it had felt remote, as if there might be time for Tom to persuade Jack to find an alternative solution. Now they had a deadline, and Jack would be focused on making sure the heist went ahead without a hitch. Ava's life could depend on it.

Tom looked at his brother's strained features. Did Jack really believe these people were going to let her go? What were the odds? Whatever his doubts, Tom couldn't voice them.

Handing Tom a mug of coffee, Jack headed towards his table of computers. 'I switched on the monitors in the palazzo this morning, and there's lots of activity. The first paintings have already been taken from the vault and are being hung as we speak. Have a look.' Lowering himself into his chair, Jack waved Tom towards an upturned plastic crate. 'Sorry,' he muttered, his attention firmly on the screen.

He pressed a couple of keys and the third monitor changed from scrolling numbers to a live video stream revealing an opulent room with high ceilings and tall windows. A polished marble floor was partially covered by a huge faded Persian rug, and one wall was already hung with vibrant abstract paintings. Two men wearing grey cotton duster jackets and white gloves lifted a canvas and carried it carefully across the room towards one of the empty spaces.

The screen switched to another camera, and Tom noticed a young woman in a sapphire-blue silk blouse, navy pencil skirt and impossibly high stiletto heels standing to one side, arms folded. She was watching every step the men took, leaving little doubt that she was in charge.

'This is the salon where the reception will be held. The main body of the collection is owned by the D'Angelo family, the head of which is Vittorio D'Angelo. He's the one with the money. I've only met him once.' Jack tapped the screen, pointing to the woman, who appeared to be in her thirties. 'His daughter. She's been my main contact and is organising the reception.'

'I thought rich people had teams to do all that kind of stuff.'

Jack's mouth twisted into a parody of a grin. 'You haven't met Gabriella. She finds it difficult to trust anyone. She says people prey on her father's generosity and rip him off at every opportunity. I persuaded her to trust me, and look how *that's* worked out for her.'

There was nothing Tom could say.

'What is it about your system that's so brilliant? Not that I doubt you, of course.' Tom tried for a smile, but Jack just stared at the monitor.

'Lots of tiny cameras are placed discreetly throughout the gallery. There's visible CCTV as well, because you'd be mad to have an exhibition like this without video feeds. If all the cameras were hidden, everyone would be trying to spot where they were, and it's the tiny ones that are crucial. They feed into my behavioural analysis system, which scrutinises body language and eye movement to gauge interest in the paintings. A person staring intently at a piece of art because they love it will present a different pattern to someone looking at it for other reasons – such as working out how to steal it. The system is programmed to recognise suspicious behaviours, using gaze tracking to see if people are looking around the painting rather than at it, checking different angles, as if they're searching for security measures.'

Tom blinked. He presumed this was AI, about which he had mixed views – loving it for its numerous benefits, terrified of how it could be abused.

'What happens if someone's behaviour suggests they're not there solely to enjoy the art?'

'The system triggers an advanced facial recognition program that strips features back to their most basic form, removing modifiers – glasses, beards, hairstyles. It breaks down the facial structure to components such as the distances between features, nose shape, mouth and so on, then compares them with a huge database of images, mostly drawn from the web and social media. It's pretty accurate.'

'Isn't this illegal, Jack? Sorry – I have to ask.'

'Of course you do,' Jack said with a flash of irritation.

'Okay. I probably deserved that. In terms of rescuing Ava, I absolutely understand that you might be willing to cross boundaries, but this is about the gallery and I'm just wondering about the legitimacy of it.'

'Jesus, Tom. Still the white hat. For the record, it's a bit of a grey area here.' Jack shrugged. 'My client is willing to risk it. And anyway, how can it be illegal to use tech that might prevent a crime? We're not sharing the information or using it to target innocent people. Plus, let's be real: every move you make on your phone and your computer is being monitored and shared so companies can sell you stuff. How is that more acceptable than analysing facial expressions with the aim of preventing crime? I developed this because I believe criminals should be caught, although once again – against my will and better judgement – I'm about to become one myself.'

Tom didn't know why he was uncomfortable. If it was up to him, every man and woman in the UK would be asked to willingly submit their DNA to be held on file. If a person doesn't intend to commit a crime, why should they object? But he wasn't about to debate that.

'What do you do if you find a match?'

'There's a deeper dive – police records, finances, you know the kind of thing. Anything we can get on them to determine if they were just gazing around because they were bored, or if there's any serious intent.'

'And if there is?'

'At that point, it's out of my hands. All I can do is report the apparent threat. How they deal with it is up to Gabriella and her father.'

Tom decided to stop asking questions. He wasn't involved in Italian law enforcement and didn't know the rules, which he expected were quite different from the ones he was used to.

And anyway, sometimes it was better not to know.

Tom watched the activity in the palazzo on Jack's monitor for a while, but it told him nothing new. His eyes were constantly drawn back to the steady pulse of the countdown display as each second clicked by.

'What's the plan?' he asked.

'The reception is Monday evening, and the heist will take place at around four a.m. on Tuesday morning. About two hundred people have been invited, all desperate to set foot inside D'Angelo's palazzo. It's known all over Italy as one of the very best examples of Venetian restoration, and even the rich and famous would move mountains to get an invitation.'

'And what's your role?'

'It's relatively simple. I hack the CCTV, open doors, disable alarms – all controlled by my security system.'

'This may be a daft question, but afterwards will there be any doubt that you were involved?'

One side of Jack's mouth curved up in a reluctant half-smile, his eyes showing a mixture of guilt and resignation.

'As things stand, none whatsoever. No one on the security team knows how to override the whole system. And because the exhibition will be monitored 24/7, I'll have to hack the camera feeds and substitute video clips that show the room empty as the painting is being removed from the wall.'

'I won't insult you by asking if you can do that, although it sounds as if there's a huge risk of screwing up the timings. I *have* had an idea, though, if you're prepared to listen.'

Jack looked at him and raised his eyebrows.

'I could talk to Philippa Stanley and tell her in absolute confidence what your dilemma is. I did some research last night, and there's a squad in the *carabinieri* dedicated to combating art and antiquities crimes, including the illicit trade in high-value paintings. If they knew what was at stake, they would surely help. It has to be worth considering, Jack.'

'No.'

'For God's sake, why are you being so bloody stubborn?' Tom muttered, fighting to keep his frustration in check. 'Can't you at least consider other options, or are you committed to just hurtling headlong into the first plan that comes to mind?'

The muscles in Jack's jaw tightened. 'You know nothing about this world, Tom. Yes, you know about catching criminals, and I accept that you're bloody good at it. But I know how these bastards work. Have you any idea what they do to people who cross them? Look up Lea Garofalo when you have a moment – she was killed and her body burned for three days to make it disappear, all for being a police informant. What do you think they'll do to Ava if I call in the *carabinieri*? And it's not as if I have a shred of evidence to prove who set this up.'

'Don't you *know* who's asking you to do this?'

Jack turned back to face the computer, probably so Tom couldn't read his face. 'I know more than I knew yesterday, but it's still not enough. I've been working on it for more than two weeks, but they know how to cover their tracks. I know the main man goes by the name Renzo Moretti. It took me a while, but I finally found a weakness in the encryption he used to message me when Ava was taken. His system was leaking metadata—' Jack glanced over his shoulder at Tom, '—but I don't suppose you're interested in that bit. I've been digging up everything I can on him ever since. It seems Renzo Moretti and his gang of merry men have been operating around the periphery of organised crime in Venice – low-level drugs, extortion, the usual – but now he wants to join the major league. The top boss of the local *'ndrina* – the *capobastone* – is Bruno Contarini, and it's him that Renzo is trying his level best to get in with.'

'I thought each *'ndrina* was a tight-knit family structure?'

'Absolutely, which is why betrayal is so rare, and why it's almost impossible to infiltrate them. But Moretti is engaged to Bruno Contarini's daughter.'

'Ah,' Tom said. 'And that gives him an in?'

'It gives him an *opportunity*, but I guess he has to prove himself. They're not married yet, and if he doesn't show himself worthy perhaps they never will be.'

'What's the painting got to do with any of it?'

'It's just a theory, but maybe Moretti needs to demonstrate that his crew is good enough to join the *'ndrina* – some kind of initiation, though there's probably more to it. It could be a commissioned theft for a collector, maybe Contarini himself has his eye on it, or Moretti might need it as collateral – you know, a guarantee of future payment for a shipment of something illegal: guns, drugs or even people.'

'And he needs collateral because…?'

'Because if he's trying to hit the big time, I doubt he's rich enough to find the up-front capital for whatever he's buying. He'll be able to pay off the debt when he's sold the product on – no doubt at a whopping profit – but until then he needs to provide proof of financial security. In this case, the painting.'

'If that's what it's all about, why don't we *give* him the bloody money? He'll know how to launder it, I'm sure. You wouldn't have to steal the painting then, would you?'

Jack shook his head. 'It wouldn't help him establish his worth to Contarini. He needs to prove himself capable of executing a major crime. Contarini might be a cold, calculating, ruthless Mafia don, but from everything I've learned it seems Renzo Moretti is equally ruthless, and also a hot-headed, impetuous thug.'

Tom recognised the type – always the most dangerous because they were unpredictable.

'Could it all be much simpler? Maybe he's just stealing the painting to sell because he needs – or wants – the money?'

'All things are possible – the market for stolen art is worth billions – but from what I've discovered about Moretti, I doubt he has the right contacts.' Jack shrugged. 'Either way, these guys will stop at nothing to get what they want, and it seems it has to be this particular painting, probably because Contarini knows it's bloody difficult to steal. He's testing him – or at least, that's my best guess.'

If that were the case, Moretti wouldn't want to leave any loose ends. Would Jack become unfinished business?

Last night, as Tom had lain awake considering all possible outcomes, he'd reasoned that, brutal as the Mafia might be, they would probably release Ava if their terms were met. Threats only hold power if there is hope attached, however slim, and no one would ever again pay a Mafia ransom or bend to their will if they knew they wouldn't honour their part of the bargain.

It was Tom's best, if somewhat feeble, attempt at positive thinking.

24

Why am I here? What do they want with me?

The questions repeat in Ava's mind as she huddles in the corner of the room, but she's no closer to finding answers.

Her dad has tried for years to convince her that her past is behind her, but at the same time he says he'll do everything in his power to protect her. Doesn't that mean it's *not* over? Maybe it never will be.

He's always said that if anyone wanted to harm her it would be because she's Natasha Joseph, a girl who supposedly died in a fire years ago. But the man who tried to have her killed, Finn McGuinness, is dead, so surely the danger has passed? Yet Dad still insisted on taking precautions. She'd started to think he was paranoid, but she should never have let down her guard.

Finn was the enforcer of the gang that abducted her when she was six years old, and he terrified the life out of everyone he met. Even from prison he'd arranged to have her killed, her home set on fire with herself, her stepmother and her baby brother inside – anything to prevent Ava from giving evidence against him. They would all have died, but the man she now calls Dad got them out with help from his brother. That was when she'd become Ava

Johnson, and she'd started to believe it might be possible to be happy. But life wasn't that simple.

Finn may have been the most evil of them, but there were others in the gang who knew her and it had taken years for Ava to stop looking over her shoulder, searching for familiar faces, ready to run. She should never have stopped.

She pushes herself up from the floor. She needs to move. The food they give her is only enough to stop her from starving, and it lies in her stomach like a lump of raw dough. Her muscles ache from sitting still too long, and she's weak – as if her body's giving up on her. She should exercise, but the effort feels beyond her. She stretches her arms above her head, then half-heartedly rests one hand against the wall to support herself as she tries a few squats.

Rubbing her eyes on the sleeve of her filthy shirt, she gives up her feeble attempt and lies down on the thin, stained mattress, wrapping her arms tightly round her body – not for warmth, but for comfort – trying to block out ugly memories from her past, that other life, the one she'd rather forget. But it's impossible. This isn't the first time she's been thrown into a dark, damp hole in the ground with no food, little water and no light. Sometimes she'd lain there, starving and shivering for days until she agreed to do their bidding. Refusal was never an option. Punishment for even *thinking* of saying no to any demand was swift and brutal.

Why is this happening to me again?

They haven't asked anything of her, and she's been here for days. How many, she can't guess. Too many is all she knows, and no one's come to save her. Perhaps they don't care.

She wishes she knew what the two men guarding her want. At least back then she'd known why she was being made to grovel in the filth of the place she called The Pit. Now, there is only silence.

25

'I'm not being much help, so why don't I go and get us some food?' Tom asked.

Jack sat with his back to him, apparently focused on perfecting the algorithms that would make the CCTV in the palazzo display footage of empty rooms during the heist. He gave a small shrug, and Tom guessed food wasn't much of a priority right now.

'I know you're busy, Jack, but you said you half-hoped I'd come and find you. I'm here now, and yet you don't seem to want me to help. There must be *some* reason you wanted me here?'

Jack swivelled to face him. 'Two heads are always better than one, and while you may not be over-endowed with criminal tendencies, little brother, I think you're a good sounding board. Talking things through helps me judge whether my plan makes sense.'

'Irrelevant of what I think?'

Jack gave a half-smile. 'Pretty much.'

Tom didn't know whether to laugh or argue, but it was vintage Jack. 'I'll head out for a while, but first tell me about Clare and the kids. Are you in touch?'

'We're using encrypted messages. I'd love to speak to her, but I can't risk it. Let's face it, if they can hack Prince Harry's phone – and that was only journalists – think what the Mafia might be capable of.

I can secure my line quite effectively, but they may have found a way of accessing Clare's.'

'But she's okay?'

'Seems to be. Worried sick, of course.' Jack's lips tightened. 'You haven't spoken to anyone on an open line about this, have you?'

Tom tutted. 'Of course not. I'm a police officer, Jack, so I do take *some* degree of caution. I spoke to Louisa last night and told her I wasn't going to tell her anything.'

'Poor Louisa. How did that go down?'

'Not well, but I've promised not to lie to her, so I thought it better to piss her off by telling her nothing. I succeeded, of course, but she was over it by the time we spoke this morning. I do need to speak to Becky Robinson, though, who's acting DCI in my absence, and to Philippa.'

'*What?*' Jack practically bellowed. 'I *told* you, Tom – no police involvement. And I meant it.'

'Calm down! Becky will speak to the school and North Wales Police. Do you want them posting photos of you and Ava all over the press and TV?' Jack's eyes widened. 'No, I thought not.'

Jack scratched his head. 'Okay. But use the mobile I gave you. It's a black phone. Nothing's hackerproof, but it's as good as it gets, and I'm sure GMP has secure lines. Just don't mention names – or at least, don't mention Ethan Blake.'

Tom remembered reading about black phones some years ago. They had been withdrawn due to lack of consumer take-up, but he guessed Jack had modified this mobile in a way which was beyond Tom's technological know-how, creating his own black phone.

'What about asking Becky to go and see Clare – just to make sure she's okay.' Tom held up a hand to stop Jack from interrupting. 'We're not idiots, and she'll hardly roll up in a police car. She'd be in a Post Office van or something. Surely Clare needs some support too?'

Jack released a long slow breath. 'Another good idea. I knew you'd be useful! But for God's sake, tell Becky to be careful.'

Tom just gave Jack a look. His brother might be a whizz on

computers, but there were some things Tom was confident he knew more about, if only Jack would listen.

Hastily scribbling something on a piece of paper and passing it to Tom, Jack told him to memorise Clare's address, then demanded the paper back. Tom was about to laugh and ask him if he was going to eat it, but thought better of it. If that scrap of paper was found or taken from him, it would potentially be bad news for Clare.

Leaving Jack to his computer screens, Tom made his way back down the stairs – this time with a key to let himself back in to what Jack referred to as his HQ.

Constantly checking over his shoulder, doubling back on himself, weaving through the quietest of winding paths and alleys where he could be sure there was no one following him, Tom finally made his way into one of the many small squares off the main tourist track and found a local café. Taking a seat outside with his back to the window so no one could listen in from behind, and positioning himself some distance from two elderly local men sharing a table but sitting in silence, Tom sent a message to Becky on the black phone.

> Tom here. Need to speak. Secure line if
> possible.

The reply came in seconds.

> Will send number. Need a couple of minutes.

As he waited, Tom cast his eyes around the square. It was mid-morning and probably too late for locals on their way to work and too early for lunch, so it was quiet. A smiling woman in a wrap-around apron came out of the café with tiny cups of coffee for the two men. She disappeared for a moment, returning with two empty glasses and a bottle of clear liquid that Tom guessed was grappa. There was a murmured 'Grazie' from one man, while the other got on with pouring the clear liquid into the waiting glasses.

She walked across to Tom's table, smiled and murmured, 'Cosa le porto?' which Tom interpreted as 'What can I get you?'

'Un cappuccino, per favore.'

As the woman turned away, his phone beeped – a message from Becky with the phone number.

'Becky,' he said, as soon as they connected. 'Thanks for taking my call. I'm happy for you to report back to Philippa with everything I say – I don't want her to think I'm cutting her out – and I need to tell you something. We're secure, aren't we?' At Becky's 'Yes', Tom took a breath. 'Ava's been abducted.'

He heard a gasp. 'Christ! How the hell did that happen?'

'She was taken from the station car park close to her school. Jack was waiting for her, but he was parked round the corner. He knew roughly what time it happened so he hacked the station car park's CCTV. She was taken in a dark blue Transit van with sliding doors on the side. He doesn't trust the number plate – thinks it will have been stolen from another van. They probably switched vehicles too, as soon as they were out of the city, but I can send you what he has.'

'You mean he hasn't hacked the ANPR system too?' Tom detected a note of dry disbelief in her voice.

'He said it wasn't worth it. I guess there are lots of cameras in central Bangor, but if they headed into Snowdonia and kept off busy roads, it would be a waste of time. And there's no clear footage of the kidnappers' faces – so facial recognition's not an option.'

'Are you telling me Jack has access to that?'

'I'll leave you to draw your own conclusions. But despite what I originally thought, this abduction is nothing to do with either Jack Douglas or Natasha Joseph. This isn't their past lives catching up. It's to do with the security work Jack's been doing in the last few years – all legal and above board. I can't say any more. I'm sorry.'

'Does he know who's got her?' Becky asked.

'He thinks so. Not to say the word out loud as I'm out in the open and it's definitely a word the locals *would* understand, but it's an Italian group – the kind you don't mess with.'

'Shit, Tom. That's bloody dangerous.' There was a pause that Tom didn't know how to fill. 'What do you want me to do?'

'Could you go and see Louisa when you have time? I don't want to discuss this with her on the phone. She doesn't have a secure line, so I haven't been able to tell her about Ava, and she definitely doesn't need details of who we believe is involved. That would scare the hell out of her. Can you ask her not to try to contact Clare because it might not be safe, but can *you* check on Clare and the kids, do you think? They're living just outside Heywood.'

'Heywood? Why?'

'Jack wanted their backup safe house to be within GMP jurisdiction. Don't go as a detective, though. You'll need a cover. Jack's only communicating with her via secure messaging, and I'm sure she's out of her mind with worry. I'm not sure we can make things better for her, but it might be good for her to have someone to talk to. Do you mind doing this, Becky? I know it's a lot to ask.'

'Of course I don't mind. Poor Ava, though. Hasn't she had enough to deal with in her life?'

Tom could only agree. 'Can you also make sure Philippa has called off North Wales Police? There can't be photos of either Jack or Ava in the press, flagged as missing. I've already asked her, but if you explain what's happening she'll make up a story – not without a tinge of irritation that my brother's causing her problems again.'

'Huh. Not when she knows what's at stake. Look, I'll take Rob Cumba with me to see Clare. We'll purloin an Ocado van or something in case anyone's watching.'

'That'd be brilliant. Thanks, Becky, but careful what you tell Rob. He knows nothing about Jack, and I'd rather it stayed that way. Jack thinks his family are all fine, but he's not spoken to Clare in case her mobile's been compromised.'

'I'll get her a clean phone. I got to know her quite well during the whole Tasha episode and all that followed.'

'Yes, of course you did. I'll send you what I have on the vehicle involved in Ava's abduction too.'

'There's a lot we could do to track the van if you'd allow me to contact North Wales Police, you know. Even if the number plate's been changed, we might pick it up on CCTV, then we can track the new number on ANPR. We can also get mobile usage data for the station area to see which phones were being used at the time. That might tell us something. But only if we can reach out to NWP.'

The woman came out of the café with Tom's coffee. He smiled his thanks and took a sip. 'The fewer people who know, the better. You know how tricky this is, Becky.'

'I do, but maybe Philippa can come up with a plan – if you can live with that?'

Tom could. But he wasn't sure what Jack would think.

'I know there's a lot you're not telling me here, Tom. These people won't have taken Ava for no reason, and Jack wouldn't have gone to Venice for a spot of sightseeing. I'm guessing you can't share the details with me, but it's only a couple of weeks since I was trying to stop blood from pumping out of your chest, so forgive me if I'm worried.'

Tom was unlikely to forget that moment. Or the sound of Becky's voice, begging him not to die.

'I appreciate your concern, but please don't do anything you're not comfortable with. This is my problem.'

Becky scoffed. 'Oh, for God's sake, Tom. No one here is going to leave you to fight whatever battle you've got going on without support. Let me deal with this, but stay safe.'

26

By the time Tom made it back to Jack's room, he was feeling slightly relieved that someone other than him knew about Ava's abduction. Although he couldn't tell Becky what Jack was planning to do, someone else needed to know about Ava in case everything went wrong.

Jack was struggling, and Tom's chest tightened at the look of despair in his brother's eyes, knowing all he could do was offer his support. It wouldn't help if he was light-headed through lack of food and sleep, though, so on his way back Tom had thought that if anything would tempt Jack to eat, it would be pizza. Not the healthiest of options, but he was unlikely to be lured away from his computer by a green salad. More in hope than expectation, he'd also bought *panzanella* and *insalata di fagioli*.

Jack barely registered Tom's return and ignored the mouthwatering aroma coming from the takeaway bag. Tom cut a slice of pizza *diavola*, stuck it on a piece of kitchen roll and placed it next to his brother, along with the *panzanella* and a plastic fork. Jack reached sideways, took a bite of pizza and put it back down again without taking his eyes off the screen.

Over his shoulder, Tom could see live footage of the palazzo. More paintings had been hung and the room looked almost ready.

'What's happening?' Tom asked, gently squeezing his brother's shoulder.

'I just checked the comms between Gabriella D'Angelo and her security team. The primary insurers for the paintings have spread the risk across several companies, and they're sending a team to review the security measures.'

'That's not a problem, is it?'

'I can't see why it would be. They'll be interested in the motion detector sensors in the floor, the infrared beam barriers and the smart lock systems. Gabriella doesn't need to tell them about the behavioural analysis software, and they're probably just as worried about damage as they are about theft, so they'll want to know about humidity and temperature sensors. I'm not worried about them.'

Jack might claim to be unconcerned, but it didn't seem to have stopped him obsessively studying the details of the inspectors, which he had acquired from somewhere.

'One guy's already been and gone, and another is about to arrive. Let's hope they don't find any reason to shut the exhibition down before Monday night.' He took another bite of pizza, his eyes fixed on the scene playing out in front of him. 'Here comes Gabriella.'

Gabriella D'Angelo was accompanied by a tall, slim woman in an emerald-green silk shirt with long wavy auburn hair, tied back. Jack's body jolted, and he peered at the screen, his fingers working the keyboard as he switched from one camera to the next, enlarging the image to get a better angle on the woman's face.

'No...no...' he muttered. He pulled back on the focus so he could watch the woman as she looked around the room.

'What?' Tom asked.

Jack didn't respond. Tom could see *Serenata Selvaggi* – the painting at the centre of the heist – hanging on the wall. It was smaller than he had expected but it looked even more stunning on the screen than in the article he'd read. The women were walking towards it, and Jack flicked to another camera. Two faces filled the screen.

'*Fuck!*'

'What's up, Jack?'

Still ignoring him, Jack turned to the list of inspectors. He glanced at his watch, back at the list of inspectors, then back to the face filling one of the screens.

'Eleven thirty a.m., Elena Ferraro, Assicurazioni Nazionali,' he read out.

'And...'

'And that is *not* Elena Ferraro. Unless she has a doppelgänger, that's Tia Rukavina. And she means trouble.'

Jack had ignored Tom's pleas for an explanation, raising his hand for silence as he switched on the audio. The women were talking in Italian, and Jack continued to press keys on his screen until a text box appeared with translated subtitles. Gabriella appeared to be voice A.

A: So you see, Miss Ferraro, the system carefully monitors those looking at the painting. It's highly sophisticated and can even implement a degree of behavioural analysis, although we totally respect the regulations.

'She shouldn't have said that,' Jack muttered. 'Especially not to this woman.'

Much as he wanted to ask Jack what was making him so edgy, Tom knew better than to distract him, so he watched, read the transcript and studied the women's body language.

Elena Ferraro, or whatever she was called, seemed like a closed book. She stood tall, looking straight ahead, and neither smiled nor frowned at Gabriella's comments. Her hands were pushed into the pockets of her black slim-fitting trousers and she stared, unblinking, at the painting as Gabriella tried her best to convince her that the security systems were first class.

'She's not listening,' Jack said.

'How do you know?'

Jack pointed to one of the screens on his right, which seemed to be running some form of analysis.

'Her eye movements tell us she's focusing on the painting. No subtle nods or head tilts towards the speaker. Pupil dilation indicates visual interest rather than cognitive processing of what's being said. Is that enough to convince you? There's more.'

'God's sake – we won't need detectives to interview suspects soon,' Tom grumbled.

Jack didn't respond, his gaze fixed on the screen. Whoever this woman was, she was worrying him.

Gabriella had fallen silent, perhaps realising her words were falling on deaf ears, and after thirty seconds or so, Elena turned to her with a polite if rather tight smile.

B: Can we move on, please?

The two women walked around the rest of the gallery, stopping to look at paintings which, according to Jack, were the most expensive in the room, but even without behavioural analysis it was clear to Tom that each piece of art was getting little more than a cursory glance.

B: I've seen enough, Miss D'Angelo. I'd like to see your security control room now.

With that, the two women exited the gallery.

'Are you going to pick them up in there?' Tom asked.

'No point. She's just going through the motions. The only painting she was interested in was *Serenata Selvaggi*. As an insurance company risk assessor that shouldn't have been her main focus, but it was.'

'Who is she? Stop being so bloody mysterious, Jack.'

Jack pushed the pizza away, took a gulp of what looked like cold black coffee and grimaced.

'I'm not. At least, not intentionally. I was hoping to get a clue to what she might be up to, but ever the professional, she gave little away. She may be calling herself Elena Ferraro now, but I am one hundred per cent certain that's Tia Rukavina. Very few people have almond-shaped eyes that colour of green. They practically match her shirt. And when she pulled her hand out of her pocket, I saw the scar. She got that when she was a child, and she rubs it when she's stressed.'

'So how do you know her, and why are you worried?'

Jack spun round in his chair and sat back, arms folded. 'Tia Rukavina is Croatian. She won a scholarship to Oxford to study law, then did a masters in law and finance. I know this because I studied every detail I could find on her when she became a forensic accountant, working primarily for the National Crime Agency and occasionally the Serious Fraud Office. Her speciality was tracing and recovering assets, and a significant amount of her work involved disrupting money laundering and other illicit financial networks.'

'And you know her because...'

Jack had always told Tom he hadn't been involved in any of Guy Bentley's gang activities – drugs, prostitution or the inevitable money laundering – and he hoped he hadn't been lied to.

Jack gave him a lopsided smile. 'Don't give me that look, Tom. I kept well away from that part of Guy's business, but I was determined to bring him and his crew down and end his threats against my family. That's why I was interested in Tia Rukavina's investigation into his activities.'

'What's her involvement here, though? None of what you've said about the art theft or this private viewing has anything to do with money laundering, has it?'

Jack shrugged. 'Who knows? But I'm sure she's not a risk assessor. And she's not called Elena Ferraro either. Whichever agency she's working for, she's obviously deep undercover, and whether she's investigating money laundering, art theft or fraud, if Tia Rukavina intervenes and the painting is seized or the exhibition closed down, that would be a disaster. No heist, no Ava.'

27

Footsteps.

They're coming towards her along the stone passage – the route out of here that she eyes longingly every time they open the door. Two pairs of feet.

Why are they here? They have already left food and water. *What do they want?*

She huddles at the far end of the mattress, pressed into the corner, and pulls her knees closer to her chest at the sudden scrape of metal against metal. Her gaze is glued to the door, knowing the bolt is being drawn back. The door is pushed in with force and slams against the stone wall as the two men stomp into the room – Big Guy and Skinny Guy. They are talking and seem angry, but with each other, not her. She doesn't recognise the language – some sounds are sharp, others almost guttural. One of them is waving a phone in the air and pointing at her. It's Skinny Guy, and she doesn't like the look on his face. His black eyes seem wild and they run up and down her body in a way that sickens her. His lips part and a thin tongue slips out, slowly tracing the corner of his mouth, leaving a trail of saliva.

Big Guy punches him on the shoulder and shouts. She doesn't

know what he's saying but Skinny Guy shrugs and, with a sickening grin, makes an obscene gesture with his right hand against his crotch. She may not understand their words, but she knows exactly what's happening.

She holds her breath, her body trembling. They are both looking at her now. After what seems like minutes but is no more than seconds, Big Guy slaps Skinny Guy round the head and shouts again, and there is no mistaking the disgust and venom in his voice. He waves his finger at the mobile, shouts some instructions, and with an air of sulky resignation, Skinny Guy holds it up.

Her eyes fill with tears of relief as she realises he's taking her photo. Does he need to prove that she's still alive? Is she for sale? Maybe it's nothing to do with her being Tasha Joseph, the girl who helped bring down an organised crime group in Manchester.

Whoever the photo is for, they'll struggle to recognise her. She's filthy. Her hair is hanging in greasy matted clumps, her skin is dry, flaking, and her lips cracked through lack of water, decent food and sunlight. With only just enough drinking water, she has no way to wash. How Skinny Guy could find the idea of raping her enticing, she can't understand. She must stink.

He takes a couple more photos, the flash nearly blinding her, and shows them to Big Guy. He grunts as if with approval and heads towards the door. For a moment she thinks he's leaving her with Skinny Guy, and her pulse quickens. She's about to shout out a plea for him not to go when he turns at the door, says something in a harsh, commanding voice, and with a low snarl Skinny Guy turns too, pushes past him and disappears.

The bolt scrapes back in place, and the relief that she's safe – for now – leaves her trembling.

And then it hits her. In all the days she's been here, why hasn't it occurred to her before? Why hasn't she realised what it means? She's been around men like these before, and there were strict rules no one broke.

Cover your face. Don't let the victims see who you are. No names.

She may not know their names but she knows every inch of their skin; so well she could paint them. And that means only one thing.

They're not going to let me go. They're going to kill me.

28

Exactly sixty-two hours to go. Tom couldn't decide if he wanted time to speed up or slow down, but if there was an ongoing investigation into the painting, the chances of everything falling apart in the next two and a half days were significant.

'What else do you know about this woman – Tia Rukavina, Elena Ferraro, whatever her name is?' he asked.

'When I knew her, she was looking into Guy's finances. You know how it is with the heads of organised crime groups – the police generally know who they are, but they have no way of pinning anything on them because they hide their money so well.' Jack leaned forward, lowering his voice as if someone might be listening. 'Tia was trying to link Guy to shell companies she believed he was using to hide his dirty money. She was certain he was using smurfing techniques – you know, using lots of individuals – smurfs – to deposit small amounts of money in different banks, different accounts, different locations. Then, once it's clean, it can be channelled to wherever he needs it to go.'

'But she didn't catch him?'

'No, not the first time, which is when I met her. But I kept tabs on her investigation even after I supposedly died. She was still digging into Bentley's activities three years later and she was good at her job. I was hoping she'd expose him and save me the job of bringing him down. I'm sure she was getting close, but about five years ago she disappeared in the middle of the investigation. Hers was a dangerous job, and she was no doubt pissing off some of the world's most violent people. Finn McGuinness could easily have arranged for her to have a fatal accident – but she's here now, so clearly that never happened.'

'Did you have any dealings with her?'

'Yes, although not out of choice. I was ordered to provide her with documents relating to Guy's legitimate business to throw her off the trail. She obviously assumed I was involved in the money laundering operation, and who can blame her? I genuinely had no part in that, but my job was to waste her time by giving her irrelevant transactions to review. I've no doubt she'll remember me if she sees me, and not with any degree of affection.'

'Did you ever find out why she left mid-investigation?'

'Nope. I couldn't find any trace of her online. It was as if she'd dropped off the face of the earth. I checked death certificates in case it was Finn's work. There were none in her name. I checked the missing persons register too.'

'You hacked the NCA Missing Persons Unit?'

Jack tutted. 'Sometimes, Tom, it's necessary to do things that are illegal with no intention of doing harm. If I'd found that she'd been reported missing, I'd have tried to establish if Guy or Finn were involved. And let's face it, even as a dead person I'd have had a better chance of solving her disappearance than the National Crime Agency, given I knew the kind of people she was dealing with.'

Tom thought his brother was underestimating the NCA, but that was a conversation for another day.

'Do you think she's gone deep undercover with a new identity?'

Jack shrugged. 'It's the only conclusion I can come to, although I don't know who she's investigating – only that it seems to be related to the painting.' He turned back to his computer and started to type furiously.

'What are you up to?'

'I'm finding out where she's staying. Hotels and rental accommodation have to collect passports or identity documents and register them with the *questura* – police headquarters. Unless she's done what I did and booked via a no-questions-asked operation – unlikely, if she's supposed to be here in an official capacity – we should be able to find her.'

'How are you going to do that?' Tom asked, then held up both hands. 'No, don't tell me. I really don't want to know.'

He was rewarded with the whisper of a smile from Jack.

After no more than ten minutes, Jack pushed his keyboard away. 'No Elena Ferraro and no Tia Rukavina staying anywhere in Venice. Which means she's travelling under the radar. I told you she isn't a bloody risk assessor. She could be investigating Vittorio D'Angelo, I suppose, as he owns the painting. Maybe he bought it with dodgy money. Whatever it is, she could be about to wreck the whole plan. She may be on the side of the law, Tom, but we have to find her.'

Venice wasn't the biggest city in the world, but the cafés and pavements were teeming with tourists, so how the hell did Jack think they were going to find Tia Rukavina among the crowds?

'What about contacting Gabriella D'Angelo?' Tom suggested. 'Would she have Tia's – or Elena's – phone number? Could we make use of that?'

Jack lifted his head. 'It would be hard to explain why I want it, but you've given me an idea.'

Once again, he turned back to his computer. 'If Tia had her phone with her when she went into the gallery, it would have sent a probe request to try to connect with the network inside the gallery – you know, like when you go somewhere new and your phone shows you all the available Wi-Fi networks. The gallery security system captures all the requests. From that, I can get something called the MAC address of her device – nothing to do with Apple, in case you were wondering.'

'I wasn't. Will that give you her location?'

Jack shook his head. 'Not exactly. It just tells me her phone was nearby, not where she is now. But I might be able to pick up other data about recent access points.'

Tom jumped to his feet. 'Bugger this, Jack. I get it with the tech, but how far away is the palazzo? I could just follow her, old-style, if I can get there before she leaves.'

Jack frowned. 'Actually, that might be our best bet. I can delay her a bit – run some fake security protocols to lock everyone in for a few minutes if it looks like she's going to leave before you get there. Head out now, and I'll drop you a pin for the palazzo before you've reached the bottom of the stairs.'

Tom dashed towards the door, grabbing Jack's sunglasses from the sofa as he left, and as promised, a beep from his phone told him the pin had arrived. He set off at a jog. Fifteen minutes to the palazzo. He could only hope Jack was able to perform some magic to detain her if she tried to leave before then.

Slowing to a fast walk when he drew close to his destination to avoid attracting attention, Tom was catching his breath and rubbing the still-healing wound in his chest when his phone buzzed.

'Nearly there,' he said.

'I know, I'm tracking you.' Of course he was. 'I delayed her for a few minutes, but she's just left the building. I've accessed CCTV close by, and she turned left, heading away from where you are. I can't hack into any other cameras right now.'

Just then, Tom saw a flash of emerald green not far ahead. Her silk shirt. 'Hang on, I think I can see her.' He walked a little faster. 'It's her, Jack. I'm on her.'

Keeping a careful distance, Tom tailed Tia through the winding streets, staying close enough to keep her in sight, but hopefully far enough away to avoid her spotting him. The afternoon sun was hot, and he felt uncomfortably sticky after his jog but had no time to stop for a bottle of water.

Tia moved with purpose, her pace steady as she navigated a group of street performers – acrobats flipping through the air to the rhythm of lively music. She weaved through the crowd without giving the performers a second glance, but Tom found his path increasingly blocked by spectators. He attempted to skirt the thickest part of the crowd, but his line of sight to Tia was obstructed as bodies shifted and swayed to the music. He craned his neck, catching a glimpse of her distinctive shirt.

'Excuse me, do you speak English?' A woman stopped directly in front of him, clutching a map and looking frazzled. 'I'm trying to find the Rialto Bridge.'

'*Nein*,' he replied tersely, thinking quickly. Feeling guilty about his rude response, he gave her a brief smile as he strode past, glancing frantically about. He thought he'd lost Tia, but after a few seconds he caught another flash of the shirt.

Fluttering pigeons took flight around the square as he speeded up again, and Tom watched as she disappeared into a quiet, narrow street with fewer pedestrians. Keeping his distance, he turned to gaze into a shop window as she paused, appearing to check her phone. Tom let out a silent breath of relief when she carried on without turning round.

As she continued deeper into the labyrinth of Venice's back streets, he was forced to hang back, thinking as he turned each corner that he would find her there, waiting for him, hiding in the shadows, demanding to know why he was following her. It never happened. She crossed over a footbridge spanning a narrow canal, her footsteps quick and purposeful. He hung back until she reached the other side, his gaze fixed on her as she walked along the canal's edge. The water was dark and still, the windows overlooking it shuttered to keep out the afternoon sun. He felt exposed, but she turned into a passage between tightly packed ancient stone houses without a glance over her shoulder.

When he reached the corner, the alley was empty. He stopped, scanning the deserted pavement and the closed doors of the surrounding buildings. The only sound was the gentle lapping of water against stone walls.

He'd lost her.

29

'Okay, Rob, this is the address,' Becky said, pointing to a new-build detached house. 'Can you stay here and keep an eye out for anyone watching?'

Rob drew the borrowed Ocado van to a stop. 'Of course, but I wish you'd tell me what the hell's going on,' he said, shuffling in his seat. Keeping still was always a problem for him, and Becky knew asking him to stay in the van was a tall order.

'It's just a welfare check.'

'Becky – or ma'am, as I should now call you – even *I* know that DCIs, acting or otherwise, don't do welfare checks.'

Becky turned towards him. 'Becky's fine, and I realise I'm being unfair, but it really is a welfare check. I'm not going to give you the details, though, because it's better you don't know. Just trust me, Rob. Okay?'

DS Rob Cumba might be junior to her, but Becky had worked with him for a while now and liked him. He had endless energy and a perpetually good humour – although her insistence on telling him nothing today was stretching it to the limit.

'Fine,' he said. 'Do I need to stay in the van, or can I have a wander round?'

Becky smiled, knowing he would get fidgety if he was confined to his seat.

'You need to look like an Ocado driver, so if you want to get out, I suggest you go round the side of the van and look as if you're checking the deliveries. Or examine the tyres if you like. But don't stray too far, and stay in your role. You can get out now and pass me the crate of groceries.'

With a grin, Rob opened the door and jumped out, his normal cheery disposition restored. Becky stood to one side as he pulled out the crate.

'Sure you can carry this?'

Becky just gave him a look as she turned to carry it up the drive.

The house was situated two thirds of the way down a small cul-de-sac, and she felt sure Jack had chosen it because it was ordinary and in a family neighbourhood. He would want the family to blend in, worried about the consequences of leaving them alone in a more isolated spot. Nevertheless, the house appeared to be protected with a high-end security system.

Placing the box on the floor of the porch, she pressed the doorbell. Tom had said Clare was here with the two youngest children, and it was Saturday, so they should all be in.

No one answered.

Becky pressed the bell again and waited. Nothing.

Turning to glance behind her to check the Ocado van was shielding her from view, she bent and put her ear to the letterbox. There wasn't a sound from inside the house.

It was impossible to see anything due to a flap on the inside, but Becky put her mouth to the opening and shouted as loud as was reasonable.

'Clare, it's Becky Robinson. We met a few years ago. Tom asked me to come. Are you there?'

She put her ear to the opening. Silence. The kind of silence that says no one is in the house – or at least, no one living.

Knowing how odd this would look to a nosey neighbour, Becky went round the side of the house, signalling to Rob that she was heading to the back. He threw her a puzzled glance, but stayed where he was.

The back garden was paved and devoid of plants, a practical solution if they didn't normally live there. No toys, though. Not even a football.

Frowning, Becky peered through a window into the kitchen and wasn't entirely surprised to find it empty. She looked through the patio doors into the living room. No one there. More in hope than expectation, she pulled on the handle but it didn't budge. There wasn't a single sign that anyone was living there – not a book, a magazine, a child's toy in sight. She moved back to the kitchen window. Unless Clare was a total neat freak, this room was way too tidy for a woman with young children. Every work surface was bare, not even a dish cloth or tea towel, a jar of coffee or...

She pulled out her radio from under her Ocado fleece. 'Rob, I'm going to need to get in. Is there anything in the van's toolkit that might help? The door at the back of the garage has a glass window and Yale lock. There seems to be a door from the kitchen to the garage.'

'I'll have a look. Give me a minute.'

'Okay, but bring another crate from the van, so it looks like we've been asked to bring it round the back.'

Becky waited a few minutes until she heard Rob whistling a cheery number, as if happy in his work. He appeared carrying the first crate from the porch with a second one balanced on top. He dumped them on the ground, lifting a bag of potatoes to reveal a small pry bar, probably used to open the crates, a large screwdriver and some plastic gloves.

'Do you want me to do the honours?'

'No. If this goes badly, I don't want you implicated. If an alarm goes off, we're going to have to leg it, so can you go back to the van and get the engine running?'

'There are plenty of signs that the place is alarmed, Becky. Is this worth risking, or should we get official permission to enter?'

Becky could see his point, but that wasn't going to work. She wasn't here in an official capacity. She was, in theory, just checking Clare was okay. She debated contacting Philippa Stanley to ask if she could get permission to enter, but Philippa was probably safe at home by this time on a Saturday evening. If she was subsequently challenged for breaking into the property, she'd argue that she thought children were at risk.

'Why do we run if the alarm goes off?' Rob asked. 'Why not say we're police – flash our badges?'

'It's complicated. We can't show any connection between this family and the police. That's crucial. If it goes off, we run. If we're caught half a mile down the road, I'll explain to the officers. But the neighbours can't be alerted to the fact that we're police.'

Rob shrugged. 'And you're not going to tell me why, are you?'

Becky threw him an apologetic smile. 'The good news is that when I looked through the kitchen window I could see the alarm box. There's no sign it's active. No lights flashing, which you'd expect if it's armed. Maybe if the family don't live here all the time, they don't think it's worth leaving it on if there's nothing of value in the house.'

'What kind of person puts in a state-of-the-art alarm system and doesn't arm it?'

Becky shrugged. 'Maybe someone who doesn't want to be called out if it goes off by mistake. I don't know, Rob – but make yourself scarce. This is down to me.'

30

'I've got her!' Jack spun round in his chair to face Tom as he walked through the door. He grinned at Tom's despondent face. 'Doesn't matter that you lost her – you gave me a search area, and she's staying very close to where she disappeared, in a rented apartment at the end of that alley.'

Tom slumped onto the sofa. 'Thank God. I thought I'd blown it. I don't suppose you're going to tell me how you found her, are you?'

'I don't suppose you really want me to, do you?' Jack countered. 'Anyway, it doesn't matter. She had to be close by. The apartment's one of thirty in a huge palazzo, and I've no idea which one's hers.'

'And what do you plan to do about it? Are you going to talk to her?'

Jack's eyes opened wide. 'Are you kidding? In case you've forgotten, I'm supposed to be dead. Look, I have no idea why she's here, but she spent a long time staring at the painting. If it's stolen art or it was bought with dodgy money, I think she'd have acted by now. So I'm wondering if her investigation is somehow related to Moretti's heist.'

Tom tossed the idea round in his mind. 'I'm struggling to see how the planned theft of a painting relates to her expertise in money laundering, Jack.'

'Maybe we can't make sense of it because we don't know why Moretti's stealing it. My best guess has always been collateral for buying something – people, drugs, guns. But now Tia's snooping around, things aren't adding up. What if Moretti's going to use the painting to wash cash?'

'How? I understand how dirty money is cleaned by buying art, but stealing it? Unless maybe he plans to sell it to a shell company, then move it through a series of fake sales to make the money look legitimate. That could work.'

Jack lifted his hands, palms up. 'Your guess is as good as mine, but whether Tia's going to waltz in and seize the painting or she knows about Moretti's plans and is about to have him arrested, the outcome is the same. It's the last we'll see of Ava.'

'So, given that we don't have a bloody clue what she's up to, what's the plan? Because I'm sure you've got one.'

'I've got to stop her. I need to figure out what her game is, and then – if necessary – one of us will have to persuade her to allow the heist to go ahead. But we need more facts, and we're running out of time.' Concern was written all over Jack's face, and Tom glanced at the clock. 59:07:33. *Where the hell had six hours gone?*

'What can I do, Jack?'

'You're going to have to make contact with her.'

Tom blinked. 'In what capacity, exactly? As a police officer? Wouldn't that be risky? I might blow her cover.'

'It would, so that's not what I want you to do. I want you to gain control of her mobile phone so I can monitor what she's doing.'

Tom stood up and paced the room. He had the unsettling feeling that he was in way over his head.

'Maybe this is when we rethink the decision about the police. If I can get you a one-to-one meeting with the head of the unit that deals with Mafia crimes, you can explain everything to him.'

Jack's jaw clenched. 'I'm not going to have this conversation with you again, Tom. You don't know these people. I don't either – but I do know their type. The very first sign of a problem, Ava is dead. Me too, if they can find me. I don't know if there are any leaks in this elite unit, but I'd be very surprised if there aren't. Neither do I know how efficient they are. If they stop Moretti's heist, we're done. If there's a leak, we're done. I'm not prepared to give up control.' Tom was about to interrupt, but Jack held up his hand. 'If you don't like it, then do us both a favour and bugger off back to Manchester. Either shut up and help me, or fuck *off.*'

With that, Jack swivelled back towards his monitor, his back to Tom. Resting his elbows on the desk, he lowered his head onto his cupped hands, breathing heavily, as if he'd run a race.

Neither man spoke, and as the silence lengthened Tom thought about the times he and Jack had seen each other since his brother had 'risen from the dead', as he always referred to it. Tom had felt anger and joy in equal measure when he discovered Jack hadn't been killed in a freak boating accident. Anger at the pain he'd suffered at the apparent loss of his brother, joy that he was alive. He remembered Jack moving to stand in front of him years ago when a gun was pointed at his chest, prepared to take a bullet for him, and how he'd helped rescue Ava and her little brother at risk to his own life. Whatever his methods, Jack had consistently helped those he cared about. And Tom knew, without a doubt, that if this were Lucy, he'd stop at nothing to get her to safety.

'Bollocks to this, Jack. You need to at least listen to me – *hear* me – because I'm trying to strike a balance between achieving what we all want – rescuing Ava – and making sure you stay out of prison for orchestrating an art heist. Or, of course, you could seriously piss this gang off and end up dead yourself. It's true that I've questioned your approach – and it's right that I should. It's called *balance*, and I will *not* stop making more rational suggestions, even if you choose to ignore them.' Tom took a deep breath. 'So let's get this straight. I will *not* fuck off back to Manchester. I will stay here and help in any way I can, or at least, any way that my conscience will allow. And that bit of me is feeling quite flexible right now. But I'm not going to stop telling you if it's a step too far, and I won't stop offering alternative suggestions – even if you shoot them down in flames. Okay?'

Jack lifted his head and spoke without turning round. 'Well said, little brother. I have a conscience too, but there's not much I wouldn't do to save my daughter. She doesn't deserve any of this. And the time might come when you *do* have to fuck off back to Manchester – because I might cross a line that your conscience won't accept.'

Tom released a long breath. 'Well, we're not there yet, are we? Until we are, tell me what you need me to do.'

31

It's getting close now, and only time will tell whether I'm as good at my job as I have led them to believe. The pieces are slotting into position, but let's face it. I'm playing a part. One false move and I'm dead.

I fling open the tall windows of the apartment and lean against the railing of the Juliet balcony, looking down at the canal shimmering in the last of the sun and alive with activity. A vaporetto with bold blue stripes cuts smoothly through the water, its deck crowded with passengers, their lives untouched by anything darker than the fading light of an evening sky.

The silhouette of a gondola drifts into view, its black hull contrasting with the colourful scenes around it, and I close my eyes for a moment, letting the sounds of the canal wash over me – the gentle lap of water against stone, the excited chatter of tourists – knowing that if I fail, this may be my last opportunity to experience one of the world's most breathtaking cities. In fact it might be my last chance to experience any of life's pleasures, because I don't know what they'll do to me if they find out who I am.

It's taken months of planning, years of integrating myself into this world. My past has been eradicated, a new persona created, and no one – not even the mighty 'Ndrangheta – will find a hole in my story.

What do people see when they look at me, I wonder? My Italian is flawless, thanks to inviting a group of native speakers into my home and *speaking only Italian for three months. They were instructed to stop me each time my accent wasn't perfect, or when I failed to use the slang of the region I'd chosen as my birthplace. I mimicked their expressive, animated body language, using my hands to emphasise points, punctuate sentences and convey emotions. I tried standing closer to people, keeping strong eye contact, but it felt alien to me, a woman brought up in a world of conflict. I am by nature reserved, guarded, and I couldn't maintain the façade. My mannerisms – the detached smile, the unwavering gaze – now defy their expectations of women in their culture. I don't stand close, I don't touch, and I don't use my hands expressively. I am calm, distant, composed, and I never show a moment of fear.*

The surname Ferraro was a strategic choice. Not an uncommon name, but I wanted to be associated with Rosa Ferraro – one of the few women who made a significant impact as a leader within the 'Ndrangheta. It has taken months to gain their trust, but now I have it. Whatever their demands, I haven't wavered.

It's the end game that really matters, though. And I will not hesitate. I will play my part exactly as planned.

But it's my plan. Not theirs.

32

Rob stood, hands on hips, glaring at Becky. 'If you're going into this house without any knowledge of what might be waiting for you inside, I'm going with you. You wouldn't be doing this if you didn't have a very good reason and you don't need to tell me what it is. But you're worried, which means I am too. So stop arguing and give me that pry bar thingy.'

Becky knew this wasn't a good idea, but in the unlikely event that Clare was in the house, she would ask Rob to go back to the van. He didn't need to know any more. And the truth was, she was glad to have him with her.

Blowing out a long breath, she pulled the pry bar from the crate and passed it to him. 'Here you go, if you're sure. All I can tell you is that I was doing someone a favour by checking up on this family. I seriously expected them to be sitting round the TV watching *Britain's Got Talent*. But they're not, and I need to know why.'

Rob just gave her a look and took the tool in his hand. 'In we go, then. Do I need gloves?'

Becky nodded. 'I think so, but not to avoid leaving traces of ourselves. We don't know what's happened here and I don't want to destroy any evidence.'

'Shit, Becky – this is serious, isn't it?' Rob said over his shoulder as he carefully inspected the door to the garage.

She didn't know how to answer. Was it serious? Or was Clare insanely tidy and they'd all gone out for a burger?

'Let's see.' Rob peered closely at the lock, then back at the pry bar. 'I'm going to slide the flat end between the door and the frame near the lock and try to separate the mechanism from the frame. Can you push against the door for a bit of extra leverage?'

Becky did as he asked. After a few seconds, the door popped open with a sharp click, fortunately with minimum damage done.

There was no car in the garage, just a washing machine and a tumble dryer, both empty. Knowing how much washing one child created, let alone two, Becky was surprised. She sniffed. No lingering smell of detergent, and the inside of the washer was bone dry.

She turned to find Rob examining the door to the kitchen. 'This one's a bit tougher,' he said. 'It's a Yale, and contrary to popular belief, the old credit card trick doesn't work. The security on this type of lock is way beyond that nowadays. I was hoping the hinges would be on this side so I could remove them and lift the door out without damaging it. But they're not. What do you think?'

Becky groaned. 'I don't want to wreck their door, but I can't just leave, Rob. I need to know what's happened to them – even if they're just out for the evening.' She didn't want to think of the alternative. 'If we use the pry bar again, we're going to wreck the frame, but it's better than kicking the door in.'

'And I don't suppose you have a bump key handy,' Rob said with a grin.

'I wish.'

'Well, let's not worry just yet. If we make too much mess we'll have to call someone out to put it right.'

Becky was even more glad she wasn't doing this alone, but she was going to have to tell Rob something.

'Before we do this, you need to know that this is related to Tom – to someone who was a CHIS for him in the past. Okay? I'll tell you more later, but that's why the locals can't know there's any police involvement. We don't want to blow anyone's cover. Right now, it's the wife and family we're worried about.'

Rob lifted his hands, palms up, and shrugged. 'You don't have to explain. If you say we have to do it, you won't get any more questions from me. Let's just get it done.'

Becky cringed at the splintering of the wood as they prised the door open, but they were in within minutes. She stood still just inside the door, breathing in the scent of the house.

Realising Rob was watching her, she had to come up with something plausible, not wanting to admit her first instinct had been to check for the whiff of death – that sweet, sickly stench of decaying human flesh.

'I'm just trying to get a sense of the air in here,' she said, her voice steady but distracted. 'I would have expected something – coffee, maybe. Traces of food, the familiar scents of a lived-in family home. What do you smell?'

'Nothing,' Rob said. 'Stale air. Like the place has been locked up for a while.'

She breathed again. Rob was right. Neither the doors nor windows had been opened for a long time. She looked around the room. The cupboards had a shiny dark red finish with no trace of the sticky hands of small children. A breakfast bar separated the kitchen from the living room, and there was a small dining table. All surfaces were completely clear and clean.

'We need to search.'

'Okay. What are we looking for?'

'Signs of human life – that someone has been here, and if they have, that they left voluntarily. You look down here. I'm going upstairs.'

Becky didn't want to do this. She had no idea what she was going to find and could only hope that her sense of smell hadn't missed something ominous.

33

Despite telling Jack that he was in and would do whatever was necessary – to a point – Tom wasn't comfortable with Jack's latest instructions. He was getting close to the area where Tia was staying, and had to hope he could find her, maybe in a café or restaurant nearby.

'She'll have to eat, Tom, and the place she's staying doesn't have cooking facilities, according to the website. It provides a list of restaurants within ten minutes' walk, though, and her new name suggests she's playing at being Italian. If she's acting the part, she's likely to pop out to a local *osteria* – of which there are many. It's probably worth checking the recommended ones first; I doubt she'd go to anything with a tourist menu. Nevertheless, I need *you* to be a tourist asking questions. And then I need you to find a reason to sit at her table.'

'Christ, she'll think I'm trying to pick her up.'

'Probably. She might be flattered – although unless she's changed from the person I met a few years ago, you're more likely to get a very cold look, if not simply told to piss off. You need to use your charm—' Jack attempted a grin, '—of which you have plenty. Tell her you're trying to find a specific place in Venice – you'll have to come up with something. Use your imagination. The point is, you need to keep her occupied for a few minutes with your phone – or rather, the one I'm going to give you – in close proximity to hers.'

Tom didn't like the sound of this one bit. 'What law, exactly, am I breaking this time?'

Jack ignored the question. 'First thing, don't use this phone for anything else, only for putting close to hers on the table. And switch off your black phone. There's no bigger giveaway than a phone ringing in your pocket when another one is sitting on the table.'

'Okay, I can manage that.'

'When you've identified her – and she's pretty hard to miss with those green eyes – you switch on this phone.' Jack held a mobile in the air that looked no different to the one he had previously given Tom.

'And then?'

'Find a reason to speak to her. Ask if she speaks English – in bad Italian.'

'I don't know *good* Italian, so that's not hard.'

Jack ignored him. 'I suspect she'll say she doesn't, so your obvious opening is gone. But not a problem. Look frustrated, then pull out this phone. Hold up your finger to indicate you're trying to look up some words in Italian. She'll be irritated, but that's tough. Press this icon.' Jack leaned forward and showed Tom the screen. 'Then shrug, put your phone on the table – even if hers isn't there it will probably be in her bag – and leave it there as long as you can. Keep her occupied for at least a couple of minutes. That's all I need for the first part. For full implementation, five minutes would be better.'

'Then what happens?' Tom asked.

'This device, which isn't really a phone at all, does its work.' He handed it to Tom.

'Which is?'

'Are you sure you want to know? Okay, okay!' He held up both hands as if surrendering. 'It has some tools installed specifically for exploiting Bluetooth vulnerabilities. Once it makes a connection – and she won't know that's happened – it will extract data: contacts, messages, files. Limited information, unfortunately, which is why I ultimately need to install spyware to monitor her comms. There's a lot of security around apps nowadays, so it's not guaranteed, but we'll install the spyware and I'll see if I can trigger its activation remotely – maybe send her a fake app update prompt. It's tricky and time is tight, but it's our best shot.'

Tom had run through Jack's instructions in his head several times in the hours before it was late enough in the evening to begin scouring the restaurants. Now, as he walked through the area close to Tia Rukavina's apartment, he went over them again. Had this been an undercover operation for Greater Manchester Police he'd have relished the challenge, but the stakes were so high. He couldn't afford to get it wrong.

He'd just reached the fifth of his target eateries and was beginning to think he needed to do another circuit when his phone rang – his real phone – which he hadn't yet switched off.

'Hey, Becky. How did it go?'

Becky's voice was low and fast. 'Tom, I know you don't want to speak on an open line, but I don't have a choice. Rob and I visited the address in Heywood. You need to get to a place where we can speak properly, because the house is empty. And the occupants weren't just out for the day. There were no clothes, no food, no sign that anyone had been in the house for months.'

Tom stopped dead. 'You're sure you got the right address?'

'Certain. We went next door and told them we were trying to deliver some shopping. They said they'd met the people who own it just once. A couple with three children – one girl a lot older than the other two, so that sounds right. They told the neighbours they work abroad and the house is just for when they are in the UK. Since that first visit several months ago, they haven't seen them at all.'

'Shit!' Tom hissed under his breath.

Every instinct told him to turn back, to find his brother and break the news. Jack said he'd been in touch with Clare and all was well. So where the hell was she?

On the other hand, this might be his only chance to find Tia.

'Where are you, Tom?' Becky asked.

Tom looked around. He was standing in the middle of a square, pedestrians weaving around him. He glanced at the small *osteria* directly ahead of him just in time to see a woman in a vivid green silk shirt take a seat at one of the outside tables. Her long wavy hair was tied back loosely, and although he couldn't make out the colour of her eyes, he had no doubt that this woman was his target.

She spoke briefly to the waiter and then pulled a mobile phone from her bag, glanced at it, and placed it on the table.

'Tom?'

'Sorry, Becky. I can't explain now, but I have to go. Can I call you back in perhaps an hour?'

There was a brief silence from the other end of the phone. 'Sure, but do you want me to do anything in the meantime?'

He understood her bemused tone, but there was nothing he could do about it. 'Not right now. Look, I can't explain. I'm really sorry.'

He hung up, turned off his phone and tried not to stare at the woman sitting outside the *osteria*. Should he head back to Jack? Or should he take this opportunity to try to capture the contents of Tia's phone?

Every bone in his body was telling him to spin on his heel and rush back to Jack. Despite Clare's messages, which suggested she was safe and well, if she'd never been to the house it seemed likely she'd been missing for some time, possibly since Jack left for Venice. Alarming as that thought was, Tom's rational brain told him that one hour was unlikely to make any difference. And if he lost this opportunity to pursue Tia, he might never get it again.

Decision made, Tom tried to relax his muscles and slow his breathing. He couldn't let the woman sense how shaken he was.

Luckily for him, the small tables of the *osteria* were mainly occupied by couples, and the only spare seat in the outside dining area was at Tia's table. Taking a deep breath, he walked to her table, which was thankfully at the edge of the small terrace.

'Excuse me, do you speak English?' he asked, deciding not to try a poor attempt at Italian.

The woman looked up without a trace of a smile on her face and shook her head. There was no doubt this was Tia. Her eyes were definitely green, almond-shaped. And sharp.

'Damn,' Tom muttered. He put his hand on the back of the chair. 'May I?' he asked, pulling it out before she had a chance to speak. He switched on the fake mobile and sat down. She glared at him, clearly incensed, but could hardly ask him to leave in English.

Tom rubbed his back. 'I know you don't understand me, but I've been standing for too long. Got a back problem.' He reached behind him and massaged the small of his back. 'If I can just ask the waiter for some help when he's free, I'll leave you in peace.'

Tia's eyes narrowed. 'Please go,' she said, her voice barely disguising her irritation.

'Oh! You *do* speak English.' Tom gave her his widest smile. 'That's lucky. I guess you thought I was going to chat you up, but that's not it at all. I'm on a mission for my wife. She wants me to take a picture of something called the *Sotoportego dei Preti*. Did I pronounce that right? I'm in Venice for a conference and she wants me to visit this archway. They say that walking through it with a loved one brings good luck – even better if you touch the hidden heart – and she's hoping it will work even if she's not here. She's going to join me on FaceTime as I go through.' Tom chuckled. 'I know. Total nonsense, but it would make her really happy. Do you know where it is?'

Tom fished a crumpled map from his pocket and started to open it.

The woman glared at him. 'If you can use FaceTime, you're also capable of using a maps app. Better than this.' She waved long thin fingers dismissively towards the map and Tom noticed the scar on her hand. Further confirmation that he had the right woman. 'It will show you where your destination is and how to get there from where you are now. So, if you'll excuse me.'

Tom pulled a guilty face. 'Sorry. I'm not great with technology, but I'm sure I can work it out. I'll just ask the waiter to point me in the right direction, and I'll be on my way.'

Tom was trying to gauge how long he'd been at the table and guessed it wasn't long enough.

'Can I get you something, by way of an apology for interrupting you?'

Tia closed her eyes briefly. 'No. I would rather you just left.'

'Oh,' Tom said despondently. 'I'm sorry. I've obviously disturbed you. Your English is perfect, by the way. Are you Venetian, or from another part of Italy?'

He was pushing his luck. Any minute now she would ask the waiter to remove him.

'Please leave my table, or I will tell the waiter you're making a nuisance of yourself.'

Tom made a point of struggling to his feet. 'I *do* apologise. I didn't mean to give offence. I thought Venetians were friendly to tourists. Look, I'm going to find the bathroom, then I'll leave you in peace.' Tom stretched and groaned to remind her of his supposed back problem. 'I'll leave my stuff here, if I may. Nowhere to put things down in a gents' toilet, you know.'

Smiling broadly at the unresponsive Tia, Tom put the phone and his crumpled map on the table and made his way into the *osteria*.

Standing just inside the door where he was able to see her through the window, he watched and waited. There was a risk she would pick up his phone, but even if she turned it over, the home screen was blank. She didn't know the password, so he was confident she wouldn't recognise it as a fake.

Just as he thought he might have been gone too long, the waiter passed him on his way out to the terrace, putting a plate of *cicchetti* on the table in front of Tia. On any other evening Tom would have been jealous of the tiny portions of grilled seafood, marinated vegetables and *crostini*. But now he just saw it as an opportunity to delay his return slightly, hoping the food would distract her.

He waited a few more moments, and then headed out, picking up his belongings from the table.

'Sorry, it was probably a bit much asking you to keep an eye on my things. I'm constantly terrified my phone will be stolen here, with all the pickpockets. I'd be lost without it, even though I clearly don't know how to use it.' He gave a self-deprecating smile, but Tia didn't even raise her eyes from her food. 'Enjoy the rest of your evening, and I'm very sorry to have disturbed you.'

Getting no reaction whatsoever, he decided that playing the foolish tourist had gone on long enough and, heart pumping, he hurried away from the *osteria*.

34

Tom walked slowly across the square, pretending to look at his map in case Tia was watching him. Tempted as he was to break into a run, he realised he should stay in character until he was out of sight, so with his eyes still on the map, he set off towards the *Sotoportego dei Preti*, which was unfortunately in the opposite direction to Jack's room. Glancing over his shoulder as he crossed a bridge, he could see Tia staring straight ahead, apparently looking at nothing in particular as she ate her food. She didn't seem remotely interested in what he was doing.

Resisting the instinct to race back to reveal Becky's distressing news about Clare, he decided it would be better not to tell Jack half a story. If the family had never been to the house, Tom needed to devise a strategy for finding them before he returned to his brother so he could present him with a plan. And first, he had to talk to Becky.

Call on this number from a secure line

Aware that she would normally be home by this time on a Saturday evening, he could only hope she'd stayed in the office.

While he waited for her call, Tom worked out a way back to Jack's room without passing through the same square a second time, and he was halfway along his convoluted route when the black phone rang.

'Becky, thanks for waiting. I'm sorry I don't have time to explain everything now, but tell me about Clare and the kids. What did you find?'

'There was no sign that they'd ever been there, Tom – exactly as I told you. I can talk freely on this line, can't I?'

'You can, yes. Jack said he saw them off from the farmhouse before jumping in his own car to head to the airport. But he hears from her every day. They use secure messaging. He doesn't think it's safe for them to speak; he's worried about listening devices. To be honest, the complexities of being Jack make me dizzy.'

'He's sure the messages come from Clare?'

'He hasn't had any reason to doubt it, as far as I know. Can you talk me through what happened?'

Becky told him their original plan: the Ocado van, the delivery. And then the fact that no one answered the door.

'Rob and I got in through the garage. The alarm didn't appear to be armed, which surprised me.'

'That makes sense, knowing Jack,' Tom said. 'They don't need protection if they're not there. She'd have armed it when she arrived, though, and then I'm certain no bugger would have got in. Tell me everything you saw.'

Becky paused for a moment. 'Look, I know this is going to wind you up, but I had to tell Rob something.'

Tom took a breath. He trusted Rob as much as he trusted anyone he knew professionally but he couldn't forget that, not too long ago, one of his team had been guilty of passing information to suspects, something that had surprised everyone and devastated Becky.

'I understand. What, exactly, did you tell him?'

'I said you had a contact who'd been an intelligence source for a long time. Over the years you'd got to know the family well, and although your contact wasn't working on an active case right now, you'd been concerned when you tried to contact him and had no response.'

'Quick thinking, Becky. Okay, you said Clare wasn't there and there was no sign she ever had been, but was there a car in the garage?'

'No, not on the drive either. If you can get the registration and the date they left North Wales, I can get ANPR data to see where the car disappears from traffic cams, but I'm going to have to clear this with Philippa. I don't want to go behind her back, and she won't help if she thinks we're keeping her out of the loop.'

'Agreed. Are you happy to fill her in? She can call me if she needs to – but on this number only. Jack's paranoid about phones.' Given what he'd just done with Tia's phone, Tom could quite understand his brother's concerns.

'Okay. I'm guessing you want to keep names and photos out of the press in Manchester as well as North Wales?' Becky asked.

'We have to. It might be safe to use Clare's photo, but not Jack's or Ava's. I'll speak to Jack and see what he thinks, and I'll ask about tracing her phone. He'll have tracking on it, without a doubt.'

'Yes, but if someone's taken her, they're bound to know that,' Becky said, frustration showing in her voice.

'Maybe we can do some analysis of the messages he's received. He said they were from Clare, but he could try sending a message with a question – see if it's really her responding.'

Becky sounded more upbeat: 'Yes, something only she'd know the answer to.'

'Exactly. In the meantime, are you happy to sound out Philippa, get the ANPR checks done? And I'll talk to Jack about tracking Clare's phone.'

'I'm on it, Tom, and you take care of yourself. Okay?'

Tom almost laughed. He had rarely felt less in control of his own destiny.

35

'You did it!' Jack called out without turning round.

Tom sank onto the sofa, out of breath, his hand pressing against his throbbing chest wound.

'The device sent me exactly what I wanted. I've got her mobile number, which gives me options, and I've downloaded her messages and contacts. I need to go through everything, see if I can find a way to get the spyware functioning, but well done, Tom.'

Jack turned to look at him, his face clouding with concern. 'You okay?'

'I'm fine. Just aching a bit. Glad the phone hack worked, but Jack, there's something I need to tell you.' Tom hated to burst Jack's balloon, but he had no choice.

'Not liking the sound of that, little brother.'

'It's not good news, I'm afraid. Becky did a welfare check on Clare, as we discussed. She was careful – don't worry about that – but Clare's not there.'

Jack's eyes narrowed. 'I'm guessing Becky didn't think she'd just gone shopping, then?'

'She broke into the house. It's empty. No food in the fridge, no clothes – nothing. She doesn't think Clare's even been there.'

Jack jumped to his feet and started pacing, hands clasped at the back of his neck. 'What the *fuck*…'

'Look, before we all go into meltdown, Becky's going to speak to Philippa about accessing ANPR. We can try to track Clare from the time she left your place in Wales. I'll need the exact time and date that they drove away from the farmhouse, and if you know what route she was likely to take, that's even better.'

'She left on April the twenty-fifth at about seven in the morning. She would have gone the obvious route to avoid driving too long with the kids – the A55 and then the motorway.' He stopped and swivelled to face Tom. 'This doesn't make sense, though. She's been messaging me. I can track her phone. All our devices are set up that way.' Jack hurried towards his computers. 'Let me check her location.' His hands shook slightly as he typed frantically. 'Shit,' he muttered. 'Someone must have tampered with her phone. Hang on.'

Tom waited, hoping Jack would be able to perform his usual magic.

'Fuck! I can't get anything, and that's on me. I set her phone up with a VPN to mask its location.' He slammed his hand on the table. 'It was meant to protect her, but now it's working against me.'

'Is there anything you can do?'

Jack took a deep breath. 'I installed a remote management tool on her mobile for emergencies, but her phone needs to be switched on and connected to the Internet.' Tom waited, hoping this was the solution, but Jack lifted his hands to his face in despair. 'It's off. Her bloody phone is *off*. We never turn our phones off.'

'Okay, let's not panic yet. When did you last hear from her?'

'Just after you went out in search of Tia Rukavina. She said all was well, the kids were fine. If she has a problem, we've got safe words so we can tell each other there's something wrong. And there were none of those.'

'But does it *sound* like her? Her language, the phrases she uses?'

Jack scoffed. 'Of course it bloody does. They're probably using AI to mimic her tone and vocabulary. They'll have fed previous messages between us into the system and asked the software to respond using her language structure.'

This wasn't sounding good. 'When are you expecting to hear from her again? Her phone would have to be on for that.'

'Not until tomorrow. I can't wait until then. I need to *do* something!'

'Okay, so Clare's phone was switched on no more than an hour or so ago. We might be able to work with that. Leave that with me. Can you check when she last used a credit card?'

'Waste of time. We don't use conventional banking. She had a lot of cash and about twenty anonymous prepaid cards. It was all meant to keep her safe from *others* tracking her. And now I have no way to find her.'

'I'll contact Philippa. I'll have to tell her exactly what's going on with Clare and the kids, Jack. If she knows they're in danger, she can get authorisation for cell-site analysis. It's not as precise as GPS, but it should give us a good idea of where Clare is now, or where she was the last time the phone was used. I'll deal with that. You focus on finding out if this Tia woman is about to sabotage Ava's rescue.'

He needed to keep Jack focused on something positive, because for once the technology seemed to be letting him down. Pulling out his phone to call Philippa, Tom heard a quiet voice.

'Can't tell you how glad I am that you're here, little brother.'

36

While Tom waited for Philippa to call him back on a secure line, his eyes were drawn to the clock again.

54:14:02. Time was suddenly ticking away at an alarming speed and the walls of Jack's makeshift HQ seemed to be closing in.

An image of Louisa, Lucy and Harry flashed into Tom's mind. If they had been missing, he'd have been incapable of coherent thought. He didn't know how Jack was still functioning. His brother had been confident that if he helped Moretti steal the painting, Ava would be released. But now Tia – an undercover investigator – was sniffing around, potentially about to sabotage the plan, and Clare, Billy and Sophia were missing too.

His thoughts were interrupted by his phone.

'Tom, it's Philippa. I'm on a secure line. I hear things are going from bad to worse. Becky's told me about the girl, and now apparently the mother and the other two children are missing. What else can you tell me?'

Philippa might sometimes be a pain in the neck, but she always got straight to the point.

'Jack can't trace his wife's mobile. He put heavyweight protection on it to try to stop anybody finding them, but whoever has her is now using that against us. The phone's currently switched off, but she messaged him a couple of hours ago. The only hope we have is cell-site analysis.'

'Okay, let's be clear about this. The woman – Clare, I understand – is missing with the two youngest. The eldest has been abducted and is being held in a tiger kidnap to force Jack to do something for them, whatever that is. I'm assuming you've discussed working with local law enforcement to free the girl?'

Tom kept his voice low. 'We've discussed it, but Jack's thinks there's a fair chance of a leak, given who we're dealing with, so he won't contemplate it.'

'And I assume he realises it's likely she'll be killed anyway. Especially if what you suggested to Becky about the Mafia connection is correct.'

Philippa was not one to pull her punches, but Tom could only agree. 'That hasn't been voiced as a concern – he wouldn't want to say the words out loud.'

'Hmm. I can find you someone who I believe is trustworthy in Italy, but this is out of my jurisdiction so I'm not going to insist.' Tom was about to mumble some excuses for Jack, but Philippa continued: 'I can do something about the rest of the family, though. They were supposed to be in Heywood – which *is* my territory – so I'll start some enquiries. You said you don't think this is anything to do with your brother being the infamous Jack Douglas?'

Deciding not to comment on the unnecessary adjective, Tom responded in a calm voice. 'No. He was targeted for his skills as a security systems expert. He doesn't think those involved know about his past. Having said that, there's a woman here who he's panicking about. Her name is Tia Rukavina, and in the past she worked for both the NCA and SFO as a forensic accountant. Jack came across her because she investigated money laundering in Guy Bentley's set-up, but he can't find any trace of her online for the past five years. Now she's turned up here using a different name – Elena Ferraro. He's worried she's working undercover for one of the agencies and is about to expose the gang that has Ava. Then we'll never get her back.'

'You said Jack's been targeted because of his security expertise. I assume they're making him do something highly illegal, and you're not intending to tell me what that is?'

'Best if I don't. For your sake, more than anything.'

'My God, Tom, this situation is beyond complex. Think carefully before you get any more involved. I understand there's a girl's life at stake. I get that. And I understand that it's family. But we both know there's a right way and a wrong way of handling this. I assume Jack's more inclined towards the wrong way – so yes, it's best I don't know. You, however, are putting your life and career at risk, and you should be capable of finding a better way.' There was a brief pause, which Tom wasn't sure how to fill, then Philippa continued: 'Okay. Lecture over. Send me everything you have on the wife. Becky said you'd know the times, routes, phone numbers. And send me photos – not to be distributed. For information only.'

For a moment Tom wondered if she meant for identification purposes, should the whole family be found dead, and he swallowed hard as she continued.

'I'll look into this forensic accountant woman – see if I can find out what she's doing. I have some contacts at the NCA who deal specifically with money laundering and they may know why she's apparently disappeared off the face of the earth. Any idea who she might be working for now?'

'None, but given who we're dealing with, it could be INTERPOL or Europol. Maybe both, depending how deep it goes.'

'Hmm. As there's so much you're keeping to yourself, I can't really comment on that, so for now I'll get someone checking the wife's route on ANPR and sort out cell-site analysis as soon as you send me through all the details. See where that gets us.'

'Philippa, I really appreciate this. It's good of you to do so much to help.'

'I'm doing my job, Tom. A woman and two children are missing from my territory.'

Tom knew this was Philippa's way of saying that she wasn't aiding and abetting any illegal activity, nor did she want any knowledge of it.

Jack was pounding away on his keyboard but kept frantically rubbing the back of his head, a sure sign he was stressed. Hearing Tom approach, he swivelled to face him.

'And…?'

'I've spoken to Philippa and sent her all the details you gave me about Clare's likely route. She's going to see if they can pick her up on ANPR. The roads you thought she'd take are well covered by cameras.'

'That's something, I suppose,' he muttered, turning back to his screens.

'How are you doing with analysing Tia's contacts and messages?'

'I can't work out what her game is. The access we secured is very limited. I'd hoped to be able to read her most recent messages, but it seems she uses Signal. It's like a digital fortress – unbreakable, private, built for those who need absolute security.'

'And does that tell you anything?'

Jack gave a half-hearted laugh. 'It tells me she's either working for a government intelligence agency or for organised crime. Maybe both, as she's undercover. So not helpful.'

Tom was at a loss. Had all his efforts with Tia been for nothing? 'You didn't find *anything* useful?'

'She has Renzo Moretti's burner phone number in her contacts – the same number that I have. I wouldn't expect her to have this number if she's working for law enforcement, but it depends how deep undercover she is. She also has a number with a +502 country code. Guatemala, although that might not mean much.'

'What do you mean?'

'Whoever the number belongs to could be using a SIM card from a different country. There's no saying it really is a Guatemalan contact. She has other numbers – I'm doing a reverse search – but up to now they've all been untraceable. What the hell's she doing here, Tom?'

The only solid clue seemed to be Moretti's burner phone number, and Tom wondered if this was something they could work with. Was Moretti her target? He grabbed an A4 notepad from Jack's desk.

'I wish we had a whiteboard so we could put all this stuff up,' he grumbled as he pulled a pen from his pocket.

Jack raised his eyebrows. 'If you want to brainstorm, computers are pretty good for that, you know. Maybe forget the pen and paper?' The largest of Jack's monitors cleared to an empty white screen with a tool bar on the left. 'Let's start with what we know. Try to organise it as we get further in. You're the detective – you lead this.'

After half an hour they had created multiple strands, boxes in different colours and links between them, but there were so many questions. Why did Renzo want the painting? What was Tia investigating?

They filled in the details of Ava's abduction – where, when and how – with different colours showing what they knew, what they needed to know, what investigations were under way, and what they were guessing at.

Tom pointed at the screen. 'You said Renzo Moretti's crew are small time. He's trying to up his game and worm his way into the 'Ndrangheta. So how the hell did he orchestrate at least one, if not two, abductions in North Wales?'

Jack stared at Tom, the silence in the room only broken by the hum of a motorboat echoing up from the canal below.

'Shit,' he murmured. 'Why didn't I think of that?'

'Maybe because you've had rather a lot on your mind. We know the 'Ndrangheta has Manchester affiliations, and that isn't so far from North Wales. Could they have set it up for him?'

Jack shook his head. 'That would defeat the object. If Moretti's trying to break into the local *'ndrina*, he needs to prove himself capable – and that can't involve pulling in Contarini's help.'

'So the big question is: who did he recruit to get to Ava? And how?'

37

Ava knows she needs a plan. If she can't find a way out of this dungeon, she's going to die. She knows the rules. *Cover your face.* Why have they ignored that?

She won't beg. That never works. Her stomach churns every time they walk through the door, but she has to stay strong.

Flashes of the journey here have come back to her. She was drugged, but there were moments when she knew she was no longer in the van. Was she on a plane? Did she imagine the roar of an engine? She's guessing she's not in the UK, given her captors speak some foreign language. Why would they fly her somewhere if this was punishment for things that happened years ago in Manchester? And why now? And why take photos of her? For ransom? But that doesn't make sense either. There are kids from far richer families who would be a much better choice than her – not only younger, but an *actual* child of the family.

She told them days ago that no one would pay to save her. 'If it's money you want, you're out of luck,' she yelled at the top of her voice, hoping they would hear her through the door. 'I'm nothing to them – I'm not even their kid! They'll be glad to be rid of me.' But then she stopped.

If they don't think they'll get any money, what will they do with her? If they don't kill her, will she be sold? The skin on her arms prickles with goosebumps. She knows what happens to girls who are sold. They're made to look cute, appealing to buyers. She's seen it happen with her own eyes, and when she was twelve it was her worst fear. But she's seventeen, and there is nothing remotely appealing in the way she looks right now.

So why did they take her?

Think, Ava. You know guys like this. What do they want?

One thing is on her side. Ava has been beaten, starved and thrown into a dark cellar before, and she isn't going to be broken by these men. She'll cry if she needs to, but only to manipulate them. Not because she's weak.

'Crying won't get you anywhere,' she was told repeatedly in that other life – the one she's been working so hard to forget. But maybe these men are more susceptible to tears. Either way, she's determined to survive – to come out of this stronger. If they think they're dealing with a normal kid, they're wrong.

She needs to persuade one of them to let her go. She can't escape without help – there's no window and only one door, bolted and guarded. Which one should she work on?

Her dad's words come back to her.

Every face is a story.

Does either man's face tell a story that might give her hope?

Skinny Guy permanently scowls, as if life has been unfair and he wants to spend every moment trying to make others pay for it. There's a sense of disappointment in Big Guy's face, as if he'd expected life to turn out better than it has. But he stopped Skinny Guy from doing whatever was in his mind, so maybe she can appeal to the man he'd once hoped to be.

It would be easier if she understood their language. Her only hope is to find a way to gain Big Guy's sympathy. Even if he doesn't understand her words, he'll recognise the desperation in her voice.

Her thoughts freeze. There's a sound outside the door.

Someone's coming.

Ava holds her breath. The door swings in, and every muscle in her body tenses. Is it Skinny Guy, back to finish what he was hoping to start?

She lets her breath out slowly when she sees it's Big Guy. This is her chance.

'Please,' she says softly. 'You don't seem like a cruel man. Can't you let me go? You can say I escaped, can't you?'

He stares at her silently.

'Please,' she whispers again.

He flings a plastic bottle of water towards her, shrugs and turns back to the door as she starts to cry. He glances over his shoulder, bites his bottom lip, then shakes his head and stomps out of the door.

Ava's body sags, but she's not giving up.

Stay strong, Ava. You will survive.

Frustrated that her performance achieved nothing, she pulls down the sleeve of the school shirt she's still wearing and wipes her eyes.

38

It was Sunday already, albeit only four in the morning. The heist was scheduled for the early hours of Tuesday morning – just two days away – and there was so much they still didn't understand.

A full night's sleep was out of the question, but Tom needed a shower and a change of clothes. He'd returned to his hotel by a circuitous route, wandering the almost silent streets, the eerie still-ness forcing him to glance over his shoulder at the slightest sound. Other than a few city workers cleaning the streets ready for another busy day of tourists, there was no one around.

Philippa had given authorisation for the cell-siting of Clare's phone, but it hadn't helped. The last time the phone was switched on, the signal had come from Heywood – exactly where they would have expected. Either Clare was being held somewhere near the house, or her mobile had been passed to a third party tasked with maintaining regular contact with Jack.

Before heading back to the hotel, Tom told Jack to try to get a few hours' rest, but his words fell on deaf ears.

'You've no idea how many times I've grafted through the night, Tom. When I'm working on some new idea – a complex app, an innovative security measure – sleep is impossible. My mind doesn't rest. And that's just a *tad* less stressful than knowing your whole family is in danger.'

Even if Jack could go without sleep for the next forty-eight hours, Tom wasn't capable of it – not if he needed to be even vaguely coherent. The ache in his chest was a constant reminder that he wasn't yet fully fit, and the blood loss still left him battling exhaustion. He needed to lie down, even if only for a few hours.

In the hotel foyer, the young man behind the reception desk didn't look remotely surprised to see Tom come in at this godforsaken hour. Either he was trained to keep a straight face, or he was used to tourists staying out for most of the night.

'Good evening, Mr Douglas. Can I get you anything? We do have a twenty-four-hour kitchen.'

'I'm fine for now, thank you. But could you arrange to have someone bring me breakfast at seven, please? Just fruit, pastries and a double espresso, if that's okay.'

'Certainly, sir. Have a good night.'

Tom smiled. There wasn't much of the night left.

If Tom had hoped to grab three hours' sleep, he was out of luck. His mobile rang at 6.30 and he groaned. It was his black phone, and the only people with that number were Jack, Philippa and Becky.

'I have news.' Philippa didn't bother to announce herself.

Tom shook himself awake. 'Okay, tell me.'

'Are you awake? You don't sound as if you are.'

'It was a late one, Philippa. I just grabbed a couple of hours. What's happened?'

'It's five thirty in the morning here, and I was hoping for an extra hour or two myself. Do you want me to call back when you've had coffee?'

Tom knew she didn't mean that. It was her way of telling him that if she was awake, he should be too. 'I'm fine.'

'Right, well if you're fully conscious, I can tell you that we managed to track the kidnap van.'

Tom was now well and truly awake. 'That's excellent news.'

'Don't get too excited because it's been set on fire.'

'Where?'

'Penrhyn Quarry, just outside a place called Bethesda. It's about twenty minutes' drive from where they picked up the girl.'

Tom quickly pulled up Google Maps on his personal phone. 'But that's heading inland, away from anything much.'

'It is, but with some help from North Wales Police—'

Tom felt a moment of concern, knowing how Jack felt about involving the police. 'What exactly did you tell the Welsh guys?'

'Tom, will you please give me some credit? I *do* understand what's at stake here, so you don't need to question my every move. For the record, I told them we're concerned about the family of an important informant – not a million miles from the truth, but I'm not a fan of lying to fellow officers.'

'Sorry. Put my interruption down to lack of sleep. What did they discover?'

'The local police contacted a couple of delivery companies and a taxi firm. The delivery companies both use dash cams, and two likely vehicles were identified driving away from the quarry area at around the right time.'

Tom felt a moment of elation. 'Where did that lead us?'

'One car headed deeper into Wales, and there aren't many cameras there so we lost it. But the other vehicle, another van, went back towards Bangor and over the Menai Bridge. We lost that too for a while – maybe they had the sense to stick to back roads – but we picked it up in the early hours of the morning just outside Holyhead.'

'They were taking the ferry, I assume?'

'It seems so, yes. Did you say you think the girl's in Venice?'

Tom swallowed a sigh. 'We don't know for sure. Jack's making that assumption from the shape of some bricks or something. But he may be clutching at straws, thinking that if she's close he can rescue her.'

'Hmm. Ever the hero.' Once again, Tom chose not to comment.

'We have to assume that they took a ferry to Dublin, probably concealing her in a hidden compartment, and we're investigating ways they may have taken her on from there. I doubt they'd have travelled on a commercial flight, so it's either a boat or a plane from a private airfield. There are several options and we're looking into them.'

It was some progress, and at this point Tom was grateful for anything that appeared to be a step forward.

'Thanks, Philippa. It's a start, even though we've no idea where she ended up.'

'It might be a bit more than a start, Tom, because although they set fire to the van, they messed up. A cap was found in the undergrowth, probably from the can of petrol they used to douse the vehicle. Maybe they had to take their gloves off to unscrew it, then dropped the cap. With the van on fire, they wouldn't have had time to search for it.'

'You're saying it had prints on it? Can we identify someone?'

'Oh yes,' Philippa said, a smile in her voice. 'We can indeed. He's well-known to us in Manchester. But here's the thing, Tom. He's not Italian. He's Albanian.'

39

Tom hurried through the early-morning streets of Venice, already busy with locals heading to work and tourists getting an early start to the day. Relieved that no one seemed to be taking the slightest interest in him, he still took a different winding route to Jack's room, constantly checking to make sure he wasn't being followed.

'I'm not sure Moretti's lot are particularly interested in where I'm staying,' Jack had said. 'As long they have Ava and I do my job, why should they care? But I don't want them to discover there are two of us and they're no longer just dealing with a desperate father.'

With one final glance over his shoulder, Tom let himself into the apparently deserted building at the end of the alley and rushed up the three flights of stairs.

'I've got news,' he said, bursting into the room. As always, his eyes were dragged to the countdown displayed at the top of one monitor. 43:21:09. *Shit.* Less than two days.

Jack looked feverish when he turned, his eyes red-rimmed and burning too brightly. He didn't ask any questions, just raised his eyebrows as Tom filled him in on everything Philippa had told him.

'Albanians,' Jack said softly when Tom had finished, his gaze now fixed on the floor, frown lines creasing his brow. 'We already thought it strange that Renzo had contacts in the Manchester mob, but *Albanians*?' He looked up at Tom. 'He wouldn't have the connections. No way. He must be using a fixer. It makes sense on so many levels and answers some of the questions that have been puzzling me all night.'

'Such as?'

'Such as how Renzo Moretti has managed to coordinate something this complex. I'm working on the assumption he's trying to ingratiate himself with Contarini – his future father-in-law. Given Moretti's background, it's probably a drug deal. That's the kind of thing that would impress the *capobastone*.'

'Would Contarini allow that?'

'As long as Moretti's not setting up in competition, I guess so. The 'Ndrangheta controls a huge share of the drugs market across Europe, so if Moretti's trying to get involved in the supply chain, the product is probably coming from one of the South American cartels they collaborate with. As I said, I doubt he has enough money to buy a shipment outright, which is where the painting comes in – to cover the seller's risk. If something goes wrong – the shipment is seized, the boat sinks, no end of possible cock-ups – Contarini wouldn't bail him out. Instead, Moretti hands over the painting as payment.'

'And you don't think Moretti's up to organising all this himself?' Tom asked.

Jack shook his head. 'From everything I've learned, I seriously doubt he's got the contacts to handle something this big, which is why he needs a fixer – someone with the know-how to handle the logistics, broker the deals, navigate the risks. Moretti's been a small-time dealer until now, pushing MDMA, ket and benzos to tourists. If he wants to prove himself to Contarini, he'll need someone who knows how to play the bigger game.'

'I know you think it's probably drugs,' Tom said, 'but the Albanian connection might suggest something else – illegal arms, maybe? Weapons from eastern Europe would make sense.'

'I don't know, Tom,' Jack replied, rubbing his forehead. 'Venice isn't a hub for the illegal weapons trade as far as I'm aware, whereas the demand for cocaine is huge across Europe. Given the 'Ndrangheta's dominance of the market, drugs seem the more likely option.'

'And the Albanians?'

'If Ava was taken by Albanians, it's likely that this fixer, whoever he is, arranged that too. Somewhere along the line, the fixer linked Moretti to the Albanian mob in Manchester. We're looking for someone with excellent planning skills who also has contacts in UK organised crime. If we can identify him, we might be closer to finding Ava.'

Maybe. But they weren't there yet.

Time was hurtling by, and Tom could feel it passing with every beat of his heart. The intelligence that Philippa had been able to gather about Ava's abduction was useful, but it wasn't going to help them find her and secure her release before the heist.

Jack's tension had already felt explosive, but now there was the added concern that Clare and the little ones were not where they should be, and Tom was seriously worried that his brother would become so stressed he wouldn't be able to function at all.

Why had they taken the rest of Jack's family? Tom could only think that Renzo Moretti's accomplices had discovered that Jack wasn't Ava's birth father. Maybe they saw kidnapping Clare, Billy and Sophia as added insurance, should he refuse to bow to their commands for a child who wasn't his.

They obviously didn't know Jack.

The large monitor was still showing the mind map. Jack was staring at it.

'I'm going round in circles, Tom. Terrified for Ava one minute, panicking about Clare and the kids the next. Any more from Philippa?'

'No. She'll call when they have something.'

'And now we've got bloody Tia Rukavina thrown into the mix. If she blows the whistle on whatever she's investigating before Moretti's crew steals the painting, I could lose my whole family.'

Hearing the raw despair in Jack's voice, Tom felt impotent, but there were questions he needed to ask.

'Let's assume you're able to bypass the security system in the palazzo and the theft of the painting goes to plan. What do you see happening next?'

'I hope and pray they let Ava go, and that whoever is holding Clare, Billy and Sophia does the same.'

'And you? Do you think the D'Angelo family will come after you?'

'Almost certainly. If I want to escape prosecution I'll have to create a flaw in the technology and be able to demonstrate how the thieves exploited it. My bad – I wasn't as good as I said I was. But you know what? Losing my reputation and my business is the least of my worries.'

'And are you ready for the heist? Is everything set up?'

'More or less. It feels like the easy bit now. The paintings have all been hung, so I've been able to grab CCTV footage of the empty rooms during the night to make sure the lighting is the same, although sadly I'm not capable of controlling how much cloud is covering the moon. We'll just have to hope for the best.'

Before Tom could ask any more questions, his black phone rang.

'Philippa, do you have news?'

'Yes – of sorts.'

'Clare?' Tom asked, walking to the other end of the room where Jack couldn't hear Philippa's occasionally strident tones.

'Not yet, but here's what I propose. The cell-site analysis indicates the phone connects to a tower close to their home in Heywood, but we know they're not there. This suggests they're either in another house close by, though that's unlikely, or someone's going somewhere close to the house at the crucial time, receiving the messages and manipulating the responses. This seems the most plausible scenario, although not a certainty. However, we'll send unmarked cars to the area. TSU have kit that will help pinpoint the phone's location.'

'Then you'll follow them?'

'If we can identify them, yes. I'm guessing, though, that if we locate them, you don't want the family rescued immediately?'

Tom glanced at Jack again, relieved that he had turned back to his computer.

'We need to give this a bit of thought. I'm not sure what will happen if that particular cage is rattled too soon. Will our guy be freaked out by the involvement of the British police, and will that have ramifications for Ava?'

'My thinking precisely. Let's find them but hold off until we work out the most appropriate plan. Or rather *you* work one out, as only *you* appear to know exactly what's going on.'

Despite the irritation in Philippa's voice, Tom didn't respond. She couldn't be party to their plans.

With an impatient huff at his silence, Philippa carried on talking. 'I'm not only calling about Clare, though. You asked me to see if I could find out anything about Tia Rukavina, so I've asked a few questions. Five years ago, her partner, Alessandro Broglio, left her. He was a private wealth manager at the top of his game, dealing with high-net-worth individuals, and nobody at the NCA knows anything about the breakdown of their relationship, just that she requested a leave of absence after he left. In view of the excellent work she'd done for them, it was granted. Six months, apparently. She subsequently resigned and asked the NCA to scrub her name from all records of her investigations. She was concerned that some of the people she'd investigated might be keen to seek revenge, and it seems she had the expertise to cover her tracks and remove any digital footprint. The person I spoke to says they have no knowledge of what she did next, but they assume she changed her name.'

'Do you think it's possible she's still working for them, but undercover?'

'Tom, I have *some* influence, but do you honestly think a telephone call would result in my contact divulging the fact that she's operating covertly?'

'Sorry – daft question. I think we're grasping at straws here.'

'And you're still not going to tell me what exactly is going on?'

Tom swallowed. 'No. It's best for you if I don't.'

He heard another tut down the phone. 'Tread carefully, Tom. Remember who you're dealing with, and acknowledge that you don't necessarily understand their rules.'

With that, Philippa hung up.

40

Tom couldn't fail to notice the anguish in Jack's eyes when he said Philippa was no closer to finding Clare.

'But she has a plan. She's a right royal pain sometimes, but she's good at her job, and this is a genuine case. She can throw resources at it; no one likes missing children. Becky and the team will work with her, but they'll be discreet. They know what they're doing.'

Tom explained Philippa's plan to attempt to identify where the phone messages were coming from and saw a flash of hope in his brother's eyes.

'Sounds a decent idea.'

'It does, but we need to confirm that Clare's being held against her will. It's possible she just hasn't told you that she's staying in another house, or at a bed and breakfast somewhere. Maybe there was a problem at the house and she didn't want to worry you.' Jack gave him a look that said, 'Yeah, right,' but Tom carried on. 'If they *have* been abducted, these guys are smart enough to know that Clare's phone can be tracked with cell-siting. Why else would they take it to the approximate location of your house in Heywood? And we don't know what else they might have up their sleeves. Have you worked out what to put in your next text to Clare? We need to be one hundred per cent certain she's not in control of her own messages.'

'Nope. I can't ask a direct question that's obviously intended to trip her up, such as "What's Sophia's favourite song?" They'll know instantly that it's a test. I need to come up with something Clare would answer in a very specific way that doesn't set any red flags waving. I'll think about it, but let's move on. You said she had news of Tia?'

Tom repeated everything that Philippa had told him. 'Not much help, I'm afraid.'

Jack swivelled back to face his computer. '*Christ*, I wish I knew what her game is. Until she appeared on the scene, I thought I had this under control. I'd do what Moretti wants, get Ava back, and we're done. Not only am I in a blind panic about Clare and my kids, but I now have this woman – this *investigator* – lurking around. If that painting's involved in some other crime or it was bought with laundered money, she could seize it before tomorrow night and then all bets are off. No painting, no heist, no rescue. *Shit!*'

Tom said nothing, just walked over to Jack and put his hands on his brother's shoulders. No words were necessary. He felt the full weight of Jack's frustration and despair, and platitudes weren't helpful.

Jack rubbed his face vigorously with both hands. 'Right, shouty moment over. Let's get back to it. Take a seat on your comfy chair, Tom.'

Pleased to hear a trace of humour – forced or otherwise – in his tone, Tom sat down on the crate as Jack pointed to a screen.

'I searched for Tia Rukavina and went pretty deep to see if there was anything hidden in the depths of the web. But she – or someone – has done a great job of erasing her history. This backs up what Philippa told you. I've looked into Elena Ferraro too, but I didn't think it was worth digging too much. If she's deep undercover there won't be anything to find, unless...' He sat back in his chair, scratching his cheek, clearly miles away. 'When you send someone undercover, Tom, what do you do?'

'Create a backstory – a history. They need to have something of value to offer whoever's employing them, be able to demonstrate they have the expertise to do whatever they're tasked with. They also need to check out – seem to be who they say they are. Is Tia *really* undercover as an insurance assessor, though? It sounds a very bizarre place to put her, given her skills.'

'Maybe her employers think D'Angelo's setting up someone to steal his own painting, then claim the insurance. Who knows? But whatever she's up to, she needs a bloody good backstory. I just need to find out what that is.'

Tom glanced at the clock. An hour had passed, and despite going over every piece of information they had, he was no closer to working out which agency Tia might be working for. He plonked a mug of coffee down next to Jack and looked over his brother's shoulder.

'What are you up to?'

'Not sure you want to know. Depends how far you're prepared to go down this particular rabbit hole with me.' Jack didn't take his eyes from the screen.

How far *was* Tom prepared to go? What risks would he consider reasonable to save the life of an innocent seventeen-year-old girl and rescue a woman and two children? Did he really care about whether a painting was stolen or not?

The answer to the last question was easy. No, he didn't. A painting was merely a *thing*, its value an illusion created by the desires of those who want to possess it. It was just canvas and paint. A person's life was priceless.

'I'm in, Jack. All the way.'

'Okay.' Jack attempted a smile. 'Despite being out of the picture for so long, I still have contacts. None of them know I'm Jack Douglas – that would be insane. But when Jack died, I created a whole new persona online and gradually, over time, I've gained the trust of people I'm sure you'd love to arrest. If you remember, that's how I discovered what Guy Bentley was up to all those years ago. But I only knew what was going on because I kept – and still keep – my ear very close to the ground.'

'I get that, but why didn't you know anything about what's going on here in Venice?'

Jack groaned. 'Because I'm a bloody idiot. I've never attempted to keep up with the Mafia – especially not in Italy. They didn't have such a hold in Manchester when I was working for Guy, and my main aim nowadays is to keep on top of who's doing what, who's working for whom, to make sure none of Guy's ex-mob are looking for me. That doesn't really involve Italians.'

Jack could clearly have been a much more valuable intelligence source than Tom had realised, and he had to ask himself if he should have made more use of his brother's knowledge and experience.

'I can read your mind, little brother. You're thinking I could have fed you info, but showing my hand over something relatively trivial would have been stupid. Now I'm going to dig deep. Did Philippa give you the name of the Albanian? One of my sources is bound to know who recruited him.'

Tom could imagine that conversation with Philippa. She would want to know why he needed a name, given that – in her mind – he wouldn't be able to do anything with it. But he had just told Jack he was all in, and that meant he was going to have to do what he'd sworn he wouldn't. Ask Becky.

41

Ava squeezes her eyes shut, blocking out the cold, damp air around her, imagining herself in her room at home. Giggles drift from downstairs; her brother is tickling her little sister. She listens for noises from the kitchen, wonders what might be for lunch. Maybe chicken tacos, with lots of tomato salsa and sour cream. Her favourite. Or macaroni cheese, the way only Mum can make it. She can almost taste it now, and her mouth begins to water. In her imagination, she hears the crunch of tyres on gravel. *Dad's home.* She breathes a big sigh. *Safe. She's safe.*

Only she isn't safe. Her dad isn't about to walk through the door and set her free. He's not coming. This time there's nothing fake about her tears and she curses herself for beginning to trust. She'd spent her life until the age of thirteen knowing she was unloved, unwanted. But she's become soft, lulled into a false sense of security. She'd thought she was safe walking the streets alone, and she'd believed she had a family that loved her. Wrong on both counts.

More fool you, Ava. If they loved you, Dad would have been here by now.

The silence is suddenly shattered by the high-pitched blare of a siren, steadily growing louder as if it's coming closer. Its tone is foreign, unfamiliar, unmistakably different.

Is it the police? Are they coming for me?

She waits, holding her breath, terrified of missing something, praying to hear the sound of footsteps, shouting, banging on the door. *Police!* But all she hears is the beat of her heart, and the sound fades gradually into the distance. Whoever it was, they've gone.

She curls up tight, trying to stop the shaking. She has to think of something – come up with a plan. If no one else will save her, she has to save herself. Perhaps when Big Guy comes, she will plead with him again, ask him if he has any children of his own. He might not understand her, but she'll *make* him.

Ava starts to plan her performance. She could shiver as if she's sick. Perhaps she should lie down, rock from side to side as if she's in pain. It's worth a try if it makes him feel sorry for her.

She chokes off a sob as she has another thought. If they believe she's seriously ill, they might just kill her. It would probably be easier for them that way.

Her thoughts are interrupted by sounds coming from beyond the door to her prison. She hears shouting. Big Guy sounds angry. Then the high-pitched whine of Skinny Guy. He sounds like he's pleading – but who with?

Suddenly, a sharp voice cuts through the cacophony and they fall silent.

'Shut *up*! *Zitto!*'

Ava freezes. It's a voice she's never heard before. Someone's speaking English and another language. And it's a woman.

42

'Un cappuccino e un brioche alla crema, per favore.' Tom smiled at the waiter, thinking he was going to be suffering from a serious caffeine overdose if he carried on like this.

He'd come out to a café to make his phone calls, having decided it was better not to distract Jack, who would have listened to every word, trying to glean clues from each question Tom asked.

Delaying what needed to be done, he sat for a few minutes in the late-morning sunshine, taking in the bustling scene. The square was full of tourists mingling with Italians in their Sunday best, heading for church and perhaps a family lunch afterwards. He'd always envied the way Italians share family life, with all generations mixing, supporting and caring for each other. At that moment there was nothing he would have liked more than to be home with his own family.

With a sigh, he picked up his phone. He felt uncomfortable asking Becky for favours but he had no choice, and when she called in response to his text, he wasn't surprised to find that she was at work.

'I'm going to apologise again for asking so much of you, Becky, but the situation is serious, so I'm pulling in any and all favours I can.'

'Stop beating yourself up! I have history with Jack, and I'm not about to turn my back. What do you need?'

Tom wanted to say thank you again, but there were only so many times he could tell her before she got fed up with hearing it. 'Okay, can you get me the name of the Albanian whose prints were lifted from the petrol can cap? And can you get an update from Philippa on everything she's doing – both with North Wales Police and in the hunt for Clare? I don't want to keep asking, but it's driving me insane. I'm not used to being in the dark.'

'I can imagine. How's Jack bearing up?'

Tom groaned. 'He isn't. I've never seen him like this. He feels helpless. In the past he's always had an angle, the ability to get under the hood.'

'And he can't this time?'

'It's the bloody 'Ndrangheta, Becky. The Manchester mob are bad enough, but the 'Ndrangheta… Not only does he not speak the language, but their security will be ridiculously tight so he's struggling to get a grip on anything.'

'He must be going nuts.'

'Ava's kidnap was bad enough, but with Clare and the kids missing too… And there's this woman, Tia Rukavina, who Jack's convinced is going to scupper the deal. She must be working for some agency or other. Philippa's looked into her but reached a dead end.'

'How do you think the Albanian fits in?'

'Not a clue. But it's another piece, and who knows, it might be the key.'

Becky was quiet for a moment. 'I saw Philippa's car in the car park, so she's around. I know she had a meeting with North Wales Police and, before you go off on one, we need their help, Tom. Only the heads of crime in both GMP and North Wales Police know Jack's true background. She's told me that much. They also know the CPS dropped charges against him and Ava – Natasha, as she was then – on the basis their crimes were largely committed under duress, and Jack's been a useful informant over the years. The rest of the team involved in the hunt for the family will only know their pseudonyms.'

Tom really hoped he didn't have to explain all this to Jack. The idea of so many people knowing about him could push him over the edge.

'It's a shame you never persuaded him to go into witness protection after Guy Bentley's death. It would have made things a lot easier,' Becky said.

Tom gave a derisive snort. 'Jack? In witness protection? I realise you don't know him, Becky – other than by reputation – but the thought of being under someone else's control would totally freak him out. He's never responded well to authority of any kind. He needs the freedom to go where he wants, when he wants. He normally has an excellent idea of who's looking at him, but the Italians have never been part of his world. They sneaked up from behind and bit him in the neck.'

He heard a sigh down the phone. 'I get it. Give me a bit of time and I'll get back to you with the name of the Albanian. I'll see if we can get something out of local informants – find out who was paying them and how it was set up. Traffic cams are being scrutinised to work out at what point along Clare's journey she disappeared, but it's tricky. Not too many cameras in rural Wales.'

There was little more to say, so Tom ended the call after Becky promised to give him text updates on anything and everything as soon as she had any news.

Using his normal phone, he called Louisa.

'Morning!' he said, trying to sound chirpy.

'It's good to hear your voice,' Louisa said. 'Becky came to see me. She's explained what's happening – as much as she knows, that is. And at a guess, that's not everything. I know we can't talk about it on the phone, but I need to know you're okay. Both of you. I'm so worried.'

'I'm glad you've seen her, and we're coping. Just. The level of tension is off the scale.' Tom let out a long breath. 'But enough about me. How are you all doing?'

'Pretty much as normal here. Harry's being his usual chirpy little self, pottering around with his toys, giving me a big grin when he sees me looking at him. He's so self-contained. Lucy's been playing with him even more than usual. Despite my efforts to smooth things over with Kate, she's still here more often than she's at her mum's.'

'Hmm. Any repercussions?' Tom asked, knowing his ex-wife's tendency to try to stir things up when life wasn't going to plan. *Her* plan, that is.

'I don't think Kate's speaking to me, and I'm guessing she's said something negative about me to Lucy, too.'

Tom groaned. 'I'm sorry, love. You and Lucy have been getting on so well.'

He heard a soft laugh down the line. 'Oh, don't worry. Lucy and I are fine. She's worried about you, but I haven't told her what's going on. I thought it was too much.'

'I agree. There's nothing she can do. When I think how I would feel if this was happening to her, I—'

At that moment, his black phone beeped with a message. It was Jack.

> Renzo wants to meet. Can you get back
> here?

'Sorry, I have to go. I'll try to speak to you soon. Kiss the kids for me.'

With a few last words, Tom hung up, wrapped his uneaten brioche in a paper napkin and hurried back towards Jack's room.

43

'I don't know why Renzo's demanding a meeting a day and a half before he steals the painting. I guess it's to threaten me face to face, and I need you with me,' Jack said the minute Tom walked through the door. 'I want you to check him out. I need to know if you think they're going to let Ava go.'

Tom knew Jack wouldn't be able to make any accurate assessment himself. He was way too close and would find it impossible to be objective. He also might try to strangle Renzo Moretti on the spot.

'Have you ever met him?'

'What do you think? The little shit's run the whole operation through encrypted messaging. He doesn't know I've worked out who he is and that I've a fair idea what he's up to. He probably doesn't care much. He thinks I'm a nerdy security expert, and he's got my daughter. He no doubt thinks using the word 'Ndrangheta will terrify me.'

Whether it terrified Jack or not, it scared the hell out of Tom.

'Whatever you do, Jack, don't let him realise that you know his name. That could be fatal.'

Jack gave Tom a look. 'This was my world once, Tom. I know how to play the game.'

There was no answer to that. Two brothers with huge experience of dealing with criminals, but from different sides of the fence.

'What do you want me to do?'

'Be my wingman. Read him when I ask questions. Use everything you've ever learned about criminal behaviour. We need to see if there's an angle – some way we can get control of the situation.'

'And you're happy for him to know you're not in this alone?'

Jack chewed his bottom lip. 'I've thought about that. It's not ideal, but it might throw him off balance.'

'And what if he grabs a photo of me and feeds it into a facial rec program? He's going to find out who I am. Let's face it, even Google Images would find a match at the moment, given I've been all over the press.'

'Oh crap. What is *wrong* with me? I should have been the one to think of that.'

Tom walked over to the window and looked out at the canal below, the walkways on either side thronged with tourists having the time of their lives in this glorious city. All he wanted was for Ava to be safe; for Clare and the little ones to be found; for them all to be home.

He turned back. 'I'll come with you, but let me go in first and check the place out. He doesn't need to see us together. If he's alone, you go in. If he's brought a full crew, though, you need to walk away.'

'*You* can walk away. That's your prerogative. But I can't. You know that.'

'No, I don't. He needs this painting, whatever the reason. And for that, he needs you. In many ways he has the upper hand because the Mafia are evil bastards, but don't forget how essential you are to everything he's trying to do. If you've worked this out correctly, Moretti can't afford for you to walk away.'

Jack nodded as if he agreed, but his eyes told a different story. He was, by nature, reckless – and brilliant as he was, common sense had never been his strong suit.

'Where are we going?'

'A bar in an alley just off Campo Ruga, fifteen minutes' walk. They're expecting me in thirty minutes.'

'Fine. If it's a bar, it's easy enough to go in separately. I'll play the dumb tourist again. Then we can decide what happens next.'

The bar looked dingy and unappealing, the last place you'd expect a tourist to venture, and Tom's view of the interior was blocked by a dark brown beaded fly screen. Would he be taking a risk by walking straight in? He couldn't think of any reason Renzo Moretti would know who he was, and it was fifteen minutes to the meeting time, so he might not have arrived yet.

As he eased the screen gently to one side, a beam of sunlight hit the counter and the barman looked up. The place couldn't have been less welcoming, with nothing other than the bar on the left and a shelf on the right with some mismatched stools pushed underneath. There didn't seem to be any food on offer, and Tom guessed it was the type of place where customers leaned on the bar while they slurped a quick coffee. How the place kept going, Tom couldn't imagine. Unless, of course, it wasn't a functioning business, merely a front for Moretti's crew.

Tom's eyes took a moment to adjust to the light, but he had already noticed the dark shadow of a man at the far end of the room, standing legs apart, hands clasped, blocking an open doorway. Did that mean Moretti was already here? Tom let the strands of the screen fall quietly back into position.

He was about to ask for a coffee when the bartender looked at him and waved one finger from side to side.

'Chiuso,' he muttered. Tom assumed that meant 'closed', which they clearly weren't.

'Caffe?' he asked, to try to delay his departure.

'Chiuso! Closed.' He pronounced it *clo-zed* and Tom guessed it was probably the only English word he knew. And that he used it often.

Tom glanced at the man in the open doorway of the back room, who took a step towards him. Had he been a random tourist, the posture of the man and the way he moved would have made him turn and run – clearly what the man was expecting. Tom was just debating whether to bait him by advancing further when the man took another step.

From where he stood, Tom could only see a sliver of the room beyond the doorway, but it was enough to make out a table with a woman seated on the far side. Speaking quietly to someone he couldn't see, she wasn't looking his way. Tom could see a trace of a sneer on her face and got the sense that – had he been able to hear her – there would be a derisive tone to her voice.

She lifted her hand and pushed her long hair behind her left ear.

Tom turned away quickly.

Tia Rukavina.

Heart pumping, walking as calmly as he could, Tom left the bar and headed back to where Jack was waiting in Campo Ruga. Any temptation to run was curbed by his suspicion that the goon at the door had followed him out to watch as he walked away. He wanted to turn to check, but he couldn't – not if he was to maintain the illusion of being a tourist.

Had Tia seen him?

He didn't think so. He had little doubt she would have recognised him if she had, but despite the disdainful expression on her face, she'd seemed engrossed in the conversation – presumably with Renzo Moretti.

What the hell was going on? Jack had found Moretti's phone number in Tia's contacts but had thought she was investigating him – either because she knew about the planned heist, or because he was involved in money laundering.

How could Jack walk in there with her in the room? Tia had met him. It was years ago, and Jack had changed considerably, but would she recognise him? Could they take that risk?

As Tom turned the corner into the square, he could see Jack

sitting on a bench, staring at his phone. He looked like a coiled spring, foot tapping, shoulders hunched.

'Well?' he said, jumping to his feet.

'Sit down, Jack. There's a chance I was followed so I'm going to sit by your side and not look at you as I speak.' They both sat. 'We have a problem. The bar's a cover – customers not welcome. Maybe they deal drugs there, and there's a goon guarding a room at the back. I could hear voices and I guess Moretti's already there. But that's not the problem. Tia Rukavina's there too.'

'*What?* Shit!' Neither man spoke for a few moments. 'Although perhaps it makes sense.'

'What do you mean?' Tom asked.

'While you were out earlier, I finally did a deep dive into the identity Tia's using – Elena Ferraro. As I'm sure you know, there's a network of people who operate freelance in the criminal world – everything from hired assassins to crypto launderers. Buried deep, I found references to Elena Ferraro, and her undercover persona is that of a fixer – arranging logistics, bribes, corruption, crisis management – none of which has anything to do with insurance.'

'And you think she's Moretti's fixer?'

'Could be. She seems to have a good reputation. She's worked her way up from small-time ventures in London starting about five years ago – which ties in with what we already know – gradually attracting international clients. I only had time to unearth a limited amount, but she's apparently the person to go to if you have a difficult job on, and she could certainly organise the logistics of shipping some product, or maybe selling a painting.'

'So, if she's working undercover for some law enforcement agency – either UK or international – you think she's been sent in to work for Moretti with the intention of exposing him?'

Jack nodded. 'Yes, and the insurance risk assessor role was just a cover so she could check out the gallery. I always believed Moretti had to have someone helping him. He's a vicious thug and he hasn't got the brains to organise the theft of a painting, let alone figure out the logistics of transporting whatever product he's buying to Venice.

It's a reasonable assumption that Tia Rukavina aka Elena Ferraro is that person.'

Tom let out a slow breath. 'God, she's playing a dangerous game, but if she's deep inside Moretti's operation then it's good news for us. The heist will go ahead and Ava will be released.' Then he frowned. Something about this didn't entirely add up. 'Hold on, Jack. You said Tia has been working her way up for about five years.'

'That's how long it probably takes to develop a reputation good enough to work at this level.'

'Yes, but she'd only be tasked with operating undercover for that long if whoever she's working for is out to catch a big fish, and that's not Moretti. He's only been involved with the 'Ndrangheta for five minutes. So who's she really after?'

The two men sat quietly for a moment. It was Tom who broke the silence. 'But then, whoever it is, does it actually matter as long as the painting is stolen as planned?'

Jack gave a tight, frustrated shrug. 'Not really, no. I don't care who her ultimate target is, nor do I have time to even think about it. I need to get into that bar and meet the bastard who has my daughter.'

Jack made to stand up and Tom reached out a hand to stop him. 'Remember, you don't know him. You don't know anything about him. All you know is that you're going to help him so he'll let Ava go.'

Jack gently moved Tom's arm out of the way. 'I know what I'm doing, Tom. From what I've learned, this guy's probably even more menacing than most because he's impulsive, so I'll play the tech superstar with zero knowledge of the workings of organised crime.'

With a wry smile, he patted Tom on the shoulder and walked towards the bar.

44

I'm feeling a little unnerved, and that's not like me. I can't allow it to show, so I sit taller, my face impassive as I wonder who that man was – the one who walked out of the bar a few minutes ago. Most people take one look inside and scurry away. But he didn't. I didn't hear him come in because Renzo was hissing at me, demanding answers I didn't want to give, and I failed to glance into the bar until I heard the rattle of the fly screen and caught a glimpse of his retreating back. Tall, dark blond hair, wide shoulders.

Familiar.

Did he hear anything I said? How long had he been there?

I push the thoughts aside to concentrate on why we are here in this seedy bar. I had almost walked past the entrance – little more than a narrow slit between buildings – my eyes taking time to adjust after the fierce sunlight of the street. As I moved through the room the bartender silently watched me, polishing a small glass and pouring clear liquid into it. For Renzo, I guessed.

The noise from the tourists crowding the streets faded as I headed towards an open doorway at the back. A man stood guard, thick-necked and stocky, his hands clasped in front of him, one palm resting over the other. He moved to one side to let me into the room, his eyes hard and unblinking as he looked me up and down. On the back wall was a two-way mirror so I could watch the conversation with Blake without being seen, but while I waited, I took a seat facing the door so I would see Renzo before he saw me.

Less than a minute after I arrived, I heard the clatter of the fly screen and saw the apple-shaped silhouette of a man outlined against the bright white light from the street beyond.

Renzo.

He picked up the glass waiting for him on the bar, downed it in one and gave a signal to the barman that indicated he wanted more. He didn't wait for his drink but headed towards me. The grinding of coffee beans hummed in the background as the barman poured another glass. I doubted Renzo had ordered anything for me.

'Elena,' he said, taking the seat opposite. His thin, sharp features gave him a birdlike appearance, the hawk-like nose casting a shadow over his pale lips and chin. I remember when we were first introduced. He had attempted to greet me the Italian way – a kiss on both cheeks – but I had jerked my head out of the way and held out my hand. I hadn't wanted his clammy face touching mine. Now we didn't even bother with a handshake. 'A che punto siamo?'

Before I had a chance to respond to his demand to know where we were up to, the bartender was allowed through by the man at the door to place another glass of clear liquid and a coffee in front of Renzo.

'Un ristretto, per favore,' I said, not waiting to see if Renzo was polite enough to offer me anything.

The barman dipped his head in acknowledgement and left the room. Renzo looked at me, still waiting for an answer to his question. He's out of his depth, drowning in details he doesn't understand.

'We're exactly where we should be,' I told him in English, my voice flat. I didn't need to try to impress. 'And we should speak English. We don't want to be overheard.'

I nodded my head towards the heavy, standing at the door.

Renzo narrowed his eyes, irritated that I was dictating terms. He thought of himself as a 'Ndrangheta superstar already. He had no idea that I was going to bring him down.

'All you ever tell me is that "everything is in hand". That's not good enough. I need to understand the process.'

Renzo Moretti was fully capable of pulling a gun on me – or at least, getting one of his men to do his dirty work. He'd made sure that I knew it. In an early demonstration of his power, I was invited to watch as he tortured one of his dealers for stealing from him. I knew who he was, and what he was. But he wasn't going to hurt me – at least, not yet.

'The cutting agents are already in the laboratorio. The main product is in the warehouse in Guatemala, but I can't arrange its release until the collateral is in place.'

'I didn't ask where it is now,' he snapped. 'I asked about the arrangements. Contarini will want to know how I'm getting it here.'

I couldn't afford to show any fear, so I smiled. 'You employed me. That's how you're getting it here.'

Renzo's mouth tightened. He wanted to strangle me – I could see it in his eyes – but his attempts to assert control were clumsy, betraying his inexperience. The last stage of his plan wouldn't work without me. He knew that. If he's going to make me suffer, it will only be when my job is done.

The planning had been intricate. Contarini had agreed that Renzo could buy two hundred bricks of uncut cocaine from the 'Ndrangheta's regular sources, but Renzo had to arrange the shipping to prove his worth. I had organised every step – not him. The product had been delivered to Guatemala, and I'd had it moved from a safe house in Puerto Barrios to a small coastal town. I wasn't going to share my contacts: the owners of the lanchas – the small fast boats that could evade radar detection – who would deliver the product to the freighters. And I wouldn't give him the names of the people I'd bribed, or the route from Guatemala through the Azores. Because then I would have no value.

'Can I remind you that I'm paying for this?' Renzo snarled. He lacked the authority and the cool calculation of a seasoned 'Ndrangheta boss, but his raw, unchecked aggression made him dangerous.

'You're paying for the shipping, Renzo, and paying me to implement it. Let's not forget you don't get the goods until you have the painting – Contarini's insurance against anything going wrong.'

There were so many ways he could fail. The shipment could be intercepted or, if it arrived here safely, it still had to be cut, stored and sold without detection. Maybe his stash house would go up in flames and he'd lose the lot. Who knew? Either way, he had to pay back the two million dollars he owed Contarini – either with the money he made through dealing the drugs, or, if it all went wrong, by handing over the painting.

'When we have the Serenata Selvaggi and it's stored safely, I'll confirm it to Contarini. Then the cocaine will leave South America. My job's finished when it's delivered to the cut house – the laboratorio. The team is standing by. They know what to do, how to cut it. They've been well briefed, and they're an experienced crew.'

'You're sure about the ratios?' he asked. I resisted the temptation to smile again. I was absolutely sure.

'Adding a little extra agent—' I glanced warily at Renzo's henchman at the door, '—will increase your profit. I've told you. It's cheap and no one will know.'

I didn't trust Renzo's men. He thought they were incorruptible, but given what they did for a living, that was laughable. I was hoping Renzo was too stupid to realise that if Contarini found out how he'd cut the drugs, his punishment would be swift and harsh. The 'Ndrangheta prided themselves on providing quality, and he was about to violate that standard.

'Remember, Renzo, you have to give Contarini half your profits – or at least the profits he knows about. If you cut the product the way I've said, you'll make an extra six or seven million euros he never needs to find out about.'

Renzo's mouth turned up at the corners. He liked the sound of that.

But Contarini would find out. I'd make sure of that.

45

The fly screen rattles. Blake's arrived, and I slip into the other room to watch through the mirror. I don't know what I expected: maybe some nervous-looking geek, awkward and pale. Instead he's a man of above-average height, perhaps in his late forties or maybe a little older, with black curly hair. There's a confidence in the way he holds himself, and although dressed casually in a cream-coloured linen shirt over dark blue jeans, his clothes hang well on him.

I want to see his eyes, but he's wearing sunglasses and he doesn't remove them. I'm guessing he doesn't want us to be able to read what he's thinking, to see the undoubted loathing in his eyes as he looks at Renzo. For a moment, my resolve falters. I don't blame him for his hostility, but I have a job to do. There's too much at stake.

Although it's clear Blake's not carrying a weapon under those clothes, Renzo's goon pats him down, takes his mobile and places it in his own pocket, then checks inside Blake's shirt to see if he's wired. But this man is a tech expert. If he's recording this, I can guarantee he won't be using wires taped to his chest.

Blake steps into the room and looks around as if something is missing. He waits to be told to sit, but somehow he's not entirely carrying off the role of a supplicant.

I've researched Ethan Blake. His real name is Peter Johnson, so Ethan

Blake's a fabricated name to match his company profile. Digging into Peter Johnson proved interesting. There's something that doesn't sit right. On the surface, his history is solid – almost too solid. His education checks out, his work references hold up, and yet there's an odd lack of traceable connections. For someone with his supposed brilliance in security, his digital footprint is unnervingly light. No old colleagues sharing success stories, no academic mentions, no whispers of him in the circles he's supposedly worked in, other than the most recent. And no photographs. Not a single one. It's as though Peter Johnson stepped out of nowhere, fully formed. And that worries me. People like him don't just appear – they're constructed. I should know this, if anyone does. The question with Johnson, though, is why?

Renzo is convinced we can trust him – we have his daughter, after all – but I need to form my own opinion because Blake, Johnson – whatever he's called – has to make the heist run smoothly. If he botches it, Renzo Moretti won't get another chance.

And neither will I.

'Mr Blake,' Renzo says, a sneer on his face as if to show his disdain for this man – *a man he needs, if he's to succeed in his plan. Sadly, he's also a man I need if I'm to succeed in mine.* 'Sit.' He points to a chair at the end of the table.

'Aren't you going to introduce yourself?' Blake asks.

Renzo tilts his head to one side and gives a dismissive smile before snapping his fingers. The goon goes to a briefcase lying on the floor and extracts a large document which he unfolds on the table. It's a blueprint of the palazzo. Renzo flattens it out.

'Explain the plan,' Renzo demands. 'My team has to be briefed before tomorrow night.'

'You mean Tuesday morning, don't you? Or has it changed again?'

'Monday night, Tuesday morning – same thing. Around thirty-six hours from now. You need to convince me that everything's in place from your end.'

'It is.'

Renzo doesn't like the brevity of the answer. He wants details, but Blake is failing to dance to his tune.

There's something about this man that I recognise, and it's making me even more unnerved than I already was. If he would take his sunglasses off, I'd know for sure.

'Show me the route,' Renzo demands, tapping a finger on the plan. 'And don't fuck with me.'

Blake doesn't look at it. 'Where's my daughter?'

Renzo smirks. 'Safe. And we know she's not your daughter. She told us. She said you won't do what we ask because you don't care about her. I want to know if she's right.'

Blake's jaw tightens and for a moment he doesn't speak, as if he wouldn't be able to contain himself.

'I'm here, aren't I?' He's playing it cool, but I don't believe for one moment that's how he's feeling. 'I want evidence that she's alive. And I mean today – not some video you could have filmed days ago. I'll do what you ask, but let me speak to her. Then we can agree the time and place for the handover.'

'You'll get the girl when the painting is out of Venice,' Renzo says. 'Twelve hours after we take it.'

Renzo's wrong. The painting will be outside Italian jurisdiction within three hours, but I'm not sure I want Renzo or Blake to have this much information.

I go over the plan in my head.

The painting will be transferred from the palazzo onto a food delivery boat, which will head to Torcello. Renzo's guys can't be trusted to stick to the speed limits, so from the minute it leaves the palazzo the painting will be under my control. In Torcello it will be transferred to a faster boat which, once clear of the lagoon, will head out into the Adriatic, beyond the reach of the Italian authorities, to rendezvous with a motor yacht apparently carrying a group of holidaymakers. The yacht will make its way to Croatia and within a further four hours it will be safely stored. Neither Renzo nor Contarini will know where the painting is, unless it's needed. As the fixer, that is entirely my responsibility.

The blank sunglasses turn towards the mirror and I can feel his eyes boring into the glass, wondering who's watching and why. He won't be fooled by the fake mirror, but he won't ask. Any sign of concern would be a show of weakness. And I don't think this man is weak.

'The plan, Blake.' Renzo bangs his fist on the blueprint. 'You will meet us here, which is where we enter.' He points to a side door to the palazzo, hidden from view from both the street in front and the canal at the back. 'I'm told you have an encrypted key, so you'll open the door and disable the main alarms. I need to hear you confirm that you can control all other security measures, as required.'

Renzo doesn't really understand all this – he's only repeating what I told him, but Blake doesn't try to test his grasp of the details.

'What time?' Blake asks, ignoring Renzo's demands for reassurance.

'Four a.m. The party tomorrow night may well last until midnight, perhaps later, and then the staff will be cleaning up. I have someone on the inside who will make sure every surface is cleared. I presume you need that for your video footage.'

That was my idea too. I have visions of a glass left on a table. The footage switches from live – the glass is there – to pre-prepared – the glass is gone, then it miraculously reappears when the footage is live again. Even the dumbest security guard should spot that on a monitor.

Blake is looking at the mirror again. I can't see his eyes, but I can see slight wrinkles on either side as he tries to work something out in his mind.

'You haven't answered my question,' Renzo growls. 'Can you control the locks on this door or not?' He points to the entrance, exactly as I briefed him.

'Of course.'

'And there will be no problems with the other security? You can clear my team's pathway through the palazzo and into the exhibition room?'

'I can.'

'Then this is the route we will take.' Renzo uses his finger to point out the corridors, hallways and doors. 'How much leeway in terms of time do we have?'

'None, and your route isn't the best. You have to avoid these areas.' Blake taps on the plan. 'That's all you need to know.'

Renzo leans forward. 'Are you forgetting what's at stake? Tell me what you will do, and when. I must understand all of it.'

Blake tuts. *'That would be a waste of your time and mine. You won't understand the technology. All that matters is that I can follow your route through the building. At each point, I'll turn off the relevant security remotely. The fake video will have been mapped on to the security cameras so the night team won't see anyone on their monitors. I'll turn off the sensors in the floor that flag movement within the rooms, and any infrared beams. There are no heavy doors for you to break through. D'Angelo is relying on my security system.'*

Renzo beams. *'Che peccato. He's going to be so disappointed.'*

Blake says nothing.

'How do we coordinate timings?' Renzo asks, recovering from his brief moment of glee.

'We don't. I'll be there, watching.'

'And you expect us to assume when we reach each door that it will open?'

Blake gives a frustrated grunt. *'I want to save my daughter, so provided I know she's alive and we agree the handover, I have nothing to gain by giving into the temptation to lock your men inside. You – for reasons best known to yourself – want to steal a painting that will be very difficult to sell for its full value. But I'm sure you think you know what you're doing.'*

I hear the underlying sneer in that little speech. Am I right about him? Is he more than just a technical wizard?

'May I suggest, Mr Blake, that you consider what will happen to you or those you love if you either disrespect me or fail in your task?' Renzo snaps.

The heavy at the door, picking up Moretti's tone if not understanding his words, moves towards Blake. For a moment I fear Renzo's volatile temper could take over and ruin the whole operation, but he raises a hand and the man retreats.

'We're done, Blake. You can go.'

'We're not done. I want to speak to my daughter. A video call. Non-negotiable. If I haven't spoken to her by eight this evening, you don't get your painting.'

A flush creeps up Renzo's thick neck. He doesn't think this nobody should be challenging him. But the heist has to happen. He can't allow it to *fail, and neither can I. I call Renzo on his mobile and watch his mouth tighten with irritation when he sees it's me. I speak for a few seconds, and he hangs up.*

'We'll set it up,' he says. 'We'll use Signal. I'm assuming that's not an issue for you?'

'No,' Blake answers. 'And the number you've been using to contact me is still valid?' Renzo nods. 'What about the person filming the video? I'm guessing that won't be you.'

'You don't need to contact her,' he says.

I want to scream at him for his use of the pronoun, but Blake doesn't react, he just tilts his head to one side. 'Oh, I think I do.'

I don't want Blake to have my number but I'll lose the phone as soon as we're done. I pick up my mobile and Blake's phone bleeps from inside the pocket of the man on the door.

'I guess I've got it now,' *he says, with a lopsided smile.* 'I'll send an encrypted QR code that will give you access to a secure video chat. If I haven't heard from you and spoken to Ava by eight p.m. this evening, the deal's off.'

Renzo's fury is barely contained and he leans forward, his fists clenched on the table. 'You're in no position to call the shots, Blake. Do you have any idea what I do to people who don't deliver?'

Renzo doesn't have the relaxed, unwavering confidence of a true Mafia boss. He fumbles under pressure, his nervous energy palpable. It's what makes him so reckless. It's also the very thing that's made him so malleable.

Blake, on the other hand, is perfectly calm. His mouth turns up at the corners in a hostile smile. 'I think you'll find my position is every bit as strong as yours. Without me, your scheme will fail, so let's stop pissing around, shall we? I don't accept that my daughter has to remain with you until the painting is out of Venice. Once you have it in your hands, I'll be done, finished, so you will have her ready and waiting for me before you exit the palazzo. If she's not there, I'll leave your men trapped inside, waiting for the police.'

Renzo slams both hands on the table. 'Remember who you're dealing with, Blake. Do you think I'm stupid enough to hand her over so you could go scurrying to the polizia?'

Blake pushes back his chair and stands. 'And what would that achieve? I don't know your route out of the city. I'd have to prove I wasn't complicit, and by the time I've told them everything – in English – and they've decided to take me seriously, I'm guessing the first phase of the painting's journey will be complete. This is non-negotiable.'

He stares straight at the mirror. It's as if he has a message for me, as if he not only knows I'm here, but that he knows me. After a long few seconds, he turns and leaves the bar.

I wait until I'm sure he's gone, and I'm about to come out from behind the mirror when Renzo, jaw rigid with anger, thrusts back his chair and marches over to his goon by the door.

'Segui lo stronzo. Stai vicino, ma non toccarlo. Non ancora. Ci sarà tempo dopo.'

Follow the arsehole. Stay close, but don't touch him. Not yet. There'll be time later.

46

Tom couldn't sit still. He paced up and down the square, hands in pockets, watching the entrance to the alley from which he expected Jack to appear. Realising he was probably drawing attention to himself, he finally sat down again and after no more than fifteen minutes he saw his brother walking towards him.

About to leap to his feet, Tom realised Jack wasn't looking at him but past him, ignoring him. Tom turned his head away and pretended to stare at something on his phone.

Seconds later, a man appeared at the entrance to the alley; the heavy who had stood guarding the back room of the bar. Tom dropped his head, but the man wasn't looking at him; he was watching Jack. Without raising his eyes again, Tom sent a quick message.

You're being tailed. Will try to derail.

Jumping to his feet, he decided to take advantage of the fact that the man might recognise him, and with a smile he walked towards him.

'Hi,' he said. Then, touching his forehead with his fingers: 'Ciao, I should have said. I think I saw you in the bar. Sorry. Do you speak English?'

The man stared at him, deadpan, his eyes hard as pebbles. 'Vaffanculo!' he spat, trying to step around Tom.

Tom was fairly certain he'd just been told to fuck off, but he had to delay the man for longer.

'There's no need to be rude!' he said, moving to stand, arms folded, in front of him. The Italian's muscles bulged through the shiny jacket of his cheap suit, and despite Tom being a good four inches taller, he wouldn't have fancied his chances if it came to a fight. The man reached forward to shove him aside.

'Hey!' The shout came from a woman in her fifties wearing a shocking-pink visor and a floral print T-shirt over pale blue cropped trousers. With one hand on her hip and a determined squint, she stepped towards them and frowned at the Italian. 'There's no need to get all worked up, is there? We're all just trying to enjoy the day here, right?' she said in a strong American accent.

The man glared at her and, with some force, pushed her out of the way. But Tom had blocked his sight of the far end of the square for long enough. There was no sign of Jack.

'Charming,' the woman muttered.

'I'm so sorry,' Tom said. 'That was unbelievably rude of him, but thanks for coming to my aid. I thought I was going to get punched.'

'Oh, don't mention it. Can't stand ignorant behaviour.' She glanced over Tom's shoulder and raised her hand in a wave. 'There's my husband. Better not tell him what I did. He's always telling me to butt out – not that I take much notice. Got to go, but glad if I helped.' With a grin, she hurried off.

Satisfied that he'd managed to shake the man off Jack's tail, Tom headed in the opposite direction and made his way to the nearest vaporetto stop to take a circuitous route back to Jack's room. It would give him time to think about whether they were making the most rational decisions.

Now that Jack had met and could identify the man behind the plan, Tom's logical mind leaped to the thought that they could incriminate him. But did the fact that Jack could pick Moretti out of a line-up make any difference, if he had the backing of the 'Ndrangheta? The rules here felt very different, the risks so much greater, and they were up against powerful, ruthless criminals. Tom realised with sudden clarity that if his own family were under their control, he'd follow the same path as Jack – doing whatever it took to bring them home safely.

A text from Becky arrived as Tom stepped off the vaporetto.

Message me when we can speak

Now was as good as any time, so he typed a quick response.

His black phone rang as he headed into the chaos of St Mark's Square, tourists swarming around him, buzzing with excitement, cameras clicking, voices mingling in a mix of languages. The sheer volume of chatter would make it impossible for anyone to pick up his conversation.

'Any news?' he asked, heading towards the side of the square out of the hot sun.

'Quite a bit. The name you asked for is Arjan Kodra. He heads up a small but vicious Albanian OCG in Manchester, and he was definitely involved in Ava's abduction. We think his crew could have been involved in taking Clare too. It seems unlikely that an entirely different team would have been recruited. The problem is, we can't find any direct links between the Albanians and your Italian families.'

'Any idea where Kodra is now?'

'None. Philippa's involved ROCU, which is great given they cover North Wales too. She says there's one person in particular you trust, and if anyone knows where Kodra is, his team will.'

Philippa must mean Paul Green, a senior officer in the North West Regional Organised Crime Unit. Paul was one of the very few people who knew Jack was still alive.

'Okay, so we just wait to hear?'

'For now. We need to consider that if Kodra was involved in Ava's abduction, he may very well have transported her to her final destination.'

'Jack thinks she's in Venice, although that's a guess. He's just had a meeting with the guy who's behind this. I'm on my way to find out what he's learned. There's one thing we're struggling to understand, though. Philippa checked Tia Rukavina out and couldn't find any information about her working undercover – although that's understandable. But she was *there*, in the bar where the meeting was being held. We think she must have infiltrated his crew.'

'And you don't want to blow her cover?'

'The more I think about it, the more I don't even *understand* her cover. She's been off the grid for a few years. Jack says she appears to have been involved with low-level crime groups, then somehow worked her way up to where she is now – liaising with the 'Ndrangheta.'

'Under the direction of the National Crime Agency? Is that weird?'

Tom understood Becky's confusion. It might make sense if she was trying to break into a UK *'ndrina*. But here? In Venice?

'I agree that the NCA seems unlikely, Becky. Maybe she's moved to INTERPOL. But you know how it is with undercover operatives – if Tia's been building her profile for years, there must be a greater objective. I'm assuming the small-time crooks she's worked with have been allowed to get away with their crimes, otherwise Tia's UC status would have been exposed. So she must have been put in place to reel in an important player. But Renzo Moretti isn't a big fish. He doesn't seem consequential enough to justify years of undercover work.'

'Maybe he's not the end game, Tom. Maybe Moretti's a route into the 'Ndrangheta.'

'I thought of that too, but why? Tia worked for the NCA as a forensic accountant. Why choose her to infiltrate one of the biggest crime organisations in the world?'

'I can't answer that, but I do have some other news. On Clare.'

Tom felt a surge of hope. 'And...?'

'We've identified some of her route. We picked her up in Bangor on the A55, then at Llanfairfechan, then Penmaenmawr. We lost her for a bit after that. Nothing in Conwy or Llandudno Junction, but there was a lot of traffic and she may have been blocked from the cameras by a lorry or a bus. Anyway, we picked her up again after that and followed her all the way. She came off the M62 at Birch services and hasn't been picked up since. I'd have expected her to leave the motorway at junction 19 for Heywood, but we can't find any trace. We're checking the car park at the service station to see if her car's still there.'

'Is there a service road?'

'There is, but would Clare know about that?'

Tom thought not, unless Jack had told her. If he had and she believed she was being followed, she might have decided to take it.

'Clare's car is electric. Apparently it was fully charged and would have had enough power to get to Heywood, so why would she stop at a service station?' Tom said.

'Maybe she wanted to pick up a snack or something for the kids, but as you said, we can't trace any credit cards so that doesn't help.'

Tom swallowed back a groan. It was two weeks since Clare had set off for Heywood, and the only contact had been her regular messages to Jack, which it seemed might be fake.

Becky was silent for a moment, and he knew she was waiting to share something with him.

'Spit it out, Becky.'

'Okay. Look, don't shoot me, but Keith's involved now. I had to tell him something, so I gave him pretty much the same story I gave Rob – about your long-term CHIS – but Keith's known you a lot longer. He's happy to play along with the backstory, so you don't need to worry. And he's good at this stuff, Tom.'

Tom felt a stab of guilt. These guys had stuck with him for years and had shown nothing but total loyalty. He was certain they would do everything they could to help.

'Are they both in today?'

'They are, yes. We're just tying together some loose ends on a case.'

'Can you get them together and call me back on speaker? I want to tell them the truth. They deserve it, and I trust them implicitly.'

He could hear Becky let out a long breath. 'Thank God. I'll go and get them.'

47

'Where the hell have you been, Tom?' Jack grunted without turning from his computer screens.

Tom decided not to mention that he'd been standing in St Mark's Square, staring absently at the intricate mosaics on the soaring domes of the basilica as he spoke to his former colleagues, filling them in on the situation as far as he could. It was the right thing to do, and Rob and Keith had been a hundred per cent supportive. But Jack wouldn't see it that way.

'I was trying to make sure I wasn't followed. That heavy of Renzo's took a bit of shaking off, and if it hadn't been for a helpful if rather foolhardy American woman, I'd probably be in hospital by now.'

Jack spun round. 'Sorry, Tom. I'm being a dick again. You okay?'

Tom nodded as he pulled up the plastic crate and sat down. 'Forget it. I'm fine. We're all stressed beyond belief. Before you tell me about Renzo, I have news about Clare. Not sure how helpful, but news nevertheless.'

Jack's face was a mask of controlled calm, but his eyes flickered with fear as Tom explained where Clare's car had last been seen.

'Why would she have gone to Birch services? There was enough charge in the car to get her all the way. I *checked*. And I told her not to stop.'

'I don't know, Jack, but we're on it, I promise. They were so close to the safe house too.'

'Safe house!' Jack scoffed. 'That seems a bit of a misnomer. *Shit*. I should have done more – found a way to speak to her. I was so bloody focused on Ava, I lost sight of everything else.'

'Of course you did. They're checking to see if her car's still at the services, and accessing any CCTV. But it's nearly time for Clare's daily message, and Philippa's on it. I spoke to Becky about thirty minutes ago. There'll be four cars in the area: Becky, two other members of my old team, plus an officer Philippa has co-opted, and someone from the Technical Support Unit. You do know this is a bit of a long shot, don't you?'

'I know, but doing something is better than doing nothing,' Jack muttered.

'If they *do* find where she is, what do you want them to do?'

Jack looked at Tom as if he were mad. 'What do you *think* I want them to do?'

'I suspect you want an armed response unit to race in and save the day. But let's pause for a minute and think about what that will mean.'

Jack dropped his head. 'I know what it will mean. Three of my family will be safe, but as soon as Renzo knows the police are involved, Ava may never be seen again. Now I've met him, I'd say he lacks the detached, merciless mindset of a Mafia don. He's quick to anger – a hot-head and, at a guess, a vicious one. He wouldn't stop to consider the consequences, he'd just react.'

'So we have to be smarter. Look, I need to ask, but is there any chance that Clare chose *not* to go to the safe house and decided to go somewhere else close by?'

Jack looked up with a confused frown. 'Why would she do that?'

'No idea, but you've been messaging and you didn't think there was anything odd about her responses?'

'I told you. They'll be using AI to clone her style, mimic her tone.'

'In real time?' Tom asked.

'More challenging, but we've kept our conversations fairly neutral in case they're not secure, so it wouldn't be too difficult. I need the conversation to take an unexpected turn – something that might cause them to screw up. And I think I know what it is.'

'Go on?'

'I'll say I'm hoping we'll be back home in Wales before Archie's party, and that I assume she hasn't mentioned it to Billy in case we're not back in time. Then I'll ask if she remembered to pack his costume so he can go straight there if necessary.'

Tom nodded. 'I'm guessing Archie is Billy's friend, and they can't ask Billy because he doesn't know about the party yet. How will Clare know it's a test?'

'Because Archie's family emigrated to Canada two months ago.'

'Good. Two birds with one stone. While Becky and the team look out for people in cars typing on their phones somewhere near the safe house – for want of a better term – TSU will monitor phone signals and you can confirm if it's Clare who's answering your message.' At that moment Tom's phone pinged, and he looked down at the screen. 'Sorry, Jack. No sign of Clare's car in the car park at Birch, and the CCTV doesn't show it leaving. That means she must have left by the access road.'

'Which tells us precisely nothing. Maybe she thought she was being followed and chose somewhere else to stay. If she did, she'll ask, "What party?"'

'And we'll all heave a sigh of relief,' Tom said, not believing for one second that this would happen.

Jack filled the nervous minutes waiting for Clare's message by outlining what had happened at the meeting with Renzo.

'One thing is abundantly clear: Renzo Moretti isn't the brains behind this. He's a weasel-faced man – small eyes too close together, thin lips, pointed nose – and I'd guess he's reached the position he has by sheer brutality. He doesn't try to hide his ruthless streak, and the darker corners of the web are rife with chatter about his penchant for violence. I'm sure Tia is his fixer. She wasn't in the room, but I'm certain she was the other side of the mirror. She's a clever woman. The logistics wouldn't faze her, and why else would she be there?'

'Do you think she recognised you?' Tom asked.

'I doubt it. I kept my sunglasses on and my hair was wild when she knew me, but the good news is that I've found a way to force her to activate the app I put on her phone – or rather, *you* put on her phone.'

'How?'

'I told Renzo I'll set up a private Signal group chat so I can see and talk to Ava. I need to send an encrypted QR code and I've tweaked it so that when Tia accepts it – which I'm hoping she will – it will authorise the chat access but also activate the app. Then I can monitor everything she does. With luck, it'll help us figure out who she's working for and why she's so deep undercover, and maybe we can use her to our advantage.'

Tom got to his feet and walked to the window. Everything seemed to be slipping further beyond their control, and Moretti's unstable nature was adding to his growing sense of alarm.

Jack was watching him. 'You can still run, little brother, if that's what you need to do. I won't hesitate to break the law if I have to, because if I don't, you and I both know Ava's as good as dead. Morality isn't black and white, Tom, and I'm not going to let her die.'

'It's not the morality that's bothering me. There just seems to be so much that we don't understand. But don't waste time wondering how I'm feeling – it's a distraction. Just tell me what you're planning.'

Jack stood up, walked over and grasped Tom's upper arms. 'I do have a plan – one I can't implement without your help. You're not going to like it, but if it works, no one should get hurt.'

Tom frowned. 'Go on…'

He looked at Jack's face. Despite the brotherly gesture, Jack wasn't quite able to meet his eyes, his gaze flickering away. He dropped his hands and turned back towards his computer.

'Not yet. There's no time. I need to get ready for Clare's message.'

Classic avoidance tactics. *What was Jack up to?*

48

The buzz of Tom's phone seemed startlingly loud in the almost silent room.

'It's Philippa,' he said as Jack twisted to face him. 'This might be it.' He put the phone on speaker.

'The team's ready and in position, Tom,' Philippa said. 'Clare's phone is switched on, connecting to the same tower as before. But since Heywood's semi-rural, only a single tower is in play so we can't triangulate. What's the usual protocol between her and Jack?'

'Clare messages Jack, and he responds.'

'Any time now, then. Did you say he'd tried to contact her and failed?'

'Not exactly. After Becky found she wasn't at the safe house he tried to exploit some of the features he'd added to her phone, but everything has been deactivated.'

'It wasn't a call or message? When they switched the phone on, they'd have been alerted to any missed communications. Check with him, will you?'

Tom turned to Jack, who shook his head. 'There's no way they'll know I've been trying to get in touch.' Jack straightened up, suddenly more alert. 'It's arrived, Tom. Her message. She's just asked if I'm here.' Jack quickly typed his response.

'Jack needs to keep her chatting as long as possible, Tom, so the team can check the area. The cell tower covers roughly a kilometre in radius, but with any luck they won't know that and they'll have parked close to the house. We have TSU nearby and they should be able to identify an exact location.'

Tom could see Jack typing away, his thumbs busy. He could hear Philippa talking to the team in Heywood. On his own phone he had a map of the area around the house, but there was nothing useful he could do, and as each minute passed without news, his optimism faded.

He heard a gasp from Jack, who glanced up from his screen. 'The Archie question. She says she's got Billy's outfit. It's not her, Tom.'

'Change the subject to ordinary stuff, bearing in mind you're both stressed about Ava. Tell her what happened today – the meeting, the plan to get a video of Ava. Everything you might say if this really was Clare, but don't name names or voice suspicions.'

Jack shot him an exasperated look, as if to say, 'Really? You're explaining this to me?'

'Tom, I think we might have something.' There was an unusual note of excitement in Philippa's voice. 'Jack needs to ask Clare to hang on, say there's someone at the door or something, tell her he won't be a moment. We've located a stationary vehicle with a man inside. The TSU equipment is telling us this is the guy – or rather, this is the phone's location. If he looks away and then back when Jack starts typing again, we'll know for sure.'

Jack had heard Philippa's suggestion, his thumbs moving furiously. 'I've told her not to go away. How long do we give it?'

'A couple of minutes should be enough. We want the guy to get bored and start gazing around. Keith's watching him from a bus stop down the road, and he doesn't miss a trick.' Philippa broke off, then resumed after a few seconds: 'The man's staring at the phone, but nothing else. Tell Jack to send another very brief "Are you there?" message.'

As Jack typed, Tom could hear Philippa talking over the radio. Then: 'Tom, we've got him. Both TSU and visual confirmation. Jack needs to end the message the way he normally does. We have everyone in position to follow, after this man turns the phone off. Tell me the moment it's over.'

Tom nodded to Jack, who typed a few more words. 'Done,' he said.

'Done,' Tom repeated.

There was a pause.

'Yes. He ended the call, threw the phone on the passenger seat, and he's on the move. I'll be back when he's reached base.'

'Don't lose him, will you?'

'I refuse to respond to that. I'll speak to you soon.'

Becky was in the lead car following the suspect's five-year-old grey Nissan Qashqai, which was heading away from the more built-up areas of Heywood. She was keeping as far back as possible, but avoiding detection became more difficult when he turned onto the narrow lanes leading into open countryside.

'Rob,' she said over the radio, 'I've been behind him too long. I'm going to find somewhere to pull off the road. Can you take over? Keith, there's a junction about a mile ahead. If he hasn't turned off by then, can you pick him up from there? Abir, can you come up behind Rob?'

She hadn't worked with Abir before, but she'd been assured he was one of the best and hoped it was true. This couldn't go wrong.

When all three officers had responded, Becky pulled onto the drive of a bungalow. A face appeared at the bay window and Becky raised her hand as if in apology, hoping to avoid someone coming out to check what she was doing. Seeing Rob's car speed past the end of the drive behind her, she reversed out into the road to follow at a distance.

'The suspect has turned onto a track,' Rob said. 'He's heading towards what appears to be a small deserted mill about two hundred yards back from the road, next to the canal. I'm not stopping. There's a passing point ahead. I'll pull over. I can watch the entrance to the track from there.'

'Ma'am,' Becky said to Philippa over her radio, 'we have the location. Access is very exposed.'

'Maintain surveillance from a distance,' Philippa said. 'Check if there are any other exits – they may not show on a map. I'll organise the Force Intelligence Unit to gather info and conduct a risk assessment. They can loop in the TSU to install probes during the night. Hopefully we can get audio and video in there. For now, keep watch – nothing more.'

'Okay. Rob Cumba's in position. Keith will check other exit points and get back to you. Abir can wait at the junction to back Rob up if the car moves. I'll wait to hear when the FIU will arrive. Are you informing Tom, or should I?'

'I'll speak to him. Good work, and pass that on to the rest of the team.' Philippa hung up.

Becky sat back in her seat and allowed herself to breathe. If they had messed this up, she didn't know how she would have faced Tom. Thank God they hadn't. Nevertheless, she had a feeling it was going to be a long night.

Tom had continued to pace the room, waiting for news, while Jack pretended to focus on his computer, his left leg jittering uncontrollably.

He answered his phone on the first ring. 'Philippa, how did it go? Jack's here too. You're on speaker.'

'In which case, thank goodness the news is positive, Tom,' Philippa said, a note of irritation in her tone. 'We know only one thing: the location of the man who has access to Clare's mobile phone. I'd love to say we know Clare and the children are there too, but frankly, we don't. He drove to a disused mill next to a canal a couple of kilometres from the housing estate, and I've organised resources to gather intelligence. TSU can't do anything until it's dark, and it being May, we have quite a wait. But the canal's handy.

There's a tow path, so no need to approach up the main track. What's happening where you are?'

Tom pulled a face at Jack. What could they tell Philippa?

'Detective Superintendent Stanley, this is Jack. Thank you so much for your help with my wife and family.'

'Ah, the ever-elusive Jack Douglas. You have caused me no end of trouble over the past few years, as I'm sure you know. But a crime's been committed on my patch and it's my job to rescue your family, regardless of the reason for their abduction.'

'If it helps, it has nothing to do with any criminal activity on my part, either past or present.'

Tom really wanted Jack to shut up, but he had the feeling that Jack and Philippa would get on rather well, were they ever to meet.

'I'll take your word for it. We also have news about Ava.'

Jack leaned forward, as if being closer to the phone would make a difference.

'Go on,' Tom said.

'We've discovered that a flight departed Weston Airport just outside Dublin within our time frame. It's a private airfield and it was a small jet, a six-seater. Initially, they filed a flight plan for Milan Malpensa Airport – probably to make the flight appear legitimate. Mid-flight, the flight plan was altered and they diverted to Lucca-Tassignano, another private facility with less scrutiny than an international airport. They possibly cited technical issues, but more likely it was to avoid detection by authorities, and no doubt it's easier to find people there to bribe. If they're in Venice now, they probably travelled by road – about four hours. But that part is nothing more than a guess.'

'It would have been a whole lot easier and cheaper to hold her somewhere in the UK. Why bring her to Venice?' Tom asked.

'I might be able to answer that,' Jack said, his voice lacking its usual conviction. 'They'll have secure hideouts here, and much more control. And they may have contacts in the Italian police. It's harder for her to be rescued in Venice, and – not to beat about the bush – it's easier to dispose of her, if that becomes the only option.'

There was a pause, with no one apparently able to think of a suitable response.

Philippa broke the uncomfortable silence. 'I guess we have to accept that you're the most knowledgeable of us when it comes to understanding the mindset of organised crime groups. I'll be back in touch when we know what the plan is for Clare and the children.'

With that, she hung up.

49

'Ouch!' Tom said after Philippa's parting shot, but Jack shrugged.

'I don't blame her for what she thinks of me. At least she's doing what she can to find my family. But what do we do when we know for sure that Clare and the kids are in the mill?'

Tom took a deep breath. 'It's a tricky one. Whoever's holding them is probably in touch with Renzo Moretti on a regular basis, so if we extract them it could have an impact on what he does with Ava.'

'You mean he'll know we've involved the police. Even if it's only the UK police, we're stuffed. What are we going to do, Tom?'

'We've got some time. They can't put video and audio probes into the house until after dark. If we want to hold off from rescuing your family, though, we're going to have to give Philippa a bloody good reason, and I don't want to tell her what you're being asked to do.'

'Yeah. Bad idea, I guess,' Jack murmured.

'Absolutely. She couldn't know that without sharing it with the police here in Italy. She's bent the rules in the past when lives were at stake, but I'm pretty sure I know how she'd react to this situation. All she needs to know is that there's a plan to rescue Ava, and the moment we have her safe they can go in and get Clare, Billy and Sophia out. But it's a difficult decision, Jack.'

'I know the risks. Every bone in my body is screaming that your team should kick the fucking door down and get my family out. But it feels like that'd be sealing Ava's fate.'

'What's happening about handing her back to you?'

'I've told Renzo that Ava has to be there, waiting, when his men are ready to exit the palazzo with the painting. I've told him I won't open the doors to let them out until she's safe.'

'And his response?'

'Oh, he hates the thought that I have any control of the situation, and if he thinks I've in any way undermined him, made him look stupid in front of his guys – or worse, Contarini – he'll probably shoot Ava in front of me.'

'Shit! You don't really think that, do you?'

'If it was up to him I think he would, but I don't think it is. I think Tia's running everything, and I wish to God I knew what her game is. She must *know* my family's been abducted. How can she be okay with that?'

'We don't know she had anything to do with it. She may only be involved in shipping the product. Whatever she's up to, whoever she's working for, they wouldn't allow her to get involved in kidnapping children. Renzo must have had someone else for that job. But she undoubtedly knows about it by now, so I'm sure she'll have a plan to prevent any harm from coming to your family.'

'Yeah, well, being sure isn't good enough, is it?'

Tom had no reassurance to offer. 'When will you be able to access Tia's phone? That might tell us more.'

'I've sent the QR code. We'll just have to wait and see.'

'I suppose all this tells us one thing,' Tom said. 'Ava must be in Venice if your code has only been shared with those two phones. One of them will have to be with her when she speaks to you.'

'I know, and thank God for that. At least she feels within reach. Let's hope it's Tia who films her. I can't stand the thought of Renzo being within a mile of her.'

. . .

The late-afternoon sun poured through the windows, casting sharp angles of light across the room. Outside, the muted sounds of Venice – the murmur of passing boats, the distant chatter of tourists – seemed like a different world.

Every second was dragging, and Tom's eyes were drawn to the ticking clock. 32:37:55. So little time, and he felt powerless.

Jack swivelled in his seat. 'Tom, I need you to go shopping. We need masks.'

Relieved to have something to do, Tom nevertheless didn't like the sound of this. 'What sort of masks? Do you mean balaclavas?'

Jack managed a weary chuckle. 'Nope. Venetian masks, the type worn at formal receptions – subtle, elegant, covering the eyes and the upper face. They need to be top end to fit in with the crowd at the reception.'

'And you said masks, plural?'

'One each, not matching. We're going to the reception tomorrow night. I've created passes for us, and I've located a mask shop. I'm dropping a pin on your phone. They need to be authentic, expensive. We'll stand out a mile if we get it wrong.'

Tom's phone pinged with the pin. He wanted to ask why they needed to be at the reception just hours before the planned heist, but whatever Jack was doing, he clearly didn't want to be disturbed.

Grabbing his wallet from the table, Tom was heading towards the door when Jack called out, 'And a bottle of Scotch.'

Given that neither of them had any appetite for food, this didn't seem the most sensible suggestion but Tom said nothing – mainly because, stupid as he knew it was, he could really do with a large Scotch himself.

As he made his way beyond the lane and into the centre of the city, the bustling crowds felt distant, almost dreamlike – as if they were actors in a scene from a movie he wasn't part of. Laughter spilled from bars and drifted towards him, unreal and out of place.

There was something about Venice that seemed removed from reality, even without the chaos he was living through.

Shaking his head at his fanciful thoughts, Tom headed for the mask shop close to the Rialto Bridge, passing a bustling *rosticceria* on his way. The air was filled with the scent of roast meat, rich tomato sauce and melted cheese. He felt a pang of hunger as he walked by but ignored his grumbling stomach.

He didn't know what he'd been expecting of the shop – maybe a small, cramped place tucked away down a back street. Instead, he found three large brightly lit windows displaying an array of elaborate masks, some whimsical, others haunting, their feathers and jewels glinting in the light. Many seemed designed for the carnival, full of mystery and decadence – not, Tom was sure, what Jack had in mind.

He pushed open the door to the sound of an old-fashioned bell, and an elderly man walked through from a back room. 'Posso aiutarla?' he said with a smile.

Assuming that meant 'can I help you', Tom returned the smile. 'Do you speak English?'

'Of course. How can I help?'

Tom gazed around at the hundreds of masks attached to the walls. How on earth was he going to choose?

'I'm going to a reception at a palazzo. A masked event. I don't know exactly what I'm looking for, or what would be appropriate.'

'Elaborate or simple?'

Tom had no idea, and realising he was bemused, the shopkeeper helped him out.

'Let me show you a few options.'

There was a bewildering choice, all stunningly detailed, but one caught his eye. The mask covered most of the nose and upper cheeks, rising up the forehead with two almond-shaped gaps for eyes. Black, mysterious and decorated with delicate gold scrolls and flourishes, it would be perfect for Jack.

Having no idea what to choose for himself, the shopkeeper picked one from a display on the wall.

'Would you like to try this one?'

The mask had a metallic finish with sharp angular lines and geometric patterns. It looked like something a gladiator might wear and was very different from the one he'd chosen for Jack.

'It's perfect. Thank you.'

As he paid, he gave himself a moment to worry about why they were attending the reception. He couldn't think of any reason for them to be there.

'I have a plan,' Jack had said. 'One that you're not going to like.'

50

Ava hasn't heard the woman's voice again. In fact, it's eerily quiet. She can usually hear the deep murmur of the men's voices coming from the next room, but there's silence, and no one has been in to check on her for hours. The last time she saw them, Big Guy brought her a sandwich and a plastic bottle of water, but she's scared of drinking it, certain it's drugged. It's a choice between staying alert – particularly if Skinny Guy is around – or sinking into oblivion. She doesn't know which she prefers.

The days have blurred into a haze, and she thinks of the strategies she employed when she was thrown into The Pit to keep herself sane. She was never there for as long as this, though, and the number puzzles she used to create in her head no longer seem to do the trick.

She's weighed up every option for escape, but there's only one door with two men on the other side, and if Big Guy won't help her, she doesn't have a chance. It doesn't stop her imagining freedom. In her mind, she's painted pictures of the places she wants to visit, the things she wants to do. She can imagine herself posing in front of the Taj Mahal, sunbathing on a Greek island, skiing down a mountain in Switzerland. In the last few days, she has taken all these holidays. And one day those dreams will come true. She's determined.

She has passed the time making up stories to tell Billy and Sophia, inventing characters in a mythical world with herself as the heroine, protecting her brother and sister from the creatures that inhabit the woods around their house. Her favourites are the shadowmoths – small nocturnal creatures with wings that resemble spiders' webs, and huge orange eyes that glow in the dark. If you catch those eyes, they pull you into a trance. She has created magical potions to drive them away, and has even composed the spells she will cast.

Her fantasy is interrupted by the scraping of the bolt as it's pulled back. Her eyes lock onto the opening, hoping as she always does that this time the person walking through the door will be her dad. But it's not. It's Skinny Guy, and her heart thuds. He's alone.

Half-lying on the filthy mattress, she feels vulnerable and jumps to her feet, water bottle in hand. She doesn't stand with her back to the wall. She wants space around her – room to move, to get away from him.

He walks towards her, the smirk on his face suggesting he thinks he's in luck because this time Big Guy isn't here to stop him. Just as before, he rubs his hand up and down his crotch, but now his other hand reaches to unfasten his jeans.

Ava watches, a tight knot of fear in her throat. She doesn't take her eyes off him, but she can see behind him. The door is open. This could be her chance.

She moves to one side. He mirrors her steps, laughing as he blocks the way. He steps closer, expecting her to back away, but she stands her ground. There's a hint of confusion in his eyes as she stops trying to dodge around him and instead takes a slow step towards him, her hand gripping the neck of the bottle.

The acrid scent of stale cigarettes clings to him, and she tries not to react. She stops with barely half a metre separating them. Close enough. His pupils darken and he stands, legs apart, nodding his head at her shirt as if he's expecting her to unbutton it. She lifts her left hand to the top button. His gaze is fixed on that hand, his tongue once again darting from his mouth to lick his bottom lip.

He doesn't see her right arm as she swings the full water bottle with all her strength up between his legs. It connects with a sickening thud and he shrieks, falling to his knees.

She bolts for the open door but, in her haste, she strays too close. His hand shoots out, gripping her ankle in a vice-like hold. She loses her balance and tumbles to the ground, her head hitting the rough stone. Blackness settles around her.

51

By the time he got back to Jack's room, Tom was weary. He was used to working long days, but he was also only just out of hospital. With less than four hours' sleep the previous night, he could only hope he was still capable of making rational decisions.

Jack merely glanced over his shoulder and grunted in acknowledgement at his return, so Tom found two mugs, swilled them out with water and poured a small amount of Scotch into each. At the same time, he emptied another bag onto the only plate that the place seemed to possess.

The smells from the *rosticceria* had been too tempting and Tom hadn't been able to resist buying some *mozzarella in carrozza* and mushroom *arancini* on his way back. He placed the snacks by Jack's right hand.

His brother looked up with a lopsided smile to acknowledge that, once again, Tom was trying to feed him.

'I know you don't want to eat, but if you're going to down any of this Scotch, I'm not going to give you any choice. I didn't think I was hungry or that I could stomach food until I saw these. Trust me, they go down very easily.'

Jack shook his head at Tom's persistence but nevertheless picked up an *arancino* and took a bite.

'You got the masks?' he managed, his words muffled by a mouthful of food.

'I did, and I need to know what you're planning, but it can wait until you've spoken to Ava. What if Tia's with her when the call's made, Jack? You can hardly put your sunglasses on, can you?'

'I know. I haven't worked it out yet. I've been concentrating on seeing what I can find out about those bloody Albanians. And—' There was a *ping* on Jack's computer. 'Hallelujah! Tia's accepted the QR code. That's *exactly* what we need.' He clenched his fist in triumph. 'Gotcha, Tia Rukavina, Elena Ferraro – whatever the fuck you're calling yourself.'

For the first time in a while there was a genuine smile on Jack's face.

'What can you access?' Tom asked.

'The whole kit and caboodle. I can listen in to her calls, see where she is, switch on her microphone to hear what she's saying, her camera to see what she's looking at – whatever she's up to, I've got her! Give me a moment.'

Tom had a slight twinge of concern. If Tia was working for either international or British law enforcement, there would be ramifications if this was ever discovered. Technically, Jack could be charged with espionage.

No one's getting hurt, Tom reminded himself silently. At least, not yet.

Before they could discuss what Jack had discovered about the Albanians, his phone rang.

'Renzo,' he muttered to Tom as he accepted the call and switched it to speaker. 'I presume you're calling to confirm arrangements for my conversation with my daughter?'

'I will provide evidence that your daughter is alive. I will transmit a video to your Signal account.'

'Not good enough,' Jack said. 'You could have filmed it at any time. I need to speak to her.'

'Mr Blake, I have made enough concessions. I will not permit you to ask her questions hoping she'll give you information so you can find her. You can't, of course. Trust me, you don't want to upset me. I hold most of the cards. You hold only one.'

Jack looked at Tom. It was clear to them both that Renzo was alluding to the fact that he could hurt Ava and, if he chose, the rest of Jack's family.

'My one card is pretty significant, though, and I assure you the painting won't leave the palazzo until my daughter is safely by my side.'

They heard a soft dismissive breath, almost a laugh, and Jack closed his eyes. Tom knew he was desperate to tell this man that he didn't quite have the upper hand he thought he had. But the truth was, he certainly had enough.

'Eight o'clock, Mr Blake. The video will arrive in your Signal account, as agreed.'

Tom shook his head at Jack. He couldn't display any sign of weakness.

'A compromise. I'll send you some questions to read to her,' he said. 'I'll know by her answers that the video is happening now, not something you shot days ago.'

There was an elaborate sigh from the other end of the phone, as if Renzo was offering a massive concession.

'Three questions. Send them now, and my associate will ask her.'

The call dropped immediately.

'Are you okay with that, Jack?'

'Not really. For Ava's sake, I'd have liked her to at least hear my voice, but it solves one problem. If it's not a video call I don't have to disguise myself for Tia, and I'm assuming – *hoping*, in fact – that's who Renzo means by his "associate". I have control of her phone now, so not only can I switch on the audio to hear everything that's said, I'll also be able to find out exactly where she is. Maybe the plan I have in mind for tomorrow night won't be needed.'

'You still haven't told me what that is,' Tom said.

Jack gave a half-hearted smile. 'With any luck you need never know, little brother. That would probably be best for both of us.'

With that, Jack turned away and started typing his questions for Ava.

52

Relieved as he was that Jack could now monitor Tia's phone, Tom wasn't convinced it would solve everything.

'I hate to sound negative, but it might not be easy to pinpoint Tia's precise location. The buildings here are very close together with multiple floors. Plus, if Tia's working for one of the crime agencies, she'll have GPS protection on her phone.'

'Yeah, that occurred to me too. I'll check as soon as this has gone.'

Tom was tempted to ask, 'And what if we *do* find out where Ava is? Are the two of us going to storm in and rescue her?' They were dealing with the 'Ndrangheta – or at least a man who could probably summon their support if needed – and that was unlikely to end well.

Tom took a seat on the lumpy sofa, shuffling to find a comfy spot. 'What questions have you asked?'

Jack pressed Send on his phone. 'Just simple things. I don't want her to get panicky; I just want to know she's alive and coping, that they're feeding her, she's warm enough – although hopefully it won't be long until we have her out of there. It's to show I care and that I'm thinking about her. I've asked if she remembers the strategies we taught her all those years ago. I hope they ask her that, so it reminds her what to do.'

'What kind of strategies?'

'Breathing exercises, thinking of happy memories from her life; grounding techniques – you know, focusing on physical sensations. Positive affirmations – "I am strong, this is temporary", that kind of thing. They've all helped her in the past. I really don't know if the trauma of her upbringing has made her more resilient or more fragile. Honestly, Tom, it breaks my heart to think of her going through more unutterable crap. Hasn't she been through enough in her short life?'

Tom couldn't disagree, and it was hard to see how Ava could ever feel safe again, despite everything Jack and Clare had done to give her a life that was as close to ordinary as possible, albeit with inevitable restrictions.

'She'd have been better off being adopted by someone normal, you know,' Jack said. 'But Clare wouldn't hear of it. She wanted to lavish love on the kid from the start. Ava lost her mum, was kidnapped and forced into all kinds of horrific crimes, only to discover that her dad was a total scumbag and the cause of the misery in her life. She'd have been better off as part of a conventional family.'

Tom leaned back. 'That's nonsense. She was thirteen, severely traumatised by all she'd seen and had lived for months on the streets of Manchester stealing food whenever she needed to eat. Come on, Jack. How many parents would know where to start? It's bad enough if those things happen to a child you've loved from birth, but to be faced with that level of trauma in a child you don't know and then somehow have to figure out how to help her through it? That takes someone special. There may have been restrictions because of who you are – or were – but there's been no end of love and understanding. So let's forget you said that, shall we?'

Jack shrugged. He was opening his mouth as if to respond when his attention was drawn to his monitor and he sat bolt upright. 'Tia's phone – incoming call.'

Tom jumped up from the sofa and went to stand behind him.

'Pronto,' he heard, the standard Italian way to answer a phone call.

Jack immediately switched his translation app on so they could follow the conversation.

'Ho la lista delle domande. Devi andare a filmare la ragazza.' It was Renzo's voice.

'Perché non usi uno dei tuoi scagnozzi per farlo?' Tia responded.

It took a moment for Jack's translation app to catch up. When it did, the words appeared as a dialogue between A and B.

A: I have the list of questions. You must go and film the girl.
B: Why don't you use one of your minions to do it?

Tom stopped listening to the Italian conversation and focused on the onscreen translation.

A: Because the men guarding her aren't my minions. They're yours, Elena. You recruited them, it's your job to manage them. And I don't speak Albanian.

Jack spun towards Tom, a look of shock on his face, then turned back to the ongoing translation.

B: Neither do I. They understand English perfectly, even when they pretend not to. I'll do it, but my job is to facilitate every aspect of securing the cocaine, and while that includes setting up the theft of the painting as collateral, I'm not one of your minions. I will do this only because I want to check that the girl is ready for the handover. We can't afford for anything to go wrong.

There was a slightly manic cackle from Renzo.

A: We're not turning her over, Elena. Blake has disrespected me, and no one treats Renzo Moretti like that. Speak to your Albanian friends. They can dispose of the girl after the video's made.

Jack's body was completely rigid, and Tom gripped his shoulder.

B: That's a mistake.

He cackled again.

A: My father-in-law will be proud of me. No loose ends. Just the way he likes it. And why do you care what happens to her?
B: I don't. It's your decision, but will Contarini believe the situation is extreme enough to warrant killing the kid?
A: So don't have them kill her! They're Albanian – isn't people trafficking one of their specialities? They can have her. Do what they want. See how much they offer for her, but her father's insolence has cost him.
B: And you'll do what, exactly, if he decides he's not going to let your men out of the palazzo with the painting?
A: Backup plan, Elena. You're the one that set it up, after all. A stroke of genius, taking the whole family. Tell the team in England to get ready to film them the moment Blake becomes difficult.
B: It's a bad idea to sacrifice any of your assets, Renzo. Not yet. Save your vengeance for later.
A: Don't argue with me, Elena! Deal with it!

The line went dead.
Jack folded his arms on the table and lowered his head.

53

'What the fuck...?' Jack groaned, finally lifting his head to stare at Tom. 'I don't even know where to start unpicking that. What the hell is Tia playing at? *She* recruited the Albanians? That means she planned Ava's abduction and organised for Clare and the kids to be taken. What kind of undercover operation calls for that level of criminality?'

Tom knew the answer and dreaded delivering the truth, but he had to.

'She's not undercover, Jack. Until now, we've assumed she may have been *aware* of what was happening to Ava and that she'd have a plan to rescue her without jeopardising their bigger plan, whichever agency she was working for. But we were wrong. No law enforcement agency in the Western world would order an operative to plan and execute the abduction of a teenage girl – or a family with two small children.'

'So, you're saying...'

'I'm saying that whoever she was when you knew her before, she's not that person now. Tia Rukavina is, to all intents and purposes, Elena Ferraro. And she's in this up to her neck.'

Both men were silent. They had believed the biggest threat was Tia exposing Moretti's plan to steal the painting before Ava could be freed, but this was so much worse. Tia was central to the whole plot, and far more dangerous than they'd thought.

'Do you remember the research I did, Tom? I said she'd been involved as fixer in several jobs and none of them seemed to have turned sour. No arrests, as far as I could make out. We thought it strange but assumed it was all about catching a bigger fish.'

'We did and we didn't,' Tom responded. 'I thought the whole link with Renzo Moretti was odd. When she started down this road he was a nobody, so she couldn't have been building her credibility for years just to catch him. The only possible explanation was that Contarini was the big fish they were after, and Renzo suddenly presented himself as a route into that world. But I struggled with the idea.'

'Then who is she, and what's her game?' Jack asked, a hint of despair in his tone.

'If you hadn't known who she was before, I'd have said she's a very clever criminal who's used her brain to work her way up from small-time crime to the big league. I'd also guess she's being paid a six- or maybe even seven-figure sum for this. It probably depends on the ultimate street value of the drugs, but the painting provides collateral of at least a couple of million even at its reduced black-market value. If the uncut cocaine's worth the same, this is a significant operation. At least we now know for certain what the product is, although I'm not sure that helps.'

Jack rubbed his cheeks. 'Tia's in this for the money, then.'

'And maybe the thrill,' Tom responded. 'Who knows. But we need to do some serious rethinking.'

'First, I want to see if she'll lead us to Ava. Then we'll decide what to do.'

Jack turned back to his computer and started to type. It took less than a minute for him to crash his hands down on either side of the keyboard in frustration.

'*Fuck!* You were right. She's turned off or blocked her GPS. There are other options to track her but they take time, and my priority is to see that Ava's okay. Moretti said eight o'clock, but who knows whether they'll stick to that.'

'Can you access her camera?'

'I can only see black, so I'm guessing her phone's in her bag. There's sound, but nothing distinctive. No background chatter or even the distant chime of a bell from a clock tower or church. I'm guessing she's inside somewhere – perhaps still in her apartment.'

'If she's going to do the filming, she'll have to leave soon.' Tom leaped to his feet. 'She may have already left, but we know where she's staying and if her apartment's close to where Ava's being held, there might still be time. I'm going to see if I can find her and follow her.'

As Tom hurried towards the door, Jack shouted, 'Once you're near, call me and put your phone on speaker. I'll listen to both phones and try to identify any sounds that come through at the same moment, like a bell chiming or the blast of a vaporetto horn. It'll tell me if you're close to her.'

Tom nodded, slammed the door and hurried down the stairs. He didn't hold out much hope, but at least he'd be doing *something*.

54

Infiltrating this dark world and pursuing the life I now lead has been more dangerous than I could ever have imagined. I had to start at the bottom, working with small-time criminals, helping them launder money using skills I'd once utilised to catch people like them. Now I am on the other side, twisting the expertise I'd honed as an investigator. Each deal, every transaction, has felt like a betrayal of everything I once stood for. But I couldn't allow myself to look back. And I'm not sure I want to now.

I prowl around the apartment, knowing I have to go and see the girl very soon. I need to decide what to do. Renzo's ego is dragging us down and his recklessness could ruin everything I've worked for. At each stage of my journey, the people I've met have made my skin crawl with their arrogance, their casual disregard for laws, for lives. People like Renzo Moretti repulse me, but I have a job to do and I've played along, acted like one of them, maybe even become *one of them. And yet when all the pieces of a plan slot seamlessly into place, I experience a thrill I have no right to enjoy. Each risk feels sharper, more intense than the one before, blurring the lines between ambition and morality.*

Five minutes, and I'll have to leave. I gather the few things I need – my phone, money for the water taxi and… I walk over to the bedside table, pull open the drawer and stare inside, my hand hovering. Take it or leave it? I feel a flicker of unease, but I know there's no real choice. I grab the gun and push it deep into my bag.

Today, as every other day, I feel I'm balancing on a tightrope between obsession and fear, constantly looking over my shoulder, knowing that one slip could be my last. I have never allowed myself to get comfortable or show weakness and I'm not going to start now. I've had to stay sharp, keep my emotions buried deep, because no matter how immersed I've become, my goal has always been clear: to discover why you were taken from me, Alessandro. If that has meant losing pieces of myself in the process, so be it. And somewhere along the way, I've become good at this. Very good.

It's taken years for me to become a trusted fixer, handling not only the finances but the logistics of significant deals, and now I'm as close as I'll ever be to uncovering the truth. This has to be my last job – the one that ends it all and gives me answers.

There's so much at stake, but now Renzo is adding complications. His desperation to prove himself makes him volatile, quick to resort to violence without a second thought. If this plan is to work, I need to control him. For now, I'll film the girl and then decide her fate.

Arranging her abduction and the kidnap of the remainder of the family was the most daring scheme I've ever orchestrated. I can't deny that I found it thrilling to see the plan come together perfectly.

But no one was supposed to die.

I need to fix this. To become indispensable to the 'ndrina's operations here in Venice, Renzo must first believe I have done everything he has asked, and if that means I have to sacrifice the girl, I won't have a choice. Collateral damage. I've risked so much, I can't fail at the last moment, so maybe I need to accept the inevitable. Hers is only one life, after all.

I hover by the table, delaying the moment I have to leave, staring at my master plan – a complex web of codes and symbols indecipherable to anyone else. I tap my finger on the first hieroglyph – a symbol that relates to the date, eight months ago, when Renzo Moretti made contact. 'You're a fixer, a broker, I'm told,' he'd said.

I remember the thrill of the moment, the struggle to remain calm. I was about to move one step closer to where I needed to be.

The first time I met Moretti, a man I disliked on sight with his thin lips and eyes like pebbles, he thought he could touch me, that it was his right. I met his gaze with cold, unwavering eyes and the contempt in my expression made him back off. Without a word, I made it clear that trying the same thing again would be a mistake. Since then, he hasn't dared test me.

I wanted him to see the real me – the person who distrusts everyone, who is always watching, focused and reserved, and my aloofness seems to have convinced him that I'm exactly the cold, hard person he needs.

Renzo Moretti's plan is big. Through his future wife, Renzo wants his crew to be accepted by the local 'ndrina – to become part of the mighty 'Ndrangheta. Until recently, the Morettis have been nothing more than small-time crooks, importing small quantities of MDMA from the Netherlands. Ecstasy has a market, but the users come and go. Cocaine addicts are more consistent, offering a reliable income. And Renzo wants to be a serious player. He's been tasked with managing the importation of a shipment of cocaine, then cutting and selling it. Contarini will meet the up-front costs with the cartels, but he needs a guarantee that Moretti can repay that money on demand. That's why the theft of the painting must go without a hitch. And when the money is paid off, Contarini will keep the painting. It's D'Angelo's favourite, and I've heard Contarini covets anything that belongs to Vittorio D'Angelo – including his wife.

Renzo's plan offers me the perfect opportunity to be seen as vital to those in real power – the Contarini family. They need to know me, to trust me, to invite me to work for them. Only then will I stand a chance of finding you, Alessandro. Because I'm certain Bruno Contarini is at the centre of your disappearance. I've always believed that.

To win Contarini's trust, I've persuaded Renzo to break a cardinal rule – one the 'Ndrangheta won't forgive. I've convinced him to add a tiny amount of an extra ingredient to the drugs, assured him that Contarini will never know, so his profits will be sky high.

But Contarini will know. Because I will tell him.

That is the penultimate hieroglyph on my plan.

Then, maybe he'll trust me, allow me to work for him. Someone in his inner circle must know what happened to you. I'll find out, the last box will be ticked and the war will be won.

I throw my bag over my shoulder and head for the door.

55

Tom walked quickly towards the small square where he'd seen Tia sitting outside the *osteria*. Was that only the night before? He knew finding her was a long shot, but while Jack could perform magic with his technology, Tom could at least attempt some traditional police work.

He was struggling with the idea that, in trying to save Ava, they were simultaneously facilitating the distribution of cocaine – a drug at the centre of a war waged by police the world over. He tried to justify their actions by telling himself that the drugs would be shipped anyway – if not by Moretti, then by Contarini – but to say he was uncomfortable with his part in it was an understatement.

As he walked, he gazed around, scanning every woman who passed. He remembered Tia's hair – thick, wavy, dark. Her posture – tall and upright – might make her stand out, and he expected her to be walking alone. If he passed her he would recognise her, but what were the chances of that happening?

Fighting back his frustration, Tom headed towards her apartment building, his mind filled with dark thoughts of what might be happening to Ava. Renzo believed he didn't need her as a bargaining tool – that he could use Clare, Billy and Sophia to make Jack do as he wanted – so what would Tia do? Would she give Ava to the Albanians, knowing she would be trafficked? Would Renzo threaten to have Clare and the children killed?

Tom's instinct was to have Greater Manchester Police rescue the family as soon as Becky confirmed they were at the mill, but if Moretti discovered any police involvement and Ava was still under his control she would disappear, one way or another. Renzo would relish the thought of revenge.

In Tom's mind, the best plan was to rescue the family during the theft of the painting. That way, Renzo's only bargaining chip would be Ava. If he wanted the painting, he would have to release her.

But what if it was too late? What if she'd already been handed over to the Albanians?

'Tom, you there?' Jack's voice came through his phone speaker, bringing him back to the here and now.

'I am. Have you heard anything?'

'She's on the move but her phone's still in her bag. She left the apartment less than a minute ago – I heard the *ping* of the lift. I think she's close to a canal. Sorry – that's what's known as stating the bleeding obvious in Venice, but it's very close to the apartment building and I think it's a *wide* canal. I heard an ambulance boat, and it seemed to be travelling at speed. That suggests it's one of the major canals, but it's just a guess.'

'Okay, I'm very close to where she's been staying. If she's still in the area, maybe Ava's close by. Tia hasn't got much time if she's going to meet the deadline.'

'If...' Jack said. 'I don't think either of them care too much about that. They believe they have this in the bag.'

'Well, they don't know the Douglas brothers, do they? We're going to fix this, Jack. Listen, I've just reached the closest access point to a major canal near her apartment. There's a path alongside the canal here, and I'll...'

Tom paused and glanced to his right. *Was that Tia?*

'Shit!' he hissed. She was just ten metres away, stepping into a water taxi. 'Jack, I can see her, but I can't follow her.'

Tia was facing away, her back to him, and Tom darted to the

edge of the canal, searching for another taxi. The wide waterway was busy, but every boat was occupied, and her taxi was already edging away from the dock. Tom debated trying to follow her on foot, but the labyrinth of narrower canals and bridges would make it impossible to keep up. He watched, frustrated and helpless, as her boat picked up speed.

Then, as if sensing Tom's eyes on her back, she turned around. Her gaze locked onto his.

Slowly, deliberately, Tia reached into her bag, then raised her phone and aimed it at him.

56

Who is that man? It can't be chance that I've come into contact with him two nights in a row. Is he the man who came briefly into the bar too? Is that why he seemed familiar?

Whoever he is, whether I'm right that he's following me or it's merely a coincidence, I need to know. He has to be dealt with.

I'm about to forward the photo to Renzo to get his crew to chase the man down when I have another thought. Renzo might decide that somehow I'm to blame if someone's following me, and I can't have that. I have a better idea, so I put the phone back in my bag.

Nothing can go wrong. This is my moment, and this man – whoever he is – isn't going to ruin it.

As the boat cuts slowly through the water, I think back to the months before you disappeared, Alessandro. Your job had always taken so much of your time, so much of your mind. I would watch you sometimes as you stared at the television without seeing it, opened a book but never turned a page, how you practically had to shake yourself back into the present when I spoke to you. I understood, or I thought I did. You were dealing with vast sums and your clients had such high expectations. People think wealth management is one of those jobs where the rewards exceed the effort required. Having lived with you, I know that isn't true.

You were always stressed, knowing that unless you followed the *markets obsessively, you would lose money for your clients. In those last months you were more anxious than I had ever seen you. I looked over your shoulder once when you were working in the kitchen. The number of zeros on each line of the spreadsheet was breathtaking, and you slammed the laptop closed when you realised I was looking.*

'You can't see this,' you told me. And I understood. You had a duty of confidentiality and had to comply with strict financial regulations. Even an accidental leak could cause you serious problems.

'Sorry,' I said. 'But I'm the last person to spread rumours about invest-ments; it's my job to investigate wrongdoing, Alessandro. If it helps you to tell me what's causing you so much stress, you know you can trust me.'

'It's just a difficult client,' you said.

What you didn't know is that I'd seen the name at the top of your screen: Bruno Contarini. And an address that I didn't have time to read – only 'Venice' jumped out. Contarini was your client.

Did you know you were working for the Mafia?

57

Tom's shoulders slumped as the water taxi vanished. He'd been so desperate to stick with her, to find Ava, that he'd broken every rule of surveillance and now she had his photo.

'Bloody *idiot!*' he hissed.

What would Tia Rukavina be thinking now? She'd be in no doubt that he was following her – or at least trying to – and that when he'd sat at her table at the *osteria* it wasn't just a chance encounter. Where did that leave them?

And what about the photo? Was he going to be on a Mafia hit list now?

The answer was *probably*. He had to find a way to manage that risk. He couldn't disappear, so he'd have to disguise himself. Hurrying back towards Jack's room, he thanked God that the shops in this city stayed open late.

Armed with a bag full of slightly random purchases based almost entirely on the clothes of the American tourists mooching around the shops, Tom ran up the stairs and thrust open the door. As always, Jack's eyes were fixed on the monitors.

'I'm sorry, Jack. Not only did I lose her, but she saw me.' Tom had decided on the way back not to mention the photograph. The last thing Jack needed was to have to worry about his brother's safety on top of everything else.

'I know. I saw the photo.'

Of course he did.

Jack looked over his shoulder. 'You okay?'

'No, I'm furious with myself but I'm now the proud owner of three Hawaiian shirts, two baseball caps in different colours, plus a straw fedora and a couple of pairs of ridiculous sunglasses. She'll have trouble picking me out from the sightseeing crowd in these, and it's the best I can do.'

Jack merely nodded and turned back to his screens. There were bigger things to worry about.

'Come here,' Jack said, signalling over his shoulder. 'She's taken her phone out of her bag, but she's already inside a building. I guess it's a cellar of some sort, because there's not much light and I can't see any windows. She must be gesturing with her arms as she talks, waving her phone around, because the picture's all over the place. How many minutes since you saw her?'

Tom checked his watch. 'Seventeen,' he said. 'I spent five minutes grabbing stuff off shelves, which delayed me a bit. She was on the Canale di Cannaregio. I don't know if, or where, she turned off down a narrower one. We can come up with a search radius, but nothing specific.'

'Okay, let's park that and listen. I'm recording it so we can analyse it later.'

Tia was speaking to someone in English. Tom sense a hint of tension in her voice and wondered what was causing it. The woman he had met the night before had seemed unflappable. Was it because she'd recognised him? He glanced at Jack, whose eyes were locked on the screen, waiting to see Ava. Knowing she was safe – for now, at least – was a priority, but was Tia going to follow Renzo's order and hand Ava over to the Albanians? The thought filled him with dread.

Tia now appeared to be in another room. They couldn't see Ava, but Tia was speaking. 'I told you to look after the girl properly! What part of that did you not understand? She's our leverage.'

As the image jittered around, they caught glimpses of a room with a makeshift bed in one corner. Then, suddenly, there she was. Tom heard a quick intake of breath from Jack.

If he hadn't known for sure that this was Ava, Tom might have struggled to recognise her. Her blonde hair hung in tangled, greasy strands; her skin was pale and sallow with smudges of dirt on her face and arms. But despite her eyes being hollow with fear and exhaustion, there was a glimmer of defiance in her expression and she was sitting up straight, not cowering.

The camera swung away as Tia turned to face two men. 'Clean this place up. Straighten that bed, give her some water to wash her face. But don't touch her, Besnik.'

One of the men bore a defiant expression – Besnik, Tom assumed; a skinny man with a long body and short legs. The other man, bigger, stronger, had disappeared from shot.

'Arjan, tell me you've kept Besnik's grubby hands off her.'

Jack didn't speak, but his fingers curled into tight fists. Tom could see his eyes glinting in the reflection from the monitor. How he was holding it together, Tom didn't know.

When the big man spoke, his speech had a slight staccato rhythm and a sharp, clipped accent. This had to be Arjan Kodra.

'What's the deal? She could bring good money.'

'Not until this is over,' Tia said. 'Whatever I decide, she's to remain unharmed until I say otherwise. I need to video her and then I've got a job for you, Kodra. There's a man I need you to find.'

Tom swallowed hard, but neither he nor Jack could take their eyes off the screen.

'You make big mistake if you don't let me sell her. I keep her safe from Besnik because, who knows, maybe she's still virgin. Better price.'

Jack turned to Tom, his eyes dark with rage. 'I know you said no violence, Tom, but if I ever meet that bastard, you're going to have to stop me from killing him.'

58

Ava's head is pounding. She was unconscious for no more than a few seconds after Skinny Guy grabbed her ankle, but it was long enough to ruin her chance of escape.

As she came round, she'd heard shouting. Big Guy must have returned, and she opened her eyes to see him drag Skinny Guy to his feet and fling him against the wall, yelling right into his face. She lay there, hoping they would forget about her. If she could just crawl through the door, she could lock them both in. But by the time she'd managed to get to her knees, Big Guy had yanked her up from the floor and thrown her onto the mattress.

That happened hours ago, and they haven't been back since. But then, just a few minutes ago, Ava heard the woman's voice again, and now everything feels different. The woman is here in the room but keeping her distance, as if Ava is contagious, and she realises that if she was hoping for a saviour, she hasn't found one.

The woman is talking quietly. Ava can't catch every word, but she's speaking English, so the two guys obviously understood her when she begged them to let her go.

Ava hears Big Guy say something about a virgin and a price, and goosebumps prickle her skin. He's talking about her. She realises he didn't keep her safe from Skinny Guy to protect her; he did it to get more money for her. Unsoiled goods.

Skinny Guy thrusts a bottle of water and a grimy cloth at her, but it's the woman who speaks.

'Clean yourself up. I'm going to film you for your father.'

A sharp breath catches in Ava's throat.

He's looking for me! He hasn't forgotten me!

She feels light-headed with relief. She hasn't been abandoned. How could she have doubted him? The thought makes defiance rise inside her like a wave.

'Why should I? He knows you've been holding me for weeks, so he's not going to expect me to look like a movie star, is he?'

The woman tuts. 'Just do it.'

Ava leans forward. 'What if I won't make your crappy video?'

Her mind is spinning. She's seen this before – using a video to prove a hostage is alive. The woman says it's for Dad – but why? Ransom? He doesn't have that sort of money, as far as she knows. It must be something else – something they want him to do for them. That's how it usually works.

Do they know who he is? Do they know who I am?

'What is it you're making him do?' Ava's taking a gamble, but she's got nothing to lose.

The woman's eyes narrow. She has no idea what to make of her, and Ava feels a flicker of satisfaction.

'And what would you know about that?' the woman asks.

Ava forces a laugh, but it sounds brittle. 'More than you can ever imagine. Whatever you think you're doing, my dad's not going to let you get away with it. You do know that, don't you? And I'm not scared of you,' she continues, flicking her gaze to the two men. 'I've met worse than these two idiots.'

Despite her bravado, Ava's hands are clenched into fists so tight that her nails dig into her palms, but she keeps her gaze steady, praying the fear doesn't show in her eyes.

'Enough!' the woman says. 'I'm going to ask you some questions – ones your father has given us so he knows this isn't pre-recorded.'

Ava barks another fake laugh. 'You really don't know who you're messing with here. You don't know who he is, do you? My dad, I mean. If you did, you wouldn't be doing this.'

'I know he's not Ethan Blake, if that's what you mean. I know his name is Peter Johnson.'

'Hah,' Ava says, attempting a smug smile. 'As I said, you know nothing.'

Ava watches the woman's face. Confusion – just for a second. Her gamble has paid off.

'Be quiet!' the woman snaps, a hint of uncertainty in her voice. 'I'm going to ask you the questions he sent. Whether you answer them or not is up to you. He'll hear me ask them, see you on his screen, and he'll know you're alive. I'll edit out your nonsense before I send it to him.'

She starts with the questions, but Ava concentrates all her energy on staring at her, trying to make her uncomfortable. She refuses to answer, but the care and thoughtfulness in the wording of the questions starts to get to her, and when the woman reads out her dad's third question – the one about her coping techniques – Ava struggles to stifle a sob, remembering the hours he spent with her as she recovered from her past. She has to say something, and she looks straight at the camera on the woman's phone.

'Dad, if she's sent you this video and you're watching, do what you think is right.' Her voice cracks, and she coughs to clear her throat. 'That's what you've always told me. Don't worry about me. Whatever happens, I'll be fine. They took me because of who I am, and if I'd followed the rules, they wouldn't have been able to get to me, so—'

'Enough!' the woman shouts again, stopping the video. She takes a step towards Ava. 'What do you mean about being taken because of who you are?'

Ava pauses. Has she made a mistake? But then she smiles. 'It doesn't matter.'

Let this woman think what she likes. Let her worry. Let her think there's something Ava knows that she doesn't.

'Why do you think we might know who you are, or who your father is?'

Ava channels every ounce of anger and the scars of her past and jumps off the bed, her head jutting towards the woman. 'I've told you, it doesn't matter. So just fuck off, whatever your name is.'

Tom could only imagine what the last few minutes had done to Jack. The girl had so much spirit. He was reminded of the child she'd been all those years ago, when she'd first turned up in Clare's kitchen. Her words had stuck with him ever since:

When you come from where I do, what you're scared of is being thrown in The Pit, starved until you'd do anything – yeah, anything – for a piece of bread. Or worse, you're scared one of the big guys – the real evil bastards – is going to deal with you. Do you know what they call these men? No, I bet you don't. They call them enforcers.

The love of her new family had softened Ava over the years, but the defiance she had once relied on was still there, even if it seemed less convincing.

'Careful, sweetheart,' Jack had muttered when Ava made it clear she understood the purpose of the video. Would most girls her age know that?

They hadn't been able to see Tia because the camera was pointing at Ava, but they heard her scoff – a red rag to a bull for Ava. She wasn't going to be put down by anyone. Her apparent confidence was impressive, but Jack had zoomed in on her hands and they had seen her white knuckles, her fingers locked tightly together. She must have been drawing on every coping technique she'd ever learned.

And then she'd dropped the bombshell. 'You don't know who he is, do you?'

Jack had groaned. 'Stop talking, Ava, darling. Please just stop talking.'

They had watched in silence, listening as Tia demanded to know about Ava's dad.

But the girl hadn't given an inch, and Tom had another flashback to the thirteen-year-old Ava – or Tasha, as she was then – telling everyone, including Tom, to fuck off.

So defiant, so brave, so very damaged.

59

Getting nothing further from Ava, Tia had finally left the room – and Jack's face clearly said he needed a moment.

At least they knew Ava was not only alive but also in Venice, which felt like good news. Less welcome was the fact that the Albanians obviously thought they might be able to profit from trafficking her, and apart from insisting that she be kept safe for now, Tia hadn't given any indication of what she planned to do with her.

The feed from Tia's phone was still running, but there was nothing to see. It must have gone back into her bag.

Jack's phone pinged with a message, snapping him out of whatever dark thoughts he was lost in.

'They're going to send a link to the video,' he said. 'They'll edit it so we won't hear everything Ava said.' He pushed his chair back from the desk. 'That was probably the most harrowing few minutes I've experienced in a long time, Tom. I understand why she said the things she did, but I already had the feeling Tia was wondering about me. I'm not the tech geek she was expecting. She knows Ethan Blake isn't my real name, given her Albanian crew identified Ava *Johnson* as my daughter. But now she's going to delve even deeper into my past – and Ava's – to see what she can dredge up.'

'But what's she going to find? Nothing, I'd guess.'

'Absolutely. And if I were her, that would make me even more suspicious.'

There was no answer to that.

'What now?' Tom asked. 'What if I go to where Tia's staying, wait for her and catch her off guard?'

'And do what? Try to force her to tell us where Ava is? How? You've got no jurisdiction here, Tom. You can't arrest her, so what *can* you do? Threaten her in the street? Break your own rules and throttle her until she tells you the truth? If she feels cornered it could push her into making a rash decision, and you heard what she said. She wants Arjan Kodra to find a man. I guess that's you.'

Jack was right, but they'd seen Kodra's face on video so Tom would recognise him, and at least she hadn't asked Renzo to send the 'Ndrangheta after him.

'Why do you think she's asked Kodra, not Renzo?'

'Because as the fixer she can't be bringing problems to him. Her job is solutions, and if she's done all the important stuff he probably doesn't need her any more. He'd just have her taken out.'

'Marvellous,' Tom said, a sour tone to his voice.

He walked over to the window and looked down at the canal in the fading light, trying to clear his mind. There had to be a solution.

He spun back towards his brother. 'What if I let her know we're ahead of the game, show her how much we know?'

Jack shook his head. 'She's working for the Mafia, Tom. She'll do whatever's necessary to protect herself, even if that means handing Ava over to those fucking Albanians. We have to let her think she's still in control. We can monitor her, keep eyes on everything she does while we work out our next move.'

One glance at the haunted despair on Jack's face told Tom it was time to stop pushing. 'How do you want to play this?'

'I'm trying to look at this dispassionately,' Jack said, the words belying his expression. 'There's a significant mismatch between what they *think* we know and what we *actually* know. As far as Renzo's concerned, I may have seen his weasel face, but he doesn't think I know his name or anything about Elena-slash-Tia. Nor should I know the heist is tied to a drug shipment. He'll also think the video of Ava can't be used as evidence because the link will have a one-time-only access code, with no option to download the clip. He has no idea we have it all. Every instruction to me has come from burner phones that will be destroyed, but each message is recorded. Basically, Renzo thinks we have nothing.'

Tom agreed. 'But, in fact, we know all the players including the Albanians, and we have the video and audio recordings grabbed via Tia's phone. We need to find a way to exploit that knowledge. Normally, I'd say we have everything we need to hand the bastard in, except we still don't know where Ava is.'

'And I'm increasingly certain he's not planning to let her go. He thinks he can force me to do as he wants by revealing he has the rest of my family.'

'Tempting as it is to move in and rescue them now, if Renzo found out – which is more than likely – the situation for Ava would worsen,' Tom said.

'Yep.'

Tom hesitated, then said quietly, 'There's another concern I need to raise, Jack. We're assuming Renzo's threat is just to your family, but—'

'But he's going to turn up at the palazzo with his men, and they'll be armed. I know. He always has the option to put a gun to my head. I've known that from the beginning, which is why I'm glad you're here.'

'You want *me* to go and meet Renzo?'

Jack gave a weak smile at the unease in Tom's voice. 'No, you'll be somewhere else, waiting for Ava at an agreed handover location. When you have her, I'll let his crew out. Probably.'

Tom was puzzled. 'Is this the plan you didn't think I would like? Doesn't sound too tricky.'

Jack gave a strained smile. 'It's just part of it.'

60

With the clock showing just thirty hours until the heist, for Tom and Jack the rest of the night stretched ominously ahead, filled with nothing but anxious waiting. It was only eight o'clock in England, and Philippa couldn't even think of asking TSU to approach the derelict mill to insert audio and video feeds until it was fully dark.

'Why don't you get some rest, Jack?' Tom suggested. 'There's not much we can do until we know more. Both of us would think better after a couple of hours' sleep.'

'You have the sofa, I'll take the floor,' Jack said.

'Of course you won't. I'll go back to the hotel for a while.'

'You sure about that? Tia's got Kodra looking for you, don't forget.'

'I haven't forgotten, but she's only just given him the photo and he won't know where to start. I'll change into my tourist outfit before I go, and I'll be careful. I don't think I need to worry until tomorrow.'

Jack just gave him a dark look.

Tom conjured up his best effort at a confident expression. 'I'll ask Philippa to call me when they're about to make a move in Heywood. Once we know the situation at the mill we can decide what to do, but for all the reasons we've mentioned, a rescue operation tonight might not be the best idea.'

'I guess you're right, but how would you feel if it was Louisa and Harry?'

'Frantic, petrified, I can't even put it into words. Of *course* I'd want them rescued instantly. But I think – and I can't possibly know this without being in your position – if I knew they were being monitored, with police ready to leap into action at the first sign of a problem, I'd try to weigh up the risks. If Lucy was in Ava's position, I'd see her situation as the more precarious. Maybe plan for her rescue while monitoring the others.'

Jack tutted. 'Easy to say.'

Tom bit his bottom lip. 'I'm sorry this is happening, Jack. But there are decisions to be made, each one a bastard of a choice, and I can't make them for you. If you want me to stay and talk everything over some more, as many times as you like, it's not a problem. But I honestly think you could do with some time alone without me lurking around trying to be useful.'

Jack attempted a smile. 'Yeah, you're a bit of a lurker, but I'm glad you're here. There's one thing we need to sort for tomorrow. I'm guessing you didn't think to bring black tie with you?'

'What, a dinner jacket? I hardly thought it a priority, no.'

'Well, we need something to go with those masks you bought us. We can't go to the reception in jeans, can we? So that's tomorrow's task.'

Tom gave Jack a puzzled look. 'And tell me why, exactly, we need to go to the reception?'

Jack shook his head. 'I still have some details to work out in my head, but all will become clear when we've established what's happening to my family. Until then, go and sleep. Tomorrow is going to be a very long day – and night.'

Despite his exhaustion, it had taken Tom a long time to fall asleep and he'd only managed about three hours when his mobile pinged with a message. He sat up and rubbed his eyes. It was three in the morning.

Call me. PS.

Philippa. He was instantly awake.

'What news?' he said before she had a chance to speak.

'They're in the mill, Tom. We've seen all three of them. They're well and don't appear to have been mistreated. The men with them are confirmed as speaking Albanian, although we don't recognise any of them. We'll get the ROCU team onto that as soon as we can.'

'You got audio and video feeds in?'

'We did. Fortunately, the disused offshoot of the Rochdale Canal provided a handy approach along the tow path. The video feed was sent to Becky, and she's confirmed Clare's identity. She couldn't be specific about the children and, Jack being Jack, there are no photos of them online. However, it would be bizarre if Clare had been taken with another little boy and a toddler.'

'How many men?'

'We saw two. One is armed, so we've got Firearms on alert, standing by. What's your thinking, Tom?'

How was he supposed to answer that? There was only so much he could tell Philippa.

'Ava's here in Venice. We've seen a video of her. She's being guarded by two Albanians. Their names are Kodra and Besnik, but that's all we have. The woman – Tia Rukavina – is involved too. From what we can gather, she was at the centre of both abductions. She's the one who set it up with the Albanians.'

Philippa made a 'Huh' sound. 'I'm relieved I didn't use my contacts to try to find out which department she'd gone undercover with, then. I assume you think she's gone rogue?'

'I can't think of any other explanation. What we do know is that the man who's behind all of this wants Ava to be handed over to the Albanians, to dispose of as they see fit.'

'Christ! We know what that means.'

Philippa rarely used any form of expletive, so it was clear she shared Tom's horror of what might happen to the girl.

'Given Ava's situation, if we extract Jack's family now then the top guy will know, and there's every chance that will be the end of Ava,' said Tom.

'And you've considered—'

'Don't, Philippa,' Tom interrupted. 'Jack won't go near the Italian police. This is the Mafia we're dealing with, and who knows how many people they have in their pockets.'

'I know you don't want to tell me what's happening, Tom, and I understand it's better if I don't know. But what's the timescale here?'

'I think the action will take place during the early hours of Tuesday morning, just over twenty-four hours from now. But I'll need to confirm that with Jack.'

'I'm wondering how we're going to know Ava's safe before we pull out the rest of the family. Given what you said about the Albanians, the timing seems critical.'

'I agree. Jack has a plan, but he hasn't yet divulged what it is – only that I'm not going to like it.'

Philippa tutted. 'You know what I'm going to say, Tom. Be careful. There are many things to weigh up here, not least your future in the police.'

Tom did know. But how was he supposed to balance the life of a seventeen-year-old girl against his own career? There was no contest.

61

I'm exhausted, and yet I can't sleep. I throw back the covers and walk over to the windows, throwing them open to the night air. The gentle lapping of the water below usually soothes me at this time of night when there's no one around, shouting, laughing, enjoying the city. But there's a restless energy churning inside me.

It's been a hell of a day. I wish Renzo hadn't insisted on meeting Blake. He only did it because he likes to flaunt his power, and I still don't know why Blake makes me so uncomfortable. Then there's the other one – the one who's following me. Is Renzo having me watched? The thought makes me uneasy. And yet the man was English. Is he a face from my past? Perhaps he works for Contarini, whose influence spreads far and wide. He'll know I'm Renzo's fixer. Perhaps he doesn't trust me.

Knowing what I do now about Contarini, I can only imagine what he demanded from you, Alessandro. Did he want you to launder his money? Did you find out what he was doing and threaten to report him, signing your own death warrant? Or did he want you to manage a slush fund to bribe public officials – something you couldn't bring yourself to do?

Now I know who he is, how he makes his money, the options for corrupt financial dealings are endless, and I have to wonder whether you paid with your life. Am I about to pay with mine?

Or did you choose to disappear to save me? Because I have no doubt *that if you hadn't obeyed Contarini's demands, there would have been a price to pay.*

When you didn't come home, I reported you missing to the police. They tried to help, but there was no trace of you. The last sighting was on CCTV, leaving the office. But you didn't go to the car park as you normally did. You walked down an alley that led to the back of the building. There was no CCTV there, just a narrow lane with little traffic.

And what did your message mean?

> I thought I could escape.
> I was wrong.

Had you made a mistake, thought you'd covered it up, but they came for you, made you pay?

If the stress had become too much and you wanted to escape the world for a while, I know you would eventually have come home to me. But there was no financial trail to follow, and if anyone could have tracked you, I could. The police pointed out that, given your job, you could have hidden money, but where would it have come from? We shared our bank accounts and nothing had been taken. It can only mean one thing: you are dead. And Contarini has to have been behind it.

You always said I was tenacious, and the search for answers has become addictive. I thought it might take a few months and I was prepared for that. But the longer it went on, the more obsessed I became – the more intoxicated by my own power.

A black gondola glides by below me, a couple seated in the back. To be out at this time of night it must be a private arrangement, perhaps a special occasion, and as I watch, the man turns and holds something in a small box out to the woman. In the still night air, I think I hear a gasp. Maybe he's proposing. I quietly close the windows and turn away, tears that I rarely allow flooding my eyes.

I'm envious of their joy, of how carefree they seem in contrast to my own inner turmoil. I know the choices I've made are far from ideal. I've broken too many laws, but I've never been directly responsible for hurting anyone. At least, not physically. Until now.

You could say that what I plan to do with the cocaine will harm many,

many people. But persuading Renzo to cut it in the way I've suggested gives me an angle to take to Contarini. He'll hate the fact that the 'Ndrangheta's code has been broken and will thank me – I hope – for bringing it to his attention.

There are more hurdles to jump, but I'm finally within touching distance of uncovering what happened to you. And when I do, I will use everything I have learned in these last few years to bring down anyone who hurt you.

62

Tom finally woke again just before 7 a.m., feeling not exactly rested, but not quite so frazzled with exhaustion. He'd called Jack as soon as the 3 a.m. conversation with Philippa ended, knowing his brother wouldn't have been able to sleep until he knew his family was alive, if not exactly safe. Tom had tried to sound positive.

'It's good news, Jack. We know where they are, and they're unharmed. The place is surrounded by police and Becky has eyes on Clare all the time. We only have to say the word and they'll be rescued.'

Jack wasn't convinced. 'On what planet is it good news to know my wife and kids are shut in an old mill with two fucking Albanians, at least one of whom has a gun?' he had asked. There wasn't much Tom could say to that.

'What do you want Becky's team to do? We could make an argument that if Clare, Billy and Sophia are rescued and taken out of the picture, Renzo will have no choice but to hand over Ava, if he wants the painting.'

'And equally, we could make an argument that as soon as he knows the police are involved – even if only in the UK – he'll freak out to the point where he abandons the plan completely and disposes of Ava.'

'Bad as things seem, I know you were fearing much worse for Clare and the kids, so perhaps now you can try to get a bit of sleep.' Tom's suggestion was greeted by a soft scoffing sound. 'You're going to need your wits about you, Jack. You may have pulled lots of all-nighters when you were in your twenties, but in case you've forgotten, you're a good deal older now.'

That had been the end of the conversation, and Tom had drifted back into a fitful sleep, waking to take a long cool shower in an attempt to bring himself back to life. He was on his second cup of coffee when Jack called.

'Meet me in Saint Mark's Square at ten,' he said. 'Sit at the table next to mine. When I get up, follow me. We're going shopping.' He hung up before Tom could ask how he was feeling. Given his brother's curtness, he suspected the answer would have been 'not great'.

With an hour or so before he needed to meet Jack, Tom found a pen and paper and started to jot down his thoughts. Whatever Jack's plan was – the one Tom wasn't going to like – every alternative had to be considered.

As he scribbled ideas, crossed them out and came up with new ones, the thing that kept striking him was that Tia Rukavina had become the weak point. She knew where Ava was and could be tied to the Albanians holding Jack's family in Heywood. If she realised how much they knew, she might agree to help them. On the other hand, she might do a runner, and then the situation would be even worse.

They knew where Tia was staying and had access to her phone, but Tom still had no idea what her game was. And they were running out of time.

63

Jack was already sitting outside a café when Tom arrived, looking worse than he had the day before, his eyes bloodshot, the skin around them dark and puffy.

The piazza was noisy, buzzing, and Jack picked up his phone, apparently taking a call. He spoke quietly without looking at Tom, who had sat down at the next table. 'Anything?'

Tom studied the menu. 'Update from Becky. Clare, Billy and Sophia had a quiet night – no major upsets. Sophia's a bit unsettled, but Billy's being stoic and playing the big brother. The team's holding fire until they know what we want to do.'

Jack rubbed the palm of one hand up and down his face, thick with two-day-old stubble.

'I know what I *want* to do, but I also know why it's not such a great idea. Let's get away from here. Follow me.'

Tom waited until Jack had paid for his coffee and headed across the square before getting up to follow him, carefully watching to see if anyone was paying him too much attention. He thought it unlikely that he'd be recognised, and was fairly certain that even Louisa would fail to pick him out of a crowd in the wildest of his new tourist outfits – a floral-patterned shirt, straw fedora and large sunglasses.

Trailing Jack into the quiet sanctuary of a small church, he glanced briefly at the ornate frescoes, but there was no time to stand and enjoy them. His brother was sitting halfway down, to the left of the aisle, and Tom took a seat next to him.

Jack didn't waste any time. 'No one will be looking for us here. The reason we're out in the open is because we need to get ourselves togged up for tonight. I've been listening to Tia's calls – she's going to be at the reception, so it's a good job we'll be wearing masks. Given the number of invitations that have gone out, it'll be a packed event, so hopefully she won't notice either of us. As far as we can, we should avoid her seeing us together.'

'Why are we going, exactly?'

'I'll get to that. Right now, my head is in a huge black hole, but where's yours, Tom?'

'I've been thinking through a few options, but I'm afraid nothing I've come up with is perfect.'

Jack gave a frustrated shrug. 'Don't you think I've been through all the possibilities?'

'I'm sure you have, but let's check we haven't missed anything.' Tom took a breath. 'We know who Tia is, we know where she's staying, and we have evidence on messages and video of what they plan to do with Ava. For the sake of considering every option, I could ask if Philippa – through her sources – can find someone in the local force or the *carabinieri* who she believes she can trust.'

Jack gave a mocking smile. 'How did I know you'd start with the police? It's going to take more than one trustworthy connection of Philippa's to locate Ava. It'll take a team – and even if Renzo doesn't have eyes and ears in the police, Bruno Contarini will have. The minute they know we've reported this – and I'm as sure as I can be that they *will* know – then Ava is dead or trafficked.'

Tom had been expecting this.

'Okay. I find it hard to believe I'm saying this, but I agree.' He ignored the look of surprise on Jack's face. 'Option two: we carry on as planned but we extract Clare, Billy and Sophia today – this morning – to make sure they're safe. The Albanians can be arrested and coerced into telling us where their fellow gang members are – the ones here in Venice who have Ava.'

Jack shook his head. 'I can't begin to tell you how appealing that is, but I doubt they know where Kodra is holding Ava. Tia will be in touch with the guys in Heywood, and the minute they go silent, they'll realise the police are involved and we won't be able to save Ava. Next!'

'The only other option I came up with is to offer Tia a deal: she helps us rescue Ava, and we double whatever sum she's being paid by Renzo. The money's there, Jack.'

Jack looked sceptical. 'It's promising, but if she thinks she's cornered she could just disappear – she's bound to have an escape plan. Then I doubt we'd *ever* find Ava.'

Tom smothered a grunt of frustration.

'I know it's not without problems, but I think it's the most risk-free solution. Without understanding why Tia switched from investigator to criminal mastermind, I agree it's a gamble, but is it any riskier than the plan we've got?'

Tom paused to see if Jack had anything to add, but the two lines between his brows suggested he wasn't convinced.

'Then I'm out of ideas,' Tom said, his shoulders sagging. 'I guess that leaves us with the plan we already discussed: you control the heist, Clare and the kids are rescued while it's happening, and you demand Ava is handed over to me before you let his guys out of the building. But there's still so much that could go wrong, not to mention Renzo putting a bloody gun to your head.' He paused, racking his brain for a solution, but drew a complete blank. 'Sorry I couldn't come up with anything better.'

Jack turned towards him, a half-smile on his lips that didn't quite make it to his eyes. 'Then I'll give you a chance to redeem yourself. We're *kind of* going to go ahead with that plan, but we're not going to leave it to Renzo's goons to steal the painting. There's only one sensible option, Tom. *You're* going to steal it.'

64

In less than twenty-four hours, this will all be over – at least, the dangerous part. But suddenly I'm nervous. There are too many factors in play that I don't understand.

Having finally nodded off at about five, I've overslept. I push myself out of bed and head to the shower, my head spinning.

This should have been so straightforward – do whatever is necessary to help Renzo get a toehold in the 'Ndrangheta, persuade him to maximise his profits by adding a little extra into the mix, then expose what he's done to Bruno Contarini.

I've never worried about what Contarini would do to Renzo. He's a small-time thug who doesn't care who gets hurt. My only aim has always been to get close to the capobastone. If I can prove my loyalty and penetrate his inner circle, I can only hope that eventually someone will boast about what happens to those who defy them and let slip the truths that could lead me to understanding what happened to you, Alessandro.

But suddenly everything is more complicated. The girl – Ava – hints at another side to her father. Is this just a daughter thinking her dad is a warrior? Or is there genuinely more to him? There's something – I knew that when I watched him through the mirror – but all my searches have come to nothing, no matter how deep I've gone. And Ava's less terrified than I would have expected. She should be hysterical, but there's a defiance that surprises me.

What am I missing?

Pushing these thoughts aside, at least for now, I get dressed, ready for the day – and more importantly, the night – ahead. But as I make myself a double espresso in an attempt to drive the fog from my brain, my mind goes back to Renzo's demands. He wants me to hand the girl over to Kodra. He thinks she no longer matters, since I arranged for Blake's wife and children to be taken too. He imagines that when Blake demands Ava's release, he can taunt him by showing photos of the rest of his family, then tell him he'll never see Ava again.

Renzo really doesn't get it. The Mafia's power hinges on the certainty that, if targets do as they are told, a kidnap victim will be returned. Without that assurance, Mafia threats are empty words and their power diminishes. No one's going to comply with their demands if they believe the only thing likely to be returned to them is a corpse. Maybe I should do as he asks. It would be another black mark against Renzo's name with Contarini, but probably a black mark against mine as well.

Then there's the man who spoke to me in the osteria the night before last. I knew there was something off about him – the way he hung around even when I told him to go away. And there he was last night, by the pontile when the motor taxi picked me up, trying to hail another boat. I've given his photo to Kodra, told him to find him. But where's he going to start in tourist-filled Venice?

I can't shake the feeling that I'm no longer fully in control, and this makes me uneasy.

I take a seat at the table, staring at my master plan. I'm certain I've left no stone unturned. The shipment is all arranged and the product will be released when Renzo has the painting. Contarini is bound to be impressed with my organisational skills, but he'd be less impressed if he knew about the other chemicals already in the cut house. He mustn't find out – at least, not yet.

The cocaine will take a month to arrive, then the powder has to be cut before it goes out to the dealers to sell. The wait will be agony, but when I finally go to Bruno Contarini and declare my horror that Renzo is undermining the reputation of the mighty 'Ndrangheta, it will all have been worth it. I have all the proof I need, and there's no way of tying any of it to me. I wasn't a forensic accountant for nothing, and I can demonstrate how the extras were paid for. Apparently.

As soon as we have the painting, I'll negotiate the release of the product from the warehouse in Guatemala with Contarini's nephew. Renzo curled his lip when he told me I have to do that; he's not happy that we've been asked to deal with someone other than the main man. But that's Renzo. Does he really think the boss is going to interest himself in the finer details?

I'm supposed to meet the nephew at the palazzo tonight, during the reception. As a so-called insurance assessor I have an invitation to the event, and Bruno Contarini will be there with his entourage. He's invited to every significant event in the city, the rich and powerful eager to show him the deference he believes he deserves. They tread carefully around him, scared of provoking retaliation for any perceived slight. Even Vittorio D'Angelo, despite his wealth, doesn't appear to be exempt from that rule, and I can't help wondering if that includes turning a blind eye to the capobastone's relationship with his wife.

I've been told I'll be approached and introduced to the nephew. I must outline the plans for safe storage of the painting so he knows the debt will be paid.

On the face of it, everything is going to plan, but I have a nagging feeling that something is going to go wrong.

I can't allow myself to fail. I've tried so hard, done so many things I'm not proud of. It's all so close, and whatever it takes, this has to go the way I want it to.

65

Tom was speechless. Had he heard right? Did Jack really want him to steal the painting? *What the hell was he thinking?*

Jack stood up and turned towards the aisle.

'Hang on!' Tom hissed. 'You can't drop a bombshell like that and walk away.'

Jack looked down at him with a hollow smile. 'While that big brain of yours takes it in, we'll go and get ourselves togged up for the reception. We'll be safe in the tailor's, then we'll go back to the room and make plans. Follow me, but not too close. We'll talk when we're back.' With that, he headed towards the exit.

'Christ, Jack,' Tom muttered to himself as he jumped to his feet and hurried to follow. What had got into his brother? What made him think that was an even *vaguely* acceptable option?

As he left the church, Tom could see Jack ahead and was tempted to catch up to have it out with him immediately. But being seen together would be a mistake, so he followed at a distance, heart pumping, trying to convince himself that his brother was joking. *Steal a painting!*

His mind was so wrapped up in his thoughts that he nearly missed Jack raising his phone to his mouth. Almost instantly, Tom's phone pinged with a text message.

Kodra

One word, but it was enough.

Resisting the temptation to stare wildly around, Tom concentrated his gaze on either side of Jack. He saw him immediately – the bigger of the two Albanians on the video. And he wasn't alone.

It was obvious that one man stood little chance of spotting a target among the crowds that thronged Venice, but the Albanian Mafia had a presence in Italy and Kodra must have called in some favours. There were two of them here, but how many others were scattered around the city, staring at their phones, checking faces as they passed, asking in cafés, hotels, restaurants? Would they go to his hotel? Was it safe to go back there? What were the odds of them finding where he was staying, with over four hundred hotels in Venice? And privacy laws in Italy were strict. In theory, if shown a photograph, reception staff should neither confirm nor deny if the person in the picture was a guest.

He couldn't turn back in case he attracted their attention, but with just fifty metres to go before he drew level with Kodra, a short woman holding a bright yellow umbrella above her head emerged from an alley, followed by a troop of tourists. From their accents he guessed they were Australians, and he slotted himself into the group, turning to the woman on his left, face away from Kodra, asking how she was enjoying Venice. She didn't seem even slightly surprised, and chattered happily to him until the Albanians were way behind them.

'Enjoy the rest of your stay,' Tom said with a smile, slipping out of the group and hurrying to catch up with Jack. The sooner he was off the street, the happier he would be.

Three minutes later, Tom followed Jack through a door into what appeared to be an upmarket men's outfitters. It took just twenty minutes to find trousers, dinner jackets, shirts and some soft leather shoes for Tom, Jack breaking the silence between them when it came to selecting their bow ties.

'We need to look as if we belong. A bit of flamboyance to draw attention away from a hired dinner jacket would be ideal,' he said, choosing a bow tie to match the mask Tom had picked for him – rich black velvet embellished with gold embroidery in an intricate pattern.

Tom went for a plain silver satin tie to complement his metallic mask, lacking the energy to search for anything more elaborate. His mind was consumed by Jack's revised plan and the gnawing fear that the streets were full of Albanian thugs, every one of them focused on hunting him down.

Leaving separately, they headed back to Jack's room, this time with Jack trailing behind to check if Tom was being followed.

The minute they were through the door, Tom – for want of something better to do – headed for the kettle, switched it on and turned to face Jack.

'Perhaps now you can tell me where the hell you've got the idea from that I should be the one to steal the painting. I know things are unbelievably stressful, Jack, and I can't begin to imagine how you're feeling, but this is complete bollocks. So let's forget your moment of madness and work on one of the other options.'

Jack sat down at his makeshift desk, swivelling his chair to face Tom.

'It's not a ridiculous idea, so hear me out. If we're in possession of the painting, I won't let Renzo get his hands on it until Ava's safe. He *needs* that painting if he's going to break into the big time. Think of the money he's going to make! He's not going to walk away from that.'

Tom had already done the maths and, if his assumptions were correct, Renzo's profit could run to tens of millions of dollars. Nevertheless, what Jack was asking him to do was unthinkable.

He poured boiling water over the unappealing coffee granules, gave each mug a stir and handed one to Jack, who sniffed it and pulled a face.

'But weren't we *already* in control of the situation if you're not planning to let them out until Ava's safe? He might believe he can play his trump card – Clare and the kids – but we'll have rescued them by then, so locking his men in until he frees Ava still works, doesn't it?'

Jack winced. 'Ah. I have to confess to a massive error of judgement. I was trying to be smart by telling him I wasn't going to let them out. In fact, I was stupid.'

'Why?'

'Because although the security team can't let Renzo's crew *into* the building – they don't have the authority – they *can* let them out. It's a precaution against fire or any other emergency, and my guess is that Renzo will have bribed or threatened one of the guards. If we're to have any leverage, the only option is for the painting to have already gone.'

Tom stared at Jack. *Had he lost his mind?* 'He'll just pull a bloody gun on you!'

Jack's mouth twisted at one corner. 'Which brings me to another job I have for you. The external locks of the palazzo can only be opened using a combination of an encrypted key fob – you know, like a car remote – plus a verification code sent to my phone. The key fob's proximity-based, which is why I need to be there, within a few metres of the entrance.'

'Christ. That sounds unbelievably risky. What's to stop them from killing you as soon as they're inside? They could take the key fob from you and let themselves out.'

'That wouldn't work. To let them out, I – or whoever they've paid – will have to remotely disable a control sequence which unlocks the doors in a very specific order, all within certain time limits. That's the bit I've threatened to withhold – the bit that I now think doesn't hold water.'

'In other words, if you let them in but they no longer need you to let them out, they might shoot you anyway. *Very* reassuring!'

'Exactly why we need to change the plan. You're not only going to steal the painting, you're also going to override the settings for the proximity lock. That way, I'll be able to control the locks without the key fob. When Renzo and his crew turn up, I'll tell him I'm not coming and that I'll open the doors remotely. He'll be annoyed, but he'll still think he holds all the cards. He thinks I'll let him in, his guys will get the painting, then whichever security guard he's paid will let him out.'

'And he doesn't have to free the hostages if he chooses not to, because he doesn't need you any longer.'

'Exactly, and given how angry he is with me, he's not going to let them go. That's why this new plan is our only option. I let his guys in, but the painting's gone. I then tell him he can have it, but only if he complies with my demands. And crucially, as I won't be there, he won't be able to use the gun-to-the-head option. We'll be totally in control of the situation.'

Ignoring his growing alarm at what he might have to do at some point in the next few hours, Tom tried to run through all the possible outcomes.

'If we've already extricated Clare and the kids by then, they'll be safe, but what about Ava? Will she even still be in Venice?'

'I'm banking on the fact that Tia seems to understand how crucial Ava could be. I'm monitoring every conversation, every word she mutters under her breath, every cough, every sneeze. I'll know if she tells Kodra to take her, and if that happens I'll have to switch to a much less secure plan. Until then, Ava is the only card Renzo will have left to play.'

'Why can't *you* go into the control room during the reception and fix the override switch, rather than having me do it?'

Jack shook his head. 'Security during the event will be massive. There'll be guards everywhere, and I have no excuse to go into the control room. Anyway, neither D'Angelo nor his daughter Gabriella know I'm in Venice, and it's best they don't find out, particularly if a painting goes missing. Once everyone's left the building, the guards are reduced to two because in theory the security is one hundred per cent infallible. They'll be in the office watching their screens. You'll have to get past them and into the control room without being seen, but I can help with that by monitoring the CCTV.'

Tom swallowed. 'Assuming this goes to plan, talk me through what happens when Moretti's crew arrives to steal the painting.'

'I contact Moretti and tell him that I'm letting his men into the palazzo. He'll tell me he wants me to be there with him, but I'll say I have better control from my computers. True, actually. They then make their way to the exhibition room and find the painting missing.'

'And Renzo goes ballistic.'

'Exactly. I tell him he can have the painting when Ava is returned to me. He plays what he thinks is his ace – Clare, Billy and Sophia.'

'And when he discovers they've been rescued?'

'We can't let him find that out immediately because he'll realise the police are involved and, given the potential loss of face in front of his men, he might decide to take revenge the only way he can – by killing Ava.'

'So...'

'The painting's gone. He needs me to hand it over to him. He'll try to contact the Albanians in Heywood, believing I'll be so horrified to discover he has my family that I'll tell him where the painting is. Your team will need to create some disruption to the signal so he thinks his guys have answered, but everything's distorted.'

'Signal jammer?'

'Yes, but not completely jammed. We need a broken signal, as if there's interference on the line. Renzo won't be able to prove he has my family once he gets cut off. I'll say I don't believe him. If he wants the painting he'll have no choice but to give me Ava. He'll be livid, but he'll think he can ultimately make me suffer by having the rest of my family killed. By the time he realises they're safe, we'll be long gone.'

Jack leaned towards Tom. 'He needs this painting, Tom. Even if it's only to avoid humiliation in front of Contarini. And that's why I believe stealing it ourselves is the safest way. It keeps things controlled. No stand-offs. No chance for the situation to spiral. No guns. Clare and the kids are rescued by your team. We get Ava. And only when every single member of my family is out of harm's way, he gets the painting.'

Tom shifted uncomfortably in his seat. *Could he do this?*

He thought of the version of Ava he'd seen in the video – her courage and defiance. In his mind he replaced her image with one of Lucy – filthy, terrified, cowering in that dank cellar.

He took a deep breath. 'Okay. What do I have to do?'

66

16:00:14. Time was ticking down. Tom was still absorbing the fact that he'd agreed to take part in the theft of a valuable painting when Jack's computer pinged.

'Tia's getting a call,' he said, turning to his monitor.

'Pronto,' Tia said. Jack fired up his translation software.

A: Where are we with the arrangements, Elena?

It was Renzo.

B: Which arrangements in particular?
A: The product.
B: Ready for shipping. As soon as Contarini is confident we can guarantee payment, the product will be released from the warehouse in Guatemala.

Jack's eyes met Tom's. The Guatemala contact was real.

A: And then?
B: It's moved from Puerto Barrios to Livingstone – less scrutinised and

easier access to smaller boats. Why are you asking me this, Renzo? Do you really need to understand every single part of the shipping arrangements?

There was a note of irritation in Tia's voice which, judging by Renzo's response, he was well aware of.

A: You're being paid to do this job, Elena. You need to remember who's in charge here.

Tom strongly suspected that Tia was, but she was resisting the temptation to point this out.

B: I've told you the route. If you want a map, Renzo, I'll give you one, although I'm not sure what good it would do you.
A: And the product is in coffee tins, as agreed.

There was a soft tut from Tia.

B: Yes. There are enough beans in each tin to mask the scent if sniffer dogs are used. But there are bribes in place along the route, so that's not a significant threat.

Jack raised his eyebrows. He didn't have to mention the word 'corruption' to Tom.

A: How long until it's with us?
B: Exactly the same as it's always been – between twenty and twenty-five days depending on sea conditions and issues with any of the officials we've bought off. They need to be in the right place at the right time.
A: And you'll confirm everything with Contarini's nephew tonight?
B: As already agreed.

Tom was surprised to hear tension in Tia's voice. To this point, he had thought her calm and in control. Something had rattled her.

A: When Blake turns up for the final play, you and my men will be standing by – and trust me, he'll do exactly what we ask. You know what to do when it's done. But get the girl out of Venice before then. We don't need her.

Renzo gave a little chuckle.

B: Bad move, Renzo. We don't let any of our assets go until we have the painting. You may think Blake will give in to your threats, but he's more likely to submit if he believes a member of his family is being hurt. A single scream from any of them will make him comply.

Tom saw Jack's hands curl into fists, his knuckles white.

With no more than a few more words about the plans, the call came to an end.

'How can a woman who once worked for the National Crime Agency have turned into a monster?' Jack asked. 'At least you can now see why my plan is the only option.'

'She didn't seem keen on the idea of handing Ava over to the Albanians, though. Perhaps she's biding her time, and when it's all done she'll let her go.'

'Bollocks, Tom. She *planned* everything! She's the one who recruited the Albanians. She's just smarter than fucking Renzo, that's all. She's keeping her options open.'

'And Ava? You said if you heard Tia give Kodra permission to take her, you'd switch to another plan. What does that mean?'

Jack dropped his head and stared at the floor. 'Plan A remains the default – make Renzo realise that handing Ava over is his only option. No Ava, no painting. I did consider if plan B should be the two of us tailing Tia, but with all these bloody canals, it's a waste of time. She can hop on a boat and she's lost to us.'

'It's not entirely safe for me to be out on the streets now either, and even if we found Ava, what would we do? Charge into that cellar empty-handed and face Kodra and Besnik, who'll definitely be armed? I know we dismissed the idea of trying to turn Tia, but should we totally give up on that?'

Jack nodded. 'That's my *actual* plan B. The minute I hear any suggestion that she's handing over Ava, I'll call and threaten her with exposure if she doesn't give me back my daughter.'

'And I'm guessing that's not plan A because she might run, leaving Ava for the Albanians to do as they please.'

'Exactly. It's risky, but if I hear her giving orders for that shit Kodra to take Ava, I'll tell her who I am, how she knows me, and present her with a list of very scary people whose names she'll know, saying they'll pursue her on my behalf. It would be news to all of them that I'm alive, but she doesn't need to know that. It's a last resort, because it exposes me and we'll have to move away again. But I'll do it if I have to.'

Tom closed his eyes, overwhelmed at the thought of losing Jack from his life again – this time perhaps forever.

Jack reached out and grabbed his forearm. 'Let's not start worrying about that yet, little brother. But trust me, if my research into Elena Ferraro is accurate, she'll be far more afraid of the trouble I can bring to her door than she'll be of the police.'

The brothers paused, each wrapped in his own thoughts for a moment, but there was still too much that Tom didn't understand.

'If you're not going to be with Renzo outside the palazzo, how's he going to get Ava back to you?'

'I'll tell him he has thirty minutes to take her to the Rialto market, where someone will be waiting. That someone is you, by the way. The market won't be open, but traders will be starting to arrive. There's a café that caters for them, and I can hack the CCTV on the building opposite to watch whoever brings her. There'll be people around, so I'm hoping that makes it unlikely anything bad will happen. When she's safe – when you have her – I'll tell Renzo where the painting is.'

Tom closed his eyes and went through the scenario in his head. It might just work.

'And if he doesn't comply?'

'If we don't get Ava back, I'll reveal everything we know – names, the whole plan, the links to Contarini, who will probably put a bullet in Renzo's head if he thinks he's been in any way discredited. It's going to work, Tom. It bloody well has to.'

For two hours, Tom and Jack focused on refining the plan for the theft of the painting, with Tom trying to convince himself that this was just like an undercover police operation. Jack seemed to have considered every detail, which should have been reassuring – but wasn't.

'We're both going to the reception tonight. All guests have an electronic pass on their phones to get in, and they have to swipe it again to get out, so the system knows everyone has left. But you're not going to leave, Tom. I'll fudge the exit pass.' Jack pulled up a floor plan of the palazzo. 'Here's where we go in. For the reception, guests will enter through the front door into the large foyer. The stairs ahead lead to the first floor, where the exhibition is. This—' Jack pointed to a room that covered about two thirds of the floor space, '—is the gallery. The smaller rooms on either side will house champagne bars, but the place will be teeming with waiters offering drinks and canapés.'

Tom studied the plan. It didn't seem there were many places to hide.

Jack pointed to an area in the top right. 'This isn't a room; it's a terrace. It'll be closed off for the evening because, like a lot of Italian buildings, there are steps outside – in this case, leading down to the canal.'

'Wouldn't it be easier for me just to come in that way, rather than go to the reception?'

Jack shook his head. 'There's a wrought-iron gate at the top of the stairs that can't be opened if the security system is armed, other than by a fire alarm triggered from inside the building. There are pressure sensors in case anyone is stupid enough to try to climb over and it will be armed all evening to prevent uninvited guests. I can't disarm the gate remotely, but I *can* open the door from the salon to the terrace.'

'How long will I have to wait?' Tom asked.

'I'll let you onto the terrace when the room is busy. The kitchen and waiting staff have to clear up after everyone leaves. Only when I know they're all out will I let you back in. Could be a couple of hours.'

Tom could only imagine what would be going through his head during that time, with nothing else to occupy his thoughts.

'The other thing you need to know is where you're going to hide the painting after you've taken it.'

Tom's head jerked up, his gaze switching from the building plan to Jack's face. 'Hide it?'

'Absolutely. The painting's never going to leave the building. You're just going to relocate it.'

Tom blew out a long breath. 'Thank God for that.'

Jack gave Tom a ghost of a smile and pointed to a room next to the kitchen. 'This is where you're going to put it, in a room full of recycling bins. At the back is a small office used by the events manager. There's a cupboard. You might have to turf some stuff out, but it's not a large painting, so you can make room.'

'And then?' Tom asked.

'I'll talk in your earpiece and guide you to the control room, tell you what to do, then get you out of the building. From there you'll come back here – it would be easiest by boat – and wait until it's time to go to the Rialto market.'

Tom felt his brain was going to explode. 'So in this plan I still collect Ava?'

'Yes, it has to be you. Is that a problem?'

'Hardly. It feels like the only honest thing I'm going to do all night.'

Jack grinned for what Tom felt was the first time in days. 'Let's go over it all one more time, and then I think you should get some sleep. We'll need to contact Philippa and ask her if the team in Heywood can work to our timings. I'll tell Renzo the heist is happening at three thirty, not four. I'll blame it on the CCTV replacement footage. That's bollocks, but he won't know. If Clare, Billy and Sophia can be extracted just before then – bearing in mind the one-hour time difference between here and the UK – I think we can pull this off.'

67

It felt weird to be walking through the streets of Venice surrounded by happy tourists when all Tom could think about were the dangers ahead, not to mention the threat posed by the bodies trawling the city for him. He'd changed shirts again, was now sporting a dark blue baseball cap, and was sticking to the busier areas, mingling with the crowds. He had no idea if his disguise would work, and he constantly had to resist the temptation to look over his shoulder. If anyone was watching, that would be a dead giveaway.

It was with trepidation that Tom pushed open the door to his hotel. What if they'd found out where he was staying?

'Good afternoon, Mr Douglas. Can we get you anything? Perhaps a selection of *pasticceria*?' the young receptionist asked.

'Thank you, that sounds good. And some coffee, please.' He attempted a nonchalant smile. 'Can I ask if anyone's been enquiring about me today?'

She gave him a puzzled frown. 'Enquiring about you?'

'Yes, perhaps showing you a photograph, asking if I'm staying here.'

Her back straightened. 'I can assure you, sir, that if anyone did, we would neither confirm nor deny your presence.'

'I'm sure you wouldn't. I apologise for asking.'

Taking his key and heading for the lift, he wondered what on earth she would be thinking. What sort of guest would be concerned about being tracked down? But her misgivings were the least of his concerns, and while he waited for his pastries to be delivered, he messaged Philippa. Within a few minutes, his phone rang.

'Tom, I'm here with DCI Robinson, DI Sims and DS Cumba,' Philippa said, and Tom felt a lump in his throat. The closest members of his team.

'Good afternoon, everyone. How are things looking in Heywood?'

'Hi, Tom.' It was Becky's voice, and Tom wished he could see her. All of them. 'Everyone's in place and the family's being constantly monitored. They're all fine at the moment. We just need to know when we can extract them.'

'For reasons I don't want to discuss, it would be perfect if you could get them out at 2.25 a.m. your time,' Tom said. 'Sorry it's so precise, but if it's too early it could cause things to get complicated at this end, and too late would be even worse.'

'Sir, DI Sims here.' Tom smiled. Only Keith would behave as if they were in a formal meeting. 'When we extract the family, what is the protocol for dealing with telecommunications? I'm referring to those of the perpetrators.'

It took Tom's addled brain a moment or two to realise Keith was talking about their phones. 'Don't disable them. One of them will probably receive a phone call just after 2.30 your time, with a request to switch to video. Our perpetrator here will want to know that the family is still under the control of the Albanians. We have some ideas of how that can be managed.'

Tom went through the suggestions about the video and the signal jammer.

'I see. We're going for obfuscation, then?' Keith said.

Tom smiled. 'Absolutely, Keith. We want the perpetrators to be clueless about what's going on in Heywood. We certainly don't want them to know the police are involved.'

'Understood.'

'Boss, we've got some intel on the family car.' It was Rob Cumba's voice, and Tom could picture him strolling restlessly round the room. 'We found it on an industrial estate not far from the access road to the services. The techies think someone hacked into the car's onboard computer remotely, exploiting a weakness in the car's wireless connection – maybe the navigation system – and triggered a false battery warning. Clare would have seen a message indicating the car battery was critically low, even though it wasn't. That's why she pulled into the service station. They must have taken her from there, then driven her car to where it wouldn't easily be found.'

Tom grunted with frustration. Was nothing safe any longer? He remembered reading about the infamous Jeep hack a few years ago – white-hat hackers had taken control of the vehicle remotely to demonstrate its vulnerabilities. At least they now had an explanation for why Clare had stopped.

'No witnesses?'

'No, but they probably didn't make a song and dance about it. You know, a friendly face at the window, a photo of Ava on their phone and "Come with us or she'll suffer."'

'The whole family's had a horrendous couple of weeks. I can't tell you how grateful I am to each of you for pulling together to get them to safety.'

'Nonsense, Tom,' Philippa said. 'This isn't an exercise in sentimentality. A family was abducted on our patch. It's our *job* to rescue them. I would have preferred a more straightforward strategy rather than this waiting game you're insisting on, but I'm assuming you have your reasons. If you've got this wrong, though, and this family comes to harm because of something you and your brother are cooking up, you'll have me to answer to.'

Philippa was right, but there were eyes on the family every second, and at the first sign of violence, the GMP team would have no choice but to go in. For now, this delay seemed their only chance of saving Ava. A small voice at the back of Tom's mind whispered that if the guys guarding Clare and the kids took it upon themselves to shoot any one of them, there would be no time for the armed response team to intervene. But he had to hope they would be watching for signs of rising tension. The thought of what the family was going through made him feel sick.

With assurances that unless they heard otherwise, the family would be removed shortly before 2.30 a.m. UK time, Tom lay down on the bed, more in hope than expectation of grabbing a couple of hours' sleep.

It was going to be a long night, and the prospect of what lay ahead left his stomach churning.

68

7:06:44. Tom's heart thudded as the minutes relentlessly ticked by. In the two hours since he'd returned to Jack's room, Tom had done nothing but pace the floor and stare at that annoying clock. He should have stayed at the hotel and tried to get some more sleep, but he'd been unable to push from his mind the memory of Jack letting himself into the hotel room just three nights earlier. Maybe Kodra could do the same thing, and Tom would wake up with a knife to his throat.

He hadn't wanted to walk the streets of the city either, knowing he'd be jumping at every shadow, so he'd asked the hotel to book him a water taxi back to Jack's. There was a feeling of safety in numbers – even if that number was only two.

To his surprise, when he arrived Jack was already dressed for the night ahead – dinner jacket on, bow tie in place, mask waiting by the door.

'I felt I had to do something, even if it was only getting ready,' he'd said with a shrug. 'What news?'

As Tom got changed, he'd explained the plan for the extraction of Clare and the children from the mill in Heywood, watching Jack's jaw clench and unclench as he spoke, knowing his brother desperately wanted to be with his family the minute they were rescued, to hug them, reassure them, comfort them. Deciding now wasn't the time to tell him how Clare's car had been hacked, as he'd be sure to blame himself, Tom listened as Jack went over the plans for the hours ahead until they were imprinted on both of their minds.

Seven hours remained until Renzo's men were due to enter the palazzo, but it was actually only five hours until Tom would steal the painting. He just wanted it to be over, and with every detail confirmed, reconfirmed, and nothing to think about except all the things that could go wrong, he and Jack were prowling up and down the room, eyes pointed at the ground, checking their watches or the clock on the monitor every few minutes. They didn't want to arrive at the palazzo too early; the place needed to be heaving so they wouldn't be noticed in the crowd. But the wait was excruciating.

'You ready?' Jack finally said, after about the hundredth glance at his watch.

Tom nodded, swallowed hard and headed towards the door.

'Hang on. You need these,' Jack said, handing him a pair of black satin gloves. 'It's not unusual for men to wear gloves at a masked event, Tom, so don't look so worried. But keep them on, okay?'

Tom shot him a look. 'I do have a passing understanding of fingerprints, Jack.'

His brother ignored the tetchy comment. 'Got your mask?'

'Yep. What about the passes to get in and out?'

'Just place your mobile next to the reader when we arrive. Your pass is already on there and I'll deal with your exit pass when I leave.'

Tom nodded again and opened the door. 'After you.'

Jack had booked a water taxi to take them to the event, and Tom felt conspicuous in his bow tie and dinner jacket as they cruised past pedestrians walking alongside the canal.

'Stop worrying, Tom. Kodra and his crew won't be at an event like this.'

His brother seemed strangely relaxed, as if someone had flipped a switch and the old Jack, the man who always seemed in control, viewing the world with an almost cynical amusement, was back. Realising his brother was a man on a mission, Tom's tension eased a little. For about ten seconds.

As the taxi drew up to the *pontile* of the D'Angelo palazzo, Jack turned to Tom and clasped his forearm. 'Here we go, little brother,' he said, stepping off the boat. 'Masks on. It's show time!'

Tom looked up at the palazzo, its grand stone façade rising from the canal, an elaborately carved stone arch framing an entrance flanked with flambeaux in tall stands, flames flickering. He felt as if he were stepping back in time as he scanned his phone and crossed the threshold into the elegant foyer, a marble staircase rising majestically in front of them to the first-floor salon where the exhibition was being held. The faint sound of a piano playing something soft and melodic mingled with the gentle hum of conversation and the occasional chink of glasses from above. This was a world where affluence and influence reigned, with danger lurking just below the surface.

As they made their way up the staircase and into the salon, they were met with a sea of people, the women in vibrant floor-length gowns and delicate jewelled masks, the men in sharp dinner jackets, their masks sleek, dark and disconcerting. The soft glow of twinkling chandeliers bathed the room, each painting dramatically highlighted by discreet spotlights. Serving staff in crisp white shirts and black waistcoats weaved among them, offering champagne and canapés, and as Tom and Jack stepped into the room a tray appeared before them.

To Tom's surprise, Jack took two glasses and handed one to Tom. 'Don't look so worried,' he said. 'You'll look way more dodgy if you don't have a glass in your hand.'

Tom scanned the room. Jack was right. Not everyone was making the most of the canapés, but there didn't seem to be a hand without a glass in it.

'What are we supposed to do, now we're here?' Tom asked. He hadn't thought of it before, but it would be hours before he could escape to the terrace.

'Look at the paintings, I'd have thought,' Jack said, leading the way. 'Hmm, that's interesting,' he muttered, turning his back on the crowd.

'What is?'

'Over my shoulder. Bruno Contarini. Tall guy with black hair, greying at the temples, wearing what looks like a very expensive suit, standing beside what is probably an original Turner – or at least what I *think* is a Turner.'

'Why's it interesting that Contarini is here? If he's such a big cheese, wouldn't you expect him to be?'

'I guess most people wouldn't want to offend the local *capobastone* by leaving him off the guest list, but Vittorio D'Angelo is an influential man and I assumed he was immune to the pressure of the 'Ndrangheta. Obviously not.'

'Who's he talking to?' Tom asked, referring to a man in his early forties with short black hair and very white teeth, with whom Contarini seemed to be having an intense conversation.

Jack turned to face the room and at that moment Contarini lifted a hand and rested it on the younger man's shoulders, smiling broadly before patting his cheek affectionately, then turned away to kiss an older woman on both cheeks.

'No idea. Family, at a guess. I'll see if I can find out. Go and mingle.' With that, he sauntered across the room to stand next to the man Contarini had been talking to, staring at the same painting.

'Mingle,' Tom muttered, wondering who with. The room was full of people speaking Italian. What was he supposed to do, sidle up and mutter, 'Buona sera,' and promptly run out of conversation? Jack, however, seemed to be relaxed – in his element, almost.

Tom needed a distraction and fortunately he was in a room full of them, so he headed towards the first painting. On his estimation, given the number of paintings and the amount of time before he could disappear to the terrace, he'd have to spend at least ten minutes studying each one.

He felt, rather than saw, someone move to stand next to him. He could smell her light, citrussy perfume.

'How's the conference going?' The voice was soft, but there was no warmth in it.

'Excuse me?' he said, as if he hadn't understood the question.

He turned towards a woman wearing a black lace mask threaded with silver. He recognised her instantly. There was no hiding those green eyes.

'I knew who you were the minute you walked in,' she said. 'Your mask can't hide the way you stand, the way you move. Who are you?'

Tom cast a quick look over her shoulder to see where Jack had got to. He didn't want to risk Tia seeing them together, especially since Jack's mask might not be as good a disguise as he thought. Tia must have noticed his eyes shift, and she turned sharply to follow his line of sight.

She froze. Tom was about to say something – anything – to draw her gaze away from Jack when he heard her gasp, her hand rising to her mouth as she whipped back to face him. Her pupils were black pools. The skin of her cheeks below her mask had turned pale. She stared at Tom as if he were the devil himself and, without another word, hurried away.

69

My head is spinning. I can barely breathe. Tell me I'm imagining things, Alessandro. If ever I needed you to answer me – really answer me – it's now, because the earth feels as if it's shifting beneath me.

I should have stayed, not run away. I should have walked across the room, ripped off the mask, confirmed my suspicions one way or another. But I panicked. And I never panic. For the first time in years, I don't know what to do.

I have worked so hard to get here. I've broken too many laws, done things I wouldn't have believed possible, with one aim and one only. And now I feel as if my plan is crashing down, shattered into a thousand pieces.

I had to escape. I've locked myself in one of the bathrooms, hoping no one tries to find me, but the sound of my phone ringing breaks through my despair.

Renzo.

I take a deep breath. It's not over yet, and I need to keep control. 'Speak to me in English,' I tell him. 'Too many people might hear.'

Most of the people here probably speak English as well as I do, but making Renzo uncomfortable, putting him at a disadvantage, has become second nature.

'You got rid of the girl yet?' he asks. 'Blake has no respect. He must be made to understand I'm in charge, and Albanians will pay good money for his daughter. Let them have her – now – before we take the painting. Then I can tell Blake he pushed me too far. *Non vedo l'ora.'*

I can't wait.

I can picture the look of smug satisfaction as he utters the words.

There's so much Renzo doesn't know, and so much I don't entirely understand.

I lean against the door. It's all slipping through my fingers, and my eyes fill with tears. It was so carefully constructed: the theft of the painting, the drug shipment, the breaking of 'Ndrangheta rules, the exposure of Renzo to Contarini, winning his trust, gaining access to his inner circle, discovering the truth, piece by tiny piece.

'Are you there, Elena?' *Renzo's frustration with me is barely masked, and I've been silent for too long.*

'I'll go there now,' I tell him.

'Before you do, speak to Contarini's nephew. He's here, at the reception. As am I. Why haven't I seen you?'

'A busy place, lots of people. And you may have missed it, but most of them are wearing masks.'

I hear a tut. 'Elena, find the nephew. Tell him we'll have the collateral by the end of the night. Tell him exactly how you're going to prove it to him, and then speak to the Albanians. Give them the girl.'

'And how do I find the nephew?'

'Ask around. He's a Contarini, so everyone will know him.'

I allow myself another minute to breathe, and then I pull open the door and head for the stairs. I need to get out of here.

70

Tom had been staring, unseeing, at every painting for what seemed like hours. In other circumstances he would have loved this; so many different aspects of Venice, so many interpretations – each beautiful in its own way, from pale misty canals to vibrant sunsets over the lagoon. But he was distracted, alternating between glancing at his watch and looking over his shoulder to see what Jack was up to.

The glass of champagne had turned warm in his hand, but he wasn't going to touch it, and tempting as the canapés looked, his throat felt so tight he thought he would choke if he had one.

Finally, he heard a voice behind him.

'You good, Tom?'

He took a breath and spoke without turning. 'This is pushing my nerves to the edge. I wish we could just bloody well get on with it. Who were you talking to?'

Jack moved to stand slightly to one side of him, as if they were both studying and discussing the nearest painting.

'Various people, but first Bruno's nephew – Sandro Contarini. His sister's son, but he's taken his uncle's surname. I guess that's so people know he's a big shot, not just another minion. I hid myself away for a while to look him up. He's the money man. What about you?'

'Bloody Tia found me. When she approached me, I looked over her shoulder at you – a rookie mistake, but I wanted to make sure you weren't about to come over. She saw where I was looking and turned round. Her eyes locked on you. I don't know whether something clicked in her mind, but I'm certain she recognised you.'

'Not surprising. I saw her only yesterday.'

'No, it was more than that. When she approached me, she said she recognised me by the way I move. Maybe when she was looking at you, she suddenly knew where she'd seen you before – and I don't mean yesterday. Whatever it was, she literally turned pale, then disappeared.'

Jack looked around the room. 'Where is she now?'

'I haven't seen her since. I've not exactly been looking, though, because I didn't want her quizzing me.'

'Let's do a circuit of the room and meet back here in ten minutes. I want to know who she's talking to. Renzo's here – weaselly little man that he is. He's easy enough to spot.' Jack tilted his head towards a short, swarthy man, his belly straining against his dinner jacket. A thick neck supported a thin, sharp-featured face, eyes hidden beneath an elaborate scarlet and gold mask. 'I'm keeping out of his way, but he won't be expecting me to be here so that helps. I don't want to bump into Gabriella D'Angelo either. She'll know I wasn't invited.'

'I guess she'll be even more suspicious if the painting then goes missing.'

Jack gave a bitter chuckle. 'You think? Either way, let's try to find Tia. See you in ten minutes.'

Tom turned and started to make his way around the room, trying to look as if the paintings were still fascinating him while checking out the crowd. A couple of people attempted to speak to him, but he muttered about not speaking Italian and moved away with a smile before they launched into English.

Ten minutes later, he'd done his circuit and even been down to the foyer, but there was no sign of her. Heading back to the agreed meeting point, he could tell from what little he could see of Jack's face below his mask that he wasn't happy.

His brother nodded towards a painting that wasn't attracting much attention and Tom went to stand beside him.

'I decided to take myself off to the bathroom and listen to any conversations Tia's had in the last couple of hours. She heard from Renzo. He's insisting she hands Ava over to the Albanians now – he doesn't want her to wait.'

'Shit! What do we do, Jack?'

'She was supposed to speak to Contarini's nephew too – the guy I was talking to earlier, I presume – but I haven't seen her with him, so perhaps she's gone to sort out Ava and she'll be back. We need to go somewhere we can talk properly and not whisper. Follow me.'

Tom waited as Jack headed towards the stairs. Thirty seconds later, he followed, watching as his brother turned left down a passageway, then right into a vaulted nook below the staircase. Jack pointed to one of the elegant banquettes positioned in the space, and Tom sat down gingerly. It looked too delicate, the silk brocade too precious to be sat on, but they could see to both left and right and would know if anyone was approaching.

'We've got a couple of options,' Jack said. 'My natural instinct is to move straight to my plan B. Tell Tia I know who she is, what she's done, and she has to save Ava or I'll expose her.'

Tom frowned. 'It's so hard to see where her loyalties lie. She might alert Renzo so that he, or his future father-in-law, can come to her rescue.'

'And then who knows what will happen. It feels a huge risk.'

It seemed to Tom that Jack was in a no-win situation.

'Have you tried switching on her microphone?' he asked.

'It's never off, but right now all I can hear are the sounds of the city. She's walking somewhere – heading to Ava, I presume. What do you think we should do, Tom?'

This was a momentous decision, and the implications of making the wrong choice were terrifying.

'As soon as we know what she's planning, I'll contact Philippa. She has the firearms team standing by. I'll let her know we might need to make a split-second decision, and she'll have to authorise the Heywood extraction immediately.'

'Will she be okay with that?'

'Irritated – she likes a good plan – but she'll understand that there must be a lot at stake for me to even suggest it. If Tia's going to hand over Ava, we'll hear her telling the Albanians. That's the moment you decide whether to intervene.'

'But at that point, little brother, you might well be hiding out on the terrace, and not readily available for a rather crucial chat.'

'I presume I'll have a listening device?'

'Of course, I'll fit it before you go out there. But sound carries over water, so any conversation would have to be very muted. We don't want security to come racing up to find you.' Jack suddenly sat up straight. 'She's talking,' he said, pointing to his phone.

Despite the privacy of their location it would have been foolhardy to put the phone on speaker, so the two brothers sat, heads pressed together, phone lodged between their ears, as Tia spoke.

'You're done here.' She was speaking in English, presumably to the Albanians. 'You've been paid. So go.'

The next voice came from further away. 'What about the girl? We can get good money for her.'

'I told you to go. I'll take care of the girl, and you've been paid more than you deserve, so if you ever want to work for me again, you'll do as I say.'

There was a burst of shouting in what Tom could only assume was Albanian. Then one voice cut through.

'This isn't finished, Elena. You'll regret this.'

There was the crash of a door slamming followed by footsteps, then silence. Jack wanted to switch on the video, but their location in the palazzo wasn't private enough.

Tia was speaking. 'Use these wet wipes. Clean yourself up and put these clothes on.'

'Why should I do what you tell me? I've seen your face and I know what that means. You're going to kill me anyway, so why should I play your stupid games?'

Ava's defiance didn't entirely ring true. There was a hint of a wobble in her voice.

Poor kid, Tom thought, as Jack tensed beside him.

'Because if it was up to the man I work for, you'd be going for a ride with those two bastards I just kicked out. And now you're not. Do you know what they'd have done with you?'

'Course I do. I'm not stupid. I've told you before: you don't know who I am or who my dad is.'

'Then tell me.'

There was a brief pause, then: 'My dad's the enforcer for one of the biggest crime gangs in Manchester. His real name's Finn McGuinness.'

Tom heard a groan from Jack.

71

'My dad's Finn McGuinness,' Ava repeats, swallowing hard.

The woman tuts. 'I know who Finn McGuinness is – or was. He's dead.'

'Yeah, well, you don't know everything, do you?' Ava insists. 'That's what you're meant to believe, but it was all a massive cover-up. He escaped. The boss of his gang was called Guy Bentley. How would I know so much if it wasn't true?'

Ava doesn't have many weapons to use against this woman, but the idea that neither she nor her dad are who the woman thinks they are seemed to rattle her earlier. The name Finn McGuinness is enough to terrify anyone, and Ava's hoping it will unsettle the woman even more.

'Ava, let's get real here, shall we? Your dad is a security expert. Finn McGuinness may have had many skills, but most of them involved brute force. Whatever your dad's called, whoever he is, he has to do as he's told if he wants to see you alive. And believe me, he's trying to save you. What he *doesn't* know is that we also have your mum, your brother and your sister, so now you're surplus to requirements. My boss thinks he can make extra money by selling you; I have a different plan.'

Ava swallows a gasp at the news about her family, but she can't let this woman know how she's feeling.

'They're not my family. I've told you before, I don't belong to them. They won't care what happens to me, so why should I care what happens to them?'

'For fuck's sake, girl, I don't have time for this. You're the very least of my problems – do you understand? I've got stuff to do, to sort out, and your dad can help me if he chooses to. Get yourself cleaned up. Put these clothes on. We're leaving. And whether you consider them to be your family or not, if you don't do exactly as I say, they're dead. Understood?'

The woman's voice sounds shaky. Is she going to cry? She's different from last time, and Ava recognises misery when she sees it.

'You know *nothing*,' Ava says. 'Do you know I kidnapped the boy you're calling my brother when he was a baby? I gave him to Guy Bentley's crew. Face it, you know nothing about me, or them.'

The words spill out before she can stop them. She wants to shock the woman, unsettle her, show how tough she is. But the woman stands, arms folded, and stares at her.

Ava's heart is pumping, her throat feels as if it's in a vice. Perhaps she's gone too far, but she's not sure there's any way back.

What's she going to do with me? Why is this happening?

The question has been spinning in her head since the moment she was taken from the station car park. She'd been feeling sorry for herself, thinking the rules she had to live by – the restrictions, the secrets – were unfair. But the last few days have reminded her, as if she's ever really forgotten, how it feels to be under the control of some evil bastard who doesn't give a shit about human life. She's not going there again.

Ava hasn't moved since the woman told her to clean herself up, but then the fight drains out of her and she stifles a sob. She closes her eyes and tries to picture her dad. What would he tell her to do?

Keep your cool, Ava. Play along, don't provoke her. Save your fight for when it counts.

Glaring at the woman, Ava picks up the wipes and attempts to clean up her face, her hands, all visible areas of skin. There's not much she can do about her hair. It's gone past greasy and hangs in thick clumps, her scalp itchy and begging to be washed.

A tight band of pressure settles in her chest. 'If I'm taking my clothes off, you can turn round. I don't know if that's how you get your kicks, but you're not watching me.'

The woman sighs but does as Ava asks, and she quickly pulls on the clothes. They're not great, but they feel cleaner than the ones she's just taken off. For a moment, she wonders if this is her chance. The woman isn't looking. She could push her over and run.

They've got Mum, Billy and Sophia. She can't do it.

'Right,' the woman says, turning back. 'We need to get out of here in case those two pricks decide they're going to come back, kill me and take you. But if you try to run, Ava, your family dies. And I *will* find you. You need to believe that.'

72

Jack put his mobile down next to him. Ava had been so brave, so defiant, so heartbreaking.

'Finn McGuinness, Tom,' Jack said, his voice faint. 'Why the hell did she say that?'

'You know why. He's the most frightening man she can think of.'

'And Tia knows he's dead. She'll know there was no massive cover-up.'

'What do you think she meant about you being able to help her?' Tom asked.

'I don't know, but I'm praying that not giving Ava to the Albanians is a positive sign. She's told her to clean herself up, which means she's probably taking her out of the building. God knows where she's going, but she said she had a different plan. The only thing I can do is keep listening, and the moment I sense things are heading in the wrong direction, I'll call her – even if it's only to gain some time. For now, if Tia thinks I can help her, there's a glimmer of hope. Maybe she has her own deal to make with me.'

Or maybe she has a buyer for Ava.

Tom didn't voice this thought, but was certain his brother would be thinking the same, and he couldn't forget how Tia had reacted when she'd seen Jack. Why had that rattled her so much?

Jack frowned. 'What's she up to, Tom? There must be something else going on. This is the woman who orchestrated the abduction of my whole family, so I'm struggling to believe she has a decent bone in her entire body.'

The brothers sat in silence. Soft piano music and the buzz of conversation drifted down from the gallery, but neither felt inclined to return to the reception, and what had seemed like a workable plan now appeared to be falling apart.

Tom felt he had to say something. 'Look, Jack, we know Tia thought it was a mistake to hand Ava over to the Albanians. She thought Renzo should keep her to give him more leverage over you. Maybe she wanted Ava to clean up in preparation for handing her over.'

Jack gave Tom one of his lopsided smiles. 'Very positive thinking, Tom. I'd give everything I own for you to be right, but there's something else going on. Tia's rattled. You heard it too, but you didn't want to mention it.' He looked at Tom. 'I know and understand every expression on your face, little brother.'

'Is it time to give Renzo a warning? We know far more than he realises. Maybe he needs to understand exactly what will happen if you don't get Ava back.'

Jack nodded slowly. 'I can't reveal that we know what's going on in Heywood, but I can up the pressure – tell him I know who he is and what I'll do if Ava isn't returned safely. It might just force him to contact Tia, maybe stop her from doing whatever she's planning.'

'It's less than an hour since Renzo told her to hand Ava over, and I'm guessing he thinks she's still here, trying to speak to Contarini's nephew. If you don't think you can influence Tia directly, Renzo still has time to tell her she was right – that Ava's his best bargaining chip and she needs to keep her safe.'

Jack let out a long breath. 'If only I understood Tia's motives! It would be so easy if it's purely about money. But I don't believe that.'

'Then let's put pressure on Renzo, but if you're going to speak to him, I'm coming with you.'

'No, you're not. I don't want him to know about you. It's a piece of the puzzle he doesn't need. He won't like the fact that I'm here and he won't like what I'm going to say, but that's tough shit.'

'Why don't I talk to him, then? He's going to be shocked to learn you're not alone, assuming Tia hasn't already told him.'

Jack frowned. 'Renzo's not the sharpest tool in the box. It might panic him – and a panicking Renzo is a perilous thing. Nice idea, but sadly, it has to be me. Put this earbud in.' He handed Tom a device no bigger than a large pea. 'I'll be able to hear you too, because before you put your smart shirt on earlier, I modified the collar. There's a bone-conduction microphone in it to capture your voice through vibrations. Both devices link to your phone, so don't switch it off. I set it up so we can communicate later tonight, but now's a good time to test everything out.'

Before Tom could say a word, Jack stood up and walked away, disappearing from sight. A few seconds later, his voice sounded in Tom's ear.

'I'm guessing you can hear me, but just to check I can hear you too, say something.'

'Loud and clear this end.'

'Good. Then stay where you are. I doubt anyone will bother you there. I'm off to find Renzo.'

The sound of the crowds through Tom's earbud grew louder as Jack got closer to the grand salon. It was a couple of minutes before he heard his brother's voice.

'I see him, Tom. He's standing staring at *Serenata Selvaggi*, the prick. If only he knew that my software was analysing his avaricious facial expressions.'

Tom waited, perched on the edge of the seat, anxious to hear Jack's voice again.

'Don't turn round, Renzo. Yes, I know who you are, and you

don't want to be seen talking to me, so just listen. If you're thinking you can double-cross me in any way, let me tell you: you can't. Whatever you've planned, however you think you can threaten me, I'm not the man you think I am. I know why you want this painting. I know about the shipment. I know who you are to Bruno Contarini. But if you harm a hair on any of my family's heads, Renzo Moretti, you can kiss goodbye to the future you've got planned.'

Tom stifled a gasp. Was Renzo smart enough to realise Jack knew what was happening in Heywood, or would he think Jack was only referring to Ava?

Jack's voice stayed low, controlled, as if he was talking about the painting. 'Bruno Contarini is right here, Renzo. I can speak to him now, if you like, tell him what you plan for my daughter. Would you like that? Because I have nothing to lose.'

Renzo's voice was muffled, and Tom assumed he had his back to Jack. 'You have more to lose than you think.'

Jack laughed softly. 'Are you prepared to risk that, Renzo? That would be very stupid when all you have to do to get what you want is hand over my daughter. I suggest you make that happen.'

73

Tom took one look at Jack's face when he returned from his 'chat' with Renzo and decided to say nothing. Jack's lips were pressed into a tight line, his shoulders up round his ears.

The tension was palpable, and the next few hours were going to be some of the most nerve-racking of their lives. Tom had to somehow pull off the theft of the painting, but even more unnerving was the thought that he had to get past the security guards and into the control room to override the proximity lock.

He'd faced terrifying situations before when people were in danger, and they were always adrenaline-fuelled – life or death moments. This was something else entirely. He was about to cross a line, commit a crime, all the while knowing the stakes were unbearably high. There was no room for mistakes.

'You ready?' Jack said finally. 'People are starting to leave, and we need to get you in position before the crowd thins.'

The moment had arrived. If he was going to back out, it had to be now.

His brief hesitation was interrupted by a vibration from Jack's phone. 'Hang on. Tia's phone's ringing. It must be Renzo.'

The brothers listened, hoping to hear that Jack's intervention had been successful and Renzo was about to instruct Tia to bring Ava to the handover point. But the phone just rang out.

Jack looked at Tom. 'Shit. She's not responding. I've never known her reject a call from Renzo before.'

'She might be in the shower or something. Don't panic.'

'She's not. I've been listening since she left with Ava. Everything's muffled, as if the phone's in her bag or a pocket. I've heard her speak, but it was hard to make out any words.'

'Have you heard Ava?'

Jack gave a soft snort. 'Yes. I couldn't tell what she was saying, but her tone came through loud and clear. At a guess, she was telling Tia to fuck off, or similar.'

'Do you know if they're inside or outside?'

'From the ambient sound, I'd say they were outside for about thirty minutes. That was Ava's chance to run, but I'm betting her fear for Clare and the kids stopped her. That girl would risk her own life before theirs, any day of the week.'

'Could Tia have gone back to her apartment with Ava?'

'Only if she's stupid. She saw you following her from right outside the door, so I'd guess she's taken her somewhere secure. She's resourceful – we know that. She's very possibly got more than one safe place to stay, not knowing how any of this was going to pan out.'

'So why's she ignoring Renzo?'

'No idea, but he's not giving up. He's sent a message demanding she call him.'

Tia obviously had another plan. But with no idea what it was, there was nothing to discuss.

'Come on, Tom. We can't wait any longer. I need to get you through that door to the terrace.'

Tom could feel Jack's eyes on him, burning his skin, begging him without words not to back out, not to be the policeman but the brother, the uncle, a man who believed the life of a child was more important than the law.

'I'm ready,' Tom said, rising to his feet. 'Let's go.'

74

It was easier to slip out onto the terrace than Tom had anticipated. Jack temporarily disabled the CCTV facing the door for the few seconds it took him to sneak through, telling Tom that the security guards watching the footage wouldn't notice anything other than a blip on their screen.

Tom had a mental map of where he was to store the painting, and hoped Jack could manipulate the various alarms and CCTV as he'd promised. The trickiest bit would come when he had to get past the security office and into the control room. Jack had given him the proximity code, and he would repeat it through Tom's earpiece when the time was right. Both guards would probably be watching their monitors, their backs to the passageway, but Tom was concerned about reflections or shadows as he passed the office door.

Plenty of time to worry about that later.

He settled himself in a corner of the terrace, out of sight of anyone who might come up the steps and peer through the gate. With nothing to do for at least two hours, Tom let his mind wander. He imagined himself at home with Louisa, Lucy and Harry, relaxing after a meal together, Harry sleeping soundly upstairs after a play in the bath – one of his favourite things. Anyone who got close was guaranteed to get soaked, but his merry laugh made a drenching worthwhile.

At least he had the comfort of knowing that was what he'd be going home to – provided he wasn't arrested or caught by Kodra's crew. The smile faded as he pondered Jack's future. Despite Tom's confidence that Clare, Billy and Sophia would be skilfully extracted by the team in Heywood, there was too much that could go wrong. And there were other, more immediate concerns.

Why wouldn't Tia speak to Renzo? Why had she moved Ava?

There was something else going on. Something he couldn't get a handle on. Was it to do with her moment of horror when she saw Jack?

Does she know who he is? Does it matter?

Tom looked at his watch yet again.

He'd been hiding on the terrace for seventy-three minutes when he heard Jack's voice in his ear.

'No word from Tia. She's still not answering Renzo's calls. She didn't come back to the reception to meet Contarini's nephew, and he's crucial to the release of the drugs from South America. She's inside a building. Her phone's out of her bag, on a table because all I can see is a ceiling. No hints there – it's not ornate, so not in the palazzo. She's spoken to Ava a couple of times, asking if she wants a drink, but Ava's being stubborn. Refusing on principle, at a guess, although I wish she'd have a bloody drink of water. I can hear a keyboard tapping so Tia's using a computer, but I can't access what she's looking at. Only her phone. How are you bearing up?'

Tom kept his voice low in case the sound carried to the security team at the bottom of the stairs. 'Fine. I'm the least of your worries.'

'Course you are. I'll get back to you when the rooms are clear. They're ahead of schedule, so it might be sooner than you think.'

Tom wasn't sure if that was a good thing or not. The only positive was that it would all be over sooner.

75

'It's time, Tom. You ready?'

He wasn't. He'd *never* be ready. Nevertheless, he pushed himself to his feet, heart pounding. He had a job to do.

'Ready as I'll ever be. I'm two steps from the door into the salon.'

'You'll hear a click in a moment. That's the lock releasing. There's no one there. The CCTV facing the door has been replaced and the door won't be seen to open. At each stage over the next thirty minutes you're going to have to do exactly as I say, at precisely the moment I tell you to do it. Okay?'

Swallowing hard, Tom whispered, 'Yep. I'll wait for your word.'

Tom heard the click.

'Push the door gently but quickly, move through and close it softly.'

This was it. The moment Tom would do something he had never believed possible – break the law. But there was no turning back. As he put his hand on the door, an image of Lucy flashed into his mind. What would she think of what he was doing?

Go, Dad, she'd say. She wouldn't hesitate if this was to save Ava.

Tom pressed gently, scared the door would creak and set off some ultra-sensitive alarm. Nothing happened and he breathed again.

Stepping slowly into the darkened room, he turned to make sure the door didn't slam. He held his hand against it and gently eased it into place. The soft click as the lock activated seemed to reverberate round the space.

He turned back towards the vast room, now empty of bodies. The lively chatter and chink of glasses from earlier had been replaced by an eerie silence. A dim light cast long shadows across the space, and a faint scent of perfume lingered in the air. He stood for a moment, looking around, certain he was about to hear the pounding of footsteps and an Italian voice telling him to stand still, to raise his hands in the air. He wouldn't understand exactly what they were saying, but he'd do it instinctively.

If the salon had been one oblong room, he would have been able to see all four corners. But it had been adapted with architectural panels to display more of D'Angelo's art collection, creating shadowed recesses. Uncertainty about what – or who – lay around each corner gnawed at his nerves.

He moved cautiously, tiptoeing despite there being no one to hear his footsteps. The paintings seemed to be watching him, following his every move, their vibrant colours dull in the low light.

Jack's voice came softly: 'I can see you, Tom. You're doing fine.'

Tom couldn't bring himself to respond. The silence felt fragile, as if the sound of his voice would break it, shattering the stillness and dragging him back to the harsh reality of what he was doing.

He knew where the painting was – at the far end of a space with panels on either side, but he was tempted to check out the rest of the room to make sure no one was lurking, waiting to pounce.

'*Tom, stop!* Where are you going?' Jack's voice sounded urgently through his earpiece. 'Stick to the plan! Don't take another step!'

Tom froze. The CCTV!

Jack would only have fixed the relevant cameras; Tom couldn't roam the room without being spotted on others that weren't rigged. Realising his mistake, but still not risking a response, he turned back. His eyes landed on the painting, its frame glinting softly. The room felt charged with tension and he took a deep breath.

Jack's voice had returned to cool reassurance. 'It's okay, Tom. Nothing happened. Stick to the plan from now on, please.'

Tom wished Jack was doing the actual stealing; he would be so much more composed. But Tom couldn't manipulate the technology, so it had to be him. And he needed to get on with it.

'Gently lift the painting straight up about six inches and then bring it towards you. Nothing's going to happen. No alarm will sound.'

Tom reached out. Inside the gloves, his hands were slick with sweat. The painting wasn't large, yet his arms trembled as he lifted it from the wall. He held his breath, the painting hovering in his grasp as he waited, certain a cacophony of alarms would rip through the air. Nothing happened.

'Well done. Now turn round, turn right at the next panel and head for the door on the left. It leads to the staff area. You've got this, Tom. Not much further now.'

Holding the painting in both hands, Tom moved towards the door. How was he supposed to open it while carrying the painting? The frame was too heavy to hold with one hand.

'It's okay to put it down. Open the door, then pick it up again and push through backwards.'

It was obvious really, but not only was Tom worried about being caught, this was a beautiful, valuable painting – something to be handled with great care. He gently placed it on the floor, leaned it against the wall and reached out to grip the ornate knob. He twisted it to the right. It didn't budge. He glanced up at the CCTV monitor, blinking at him from the wall above.

'Try turning it left. It's an antique.'

Frustrated with his own woolly thinking, Tom did as Jack suggested. The knob was stiff, but it turned and he was able to breathe again. He leaned down to retrieve the painting, then backed through the door.

He had thought the lighting in the salon was dim, but the corridor enveloped him in almost total darkness. He couldn't see a thing.

Standing for a moment, hoping his eyes would become accustomed to the lack of light, he listened carefully. Hearing no movement and finally able to just make out the pale walls on either side of the passage, he began to move. Each footstep echoed softly through the silent corridor, the muted thud of his shoes on the stone floor the only sound.

I'm a thief. A criminal.

The thoughts kept coming and he gripped the painting tighter.

Just get it done. In and out. No mistakes.

The consequences of failure were too dire to consider. He had to keep moving.

As he passed the kitchen, the buttery scent of pastry lingered in the air, mingling with traces of garlic and herbs. No light showed through the round window in the door – as Jack had promised, the chefs had finished for the night.

The room he needed was next along the passageway. Its door was ajar, so he didn't have to put the painting down again, but why wasn't it shut?

Tom retreated back along the corridor.

'What's going on?' Jack's voice was tinged with concern.

Tom hadn't wanted to speak, but he had to check with Jack.

'The storeroom door's open,' he whispered. 'Do you have eyes inside?'

'No. There's no CCTV in there. Are the lights on?'

Tom looked towards the door. It was only open a few centimetres, but he thought he could detect a faint glow.

'I think so.'

Jack was silent. Tom had been hoping he'd say something like, 'It's just an emergency light – nothing to worry about.' But he didn't.

'Jack?'

'Tom, put the painting down and go to the door. Listen carefully. See if you can detect any sounds from inside. If you can't hear anything, you're going to have to check it out.'

'Is there nowhere else I can hide it?' Tom was whispering so quietly he could barely hear his own voice, but it seemed to pierce the silence.

'No. You have two options, I'm afraid. Check out the room or dump the painting and get the hell out of there.'

Fuck!

76

Resting the painting against the wall, Tom crept towards the door. It was barely ajar, allowing just a thin sliver of pale light to escape into the dark corridor. He paused, his breath held tight, as he moved closer.

Wherever the light was coming from, it was faint and definitely not from an overhead bulb. He was going to have to ease the door open. If someone was inside he wouldn't know what to say, especially not in Italian, and certainly not if they peered into the corridor and saw a three-million-dollar painting propped against the wall.

He heard what sounded like a sigh of relief. 'S'okay Tom. I just checked the building plan. The room has an outside window. The light's from the moon.'

He closed his eyes. Could he trust that moonlight was all that was waiting for him beyond the door? But he could hear nothing. Not even the sound of breathing – except his own.

With two fingers he gently pushed the door inwards, waiting for a shout, ready to run. A pale beam of moonlight filtered through a small, grimy window, casting long shadows across green, blue and red recycling bins, and finally he was able to breathe.

'*Christ*, Jack. I'm a useless criminal,' he mumbled, turning to retrieve the painting from the hall. He heard a soft chuckle. 'Glad you think it's funny.'

If this was it – if this was the end of everything he had to do – he could start to believe they had got away with it. But he knew this was the easy part, and his relief evaporated when he thought of the task ahead.

The door to the office beyond the storeroom stood wide open, and Tom made his way to the cupboard Jack had told him to use. Quickly removing a stack of folded tablecloths, he placed them on the floor and when that didn't make quite enough space, he took out a rolled-up banner. Finally, he slid the painting onto the empty shelf and shut the door.

'Done.'

'Good job. Now you need to get to the control room. This bit's tricky, Tom, I won't lie to you. I've got eyes on the security guys. They're having a cup of coffee, staring at their monitors, and I'll know the second one of them moves, but you're going to have to have your wits about you.'

'Thanks for that.'

'If they look likely to leave the office, I'll do something to the monitors so they have to stay and sort them out. Make your way downstairs. Do you remember the route I showed you? I don't have CCTV down there, apart from in the security office, so you need to tell me where you're going so I can check it's the right way. Okay?'

Tom didn't like the sound of this. There was a strange comfort in knowing Jack had had eyes on him up until now, and without that reassurance he felt horribly isolated.

'Turn left out of the storeroom. About ten metres along, the door to the stairs is on your right.'

He had begun to hate doors, not knowing what was on the other side, but when he inched this one open he was relieved to see that the stairs were lit by pale nightlights. As he took a step forward, his shadow stretched before him, a dark silhouette.

It was the bottom of this staircase that was worrying Tom. The security office was right there, its internal window facing the stairs.

One of the guards only had to glance over his shoulder and Tom would be in full view.

'I'm coming to the final turn in the stairs now.'

Knowing that the microphone was hidden in his shirt collar right next to his throat, Tom found it hard to believe Jack could hear him over the thump of his heart, the pulse in his neck.

'Okay. Remember, the top half of the wall between their room and the corridor is glass, so walk slowly, steadily. No stopping and starting. They have their backs to you, but sudden movement reflected on their screens is your enemy. If I shout "Down!" then get flat on the floor. Understood?'

Please don't shout 'Down!'

'Mm' was as much of a response as Tom could manage.

Keeping close to the wall, Tom practically slithered down the last few steps. When he reached the bottom he slowly lowered himself to a crouch, then to his knees so he was below the glass part of the wall.

Without a sound, he crawled along the wall. He was desperate to tell Jack that the door to the security room was open and they would hear if he made any noise. His feet dragged as he crawled, the soft leather of his shoes grazing the concrete floor. Would they hear the sound? He raised himself into a low crouch and, moving painfully slowly, eased past the door.

'You there yet?'

To Tom, it was as if Jack was shouting through a megaphone. He didn't reply but glanced through the open door. The guards hadn't moved.

A long thirty seconds later, breathless, dripping with sweat, he was past and able to stand again, but he had no intention of responding to Jack until he was safely inside the control room.

Another door, and this time the gaping entrance to the security office was way too close for comfort. Praying the hinges wouldn't creak, Tom pressed down on the handle, pushed slowly and tiptoed inside.

'Tom?' Jack sounded anxious.

He leaned back against the door and closed his eyes for a second. 'I'm in. What do I need to do?' he whispered.

He heard Jack exhale. 'Go to the main terminal – it's fairly obvious which it is.'

To you, maybe.

But Jack was right. 'Okay, got it.'

'In the top left-hand corner you should be able to see an icon labelled *Device Management*. Click on that and look for the settings for door C2. Can you see it?'

To Tom, who considered himself fairly computer literate, the screen was a nightmare, but finally he spotted it. 'Okay. What now?'

'Select it, then enter this code. Hashtag 731982B4.'

'Done. The screen's saying *Proximity Lock Settings*.'

'Choose *Disable*, then remember to save the changes.'

Tom prayed that he was doing this correctly and was tempted to video it so Jack could check, but it was, after all, just two clicks of a mouse. Surely he could manage that.

'All done. What now?'

Tom's heart was hammering as he contemplated his journey back past the guards.

'You're good. I'm going to get you out of there now, and you don't have to go back past the security office. Go out of the door, turn left again. The guards are both safely inside. I can see them, even though I can't see you.'

Despite Jack's reassurances, Tom glanced to his right to check the corridor was clear. There was no sign of movement, but the corridor to his left was long, narrow, and he had no idea where it led.

'How far along here?' he whispered.

'All the way, but you're fine. Just slowly and silently, then turn right at the end and you'll be at an outside door.'

Tom tiptoed along the corridor, which seemed to go for miles. The end was just in sight when a frantic shout pierced his ear.

'*Run*, Tom! *Go!* Don't stop! *Get out of there!*'

His heart raced as adrenaline surged through him, propelling him forward.

77

Ava hadn't wanted to go with the woman. Her heart was pounding at the thought of abandoning the dark, dingy cellar. She'd grown used to the constant drip of water, the musty scent of mould and the feel of the rough brick walls. However grim her dungeon was, the uncertainty of what awaited her outside seemed worse.

'Don't forget what I told you. You run, your family dies. Got it?'

Ava had felt an overwhelming urge to shout at her, to call her all the filthy names she'd learned as a child. But one look at her face told Ava that the woman was close to the edge, teetering between control and despair.

She'd told Ava to walk ahead through the heavy wooden door into the outer room – a mess of empty food cartons and discarded bottles, the air thick with the stench of unwashed bodies and stale beer. But the men had gone.

'Up the stairs.'

Feeling a firm push on her back, Ava headed up the stone stairs. Her legs felt unsteady as she reached the top and took her first hesitant steps into the open air.

'Keep moving,' the woman murmured. 'Hurry up.'

As they walked through the streets Ava kept her head down,

ashamed of her filthy body and hair, but slowly she realised there
was no traffic, not even the sound of a distant car.

Where am I?

At the sound of voices on the path ahead the woman tried to
take her arm, but Ava shook her off. 'Don't touch me,' she hissed.

The woman tutted, but didn't try again.

The voices belonged to a group of men – late-night drinkers,
their drunken shouts and swaying bodies killing any hope she'd
had of begging for their help.

The narrow lanes twisted and turned. Ancient buildings loomed
either side of dark canals, and the occasional splash of water against
stone made Ava shiver. Was she in Venice, a city she'd seen in
photos and films but never imagined visiting?

It didn't matter. If the woman had Mum, Billy and Sophia, Ava
wasn't going to try to escape, wherever she was.

They turned down another dingy alley, tall buildings crowding
in, blotting out the moonlight. A few flickering lanterns hung from
the walls, their pale glow casting ghostly shapes on the cobbled
path, and she felt a hard lump in her throat. *Where were they going?*

'In here,' the woman said, stopping beneath a faded sign –
ALBERGO BELLA – and pushing open the door to what appeared to be
a shabby hotel. The man sitting behind a sort-of reception desk just
nodded, indifferent to who they were, and Ava was ushered into a
cramped, gloomy room.

She didn't bother to look around. She knew she'd just exchanged
one prison for another.

78

Flinging himself against the wall as the outer door closed behind him, Tom fought to catch his breath in the early-morning mist.

'What the *fuck*, Jack?'

'Sorry. One of the guards got up, probably to go for a pee, so I made things go squiffy on the screens but he just muttered something in Italian and waved a hand at the other guy, as if he expected him to fix it, and headed for the door.'

'Christ, if that had been two minutes earlier, even two *seconds*, I'd have been totally stuffed.'

'Well, it wasn't, and you're not. I've got a water taxi waiting for you. Just head east and you'll find him. He'll bring you back here, to the canal-side entrance. I'll let you in. Stay inside the cabin, Tom. You can't afford to be seen. We've no idea where Kodra and his crew are.'

'Okay,' Tom said, slowly releasing his breath. Somehow he didn't think he had the capacity for any more fear.

'And Tom… Well done. You were amazing.'

Tom didn't feel amazing. He felt like a quivering wreck and thanked God that he was by nature more inclined to operate on the *right* side of the law. He didn't have the nerves to be a criminal.

As he walked the short distance to where the taxi was waiting, Tom felt drained. Despite what had just happened, this was far from finished. Jack's family still had to be rescued from the mill in Heywood, and they had to make sure Ava was returned safely, although clearly something wasn't going to plan between Renzo and Tia. There was so much still to play for.

As the water taxi moved through the dark canals, the buildings either side loomed over the water, their outlines blurred in the dim light of the few lamps along the walkways. Tom leaned back, trying to slow his racing heart. The only sounds were the low hum of the engine and gentle splashes as the boat cut through the water. The night felt heavy, a reminder that the danger wasn't over yet, and the quiet only deepened Tom's unease.

His thoughts were interrupted by the sound of Jack's voice coming through his earpiece: 'What the…'

Tom sat up straight. 'What's up?'

'It's Tia. She's sent me a message. She wants to talk. I'll prop the door open on the canal side. I want you here before I speak to her. This doesn't feel good to me.'

'I can see your building ahead. I'll be with you in a few minutes.'

Tom could hear Jack breathing deeply in and out as if he was trying to steady himself. The water taxi pulled up, Tom pushed some euros into the driver's hand, and leaped onto the *pontile*.

Racing up the stairs, he burst into the room. Jack swivelled round to face him and held up a hand. The call was about to begin, and he had his phone on speaker.

'Good evening, Jack Douglas.' *She knew who he was!*

'Good evening, Tia Rukavina,' Jack responded without missing a beat.

Tom heard a chuckle down the line. 'Touché. You're supposed to be dead, Jack. I'm guessing a whole lot of people would be delighted to know that's not true.'

'I don't suppose anyone's even slightly interested,' Jack

responded, although that was patently a lie. 'And you've also apparently disappeared off the face of the earth. While I'm sure there's a good reason for that, perhaps that means we're quits.'

'Maybe. We'll see. Your daughter is one feisty kid but given her upbringing, that makes sense. Unfortunately, she slipped up when she mentioned Finn McGuinness. I knew, of course, that you weren't him, but it made me wonder so I did some research. I remember you now. The smooth-talking bastard who tried to convince me that Guy Bentley's finances were all above board. Pity you died before I could bring you and the rest of his crew down.'

'Pity you didn't hang around long enough to finish what you'd started. That would certainly have been my preference, rather than me having to go it alone and destroy him from beyond the grave.'

Tia ignored that. 'And how nice of your brother Tom to join you, and to play the bumbling idiot. This phone, by the way, is going in the canal as soon as we're done. No more listening in to everything I say and do, Jack.'

'What do you want, Tia? I know you have Ava, and I know you're refusing to speak to Renzo Moretti, so what's your game?'

'I'm done with Moretti. You don't need to know why – it's none of your business. I'm guessing you know we have your family held near Manchester?'

Jack didn't answer.

She chuckled again, but there was a hard edge to the sound. 'I can get them out of there and return Ava to you. I don't know what your plan is for the painting, but I'd guess you're not going to just turn up and let Renzo's men in, are you?'

Again, Jack said nothing.

'Give me something here, Jack,' she sighed. 'Renzo is expecting me to meet you at the palazzo. He won't go himself – he thinks that's what his minions are for. I'm the one in control of the guns, and I'm supposed to make sure one is held to your head if you don't do as you're told. But I won't be there because I don't answer to Moretti any longer. You're on your own. But I can help.'

'How?'

'I need you to do something for me, something that requires a tech expert. I'm great with logistics and spreadsheets, but this needs specialist knowledge.'

'To do what?'

Jack was being very frugal with his words, giving away as little as possible.

'I want you to use the mighty powers of artificial intelligence to create a conversation between two people. You do this, and if I'm happy with the result, you get Ava back.'

Tom gave Jack a puzzled frown, but he just shrugged. He clearly had no idea what was going on either.

'What about the painting?' Jack asked.

'Fuck the painting. I'm not interested in that any longer.'

'Why would I let Moretti's mob into the palazzo, then? If you have Ava and you'll hand her over to me if I do as you ask, why should I do anything at all for Moretti?'

'Why indeed?'

Tom felt as if his head was spinning. Tia had Ava. Becky was ready to release Jack's family. What would be the benefit of allowing the theft to even begin, let alone tell Moretti where the painting was hidden? But he couldn't speak to Jack without Tia hearing every word.

'Who's this fake conversation between, Tia? For it to sound authentic, I need samples of both voices.'

'I'm sure you have Renzo Moretti's. You've heard him talking to me, and I've no doubt you recorded every word.'

She didn't miss much. How long had she known they were recording her? Perhaps only since she realised who Ava's dad was.

Jack neither confirmed nor denied it. 'And the other guy?'

'Bruno Contarini's nephew. You were talking to him at the reception. I saw you.'

Tom hurried to the desk, found a scrap of paper and scribbled a note: *He was talking to you when she ran off.*

'Who's he to you?'

'No one. But if I'm going to set Moretti up, it needs to be with someone close to Contarini if it's to mean anything.'

Neither Tom nor Jack, judging by the look on his face, believed her. But it didn't matter what her motives were. All that mattered was getting Ava back.

'Do you have a sample of the nephew's voice?'

There was a moment of silence. 'Only in English,' she said quietly.

Jack glanced at Tom, his eyes bewildered. 'Hang on, Tia,' he said.

He pressed some keys and the sound of his own voice came through the speakers, asking about the artist of one of the paintings. A second voice answered in English, but it wasn't one that Tom recognised.

Was that a gasp from Tia?

Jack fast-forwarded for a few seconds. The same voice was heard, this time speaking Italian.

'I was speaking with Sandro Contarini at the reception,' Jack said. 'Someone tapped him on the shoulder and he turned round to speak in Italian, so I have a small amount – probably enough. What do you want them to say?'

'I'll send you the words. We need background noise, as if this conversation took place at the reception. Get this back to me within the hour and you can forget about Renzo Moretti and the painting.'

She ended the call.

'What the *fuck*…' Tom said, not for the first time that evening.

Jack looked stunned. 'Can we get Clare and the kids out now, Tom? Is it safe?'

Tom wanted with all his heart to say yes, but he wasn't absolutely sure it was the right decision.

'Check if you can do what Tia's asked first. We've still got time.'

'Yes, but if she's got Ava and is no longer working with Renzo, what's to gain by waiting?'

'Do we believe her? And if she's telling the truth and she's walked away, is Renzo going to take that lying down? If he wants

Tia found, you can bet your life Bruno Contarini's guys could locate her in about ten minutes flat – and finding her means finding Ava. I'm sorry, Jack, but I think we have to keep all options open for now. If necessary, let Moretti's guys into the palazzo – remotely, as planned – and play for time until we have Ava.'

79

While they waited for the content of the message to come through, Tom stripped off his formal outfit and changed into jeans and one of his patterned shirts, then called Philippa. There was no way she would have gone home to bed for the night with everything going down in Heywood.

'Philippa, I'm just checking in to ask whether – if necessary – we could extract Clare ahead of schedule.'

'Everyone's in position. They have been for an hour or so, and there's been a team watching since we located the family. Why do you think we might want to go early?'

'Things haven't gone entirely as expected here. It may be a good thing, and it may not. But there's likely to be one very pissed-off Italian very soon, and I can't guarantee how he'll react.'

'I wish I knew who we were dealing with here. Is this guy a serious Mafia name?'

'No, but he'd like to be. He's not very bright, because if he was, he wouldn't dream of issuing a kill order with kids involved. The minute I think it might all go bad, I'll let you know.'

'I'll be here. And remember, Tom, you're good at this. Figure out the options. Listen to your famous gut.'

He could sense the concern in Philippa's voice. Over the years they'd had their run-ins and she'd never believed in his 'gut'. But he'd always known that she had his back – now more than ever.

Tom heard Jack muttering and walked over to him.

'Anything from Tia?'

'No, but she knows there's not much time. How much of this depends on whether we can trust her?'

Tom sighed. 'Too much, and Tia strikes me as a loose cannon. Whatever she's asking you to do, we have to remember she was an investigator for the NCA before she miraculously transformed herself into an OCG fixer. She worked for Moretti, but now she claims to have dumped him. We have no idea where her true allegiances lie, if she has any. She could be playing us.'

Jack gave an exasperated shrug. 'What do you suggest?'

'I've tried to consider all the variables and how each scenario might play out, but there are so many permutations. Will Tia really hand over Ava if you do as she asks? Do we believe she's done with Moretti? What if she's playing a double game?'

'Basically, you're saying that all our careful planning to protect everyone has just gone to shit.'

'I'd prefer to say it's difficult to predict which way people will jump. Although, based on your research and one brief meeting, Moretti's character seems pretty clear.'

Jack shook his head. 'Don't forget his phone conversations with Tia. He's on a short fuse. I saw that, the way the flush of anger creeps up his neck, and you can hear it in his voice.'

'If his heist has fallen apart, someone will have to pay. But at the moment he can't – as far as we know – take it out on Ava.'

Jack jumped up from his chair and paced the room. 'But he *can* take it out on the rest of my family. That's what you're saying, isn't it? He just has to issue the order, and even with your team watching, squeezing a trigger takes less than a second.'

Tom nodded, reluctant to voice his agreement.

Jack stopped pacing and faced Tom. 'We need to get them out now, Tom. It's a no-brainer.'

'I agree, but it does increase the risk for Ava. Renzo won't take

Tia going AWOL lying down – if she's telling us the truth. The streets will soon be crawling with Contarini's thugs searching for her – and very possibly you.'

Jack drew a shaky breath. 'My brain can't deal with this. I keep imagining the terror every single member of my family is suffering, and I don't know what to do to save them. I thought I had it all worked out, but—'

'But things have changed, so we have to be flexible. We don't know if Renzo's aware that Tia's gone off-script, so until we know more, you should continue to act as if the heist is going ahead and carry out his plans until every member of your family is safe, at which point you can say "Fuck you" to Renzo. In the meantime, we extract Clare, Billy and Sophia now.'

'And Ava, poor kid, remains at risk.' Jack's voice cracked on the words.

He was right, but the risks were so varied. Tia could be lying about setting Renzo up. She could be planning to sell Ava – even if not to Kodra and Besnik. She could cut and run, leaving Ava God knows where.

'When we extract Clare and the kids, Becky will authorise the use of the signal jammer, but remember it was only ever meant to be a temporary distraction, to force Renzo's hand at the crucial moment when he needed you to let his men out of the palazzo. He'll smell a rat if he can't establish contact with Heywood for any length of time, which is precisely why we decided not to get them out sooner. For now, he needs to believe the heist is on track and we have to hope he doesn't try to call them ahead of time.'

Jack raised haunted eyes to Tom. 'It'll be a huge relief to know they're safe. But let's be clear: whatever Tia wants the audio file for, she's not bloody getting it until she hands Ava back.'

'Agreed. The minute you receive the script, tell her to bring Ava to the Rialto market. I'll go and wait there now. Release the content to her when, and only when, I have your daughter.'

Jack collapsed onto his chair. 'Okay. Get Clare, Billy and Sophia out now, Tom, then we'll fight like crazy to save Ava. It's the right decision, and although it devastates me to say so, I'll have to leave you to organise the rescue of my family. I'd prefer to be involved in every moment, hearing every breath each of them takes, but I need to deal with Tia and handle Renzo.'

Tom closed his eyes for a second. Had he got this right? If Tia was playing them, was still working with Renzo, and was still in contact with the Albanians in Heywood, they could be signing Ava's death warrant. But on balance, the danger to Clare, Billy and Sophia seemed greater. There were no guarantees, though.

'Philippa's ready to issue the order for your family's rescue on my instruction. I'll call her on my way to the market.'

Jack's top lip was clenched between his teeth, but he nodded and turned back to his computer as Tom headed for the door.

There was a *ping* from Jack's computer. 'Hang on, Tom. There's a message coming through.'

80

Jack's screen displayed a string of text, all in Italian. It was clear from the way it was set out that this was meant to be two people having a conversation.

'Will you be able to make this audio file for Tia?' Tom asked. So much of their plan hinged on its success.

'Yep. I've started to train the AI on the voices. It's captured the tone, pitch and any subtle speech patterns, so I've fed in the text and I'm hoping it will create the conversation quickly. While the software's performing its magic, let's see what she wants these two guys to say.'

Jack typed some instructions and then pasted the text into his translator. Tom read the words over his brother's shoulder.

Renzo: We'll have the collateral by the end of the night. Elena will hold it secure until the cocaine has arrived and we've recouped enough from sales to pay your uncle.

Sandro: The cut house is ready?

Renzo: It is. Everything's in place.

Sandro: And the fentanyl?

Renzo: Don't worry – we're stretching the product exactly as you suggested. We'll double what Contarini's expecting. You'll get your cut, but you need to keep him from ordering any tests.

Sandro: Quality control is my job. He trusts me.

Renzo: He'd better. Because let's not forget this whole thing was your idea.

Tom felt goosebumps on his arms. 'Shit, Jack, they're planning to cut the cocaine with *fentanyl*! Only a couple of milligrams – like a few grains of salt – can kill someone. The margins for error are crazily slim.'

Jack frowned. 'Don't forget Tia's setting them up. They might not be planning to use fentanyl at all.'

'She's not stupid. At least some of it will be true, and she's too smart for the recording to be the only evidence against them. If they get their hands on that painting, we'll potentially be complicit in murder!'

Jack dropped his head. 'It's not going come to that. It was bad enough thinking the painting was going to fund cocaine smuggling – you know how I feel about drugs – but I convinced myself that it wasn't going to make a fat lot of difference. If Renzo Moretti didn't bring it in, Bruno Contarini would. But fentanyl's a different beast.'

Tom didn't want to ask himself how far he and Jack would have gone if they'd been aware of this all along, knowing that people – many of them possibly no older than Ava – might die. Was it ever acceptable to save one person you love at the expense of others you don't know? He pushed the thought from his mind.

'Do you think Tia always knew about it, or has she just found out?'

Jack shrugged. 'As you said, she can't be trusted, but if they were genuinely planning to cut the cocaine with fentanyl and this isn't just a set-up, she'll have known.'

'If she's using this recording against one or both these guys, she must really hate them.'

'Like you said, she'll need more than just a voice recording to incriminate them. She used to be a forensic accountant – spent years unpacking hidden money trails – so if she really wants to stitch them up—'

'Of course! She'll create a false money trail of her own – build a fake path right to their door.'

Jack shrugged. 'That's what I'd do. Set up accounts somewhere like Panama, make sure Sandro and Renzo are inextricably linked. At a guess, she wants to discredit them with Contarini, for reasons we don't understand. Renzo's a complete shit of a man, but there must be something more. And God knows what the repercussions will be.'

Tom looked at his watch. 'Whatever her motives, I need to go. I'll speak to Philippa. Make sure Tia knows she has to bring Ava to the market before you'll send the recording.'

Jack was focusing on his computer, but Tom saw him nod. 'I'll send a protected version. Then, when you have Ava safe, she'll get the final version.'

'And Renzo?'

'Leave Renzo to me. Let me know when Clare and my kids are secure and confirm when you've got Ava. If and when they're all safe, I'll go for the "Fuck you" option. We don't have much time, though – so go, Tom.'

Tom paused in the doorway and looked back. They were about to bring down the wrath of the Mafia on their heads, and he couldn't shake the fear that this might be the last time he'd see his brother.

81

The sound of Tom's footsteps echoed through the narrow, deserted streets as he hurried towards St Mark's Square. He'd been to the Rialto area to buy the masks, so he knew the route, but at this hour it felt very different. He was praying that now Tia had sent Kodra packing, the Albanians had given up looking for him, or at the very least wouldn't be out searching in the early hours of the morning.

Everywhere was hauntingly still with no bustling crowds or bright sunlight, and as Tom spoke to Philippa his voice seemed to reverberate off the buildings.

'Philippa, forget the original timings. We need them out now. I'll explain later, when you've got things moving, but we can't wait.'

Hearing the urgency in his voice, Philippa didn't ask any questions.

'On it. I'll get Becky to keep you updated.'

'Thank you. I don't know what to say…'

'Then save it for later. Stay on the line for a second.'

Tom could hear Philippa talking into her radio. 'DCI Robinson, it's a go. No waiting. Move now. And Becky, patch your radio through to Tom's mobile. Keep him in the loop.'

The call ended, and seconds later he heard a beep from his phone. An incoming call.

'Becky.'

'The team's ready, Tom. The risk assessment was done in advance of the original timing. The strategy's planned. Armed response are waiting for the go.'

Tom stayed silent – talking would just distract Becky. He'd made it as far as the Rialto Bridge, but now he stopped. He wanted to hear every word, pick up every nuance, every shift in her voice, every sign of danger. He leaned against the stone balustrade, eyes on the dark canal below – not speaking, just listening. Seconds stretched into what felt like hours before Becky's voice cut through the silence.

'In position.'

Becky's heart was thumping in her chest as she sat in the control vehicle, hidden behind a copse of trees just beyond the outer cordon. The track to the abandoned mill was too exposed, so vehicle approach had been made over the neighbouring farmland, with armed officers moving in along the canal tow path.

It was a cool damp night, the moon hanging low, casting a silvery glow over the old brickwork of the building. There wasn't a breath of air, and as the men held their positions waiting for her word, every rustle of clothing, every careful step on the gravel path, every shift of their tactical gear seemed unnaturally loud. But inside the mill, all was quiet.

She glanced around the vehicle, taking in the focused faces of her team. They couldn't get this wrong. This was Tom's family.

Each stage of the hostage retrieval had been meticulously planned over the last few hours. They knew one of the two men inside was armed, and although there was no evidence of a second gun, nothing could be left to chance.

'Final checks, all units.' Becky spoke quietly, her voice steadier than she felt. Her eyes scanned the interior of the mill via the video feeds to her screen. Entry would take place through both north and south entrances. One of the Albanians was sleeping in a room to the left of the north door. The other was sitting in an old armchair in the room to the right of the north entrance with Clare and the children. His gun lay on a table within arm's reach. The little ones appeared to be asleep but Clare, half-sitting, half-lying on a rug on the floor with her arms around them, never seemed to doze for more than a minute before jerking awake, clearly terrified of what might happen if she fell asleep.

A low buzz filled the communication channels as the final checks were completed. Becky could feel the tension radiating from her team, their silent focus mirroring her own inner tension.

'Team A, prepare to breach from the north entrance. Team B, breach south. Stand by for my mark.' The voice of Nick Weston, bronze commander, crackled through her earpiece, crisp and clear. 'Two minutes to breach. Ensure all in position.'

Becky wished she had some way of warning Clare what was about to happen. Any second now, battering rams would smash through both doors and the rooms would be flooded with armed officers. She could only imagine the cold terror that would grip her and the children at that moment.

'In position,' Weston confirmed. 'Prepare to enter.'

'On your command,' Becky responded.

'On my count,' Weston whispered, his voice steady. 'Three... two...one... *Go!*'

Becky felt a surge of adrenaline as bodies erupted from the bushes and raced around the sides of the building. The north and south entrances burst open, the doors flying inward, the noise reverberating through the mill and in Becky's earpiece.

'*Armed police!*' multiple voices shouted simultaneously, the cacophony mingling with the terrified screams of the hostages. '*Show me your hands!*'

The room was crowded with officers obstructing the video feeds, and Becky couldn't see a thing. But the audio was clear.

'*Drop your weapon! Drop your weapon!*'

The sound of a single shot reverberated through the radio.

Becky thought her heart had stopped. She held her breath, knowing Tom could hear all this but would know better than to ask what was happening.

After what was only a few seconds but felt like hours, she heard Weston's voice. 'Suspect down. Second suspect in custody. Hostages secured.' Becky breathed again. 'Clearing the building. Tactical medical assistance urgently required.'

She still couldn't see Clare and the children on her monitor, but was hoping she had heard right and only one shot had been fired – just the suspect was down. But she needed to see for herself.

'DCI Robinson, we're clear. Safe to approach,' Weston said. 'Ambulance needed.'

Becky leaped out of the vehicle and, pushing through a straggly hedge, ran across the damp grass. A firearms officer, weapon across his chest, looking composed and untroubled by the events of the previous few minutes, stood back to let her into the building. A child was sobbing, a baby crying, as she burst into the room. Clare was lying on the floor, both children underneath her.

'Clare! It's Becky Robinson. Can you get up?' she shouted, rushing across the room.

Clare lifted a pale face. 'I threw myself on them when the noise started, but I think they're okay. Billy, sweetheart, did I hurt you?'

Becky crouched down. 'We'll get you all to hospital and have you checked over, but you're safe now.'

Leaving Rob to help Clare to her feet, Becky spoke into her radio.

'You got that, Tom? Clare, Billy and Sophia are all safe. One of the suspects raised his gun and was shot, but no one else is hurt. He'll be on his way to hospital as soon as we've cleared entry for the paramedics. But I repeat, no other injuries.'

She heard a groan of relief. 'Thank God for that,' Tom said.

Still leaning against the balustrade of the Rialto Bridge, Tom was grateful for its support. The last few days had taken a toll on his already weakened body, and what had just happened in Heywood had been almost unbearable to listen to.

'Any chance I could speak to Clare – just for a second?'

Tom heard a bit of mumbling in the background, then Clare's voice – shaky but just about hanging on. 'Tom? Oh God, it's really you. Please tell me Pete and Ava are both okay?'

Tom felt a jolt at his brother being referred to as Pete, but he guessed over the past five years Clare had got more used to it than he had.

'Tell me how you're doing first. I can't imagine what you've been through. Are the kids okay? Are any of you hurt?'

'We're fine. They didn't hurt us. All the noise has left Sophia scared and confused, but Becky's giving her a cuddle and she's starting to smile. Billy's been a real hero, haven't you, sweetheart?' Tom heard a hiccupping 'Yes.' 'But you've still not told me about Pete and Ava. What's going on? Where are they?'

Given the trauma of the previous two weeks and the stress of the last few minutes, Tom decided to give her a sanitised version of the truth.

'Pete's fine. Out of his mind with worry about all of you, but he's okay. We've seen Ava on video, heard her voice, and he's just finalising the negotiations for her release. I'm on my way to the exchange point now. We've got this, Clare. Go with Becky to the hospital, get yourselves checked out, and ask Becky to sort out a phone for you. They'll need yours as evidence.'

'I've got a thousand questions, but they're waiting to put us in the ambulance.' Her voice trembled and Tom heard a soft sob. 'My heart breaks for Ava… Please bring them both home safely, Tom. I can't lose him again.'

Tom knew exactly what she meant. Just like Tom, for years Clare had believed Jack was dead. She knew what the grief of losing him felt like.

'I'll let him know you're safe. I can't tell you how much he's waiting to hear the news.'

Ending the call, Tom immediately punched in Jack's number.

'They're safe, Jack. All three of them rescued.'

All Tom could hear was Jack's ragged breathing on the other end.

'Jack?'

'Thank *Christ* for that.' Jack's voice cracked with emotion. 'Where are they? Can I speak to them?'

'Becky's getting them to hospital for a check-up, but they're fine. She'll send me a mobile number for Clare as soon as she's confident that everything's set up in Heywood, in case Moretti tries to contact his guys.'

'I don't know if Tia's in touch with him. Her phone's dead. She's sent me a new number, but obviously I don't have spyware installed on that. If Renzo panics and tries to call the Heywood crew, the disruption on the line will have to be convincing.'

'Becky knows that, Jack, and it's the least of our worries now. Tia's the one I'm concerned about.'

'You think she could be playing us, don't you?'

'I don't know, but let's celebrate one success and then do whatever it takes to save Ava.'

Could Tia be setting up Renzo and Sandro Contarini with this bogus recording while simultaneously collaborating with Renzo to steal the painting? Why would she do that?

Tom shook his head. They had never understood Tia's motives and were no closer now. They just had to play the hand they had.

'You still there, Tom? Be careful at the market. Tia may not come alone.'

'I know. Not much I can do about it, other than be vigilant. I'll be there in three minutes. How are you doing with the recording?'

'Sending the audio file now.'

'What's to stop her from using it and making a run for it?'

Jack tutted. 'I've put an audio watermark on it – a beep every few seconds. I'll send her a clean version when Ava's safe.'

'And Renzo? What's going to happen there?'

'Leave Renzo Moretti to me.'

'Jack…' Tom said, hoping Jack would pick up the warning in his voice.

'I asked you to leave him to me, Tom. Okay?'

Tom could only hope that Jack wouldn't choose this moment to make Moretti pay for everything he had done. However close they were to getting Ava back safely, it wasn't over yet.

82

Ava sits on the bed in a dreary little hotel room, wondering who had thought of naming the hotel 'Bella'. Looking out of the window at nothing more interesting than the wall of the building opposite, she's trying to work out what the woman is doing. For a while she was writing in a notebook, but kept tearing the pages out and ripping them to shreds. Finally she stopped, and started to type into her phone, checking against the words she'd written down. Now she's working on her laptop, her expression tight with concentration, every keystroke deliberate.

At first, Ava thought this room – decorated in sickening shades of orange – was better than the cellar. But she'd known what to expect there, what to fear, what to hope for. Now she has no idea what's going to happen, or what the woman wants with her. She tried to ask, to threaten her again with what her dad will do, but the woman yelled at her to shut up. She didn't try again.

There was a moment earlier when Ava thought she would lose every last bit of the control she'd fought so hard to hold onto. The woman had moved to the other side of the room to make a call, and Ava could hear the muffled tones of a deep voice responding. She couldn't make out the words, but she knew who it was. She held her breath, scared to breathe in case she missed something.

'*Dad?*' she'd whispered, earning herself a sharp look from the woman, a finger to her lips.

The temptation to dive off the bed and grab the phone was fierce, but she dug her fingers into her palms, knowing it would be a mistake. Maybe, just maybe, he was doing a deal to set her free.

Dad will save me. I have to trust him.

Since the moment she heard that he'd demanded a video of her, she'd felt hope, and when the little voice at the back of her head whispered, 'Don't be stupid – if saving you was that easy, he'd have done it already,' she forced it to be silent.

Then the woman called him Jack Douglas.

How does she know who he is? Is that my fault?

Maybe it had been a childish mistake to mention Finn McGuinness, but Ava had wanted to scare the woman, and no one in this world was as scary as Finn McGuinness.

And then she said 'Tom'. Was Dad's brother in Venice too? Ava felt a surge of hope. *Tom's a policeman. If anyone can save me, surely he can?* But the woman said she has Ava's whole family, and the thought is unbearable.

Ava wanted to scream, 'Sell me, kill me, do what you want as long as no one else gets hurt.' That would be the fairest thing, given all the trouble she's caused since she first turned up in their lives.

She stifled a gasp of despair when the call ended. Hearing fragments of his voice, just knowing he was on the other end of the call, had made her feel less alone. Now that tiny comfort was gone, and she felt more isolated than ever.

Blinking away the tears that sprang unwanted into her eyes, Ava leaned back, pretending to be sleeping, but her heart was hammering so loud she was sure the woman would hear it.

Now, she looks at her through half-closed eyes. There's something weird about her. She pretended to be in charge when she spoke to those two men in the cellar – aggressive and in control. She sounded like that when she spoke to Ava's dad too. But she's been crying. Each time she lifts her head from the laptop her eyes are puffier, a little more bloodshot.

Something's rattled her, and Ava can't decide if that's a good thing or not. She remembers something her dad said about people who blindly drifted into the world of organised crime – the life she was brought up in; people driven to do terrible things by the damage deep inside them.

Never underestimate the fury of a broken soul.

Ava sees it now in the woman's eyes: the sadness buried under an intense and barely controlled anger. Despite the tears, her jaw is clenched, her back rigid. Her fingers tap incessantly on the table or on her computer. And Ava has no idea what this means for her future. She just wants to be with her dad, her mum, her brother and sister. She will never break another rule in her life if they can all be safe.

The woman's phone vibrates and she jumps as if someone's shot her. She holds the phone to her ear but doesn't speak. Ava strains to hear. The tinny voices seem to belong to two different people. They're speaking in a foreign language. There's a *ping* every few seconds.

The woman is listening intently, her top lip clenched in her teeth, head bent as if what she's hearing requires every ounce of concentration. It ends, and she plays it again. And again.

She types something into her phone and waits – staring at the screen as if willing it to spring to life. There's the *ping* of an incoming message. She reads it, tuts and looks at Ava.

'We're going out. Same rules, Ava. Run, and your family dies. If that happens, it will be on you.'

The question Ava is asking herself, though, is what's going to happen if she *doesn't* run. No one has told her that.

83

The area around the Rialto market was quiet, with only a few early traders setting up for the day. The lights flickered on in the café as Tom arrived and he took one of the outside chairs, his back to the window, his eyes scouring the canal, the dark arches of the market, the narrow black passageways.

Boats drifted up to the dock, the low hum of their engines and the soft clatter of crates punctuating the stillness of the night. Traders moved like shadows, unloading their goods. His gaze flicked between the water, the alleys, the buildings, never resting long on one spot, trying to probe the gloom. Tia and Ava could appear at any moment – or perhaps not at all. He hadn't heard another word from Jack. All he could do was wait.

His phone vibrated in his hand, and Tom's pulse raced. *Good news or bad?*

'Becky. Everything okay?' he murmured, his voice seeming unnaturally loud in the quiet square.

'Fine, but there's been no call from your man in Venice,' Becky replied. 'He hasn't tried to contact the Albanian crew here, but we've set up the signal jammer just in case. Any news on Ava?'

Tom grunted. 'I don't know. Jack's convinced we can save her, but that might be wishful thinking. The person who has her appears to have an agenda, and whatever it was originally, it seems to have changed. Everything we've planned and done might be for nothing. I'll let you know.'

'Shit, I'm sorry, Tom. All I can do is wish you luck and say we're thinking of you. Call me if I can do anything.'

All the time they were talking, Tom's eyes had been scanning the area, trying to take in every detail. Sunrise was still a couple of hours away, and with little more than a dim glow from inside the market and the light spilling from the small windows of the café, it was difficult to see much beyond the immediate vicinity. But each shadow that moved drew his attention.

Time, once again, was passing too slowly. He checked his watch – 3.30, the time Jack was supposed to let Renzo's team into the palazzo to steal the painting. Or rather, to discover it had already gone. Was that still happening? Would Renzo go ahead without Tia? They still didn't have Ava, so was Jack going to let them in? Was he trying to delay? Were the streets going to be swarming with Mafia thugs looking for Ava? He wished he knew what his brother was up to.

Tom tensed and sat bolt upright. Had they ever told Renzo that this was the handover point for Ava? He couldn't remember. They'd *talked* about Jack telling Renzo to bring her here, but had he ever named the place? Had Tia told Renzo Jack's real name, or about Tom's involvement, or did she discover these things after her change of heart? How much did Renzo know? Already alert, Tom realised he shouldn't only be looking for Ava in the shadows.

A chill crept down his back. Would he recognise Renzo? He hadn't seen him in the bar; he'd only seen Tia, then swiftly made his way out. At the reception Renzo had worn a mask, but he remembered the thin pointed nose and the fat belly. Would that be enough?

Would Renzo turn up here if Jack didn't do as he demanded? Would he come himself, or send his men? Or Contarini's? Would they be armed?

Of course they would.

Tom scanned left and right. There were more people around

now, all moving with purpose, none of them heading towards him. Yet.

The time dragged. Was Ava coming? Would Tia let her go?

His mind was about to spin out of control when his gaze fell on the market building. Silhouetted under one of the open arches were two figures, a woman and someone who appeared little more than a girl.

He leaped to his feet, his chair clattering across the cobbles, and took a step forward.

Everything in the market had faded into the background. The boats, the early traders – gone. All Tom could see was the archway and the two figures beneath it. Ava was so close. A few dozen metres and he would be able to reach out and pull her to him. But Tia's grip anchored her in place, her left hand firmly on Ava's shoulder, her right tucked inside her coat pocket. Tom's eyes stayed locked on the girl and the woman beside her as he closed the distance between them.

Why wasn't Ava pushing the woman aside and running to him? There were people around, men who would surely stop Tia from hurting her. But Ava seemed rooted to the spot.

Tia and Ava took a step forward, emerging from beneath the shadow of the arch. Tia leaned in, whispering in Ava's ear. What was she saying?

Tom wanted to shout 'Run, Ava!' but as they drew closer, he could see the girl's eyes were wide, darting between him, Tia, and the market traders setting up their stalls. Her top lip was clamped between her teeth. She looked as if every beat of her heart was urging her to run but fear was holding her in place.

They were four metres apart when Tia spoke.

'Tell your brother the recording is acceptable. If he removes the audio watermark and sends it to me now, Ava is yours.'

'Take your hand out of your pocket, Tia, and walk towards me,' Tom said evenly.

'I don't need to do anything you say, Tom Douglas. I'm in control here.'

'Really? We know who you are and what you've done. And if you hurt a hair on Ava's head, you'll be hunted down by law enforcement all over the world. I can make that happen.'

Tia smirked. 'And the minute I'm arrested, I'll tell the criminal world that Jack Douglas isn't dead. That he's been working undercover for the police for years. And we know exactly what will happen to him.'

Tom took a deliberate step closer. 'Do you want to risk that? You know as well as I do that my brother has connections that can reach you wherever you try to hide.'

'Maybe it's stalemate, then. But remember, I know all about his family, what they're called, where they live, where they go to school. They'll be easy to track down, even if he decides to play dead again.'

Tom heard a whimper from Ava. She more than anyone would understand what might happen to Jack if Tia followed through on her threats.

'Call him,' Tia demanded.

'Take your hand out of your pocket, Tia. With everything we know about you, what you've done, what you're capable of, I want to see both hands.'

A crease flickered between her eyes, gone in an instant. Was that *remorse*? She hesitated, then slowly began to withdraw her hand. Tom's breath caught as he noticed the bulge in the fabric of her coat pocket, but before he could react, two figures emerged from the shadows behind her: one stocky, muscular, the other skinny with a long body and short legs. Kodra and Besnik. Had Jack got it wrong? Was Tia still working with them?

Kodra's deep voice resonated in the crisp morning air. 'We're here for the girl, Elena.'

Tia's grip on Ava tightened. 'That's not part of our deal,' she snapped.

Kodra advanced towards her. 'I disagree. I told you it wasn't over. Give us the girl and we'll leave. No one has to get hurt.'

Tom hesitated. Rushing to grab Ava would be a mistake. He had to assume Tia had a gun in her pocket, and the Albanians would be armed too. It felt like a stand-off, and he was the only one without a weapon.

Ava stared at Tom, her eyes wide with panic. Then her gaze shifted behind him and she gasped. Glancing over his shoulder, Tom saw a figure emerge from the gloom.

'*Dad*?' Ava whispered, her voice trembling.

Jack stepped into the dim light, his eyes fixed on his daughter, and in that instant whatever Tia had said or done to persuade Ava not to run was forgotten. She shoved the woman aside and sprinted across the cobbles. Tom turned in time to see her fling herself at Jack.

'*Mut!*' Besnik shouted, lunging forward.

Tia moved swiftly, pulling her gun from her pocket and aiming it squarely at Kodra, then Besnik, then back at Kodra. 'Back off!' she commanded, her voice cold and steady.

The two Albanians halted, hands moving towards their lower backs, where their guns were no doubt stuck in their belts.

'Don't even think about it.'

Around them, the traders froze, their conversations dying mid-sentence.

'Jack, send me the file or I walk away and let them have her.'

Holding Ava close with one arm, Jack pressed the screen of his phone, and Tom heard a distinct *ping*, the sound strangely loud in the sudden hush of the market.

With her phone in one hand, weapon in the other, Tia backed into the market, keeping her gun trained on the two men. People edged away, moving behind pillars, some ducking behind their stalls. A murmur spread: '*Pistola…*'

With the Albanians' attention on the gun in Tia's hand as they looked for an opportunity to draw their own, and Tia focused on escaping before they made their move, Tom seized the initiative.

'Jack, Ava, this way!' he urged, gesturing towards a narrow passage next to the café.

Jack grabbed Ava's hand and all three sprinted down the alley, the sounds of the market fading as they moved further into a labyrinth of lanes, their bodies swallowed by the darkness. Taking random turns, dodging down narrow paths, they finally stopped, breathless, ducking into the portico of a tiny chapel, pressing themselves against its cool stone walls.

Tom put a finger to his lips, straining to hear the sound of thundering feet as Jack wrapped his arms tightly round Ava.

Silence. Maybe – for now – they had lost them.

Tom had no idea what had happened between Jack and Renzo Moretti, but they needed to get off the streets. He was as sure as he could be that, even as the threat of the Albanians faded, neither his hotel nor Jack's room would offer a safe haven from the Italian mob.

84

They had to move, but Ava needed a moment. Her head was buried in Jack's chest, her strength sapped by weeks in a dank cellar, and she was gasping for breath.

Finally, she put her hands against her dad's chest and pushed back, looking up at him.

'What took you so bloody long?' she asked, promptly bursting into tears and wrapping her arms around him again.

'I'm sorry, sweetheart,' Jack said. 'I'm going to keep you safe now, I promise.'

'I didn't know if you'd come,' she sobbed.

Jack tutted. 'You've said some daft things in your time, Ava Johnson, but that takes the biscuit.'

There was the sound of a hiccupping chuckle from somewhere close to Jack's chest, then she leaned back, her face once again a picture of despair. 'But Mum, Billy, Sophia – she said she had them too?'

'She did, but Tom's team in Manchester have rescued them. Tia didn't know. Is that why you didn't go to Tom when you saw him?'

Ava rubbed her hand across her eyes. 'She said she'd have them killed if I ran. But then I saw you, and I forgot.'

Tom felt a lump in his throat. How many people, let alone a girl who was little more than a child, would have chosen to stay with their abductor rather than risk harm to their family?

'You are one brave kid,' Jack said, hugging her tighter, 'but now we have to go. Tom, did you leave anything at the hotel that you need?'

'My clothes, but they're not important. I've got my passport and wallet. I'm guessing it's not safe to go back?'

'I don't know for sure if Tia told Renzo who we are, so as you no doubt booked under your real name, being the honest and upright chap that you are, Renzo could easily discover where you've been staying.'

Tom decided not to mention that he hadn't realised there was any reason *not* to give his real name.

'There's nothing that can't be replaced. What's happening with Renzo?'

'Absolutely fuck all,' he said. 'Sorry for the language, Ava.'

Ava grinned.

'What do you mean?' Tom asked.

'I played for time, said we had to wait thirty minutes – made an excuse about the moon and the doctored CCTV footage. I couldn't deal with him while I was worried sick about whether Tia was going to hand Ava back. I had to be here.' Jack pulled her closer again. 'The reason for the delay was plausible, so Renzo will have held off going to the palazzo, and if Tia had been playing us and we hadn't got Ava back, I'd still have had time to let Renzo in—' he glanced at his watch, '—round about now.'

'So...' Tom began, knowing that Renzo wasn't going to take Jack's betrayal lying down.

Jack shook his head. 'Let's walk and talk, Tom. I want to get Ava somewhere safe. And walk. Don't run,' he murmured as they left their temporary sanctuary.

They turned to head further away from the market, Ava sandwiched between the brothers. 'What about our phones, Jack? Turning them off isn't enough.'

'Yeah, we need to ditch them. All but the black phone. I'm pretty sure they'll never track that.' Jack pointed to a small pile of rubbish sacks by the open doorway of a bakery, the smell of freshly baking bread mingling with the cool early-morning air. There was no one in sight, but Tom could hear the sound of laughter and singing from inside, the bakers clearly happy in their work. 'These bags will be picked up in an hour or so and taken God knows where, but a long way from where we'll be.'

They buried the phones deep inside one of the sacks and carried on walking until, after about five minutes, Tom realised he had no idea where they were.

'Where are we going?'

'Somewhere safe, I hope. I'm reasonably certain Renzo hasn't been able to trace the location we used – at least, not yet – but while "reasonably" might be good enough for me, it's not good enough for you two. I've wiped the computers except my laptop, which I relocated to a backup location on my way to the market.'

Tom wanted to be surprised that Jack had a backup location, but he wasn't.

'Where do things stand with Renzo? I know you said he can go screw himself, but what does that mean?'

'I guess he'll have realised that I'm not coming and nor is Tia, so he's not getting into the palazzo. All hell is about to break loose. We're going to have to be very careful, Tom. Whatever I might think of his professional skills, I have little doubt Renzo will summon every contact he has to track me down.'

'Did you consider letting him in with the police waiting for him – or even Vittorio D'Angelo?'

'I did, and I definitely want him dealt with for everything he's put us through. But I have a strong suspicion that Tia's about to do a better job than the police.'

'Of course! The recording.'

Jack gave what sounded like a satisfied sigh. 'Oh yes. For some reason I can't grasp, she's not just setting up Renzo – Contarini's nephew is implicated too. The 'Ndrangheta won't be impressed that their reputation for high-quality product was about to be destroyed, or that two of their own were apparently hoping to make a massive profit on the side. It's a risky move – one that'll have severe repercussions for both of them.'

'I guess that's what Tia's banking on,' Tom said.

'The punishment meted out by Bruno Contarini is going to make anything I might do to Renzo pale into insignificance. I'm guessing fentanyl was Tia's idea – maybe with the sole aim from the outset of setting him up for a fall. Don't ask me why. We'll probably never know.'

'So Moretti's heist is off. I'm *so* glad I went to the trouble of stealing the bloody painting, then,' Tom muttered.

Ava turned to him. 'You stole a *painting*? Seriously?'

'Not quite. I relocated it. Not that the subtle difference would stand up in a court of law.'

'Bloody hell,' Ava murmured, a trace of a grin on her face.

'About the painting...' Tom said.

'As soon as we're off the streets I'm going to get a message to Vittorio D'Angelo and his daughter, Gabriella,' Jack said. 'I'll tell them where to find it. I'm hoping I can make him realise I was trying to protect his painting, not exploit him. But if we're to prevent him from sending the *polizia* – or more likely the *carabinieri* – after both of us, he needs an explanation. As it is, we already have the Italian Mafia and the Albanian mob hunting us. We don't need anyone else on our case.'

With that cheery thought, Jack steered them towards a door set into a wall facing on to the narrow lane and inserted a key.

'Not luxurious, but until we've worked out how to get away from here safely, it'll have to do.'

85

The door to Bruno Contarini's ostentatious palazzo is opened by a thickset man in a black suit.

'Dica,' he says, standing squarely across the open doorway.

Speak. Not a friendly greeting.

'My name is Elena Ferraro. I have some news for Signor Contarini, and he's going to want to hear what I have to say.'

Flawless as my Italian is, speaking their language puts me at a slight disadvantage, and I know Contarini and his closest team all speak English. Let them be the ones who have to think just that little bit harder.

'Is he expecting you?'

'No, but if you give him my name and tell him that I was the fixer for Renzo Moretti, I'm sure he'll want to talk to me.'

'Wait here,' he says, closing the door in my face.

I can feel cold sweat running down my back. This is my last play – if it doesn't work, I'm done. I thought it was all over last night, that Kodra and his sidekick were going to ruin everything, but when the girl disappeared with her father and his brother they must have decided she was the greater prize and chased after them. I doubt they caught them, and I'm glad about that.

The wait seems endless, but then the door opens and I'm invited inside. I walk through an internal courtyard, the morning sunshine illuminating a beautiful arrangement of exotic plants in the centre of the space. The cheerful sounds of birdsong and the gentle trickle of a fountain fill the air, and a spike of rage runs through me at this life, and those who are living it.

I am led to a doorway then down a corridor to a grand study. Contarini is sitting behind a vast desk, devoid of clutter. Four mobile phones sit on chargers with a computer to one side, but the screen is blank.

'Signora Ferraro. You prefer to speak in English?'

I don't want him to know how fluent my Italian is. 'Yes.'

'Very well. Sit,' he says, then adds 'please.' I lower myself into the chair, slowly, deliberately, as if I have all the confidence in the world. He's watching me, and I can't let him see even a flicker of uncertainty about why I'm here. 'I understand you were Moretti's fixer. I'm surprised you have the confidence to come here, as everything you "fixed" failed to materialise. Not exactly an endorsement of your abilities.'

I nod. 'I understand why you might feel that way. Let me explain. Moretti's entire scheme depended on acquiring the painting. Every step was meticulously planned, but last night I made a discovery and stopped the shipment from going ahead. You, of course, lose nothing. The product is still in your possession in the warehouse in Guatemala. You have suffered no losses, but even though I haven't been paid – and now won't be – I thought it better to halt the plan rather than let it continue and potentially damage your reputation.'

His eyes flash at my suggestion that anyone could achieve such a thing.

'What, exactly, do you want to tell me, signora?'

'I recorded a conversation last night at the reception.'

He looks at me with raised eyebrows, as if nothing I have to say is likely to concern him. He is, after all, a capobastone in the 'Ndrangheta.

'Shall I play it to you?' I ask, my mouth dry.

He tilts his head, as if to say, 'If you must.'

'Renzo Moretti speaks first. I don't recognise the voice of the second man,' I tell him, lying through my teeth.

Raising the volume to maximum, I start the recording.

'Avremo la garanzia pronta per stasera...'

Contarini is watching me, looking slightly bored, as Renzo confirms the collateral – la garanzia – will be in place by that night. And then the second voice cuts in. Contarini recognises it and leans forward, listening intently. I say nothing but watch his face.

'E il fentanyl?'

Contarini's jaw tightens, but he doesn't say a word as he listens to the rest of the short conversation. It's the words 'Si fida di me' that seemed to hit him hardest. 'He trusts me.' Bruno Contarini trusts his nephew. Or at least, he did.

For a long moment Contarini doesn't speak. Then: 'How did you record this?'

'I've never trusted Renzo Moretti. He asked me to do things I didn't agree with. We'd taken a teenage girl hostage as part of the plan to steal the painting. Moretti wanted me to kill her or sell her to the Albanians.' I doubt it's possible for Contarini's jaw to clamp any tighter as I continue. 'So I put an app on his phone and recorded everything he said last night.'

His eyes narrow. 'And what do you want from me? Payment, I presume.'

I shake my head. 'I want nothing, signore. I just don't want men like these two to go unpunished. Fentanyl kills. We both know that, and I want no part in it. I've been to the laboratorio – the fentanyl is there. You can check.'

'Do you have any other evidence?' he asks, as I knew he would.

I look down at my hands, clasped tightly in my lap, as if I'm ashamed. 'I'm sorry that I was ever a part of this, but if I may… I suggest you follow the money.'

I say it as if I know there's something to find. Contarini will have people who will uncover the financial trail I've laid, but it will take some time. If it was easy to follow, he wouldn't believe his clever nephew had made such obvious mistakes.

I lift my eyes. Bruno Contarini is staring at me, and I don't know what he's going to say next. I keep my face set firm. He can't know how I'm quaking inside.

Finally, he nods. 'I'll see to it.' He picks up a phone. 'Find Sandro. Send him to me.'

'I'll leave you to it,' I say, standing up.

Contarini lifts cold eyes to mine. 'Do you understand the consequences of sharing such information with me?'

I do. Their code – *omertà* – demands silence and absolute loyalty. At best, both Sandro and Renzo will be exiled. At worst...

I offer only a brief nod.

'If you wish, you may stay and witness what happens to people who cross the 'Ndrangheta,' Contarini says.

'That's not necessary,' I say. There are limits to what I can endure.

I head towards the door, then out into the corridor. I hear footsteps crossing the courtyard, walking quickly, a man summoned by the capobastone, heading to his fate.

He glances my way as we pass, then stops, shocked. But I carry on walking as the rage builds, cold and sharp.

Years of searching, years of pain and darkness, the unspeakable things I've done, all leading to this moment. And now I understand what he meant by 'I thought I could escape'. He meant this life – the secret life of his childhood. Maybe he thought he could escape its pull, but in the end the wealth, the power, was too tempting. Stronger by far than his love for me.

My hands are clenched into fists at my side, but I don't stop. I won't let him see the emptiness inside me.

'Goodbye, Alessandro,' I whisper.

86

Neither Tom nor Jack managed to get any rest. Jack was either studying images on his laptop or watching Ava, curled up on the bed, occasionally going across to gently touch her back when she cried out in her sleep.

'It's going to be a while before she realises it's over,' Jack said. 'And even longer before she starts to feel safe again. Poor kid.'

Tom had no words of comfort that wouldn't sound like platitudes, but if anyone could bring Ava back from the horror of the past couple of weeks, it was Clare and Jack.

'I know we're still not safe,' Tom said. 'What's our biggest threat now, and how do we know what's going on?'

'I can still use my laptop, using secure networks. Tia's hacked phone's been dumped, and I never did hack Renzo's. There was a flurry of Signal messages from him after I failed to let him into the palazzo, but I didn't answer, obviously. I don't know what he's doing now, but I'm certain it's nothing good.'

Tom closed his eyes, not expecting sleep but wanting to relieve the ache of exhaustion. He had no idea how they were going to get out of Venice in one piece.

He must have dozed off, but woke with a jolt when he felt his shoulder being shaken.

'Come and look at this,' Jack whispered, pointing to his laptop.

It was 6 a.m. and the cameras Jack had set up to watch the street outside his old HQ showed three men approaching. It was clearly not a social call. Renzo, no doubt with help from the 'Ndrangheta, had sent his men to pay a visit.

'Not sure where we go from here, Tom,' Jack said under his breath. 'If they've found me once...'

Keeping their voices low so as not to disturb Ava, the two men went over their options, with Jack furiously searching for information and chatter via his back-door online access.

Tom didn't ask what he was doing. His brother would tell him if he needed to, and Tom was busy formulating a plan of his own. Despite Jack's concerns about leaks in Italian law enforcement, he was fast reaching the conclusion that they might have to take the risk and approach the *polizia* or the *carabinieri* to help them get out of the country. How they would explain what they'd done and why they were in danger, he didn't know. He had visions of long hours in an interrogation room, trying to account for their actions as the risk of Contarini's men getting to them grew with each passing moment.

It was just after 9 a.m. when a new message arrived in Jack's Signal account. 'Tia,' he muttered.

With a wary look at Tom, Jack opened it. The two brothers sat, shoulders touching, and read the brief message.

> Renzo dealt with. All threats over. Unless I
> hear otherwise, I'll assume we have a deal.

Jack switched back to the cameras outside his former HQ. The three men were leaving, walking back up the alley. Someone had called them off. It had to be Contarini.

'I guess she's used the recording.' Jack raised his eyebrows, whispering, 'Holy *shit*.'

'What do you think Contarini will do to Renzo?' Tom asked.

'If he's lucky, he'll be banished – as will Sandro Contarini, assuming Tia set up the evidence convincingly.'

'And if he's not lucky?'

Jack glanced at Ava to make sure she was still asleep, and shrugged. 'Dead. And probably not in the most pleasant way. Which, I have to say, is undoubtedly what would have happened to me if Renzo had got his filthy hands on me.'

Tom shuddered at the thought of how close they had come to a nasty end. And they still had to get out of Venice.

'Are you worried that Tia will spread the word about you?'

'That I'm alive? I doubt it, unless I back her into a corner. That's what she means about a deal. I relish the thought of her paying for everything she's put my family through, but if she's cornered she'll be a serious threat. If we let her go and no one is looking for her, she's not going to breathe a word about me. I know it goes against the grain, Tom, but I have to be pragmatic.'

'So we let a kidnapper go free? You do realise she might do it again, Jack, and it might not turn out so well next time?'

'I don't think she will. I think I finally understand her motives.'

'Whatever they were, I don't think they excuse her behaviour.'

'No, I don't suppose you do.'

Tom tutted. 'Are you going to tell me?'

Jack sat back in his chair. 'Philippa told you that Tia lived with a guy called Alessandro Broglio and that he'd disappeared, then she'd given up her job. It turns out Broglio was a big name in wealth management. No one knew why he'd vanished or where he went, and I think Tia's been looking for him ever since, infiltrating the criminal world, believing he'd been taken against his will or possibly killed for knowing too much.'

'That's no excuse for what she did, Jack.'

'Agreed. I'm not exactly in a forgiving mood, although we both know that when it comes to fighting for those you love, people do extraordinary things.'

'Like illegally gaining access to someone's phone and stealing a painting, you mean?'

Jack grinned. 'Exactly. You went way outside your comfort zone, Tom, and yours is more strictly defined than most. Anyway, I'm now convinced that Alessandro Broglio and Sandro Contarini are one and the same. His mother is Bruno's sister, Katerina Broglio, although the surname Contarini undoubtedly carries more power.'

'Ahhh, that makes sense. *That's* what the voice recording was for. She set them both up – Sandro and Renzo.'

'Exactly. You said she went pale when she saw me at the reception. It wasn't *me* she recognised. I was talking to Sandro and she recognised him – the guy she's been trying to save or avenge, while all the time he's been living a wealthy, criminal life, allowing her to believe he'd disappeared off the face of the earth.'

Tom thought back to the night at the palazzo. If he hadn't been so stressed about stealing the painting, he would have realised that Tia's expression was one of dismay as well as shock.

'Are you telling me I need to leave this alone when I get back to Manchester, that I can't tell Philippa that the Albanians were recruited by a woman called Tia Rukavina?' The look on Jack's face said it all. 'Crap, Jack. Whatever her justification, that goes against everything I believe in.'

Jack at least had the courtesy to look guilty. 'I know, but if she gets locked up I'll probably end up with a price on my head.'

'So you don't think she's a danger if you say nothing, and you believe Renzo's been taken care of. But what about Kodra and his chum? Aren't you worried about repercussions? They know where Ava goes to school, and roughly where you live.'

'It doesn't matter. I'll close the company. We'll move house, and I'll choose another line of work.'

'Doing what?' Tom asked, not entirely certain that he wanted to know. 'And will you actually tell me where you're living this time?'

Jack chuckled. 'We'll have to wait and see, but it will all be above board, I promise. I might develop some ideas I've had for using AI for crime pattern prediction, or develop a system that predicts and prevents cyberattacks using technology to monitor suspicious behaviour. I haven't decided, but something along those lines.'

Tom looked at his brother. 'If you're setting up a new business, won't you need an investor?' He felt a surge of hope. He couldn't give Jack's money back to him without too many questions being asked, but he could invest in a legitimate business. It felt like a perfect solution.

'Let's see, when the dust's settled. But first we need to decide how to get out of Venice.'

Two hours later, Tom was saying goodbye to Jack and Ava. He'd hoped they could all travel home together because, in spite of everything, he felt safer when his brother was around, but Jack said it was a bad idea. He and Ava would take a longer route to give her time to recover.

Now, watching his back every step of the way, travelling with no luggage and trying his best to blend in with the crowds, Tom made his way to the station. His first stop was Villach, a small town in Austria, where he would buy a new phone and change trains to head to Munich. The final leg was a flight from Munich to Manchester.

Tom couldn't wait to be back, to hear the front door close behind him, breathe in the scent of home and hug his family.

He thought about Jack, Clare, Ava, Billy and Sophia – once more having to move. Ava was going to have to start again with new friends, new explanations about her strange family. But she was alive.

'Wherever we go,' Jack had said, 'I'll make sure we're outside GMP jurisdiction so you don't have to lock me up for my past sins. But we'll be close enough to come and see you all. I owe you, Tom.'

The brothers had pulled each other into a fierce hug. 'I'm your brother, and it's what families are for. I'd like to say it's been fun…'

They'd said their goodbyes, Tom touching Ava's cheek gently. Much as he'd wanted to hug her too, he understood that a hug might be too much from anyone but Jack right now.

He thought about where Jack might move to next, hoping he'd keep his promise to stay close. If the last few days had taught him anything, it was that what he wanted most was to see more of his brother. And a little voice in Tom's head was telling him that it might not matter whether Jack lived within GMP's jurisdiction or not.

Before long, he might not be in a position to lock him – or anyone else – up.

87

Five days later

As Tom walked into the office that had felt like a second home for so many years, Rob Cumba looked up from his desk.

'Boss, you're back!' He jumped up from his chair.

At that, the rest of the team turned round, and one by one got to their feet and started clapping. It was nearly too much for Tom, and so much more than he deserved.

'Good to see you all, but I don't know what that was for. I didn't do anything!'

As far as the team knew – other than Becky, Rob and Keith – he had simply provided the intel that had helped in the rescue of a woman called Clare Johnson and her two small children.

Becky walked over and hugged him. 'Unprofessional, I know,' she whispered. 'But I wasn't convinced we'd see you again.'

Tom felt his throat tightening. Where would he have been without this woman by his side for so many years?

This wasn't the first overwhelming moment of the past couple of days. Louisa's greeting at the airport had been uncharacteristically effusive. A woman who cared deeply, she was nevertheless adept at holding her emotions in check, but as she hugged him he could feel her tears running down her cheeks and onto his neck.

'We thought you were going to die, Tom. The *Mafia*, for God's sake. Don't do that again, *please!*'

Lucy had launched herself at him, Harry had clung to his leg, and he didn't think he would ever dare to leave home again. Even Kate seemed vaguely glad he was home.

'I confess I'm relieved I didn't get you killed, Tom. I don't think Lucy would have forgiven me. Not one hundred per cent sure I'd have forgiven myself.'

Tom had assured her that none of what had happened was related to anything she had said. 'But please, Kate, no mention of my brother to your friends again.'

She had pulled a face, then smiled.

Now this. His colleagues, the people he worked with every day, who had his back at all times, smiling, welcoming him back.

'Good as it is to see you, Tom, why are you here?' Becky asked. 'No one's told me that I'm back to being a DI – not that I mind, if it means we've got you back.'

'Don't worry. I'm only here to see Philippa.'

'Course! I guess you want to thank her. She was a bit of a star, to be honest.'

'Something like that.' Tom glanced at his watch. 'And I'd better go. Don't want to keep her waiting. I'll come and see you when I'm done.'

As he walked away, he could feel Becky's eyes on his back. He'd seen the expression in her eyes, the glint of tears. She knew what was about to happen.

Five minutes later, Tom knocked on Philippa's door.

'Come,' she said in that imperious tone that had irritated Tom for years.

He pushed open the door.

'Philippa,' he said, walking across the room to the chair he had sat in so many times. Some of the team referred to it as the naughty chair, but despite her acerbic manner, Tom had a huge amount of respect for Detective Superintendent Philippa Stanley.

'You wanted to see me, Tom. If it's to thank me, there's no need. I did my job, and I'm glad your brother's family is safe. I don't like the way it went down, of course, and we do need to have a debrief at some point. But for now, it's good to have you back. When are you returning to work?'

Tom still hadn't sat down and Philippa was looking puzzled. He gripped the back of the chair.

'That's the thing, Philippa. I'm not coming back.'

'You want more time?'

'No. I'm not coming back at all. I'm resigning.'

Philippa said nothing, just stared at him. 'No you're not,' she said finally. 'Don't be ridiculous.'

Tom sighed. This was so difficult for him, but he'd thought Philippa would be the easiest person to convince.

'Sit, Tom. Don't stand on ceremony. Just *sit*!'

He did as she asked. 'I *am* resigning, Philippa. I have to. I did some things – committed crimes – which are against everything I stand for. Everything *you* stand for.'

'I guessed as much, but you weren't in the country so there's nothing I can do about any of that. And I'm sure you had your reasons – good ones.' She gave him her best attempt at an understanding smile. Then scowled. 'And, of course, you were with Jack, so what else could we expect?' Philippa held up her hands, palms towards Tom. 'Sorry. Old habits die hard.'

'I know,' Tom said with a grin. 'The thing is, it was Jack's family. *My* family. And it made me realise that sometimes sticking to the letter of the law isn't the solution. I wanted Jack to go to the police in Italy but he didn't trust them, not only because he doesn't speak the language, but because he didn't know how strong the Mafia's stranglehold is – how much corruption might be in play. He convinced me he was right. So we took things into our own hands.'

'Fine – then why tell me about it? You didn't commit any crimes on my patch, so say nothing! Does anyone else know what you did?'

'No one else. But *I* know, Philippa, and that's the point. It doesn't feel right to be chasing down people who may have committed the same crimes as me. And while I didn't hurt anyone, I would have done if it had been the only way to save Ava. If I carry on, I know I'll start trying to rationalise criminal behaviour rather than doing my job.'

'Look, Tom, it's all raw right now. Give yourself some time. Don't be so bullish. Wait until the adrenaline's drained from your system and think again.'

Tom shook his head. 'You persuaded me once before, and I'm glad you did. I broke the law then to save a family – the same family, as it happens – but I can't keep doing this and still be a policeman.'

'Yes, and last time – surprise surprise – it was bloody Jack at the heart of it too.'

'Same family, same problems. And he's still – and always will be – my brother.'

Tom stood up and pulled an envelope from his pocket. 'No shredding it this time, ma'am. I'm very sorry to say that my time with Greater Manchester Police is over.'

Tom had always thought of Philippa as poker-faced, but she had the blank look of a woman in shock as she slowly held out her hand. He passed her the envelope.

'What will you do?'

'There's a business start-up that I might invest in, perhaps even get involved with, as it's crime-related.'

'On the right side, I presume?' Philippa arched an eyebrow and Tom grinned.

She shifted her gaze back to the envelope, clutching it in both hands. Tom was searching for some final words to express how difficult it was for him to leave the job, his team and even Philippa, when she waved the envelope in the air.

'I'll keep this in my drawer for forty-eight hours, give you time to get your head straight.'

Tom shook his head. 'I promise you, it's as straight as it's ever going to be.'

She took a long breath, then stood up slowly and held her hand out across the desk for Tom to shake.

Tom just stared at it. 'I suppose it would be inappropriate to give you a hug?'

Philippa looked startled. 'You suppose right, Tom.'

He laughed, gripped her hand briefly and turned away. As he reached the door, she called out, 'But I'm always up for a drink, if you're buying.'

88

'Tom, what are you knocking for? Have you come to reclaim your office?' Becky smiled, but it was a weak attempt.

'Not my office, Becky,' Tom said, stepping into the room. 'It's yours, and I suspect you've guessed what I'm going to say. I've just handed in my resignation to Philippa.'

Becky's smile faded as she slumped back in her chair. 'Why would you do that, Tom? We need you. We all love working with you – even if you occasionally drive us nuts when you have a whistling day – though fortunately they're few and far between.'

Becky's eyes glistened with unshed tears and Tom felt a stab of guilt. Walking over to the window, he looked out at the familiar view – at Manchester streets sometimes bathed in sunlight, more often drenched with rain or occasionally blanketed in snow.

'I've realised this last week or so that life is fragile. Any one of Jack's family could have died – potentially *all* of them – and I kept putting myself in his shoes, wondering what I would do if something like that happened to Lucy, Harry and Louisa. I know I'd stop at nothing to save them.'

'Come off it, Tom. That's *normal*. Anyone would say the same thing.'

Tom felt her eyes watching him as he thought about something Jack had said: 'Morality isn't always black or white.' How was he supposed to know where to draw the line between upholding the law and following his conscience? A quote from Aristotle he'd learned in training came to mind: 'The law is reason, free from passion.' Tom couldn't disagree, but now more than ever he knew each decision he made would be tinged with emotion.

'It's not the first time I've struggled with my principles, Becky, and I can't keep pretending that I believe the law is always just. Most of the time it is, but in the last few days I've broken several laws to save lives. How can I arrest some guy who steals because he's lost his job and can't feed his family? Or a man who beats the shit out of someone who's abused his daughter because the system fails to act quickly enough?'

'We all feel like that sometimes. It's a hard balance to strike, so all we can do is enforce the law and hope that most of the time it's the right thing to do.'

He couldn't argue with her, but it didn't alter the fact that Tom had broken the law in Italy. And it wasn't the only time he'd bent the rules.

'There's something I've never told you, Becky. Never told anyone, in fact.' He took a deep breath. 'I once let a murderer go free. There was no doubt the victim died as a result of a cold-blooded, meticulously planned execution, but I thought he deserved it. If I'd done my job and arrested the killer, only the innocent would have suffered – the *real* victims of the horrific things this appalling man did.'

Becky didn't speak and, believing he had shocked her into silence, Tom turned from the window. There was a ghost of a smile around her lips.

'I know, Tom. I've always known. But I never told you because you'd probably have done the heroic thing and fallen on your sword so I didn't have to live with the dilemma of whether to report it.' She shrugged. 'And wipe that guilty look off your face. It wasn't a problem. I agreed with you.'

He turned back to the window, struggling to face the sadness in her eyes. 'I don't know what to say, Becky, other than you deserve this job. You're a great detective. You have the respect and support of the team, and I couldn't be happier handing over to you.'

'What are you going to do? You're not a man who can sit around and twiddle his thumbs, and I can't believe you'll become a gentleman of leisure – if there is such a thing any more.'

Tom felt a spark of optimism. 'I'm going to dedicate some time to my family. Life felt precarious when I was in Venice, so they're going to come first until they're bored with me hanging around all the time.'

Despite his sadness at saying goodbye to his life as a detective, Tom was looking forward to the future – not just with Louisa, Lucy and Harry, but with Jack's family too. He'd spoken to his brother often as he and Ava travelled through Italy, Switzerland and Germany using a regular turnover of burner phones – a short-term but necessary solution. Ava was apparently beginning to feel more relaxed, though she slept for most of each day, and Jack was keeping his ever-restless brain occupied by dreaming up some new technology that he promised would help them all keep in touch.

'You'll like the new kit, Tom, when I've worked out the details. We'll be able to speak as often as we want.' The enthusiasm was back in his voice as he explained the concept of quantum encryption, which was apparently the basis of his new communications system. Tom had never felt closer to his brother, and he wanted to hold onto that feeling.

Turning from the window again, he perched on the sill. 'I'm not one for speeches, Becky, you know that, and this isn't goodbye. You're family too, and I'll always be here for you – any time. And I want to watch Buster grow up; I am his godfather, after all.'

He watched as a tear finally slid down Becky's cheek. 'Look what you've made me do! I'm a DCI, I shouldn't be crying on the job!'

Stepping towards her, Tom cleared his throat. 'C'mere,' he said, holding out his arms.

Becky pushed back her chair and crossed the room, hugging him round the waist as Tom pulled her close.

'You're going to be great,' he said softly. 'A complete star, just as you've always been for me. I couldn't have done this job without you.'

They stood in silence for a few moments, Becky's head buried in Tom's shoulder.

Finally, she spoke, her words muffled but just audible. 'You still haven't told me what you're going to do.'

Tom gave a short laugh. 'Well, this is going to sound seriously pretentious, I warn you. The thing is, I don't want to solve crimes any longer. By then, it feels too late. The damage is done. I want to help *prevent* crime, and I think there are some innovative ways we might be able to turn that ambition into reality.'

Becky raised her head and gently eased herself away. 'I guess I know who "we" means. I'm pleased for you, and if anyone can do it, Tom Douglas, you two can.'

***

Want to know more about Ava and her life as Tasha Joseph?

Stolen as a child. Shaped by fear.
Never truly free.

Read The Tasha Joseph story now in this special box set, including *Stranger Child* and *Nowhere Child*, and find out where it all began.

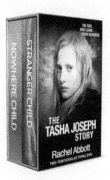

Two unforgettable stories. One lost girl.
Find Tasha's Story on Amazon

ACKNOWLEDGMENTS

Every book I complete is a result of the collaboration, expertise, and support of so many generous people. Without them, my work would never reach the page, let alone the shelves, and I'm sincerely grateful.

The research phase of a novel is a fascinating journey, and I owe a huge debt of gratitude to those who share their knowledge and experiences with me. Venice, with its labyrinth of canals and rich history, has been a source of inspiration. Although I've only visited twice - far too little for such a captivating city - I'm fortunate to have received insights and advice from those more familiar with its secrets, helping me bring its atmosphere to life on the page.

I'm lucky to have Mark Gray as my police adviser. His detailed responses to my endless questions and his insights into the realities of policing make my books what they are. He reads my manuscripts with a sharp eye, pointing out subtleties I might have missed, and I truly appreciate his time and expertise. Any inaccuracies are entirely my own.

Working with David Higham Associates has been one of the best decisions of my career. Lizzy Kremer's ongoing guidance and wise advice have been instrumental in shaping me as a writer, and I'm grateful for her belief in my work. I am equally indebted to Maddalena Cavaciuti, whose sharp editorial eye and thoughtful suggestions have been invaluable. Beyond her editorial expertise, Maddalena's unwavering support in all aspects of publishing and promoting my books has been extraordinary, and I cannot thank her enough. Together, the incredible team at DHA, including their foreign rights department, have made it possible for my books to reach readers across the globe. Thank you all.

After the manuscript is finished, the next stage of the magic happens. Hugh Davis, my meticulous copy editor, ensures my stories are polished and coherent, while Jessica Read's eagle-eyed proofreading catches the errors I've passed over too many times to notice. And a huge thank you to James Macey of Blacksheep Design for crafting such a stunning cover that perfectly captures the essence of the book.

To my wonderful readers: your support inspires me every day. Thank you for choosing my books, for leaving reviews, for telling your friends, and for joining me online. Your enthusiasm means everything. I'm especially grateful to my advance readers, who see the book before it's fully polished and offer thoughtful and encouraging feedback - it really makes a difference.

I must also give a special mention to the book bloggers who work tirelessly to spread the word about new releases. Your efforts are invaluable to authors everywhere.

Finally, thanks to David Rose for stepping in to help with my Partners in Crime Facebook group. Keeping up with social media while writing is a challenge, and his support allows me to focus on writing without the inevitable distractions.

And, as always, my deepest gratitude to my husband, John. He listens, offers suggestions, and helps me untangle the chaos, demonstrating admirable patience as I ramble on incoherently about characters and plots. Thank you for everything - you make this journey so much easier.